The Meryl Streep Movie Club

Mia March lives in Maine, USA, with her teenaged son, their sweet shepherd mix, Flash, and their lap cat, Cleo. Follow Mia on Twitter at @march_mia.

MIA MARCH

The Meryl Streep Movie Club

**SIMON &
SCHUSTER**

London · New York · Sydney · Toronto · New Delhi

A CBS COMPANY

First published in the USA by Gallery Books, 2012
A division of Simon and Schuster, Inc.
First published in Great Britain by Simon & Schuster UK Ltd, 2012
A CBS COMPANY

This paperback edition published 2018

1 3 5 7 9 10 8 6 4 2

Simon & Schuster UK Ltd
1st Floor
222 Gray's Inn Road
London WC1X 8HB

Simon & Schuster Australia, Sydney
Simon & Schuster India, New Delhi

www.simonandschuster.co.uk
www.simonandschuster.com.au
www.simonandschuster.co.in

A CIP catalogue record for this book is available from the British Library

Paperback ISBN: 978-1-4711-78573
eBook ISBN: 978-1-4711-0297-4

Printed and bound by CPI Group (UK) Ltd, Croydon, CR0 4YY

Simon & Schuster UK Ltd are committed to sourcing paper
that is made from wood grown in sustainable forests and support the Forest
Stewardship Council, the leading international forest certification organisation.
Our books displaying the FSC logo are printed on FSC certified paper.

In memory of Greg.

Perhaps he knew, as I did not, that the earth was made round so that we would not see too far down the road.

—KAREN BLIXEN, PLAYED BY MERYL STREEP
IN THE FILM *OUT OF AFRICA*

The Meryl Streep Movie Club

The Bridges of Madison County

The Devil Wears Prada

Mamma Mia!

Heartburn

Defending Your Life

Kramer vs. Kramer

Postcards from the Edge

It's Complicated

Out of Africa

(Honorary mention: *Julie & Julia*)

Lolly Weller

Fifteen years ago
New Year's Day, 2:30 a.m.
The Three Captains' Inn, Boothbay Harbor, Maine

Silkwood was on. Lolly's favorite actress, Meryl Streep, with the shag hairstyle that Lolly had gotten as a teenager, and Cher, who Lolly had always thought was spectacularly fierce. The word *fierce* had been applied to Lolly herself, usually by her sister, but Lolly didn't think she was fierce at all. There was another word for Lolly, and if only she were Catholic, she would spend every day, twice a day, in confession.

After the phone rang the first time that night, Lolly did something that would haunt her for the rest of her life, something she'd never forgive herself for. The first call had come just after two o'clock in the morning. Her sister, Allie, slaphappy drunk on New Year's Eve, laughing into the phone about how her husband was in the middle of the Boothbay Resort Hotel's posh lobby, dancing like John Travolta in *Pulp Fiction*. They'd had four or five glasses of champagne each, and could Lolly or her husband come get them? They were just five minutes away.

Five minutes there. Five minutes to get them to their

1

apartment and safely inside. Five minutes back home to the inn. That would give Lolly fifteen sweet, stolen minutes. And so she'd woken her own husband, Ted, who'd muttered under his breath about damned drunks, but put on his down parka over his pajamas and headed out to pick up the Nashes.

Lolly had done a quick check on the girls. Since Lolly and Ted's New Year's Eve plans only involved providing horn blowers and complimentary champagne to their guests at the Three Captains' Inn, they'd agreed to babysit their nieces overnight. Lolly crept downstairs from the third floor of the inn to the second and quietly opened the door to the utility room, where she kept her vacuum and cleaning supplies. Sixteen-year-old Isabel Nash had dragged her mattress, pillow, and blanket, as she did every time she visited, to the utility closet and was fast asleep, her beautiful face so peaceful you'd never imagine the hollering and cussing that could come out of that pink mouth. Just an hour ago, Isabel had come sneaking in at one thirty, despite the strict twelve-thirty holiday curfew her mother had set and the terrible argument the two had had before everyone had gone his or her own way for the evening. Lolly pulled the down-filled comforter up over Isabel's shoulder and noticed the fresh hickey on her neck. Wait till her father saw that.

Back upstairs, Lolly checked on her other niece, thirteen-year-old June Nash, who was sharing Lolly's daughter's room for the evening. The little room across from Lolly and Ted's was barely big enough for one bed, let alone the two cots Ted had squeezed in for Isabel and June, but the Three Captains' Inn was fully booked for New Year's. *Jane Eyre* lay open on June's rising and falling chest, a small, red flashlight shining up at her chin. Lolly turned off the flashlight and put it and the book on the bedside table, moving a thick lock of June's curly auburn hair off her face. June was never any trouble.

Across the room was Kat Weller, Lolly's ten-year-old

daughter. Kat had woken up when her father had come down the stairs and, within seconds, had on her coat and hat and mittens, begging to go with him. "Please, can I, Daddy? There's no school tomorrow." But it was too late and bitter cold and drunks were on the road, so Ted had tucked her back into bed.

Kat was asleep again, her purple mittens still on and her old, stuffed Eeyore under her arm. Lolly tiptoed over, grateful that her daughter was facing the wall. If Lolly had walked in and seen that sweet face, so like her father's, Lolly's heart might have burst, as it often felt like it might these days. She carefully peeled off the mittens, and Kat shifted, but didn't wake. Lolly bit her lip on the guilt that hit in her stomach, then crept back out.

She had ten minutes or so. She darted upstairs to her bedroom, closed the door, and lay down with the TV remote and the telephone on her stomach. She changed the channel; much as she loved *Silkwood*, she'd seen it at least ten times and again just a few months ago. She flipped channels, came across *When Harry Met Sally*, raised the volume just enough to mask her voice, and made her phone call. As they spoke, her heart moved in her chest as it always did, reminding Lolly of what she used to dream about. She whispered, but loud enough to be heard over Billy Crystal telling Meg Ryan just what was wrong with her.

Thirty, forty minutes later—Lolly had lost track of time— an operator broke through the phone line with an emergency. Lolly bolted up and said yes, of course she accepted. It was the Boothbay Harbor Police.

They were sorry.

Something Lolly always remembered about that night was how she'd dropped the phone, her body, her breath, going so still as she stared, in horror, at Billy Crystal's face. All these years later, she still wasn't able to watch anything with Billy

Crystal, couldn't bear to look at him, hear his voice. Her dear friend Pearl had noted that thank goodness Lolly had flipped the channel from *Silkwood*. Or she'd never have been able to look at Meryl Streep again.

CHAPTER 1

Isabel Nash McNeal

Isabel's plan to save her marriage involved three things: an old-world Italian recipe for three-cheese ravioli, the remembrance of good things past, and a vow to never again mention what was tearing Edward and her apart. She loved her husband, had since she was sixteen, and that had to be that. She stood at her kitchen counter, the recipe, scrawled in black ink she could barely read, next to the lumpy, gray blob of pasta dough she'd made from scratch. Was it supposed to look like this?

Isabel grabbed a cookbook from the shelf above the counter, Giada De Laurentiis's *Everyday Italian*, and flipped to pasta dough. Hers looked nothing like Giada's. She'd just start over. She had five days to get the recipe right. Her tenth wedding anniversary was Tuesday, and Isabel was determined to re-create the last night of her honeymoon in Rome, when she and Edward, just twenty-one years old and so in love, had come upon a tiny gem of a restaurant with outdoor seating and late hours, around the bend from the Trevi Fountain, where they'd thrown coins and made wishes. As they'd sat down at a little round table under a crescent moon on a beautiful, breezy August night, Italian opera playing softly from somewhere, Edward had said he'd wished into the fountain that life would always be like this, that she *was* his life. Her wish had been similar. Over three-cheese ravioli that they'd both declared otherworldy, Edward had told her he loved her more than anything, that he'd love her forever, and then stood, held out his hand, and dipped her for a long, passionate kiss that had charmed the owner of the restaurant into inviting them inside for the ravioli recipe. In the old kitchen was his ancient mother, who looked something like a witch with her hooked nose and severe, long black dress, a heavy black bun wound at the back of her head as she stirred big black pots on the stove. But she'd smiled at them and kissed them on both cheeks, then written down the recipe in Italian, and her son had translated below it, adding, *My mother says this recipe has magical properties and will ensure a long and happy marriage.*

All these years Isabel had kept the folded piece of paper in her wallet and had once planned on making the ravioli for every anniversary, but for one reason or another she and Edward had gone out to dinner or been away on vacation. Besides, that honeymoon plate of ravioli they'd shared had worked its magic all these years and she hadn't needed any assurances of a long and happy marriage; she'd had exactly that. Until recently.

Until their marriage had turned into some kind of cold war because Isabel had begun to want something she wasn't supposed to want, wasn't supposed to need, with a fervency that scared her, excited her, made her feel alive in a way she never had. Made her cry—in the shower, in the supermarket, in the car, and late at night in bed—because it would never be.

She threw out the lumpy dough, and as she reached into the sack of flour with her measuring cup, she heard a swishing sound by the front door. She leaned back and glanced through the hallway; an envelope had been slipped under the door. Odd. Isabel wiped her hands on her apron and headed to the foyer, her heels clicking on the polished marble floor.

The envelope, like the letter inside, typed on plain white paper, was unaddressed, unsigned:

> *Your husband is having an affair. I'm not sure if you know, or if you want to know. What I do know is that you were kind to me once, and in this town, that's saying something. I'd want someone to tell me—something tells me you would too. 56 Hemingway St. The black Mercedes is always parked in the back around 6pm.*
> *—Sorry.*

Isabel gasped and dropped the letter to the floor. She picked it up and read it again. Edward? Having an affair? She shook her head, her knees feeling like rubber, and sank down on the padded bench in the entryway. This had to be a mistake. It had to be.

Yes—a mistake, she decided. *Sorry* had delivered the letter to the wrong house. It was likely meant for her next-door neighbor, Sasha Finton, whose white Colonial, with its red door, black shutters, and impatiens-lined stone path, was identical to the McNeals'. Sasha's husband flirted openly at neighborhood potlucks and birthday parties for toddlers.

Isabel's heart went out to Sasha, who was always polite, who'd waved at Isabel with a tight smile that morning, even though Sasha had clearly been upset as she'd followed her grim-faced husband out to his car.

A black Mercedes, no? Just like Edward's.

She sucked in a breath and darted into the living room and pushed aside the heavy drapery at the far window. If she strained, she could just see the Fintons' driveway over the ornate white wrought-iron fence. Only Sasha's silver BMW was there now. But Isabel was sure Darin Finton's Mercedes was black. She glanced at her watch; it was just after six o'clock. Perhaps Darin's car wasn't in the driveway because it was parked behind 56 Hemingway Street.

She took the letter and envelope into the kitchen and set them on the counter, then put a tomato on top as a paper-weight, not that she didn't want the anonymous letter to blow away, fly up into the sky and away. But then it would land on another woman's doorstep, another woman who knew that something was very, very wrong between herself and her husband and had been for a long time now. Well before their cold war ever began. Isabel knew that.

But an affair? Edward? No.

Isabel blinked back tears and measured three cups of flour, dumping them on the wooden cutting board. She made a well in the flour and cracked open four eggs into it, careful to beat the eggs gently and incorporate the flour slowly. Once she started kneading with the heel of her palms, the dough turned lumpy instead of elastic and sticky.

She was doing something wrong.

This part of saving her marriage, the remembrance of good things past, might be ridiculous, but Isabel thought if she re-created the evening, that last night in Rome, when every-thing between Edward and her had been so magical, she would stir something inside him. The mingling of ricotta cheese and sweet marinara sauce would conjure a moonlit table in Italy and remind him of how he once felt about her, how things had once been. She planned to wear one of those sweet, old cotton dresses she'd run around in on her honeymoon and set up a café table in the backyard, under the moon and stars. Re-create the evening emotionally, if not geographically. Bring them back to the start. To the first nine years of their marriage, when everything was good, when she'd felt so safe.

Things had changed, though, over the past year. But she had a plan for that too: never mentioning what was tearing them apart, what had come between them like a sledgehammer. Something Isabel wanted and Edward didn't.

Isabel plucked up the tomato and read the note again.

The black Mercedes is always parked in the back around 6pm.

Yes, Edward had a black Mercedes. But so did Darin Finton and the Carmichaels across the street and most of the neighborhood.

She heard a car pull into the Fintons' driveway. Isabel rushed back over to the window. Darin Finton was getting out of his dark *gray* Mercedes. Not black. Goose bumps trailed up her spine as she slowly walked to the windows on the other side of the living room and peered out through the filmy curtains at the Haverhills' driveway. *Please have a black Mercedes,* she thought, then realized she was wishing a cheating husband on Victoria Haverhill. But both Haverhill cars were in the driveway—one a dark blue Mercedes.

Isabel stood still next to the baby grand piano, afraid to breathe, afraid to move.

You were kind to me once, and in this town, that's saying something. . . .

Isabel was generally kind. Sasha Finton had her good days and bad. Victoria Haverhill? Vicious.

Was the note meant for her? Her heels clattered in her ears as she walked back into the kitchen. She and Edward were both trying, though. They'd both promised to try.

"Excuse me, Ms. Isabel, but that dough isn't supposed to look like that."

Marian, Isabel's housekeeper, was putting away her supplies in the kitchen closet, her gaze on the lump of dough, her voice kind. No matter how many times Isabel told Marian to call her Isabel, Marian would shake her head and say, "No *Ms.*," with a smile.

"I'll stay and fix it for you," Marian said. "You and Mr. Edward will have a nice dinner."

Marian had been their twice-per-week housekeeper and sometimes cook for the five years they'd been living in this huge house in Westport, Connecticut. A house way too big for just two people. Marian would slyly smile and comment how one of the four bedrooms upstairs would be perfect for a nursery with its French doors and arched windows. "Like a fairy tale."

At all hours of the day and night, Isabel would go upstairs to the fairy-tale room, yet another guest room that never had guests, and imagine the graceful white sleigh crib, the pale yellow bedding, a softly tinkling mobile, the tiny ducklings she'd commission an artist to paint along the ceiling molding.

And a baby, Allison McNeal, Allie for short, named for Isabel's mother, or Marcus McNeal for Edward's father.

But there wouldn't be a baby. There was a pact instead, which Edward reminded Isabel of every time she brought up the subject of a child.

There was a pact, which she broke her own heart to abide by. So the letter had to be a mistake. There was no affair. There was no room for an affair in a pact.

Though, now that she thought about it, vows were a pact of their own. And broken all the time.

She managed something of a smile at her housekeeper. "Thank you, Marian, but I'm just practicing on this dough. For our anniversary next week. Ten years."

"You and Mr. Edward are such a nice couple," Marian said. "I hope he manages to come home before eight o'clock for your anniversary. That man works so late, so hard."

56 Hemingway St. The black Mercedes is always parked around back at 6 pm. —Sorry.

Isabel reached into her handbag for her car keys.

• • •

Isabel had been sixteen and anything but sweet when she'd met Edward McNeal at the Boothbay Regional Center for Grieving Children. He was her teen mentor, having lost his own parents in a plane crash five years earlier. He volunteered at the center every Wednesday after school. When Isabel's aunt Lolly had taken her and her sister and cousin there two days after the car accident, Isabel had one session with an adult counselor and one with Edward. The first day, she was so struck by him, by the empathy she saw in his eyes, which were the darkest brown, that she forgot for a second where she was, that she was in this place, in this hell, forever, her mother, her father, gone, just like that, while she'd slept on New Year's Eve.

She didn't want to talk about her parents. Or the fight she'd had with her mother that final night. She didn't want to talk about her sister, June, who cried all the time. Or how she felt moving into her aunt Lolly's musty old inn with her little cousin Kat, who'd lost her father because he'd gone to pick up Isabel and June's parents, drunk New Year's Eve revelers. She'd wanted to hear Edward talk about the moment he'd learned his parents were gone. So he'd talked about the nature of shock, how it had gripped him for so long he'd had a delayed reaction to the actual loss, and that when the shock did finally subside a good six months later, he found himself crying everywhere for months. At school, under the blankets at night, in church, which his older half brother, who was raising him, thought would help and sort of did, for a while. And then one day, Edward said, you realize right in the middle of whatever you're doing that you're not thinking about it, and it gets better from there, becoming a piece of you instead of everything you are.

She'd fallen in love with Edward McNeal by the second Wednesday. So had her sister, though it was more of a crush on an older boy. For a while, the Nash sisters, who'd never gotten along, had focused on that, instead of on their grief, taking their anger out on each other. "The only reason he likes you is because you're slutty," June would scream. "No, he likes me because I'm me," Isabel would scream back, "something you'll never be, Miss Ass-Kissing Goody Two-Shoes." They'd said terrible things to each other in those early days, and when Isabel would tell Edward about their vicious arguments, he'd say, "You know, Izzy, if ninety-nine percent of what June says about you isn't anywhere near the real truth, the same goes for what you say to her. Think about it." And she would, but then she and her sister would go back to arguing, and June would come out with the one thing that would drain the blood from Isabel and make her shake so badly that June would have to run and get Aunt Lolly.

Within a day, the fights would resume, June insisting thirteen wasn't too young for a boyfriend—for a sixteen-year-old boyfriend—and desperately trying to get Edward's attention by stuffing her bra and wearing peach-scented lip gloss. Aunt Lolly had to switch June to a fourteen-year-old female mentor named Sarah, whom June ended up adoring as well. But the chasm that had always been between Isabel and June widened, and they—and their aunt—had never been able to narrow it. Every time Isabel realized that all she had to do to make peace with her sister was to stop *reacting*, she would react. Badly.

And run to Edward. They'd been inseparable that terrible winter. Long walks from pier to pier in Boothbay Harbor, bundled up against the freezing-cold weather, Edward's strong arms wrapped around her as they sat staring at the docked boats, her back against his puff of navy blue L.L. Bean down jacket, his gloved hands warming her face. They walked miles in the harbor, sipping hot chocolate from take-out cups, and the farther Isabel walked from the inn, the less miserable she was. One night, in the late spring, as she and Edward lay under the oak tree in the backyard of the inn, they'd held hands and stared up at the stars, twinkling with possibilities that made Isabel feel hopeful.

"We should make a pact," Edward had said, eyes on the stars. "You and me, together forever. Just us two."

She squeezed his hand. "Just us two. Together forever."

"And definitely no kids. No kids to turn into grieving, lost orphans like us."

She turned to face him then, awed by how right he was. Just sixteen years old and so wise. "No kids."

"It's a pact then," he said. "No children. Just you and me, forever."

They squeezed hands and stared up at the stars until Isabel's aunt Lolly had called her in for the night.

For many years, she forgot all about that pact.

But now they were thirty-one. Married for ten years. Living in Westport, a beautiful Connecticut town filled with young families, with children. Isabel gripped her hand tighter around her car keys, staring at the lumpy pasta dough, remembering how, a year ago, she'd found herself peering into baby strollers at little faces, and strange stirrings would stop her in her tracks, wake her from sleep, make her think that maybe they'd been wrong about how risk worked. Until she was about twenty-eight, twenty-nine, she'd been satisfied with her life. Not a maternal instinct nipping. But as Edward started becoming distant, keeping to himself, working later and later, starting to tell her a story from work and then saying, "Oh, forget it, you wouldn't understand," she found herself beginning to need something that she couldn't put her finger on. Then came the day, over a year ago now, that she'd been counseling a family at the hospital, where she volunteered almost full-time as a grief counselor. A young widowed mother with a seven-month-old baby and a wonderful, caring extended family, and someone asked if Isabel would mind holding the baby for a moment.

That sweet, soft weight in her arms had made her gasp. She knew right then that she wanted a baby, wanted a child, that the pact she'd agreed to as a grieving teenager had no bearing on her life now. That baby in her arms had lost her father. But that didn't mean she wouldn't be loved, that she wouldn't have a wonderful life.

Isabel wanted a baby. And she'd made sure of her feelings. Slept on it for a long time until she was so sure, she wished she could get pregnant that minute.

Several months ago, she'd fallen asleep imagining what their child would look like—if he or she would have Edward's chestnut-brown hair and Roman nose, or her hazel-green eyes and heart-shaped face. She'd woken up in the middle of the night and said in the comfort of the dark, "Edward? You awake?" He'd murmured, so she'd taken a breath and said that she'd been thinking a lot lately about the two of them having a baby. He was silent and Isabel figured he'd fallen asleep and hadn't heard her, after all, but then he'd said, "We made a pact, Iz." The next morning, he'd reminded her why they'd made their pact. Gently. Then less so.

"But what if I changed my mind?" she asked.

"Well, then we're at a stalemate, aren't we?" had been his response.

She'd tried talking to him about how they weren't those same scared teenagers anymore, that they didn't have to abide by rules they'd made about the world from a place of sorrow, a place of fear.

He would stare at her, with anger in his eyes, and say, "I don't want children, Isabel. End of story. We made a *pact*." Then he'd walk away and a door would slam. After a few months of the same conversation, they both started retreating—but from each other instead of from just the conversation. She spent more time at the hospital, helping people who'd just been informed of losses. When she wasn't needed, which wasn't often, she'd stand in front of the nursery window, looking at the babies, closing her eyes against the squeeze of her heart, allowing herself to feel every inch of her wish to have a child. Her anger at his resolute stance turned her quiet, and in time he withdrew even further than just being late for dinner or having to work on Saturday mornings. He avoided rooms she was in. And stopped coming up to bed. In the morning she'd find him asleep on the sofa in the living room or the too-small-for-him love seat in his den. The rare times he'd sit down to breakfast, he made her feel a crushing loneliness when he was three feet across the table from her.

"Edward, we need to talk. We need to fix this," she'd say over and over, at breakfast, in e-mails, in phone calls, in the middle of the night, when she'd wake and realize she was alone and go downstairs to find him either watching a recorded Red Sox game or just sitting there, head in hands. She'd pause then. Scared. Unsure, suddenly, how to get inside this man she'd known half her life.

And so months ago, Isabel had stopped taking the elevator to the third-floor nursery at work to see the babies. She'd stopped drifting off to sleep thinking about tiny Roman noses and hazel-green eyes, a combination face of hers and Edward's. She'd made a pact. She'd married, made vows, under that pact. And she'd abide by it. Edward had saved her, and now she would save *them*. Save their marriage, which had been so strong, so good, for nine years. For so long, he'd come through the door and swooped her up into a hug and kiss her the way he had on their honeymoon. They'd make love and watch old movies in bed, sharing their favorite Chinese takeout. He'd listen to her stories about the hospital, sad stories, and hold her until she could breathe again. And when they'd dutifully visit her family in Maine for holidays, and it would be too much for Isabel, being in that inn, arguing with her sister, she and Edward would walk around the harbor the way they used to, hand in hand, and everything would be all right.

You and me together forever, just us two.

Edward McNeal was her everything. And so she had fought for her marriage these past couple of months. Fought hard.

At first, he'd responded. Her smile had been genuine, not forced. Her gaze upon him full of love instead of resentment. She would walk up behind him and massage his strong shoulders, breathing in the masculine, soapy scent of him that she'd loved for so long, and he'd turn around and kiss her, deeply, passionately, and lead her upstairs. But afterward, she'd notice something, something just more than subtle, in his expression, in his body language. The damage had been done, perhaps even before she'd brought up the subject of a baby, and something had been lost that smiles and sex and possibly not even time could get back.

And so she'd waited. And tried. She tried so hard that she'd burst into tears while they made love, and Edward would shake his head and get off her and leave. And not return for hours.

"You can lie, but you can't lie to yourself," her aunt Lolly had always said.

So she'd tried harder. Just last month, she'd assured Edward she'd made peace with their pact. Yes, she was thirty-one years old now, had been married for ten years, and, yes, she had changed her mind about wanting a baby. And, yes, she believed in her heart that she would be a good and loving mother. But she would put her marriage first. She would take his many suggestions—they'd get two dogs, big ones, like a

Rhodesian ridgeback or a greyhound. They'd travel, back to Italy, to India, to the American West she wanted to see so badly, to Africa for a safari, and she'd see how free they could be, just the two of them.

Just the two of them. Even though their marriage was different, even though something had been lost—perhaps irrevocably—she loved her husband and they'd weather through. Sometimes, late at night, she'd think about what her sister had muttered last Christmas at the inn, in the middle of one of their usual arguments when Isabel had deferred to her husband about something minor: "God, Isabel, do you even know who you are without Edward?" Isabel *had* been a different person entirely before she'd lost her parents, before she'd met him. And now she was starting to want things she hadn't before, big, life-changing things. Maybe she was just scared enough to let Edward win. And so that was that. There would be no baby. There would be no pitters and patters of little feet. In the deepest recesses of her heart, Isabel accepted it as enough—almost—that she *wanted* a child. That told her something. Something good about herself.

Her car keys now digging into her palm, Isabel thought about how she'd believed they were back on track, at the gate, at least, even though he'd told her that morning he wasn't going to Maine with her tomorrow. Edward never missed an excuse to go to Maine, to visit his brother and wife, and her aunt Lolly, whom he liked, despite everything. He always had, since the beginning. But when she told him about Lolly's strange call a few days ago, that her aunt had some kind of big announcement she wouldn't talk about over the phone, but wanted Isabel, her sister, June, and their cousin Kat to come for dinner at the inn Friday night, Edward said he couldn't go with her. Meetings. Client dinners. More meetings. On a weekend.

"I can't get away tomorrow, Isabel," he'd said that morning. "Go and see your family. It's been a long time, right? Stay the weekend or longer, even."

She hadn't seen Lolly or June or Kat since last Christmas, she realized. It was now August. Twice a year, at Thanksgiving and Christmas, seemed to be as much of one another as the four of them could stand.

Stay the weekend . . . longer, even . . . Did he remember their ten-year anniversary was Tuesday?

"What's Lolly's big announcement again?" he'd asked without looking at her, thumbs on the QWERTY keyboard of his iPhone.

He didn't listen to her anymore. She'd been fretting ever since she'd gotten the call from her aunt. Summoning the three—the two, since her cousin Kat lived at the inn—was unusual. Isabel figured her aunt was selling the Three Captains' Inn, and since the three girls had grown up there—well, for Isabel since age sixteen—perhaps Lolly, the least sentimental person on earth, felt the announcement needed to be made in person. Lolly would make her announcement with the same emotion she'd use to note that the lilacs had been particularly fragrant that summer. Then the four would each go about her business, Lolly disappearing in the parlor for Movie Night with her guests, June building LEGO towers in the backyard for hours with her son, Charlie, to avoid running into anyone she knew in town. And Kat avoiding . . . Isabel.

Isabel hoped her aunt *was* selling the place. It wasn't as if it held happy memories for any of them.

Hear me. Care again. Look at me, she'd sent telepathically to Edward. But her husband's attention had remained on his iPhone. "Lolly wouldn't say," she'd told him. "But I'll bet she's going to tell us she's selling the inn."

He'd nodded absently and glanced at his watch, then grabbed his briefcase and stood up.

That was it? No comment? No nostalgia for the place

they'd spent so many nights lying together in the acres of backyard, between those century-old oaks, staring up at the stars? Making plans about much more than the children they wouldn't have.

No comment. No nothing.

Now Isabel stared at the anonymous note sticking out of her bag. She read it again. Then slipped it back into the envelope.

Your husband is having an affair . . .

Did she want to know? Some wives looked the other way, for complicated and uncomplicated reasons. But it *could* be a mistake. Last year's model Mercedes. Someone who *looked* like Edward, darting through a back door. Or she'd find out for sure that Edward was cheating on her, and then what? He'd beg forgiveness? They'd work through it? He'd swear it was a onetime thing, that he loved her?

Except he didn't seem to love her lately. A long lately. And maybe he wouldn't even lie about it.

She could crumple the note and pretend she never got it. That it *was* meant for someone else. Isabel closed her eyes and let herself drop down on a chair just as her legs started shaking. No matter what she'd do, she had to *know.*

And it was just past 6:25.

Isabel took one last look at the pasta dough on the wooden board, shoved the letter back into her purse, and drove the three minutes to Hemingway Street. Number 56 was the last house, a Greek Revival with stately pillars, and she realized she'd been here before, for a meeting a couple of years ago to discuss some town referendum that was up for vote.

Who lives here? she asked herself, trying to remember as she parked several houses away and then hurried alongside the house to the back, her heart thumping, her breath coming in ragged bursts. There was a carport, impossible to see from the street. *Please don't let* his *black Mercedes be back here.*

But there it was.

The breath went out of her.

Oh, Edward. You bastard.

Anger, so sharp she felt it piercing her stomach, was moments later replaced by a sadness she couldn't remember feeling since the morning she woke up to learn her parents were dead. She leaned against the side of the house for support, glad for the majestic evergreens that shielded her. Shielded Edward and his Mercedes from neighbors. Except one, of course.

A weathered wooden sign with THE CHENOWITHS painted in various colors was hung above the sliding glass doors. Ah, yes. Pushy Carolyn Chenowith and her husband, whose name she couldn't remember, a couple in their thirties with one child, a three- or four-year-old girl. She had a nineteen-year-old Irish au pair with huge breasts, a tiny waist, and a warm, bright smile.

What a cliché. Edward was screwing the hot Irish au pair.

She closed her eyes as a rush of tears stung her eyes. Did she go home and pretend she didn't know until she figured out what to do about it? Did she call Carolyn Chenowith right now and tell her that her au pair was sleeping with Isabel's husband and likely Carolyn's, too? Or did she storm in and confront them?

With rubbery legs, Isabel walked up the deck steps to the sliding glass doors and gave the latch a slide. The door opened. She stopped and listened. Muffled voices. Coming from upstairs. Holding her breath, Isabel walked up the white-carpeted stairs, leaning heavily on the banister, her heart pounding so loudly she was surprised no one came rushing out of the bedrooms.

And the moment she landed, Edward McNeal walked out of a room wearing only his unbuttoned shirt.

His mouth fell open and he stared at her, his face going so

pale she thought he might faint. He staggered back and held on to the doorway. "What the—"

"Baby? What's wrong?" came a woman's voice.

And not an Irish accent.

Carolyn Chenowith, naked, walked out of the same room, saw Isabel standing there in the hallway, and turned white. She seemed frozen for a moment, then ran back in and returned with a bedsheet wrapped around her, her face now red.

"Isabel, I—" Carolyn started to say, her expression . . . full of sympathy.

Edward held up his hand and stared at Isabel, his eyes glistening with tears. "Iz. I'm . . . Oh, God, I'm sorry, Isabel."

Isabel stood there, not breathing, unable to move, unable to process, unable to think.

"You're—" Isabel tried to get out the words. *You're having an affair. And with Carolyn Chenowith? A mother.*

She stared at both of them for a moment, then ran back down those white-carpeted steps and out the door.

CHAPTER 2

June Nash

June had always hoped that if she ever had to see Pauline Altman again, Pauline would be forty pounds heavier with adult-onset acne, but no such luck. Still blond, still slim, still pretty in a horsey way, Pauline stood flipping through a travel guide to Peru in the Travel section of Books Brothers. June, about to reshelve *Paris on the Cheap*, which someone had left on one of the café tables, darted into the Local Maine Interest aisle and whispered to a salesclerk that she was heading into the office for a moment.

When the door closed behind her, she let out the breath she'd probably been holding for seven years.

The last time she saw Pauline, June was twenty-one years old and eight months pregnant and working as a clerk in the Books Brothers store in Boothbay Harbor, her hometown. Pauline, whom June had beaten out for valedictorian of their high school class, had come to the checkout counter with the LSAT study guide and her mouth gaping open. "Oh, my God, Juney! You're pregnant? And *huge*. Guess you're not going back to Columbia University."

Guess not, June had thought, wanting to disappear behind the boxes of new books that had just come in. She'd miss her senior year, but she wouldn't miss how lost and lonely she'd been the previous semester in New York City. She'd gotten pregnant back in November but hadn't known till the spring term had begun. And once she'd known, everything but the pregnancy—and finding the father of the baby—had gone out of her head.

Pauline had eyed June's ringless left hand, triumph blazing. "I can't believe you of all people got *pregnant*. I figured you'd be doing some amazing internship at a magazine or publishing company and set on your path to become the editor of *The New Yorker*." A customer came up behind her, so Pauline had slipped her book in her bag and said, "God, it's amazing how even the smartest people can make the dumbest mistakes." Then she and her flat stomach and her cutoff sweats with YALE across her butt had walked away in her flip-flops.

June had had to request a ten-minute break—she'd gotten as many as she needed in those days from her kind boss—and she'd sat down on the back of the toilet seat and closed her eyes and tried to breathe it out. She hadn't made a dumb mistake. Even if it looked that way to everyone else.

Now, here she was, seven years later, hiding again in the back room, though at least the Portland Books Brothers store had a much bigger office than the tiny original shop in Boothbay Harbor, which June rarely visited for a number of reasons. But mostly because the small town was full of Pauline Altmans who'd remember June as the valedictorian with the big dreams of taking over the New York City publishing world, but who'd gotten herself knocked up on a two-night stand and had spent the past seven years as a single mother working in an indie bookstore.

She was manager now, at least. She made just enough to pay her bills and tuck a little away every month for emergencies. Luckily, Charlie's college fund was set.

And she had Charlie. Which reminded her what was

important. Screw Pauline and her judgment. Screw feeling bad about what could have been. This was her life and it was good—no, *great*, with a great kid and great friends and a job she loved. June pulled her long, curly auburn hair up into a loose bun at her nape and stuck a pen through to secure it, then sat down at her desk in her tiny office and wrote a Post-it note to pick up a snack for Charlie's playdate today after camp. His beloved cheese sticks and green grapes and maybe those little mini-cupcakes with sprinkles. She smiled at the image of Charlie and his friend sitting on the moon-and-stars rug in Charlie's room, building LEGO robots, peeling their string cheese, oohing at the cupcakes.

"Oh, June, there you are," Jasper Books said as he came out of his office, which was next to hers and even smaller, since he only came in twice a week. Tall and dapper in his trademark suspenders, thirtysomething Jasper owned both Books Brothers (with his twin, Henry, who ran the Boothbay store), and she owed him a lot. Both of them. Jasper had hired her as a clerk in the Portland store when she'd had to get out of Boothbay Harbor, away from stares, away from "Oh, wow, you had your whole life ahead of you," as if she'd robbed a bank and was being sent off to prison, and away from her aunt's . . . disapproval, if that was the right word. She'd been so grateful for the two-bedroom apartment that came subsidized above the store on vibrant Exchange Street in Portland's Old Port, where the bookstore was nestled among one-of-a-kind stores and great little restaurants and coffee shops. She was raising her son in that apartment and had been able to because of this store and her kindly neighbor, a loving grandmother who babysat. And because of Jasper, who'd promoted her to assistant manager and then manager. She loved Books Brothers, loved the smell of the books, loved helping customers choose gifts or find something for themselves, loved making her shelf-talker cards of titles she recommended. She loved the scuffed wood floors and round braided rugs and overstuffed sofas, where people could drop down and read half a book, even if half the time they put it back.

"Hey, Jasper. Going over the financials again?" Over the past few months, Jasper had mentioned more than once that sales were down and he was worried, so June had come up with several initiatives to bring business to the store. Readings from local Maine authors and two bestsellers. Three book clubs. A coffee stand and the three little café tables. And story time in the children's section. Business had improved. Not much, but some.

Jasper looked at her for a moment, then sat down in the chair wedged between the side of her desk and the wall. "June, it kills me to have to say this aloud, but Henry and I came to a decision about the Portland store. We're going to have to close it."

June bolted up. "What? Close the store?"

"In a few months, we won't be able to afford rent and overhead. We've got to face facts and let it go. Maybe we can expand the Boothbay store, which is doing fine because we own the building and it's one of only two bookstores in town. It's Henry's baby, of course, and he does seem to manage it fine from that boat of his, but he'd take you on as manager, I'm sure. You know we wouldn't just let you go."

Oh, no. No. No. No. Closing the Portland Books Brothers, a fixture on Exchange Street? Her beloved shop?

And manager of the Boothbay store? It was bad enough she had to drive up to Boothbay Harbor tomorrow night for dinner with her family. Her aunt Lolly had called a few days ago and said she had an announcement and had called Isabel too. The idea of facing her rich sister and smug Edward, her all-observing cousin Kat, and silent Lolly, who'd go about her business as though her nieces weren't even there, spending the evening watching movies with her guests instead of spending time with her nieces, was unbearable in general—but when she'd just lost her job? "Three years at an Ivy and you're still stocking books, June?" Smegward (her pet name for Smug Edward) had said more than once last Christmas. "Surely you could become an editor for a regional magazine, like *Portland* or *Down East*." Right. Because it was that easy to go from stocking books to getting hired as an editor, a dream she'd let go of when a steady, secure job, paycheck, and subsidized apartment was essential. And anyway, she wasn't a clerk. She was manager. "Oh, sorry. *Manager*," Smegward liked to say with a sneer.

She could barely believe she'd once—as a thirteen-year-old—spent hours thinking about Edward's face, the length of his eyelashes, the slope of his nose, the dark brown eyes that sometimes still triggered a memory of the angry, grief-stricken girl she'd been, a girl who'd been full of dreams until the accident that had changed her and Isabel's lives and their cousin Kat's too. Once June had gone off to Columbia, she'd found those dreams again. She'd been away from Aunt Lolly, away from that old-fashioned inn that tourists seemed to think was "authentic fishing-village chic," and she'd found herself. Until one day on a stone bench in Central Park, when she'd been stood up and her life changed again.

And work in that town where she'd been *poor-Juney*'d so many times she started expecting it from even strangers? No. "But, Jasper, Boothbay Harbor is an hour and a half away from Portland. I couldn't commute that far back and forth every day. And I can't go back there, anyway. I'll just find something here. Maybe the library—"

He gave her shoulder a squeeze. "Honey, I don't know how to tell you this, but . . . when we give up the store, we give up the two apartments. They're part of the lease agreement and were well under market."

June slumped in her chair. Oh, no.

Jasper squeezed her shoulder again. "You'll find where to go, June Bug. A new job, a new home. You always land on your feet."

Then why did she feel as if they were going to fall right out from under her?

June stood at the counter in the small kitchen where she'd fed Charlie his first spoonful of peanut butter, played Go Fish with him over and over at the table, and often sat for hours late at night when she couldn't sleep, with a cup of tea and the one photo album she had of her parents. She glanced around at the old cabinets and worn black-and-white vinyl floor and knew the place wasn't much, not like her sister Isabel's *Architectural Digest* house in Connecticut. But it was hers, and she'd painted the walls a pretty pale yellow, put down colorful, cheap kilim rugs, done some decent work with slipcovers, throw pillows, and curtains, and the little apartment on the busy street had become a cozy home for her and Charlie.

Do not cry, she ordered herself, her back to the table where Charlie, wearing the Batman cape her cousin Kat had sent him for his seventh birthday, and his new friend, Parker, sat with their take-home folders from day camp. The boys were as physically opposite as could be—Charlie, with his fine, dark hair and green eyes (he did not get that from her), and Parker, with a mop of blond curls and angelic blue eyes. June grabbed two cheese sticks from the fridge, poured two plastic Batman cups of apple juice, and brought the snack to the table. She had stopped at the bakery for the mini-cupcakes, needing something to cheer her up, such as the peanut-butter whoopie pie she'd bought herself. She'd surprise the boys with their cupcakes later.

"Guess what?" Charlie whispered to Parker, scooting his chair closer. "I can't even do our camp project because I don't have a dad."

June sucked in a breath. What was this about?

"Why don't you have a dad?" Parker asked.

Charlie shrugged his thin shoulders. "I just don't."

Parker shrugged too. "I thought everybody has a dad."

Charlie shook his head. "Not me."

Both boys turned to look at June.

That same old strange fear and dread came over her as it always did when Charlie asked where his father was. No answer was right. Sometimes, especially when she'd see moms and dads together at school functions or when she heard children mention their dads in front of Charlie, she'd feel that awful sadness that used to stop her from sleeping when Charlie was a baby, which came in handy for his night feedings. She'd let herself fantasize that John *had* met her at the bench that cold November day, that they'd gone through the discovery of the pregnancy together and decided as a couple to keep the baby. That they'd gotten married, magically found a great apartment in New York, where she'd finished her last year at Columbia and become an editor at *The New Yorker*, and he'd . . . taken a year off from taking a year off, which was what he'd told her he was doing, and the three of them lived happily ever after, an intact family. In this fantasy, Charlie had a dad.

In reality, he did not.

She took in a breath and knelt down between their chairs. "What is this project about?" she asked, peering at the open folders.

"It's for the end-of-camp celebration that all the parents get to go to," Charlie said. "We're making a huge tree, like ten people tall, and we're putting our *own* family trees on it.

Do you know what a family tree is, Mommy?" He pulled out a piece of green paper from his folder.

"I do, Charlie," she said, looking over the paper with the outline of a tree and branches. There were ovals for names. Great-grandparents. Grandparents. Parents. You. Siblings. *Fill in names and in the space below, write three adjectives (words that describe) your parents and grandparents.*

Oh, Charlie, she thought, her heart breaking. She could easily fill in one side. The Nash side. Even though there would be *D* for "deceased" where Charlie's maternal grandparents and great-uncle should be. It was the other side, starting with father and up, she had no clue about. She knew Charlie's father's name, of course—thank God she knew at least that. And three adjectives? The best she could do was tall, dark, and green-eyed. Because everything else she thought would describe him—from two dates, anyway—had been blown to bits. All that was left of John Smith was a face she'd never forget, a face she saw in Charlie's every day.

"Mommy, can we talk in the other room for a minute?" Charlie asked, his face half-crumpled, half-rigid as he tried not to cry in front of his friend.

"Parker, we'll be right back, okay?" June said. "Help yourself to a cheese stick and apple juice."

They went into Charlie's tiny room, recently done up in Harry Potter. Charlie took his magic wand off his desk, his eyes teary. "Mommy, why don't I have a dad like everyone else?"

She sat down on his bed, pulled him onto her lap, and wrapped her arms around him. They'd talked about this many times, but when he needed it repeated, she repeated it. "You *do* have a dad, Charlie, but he's not in our lives. He didn't know that I was pregnant with you, and he moved away before I could tell him. And even though I looked for him, I couldn't find him." She hugged Charlie for a moment and rested her cheek on his fine hair. "If he knew about you, Charlie, if he knew you, he would be with us. He would love you. I know that in my heart."

"But how am I going to fill out the tree?" Charlie asked.

June's heart squeezed inside her chest. She knew this day would come, when what she said wouldn't be enough. She had to do something, had to find out something. Charlie deserved to know who his father was—more than a name and two dates' worth of scanty information. "Sweets, listen to me. I'm going to try to get some information about him for the tree, okay? And about his parents and grandparents too."

Charlie brightened the way kids so easily did. "Okay."

She had no idea how she'd track down John Smith after all these years, especially when her search back then had been so fruitless. But she had to. Maybe Isabel or Edward knew someone, a lawyer or a private investigator. Isabel never went anywhere without Edward, so June was sure she'd see him at the inn for her aunt Lolly's big announcement tomorrow night.

Maybe she's selling the place, June thought with mixed feelings. She'd spent the saddest time of her life at the Three Captains' Inn, but there had been *some* good times too. Lolly had told her to bring Charlie, of course, and Boothbay Harbor in August was heaven for a kid. Still, for June the inn would always be where she'd had to go when she lost her parents—and then, in a way, her sister. Coupled with how she'd felt as a scared, pregnant twenty-one-year-old, stared at by former classmates home for the summer, Boothbay Harbor hardly felt like "home."

No, June was not looking forward to tomorrow night at all. She needed to make a life plan, needed time and space to think. She wouldn't get that at the Three Captains' Inn. Or in Boothbay Harbor, no matter how beautiful and serene it was. At least she could pop in on Henry at the bookstore. He'd love to see Charlie.

She was grateful for the hug her sweet boy gave her before he ran back into the living room to his friend, his frown so easily turned upside down.

CHAPTER 3

Kat Weller

With white buttercream icing in the pastry bag, Kat squeezed out six serif initials—*L* for Lolly, *I* for Isabel, *E* for Edward, *J* for June, *C* for Charlie, and *K* for Kat—along the edges of the German chocolate cake she'd baked for that night's family dinner. German chocolate, with its gooey caramel, sweet coconut, and crunchy pecan filling, was her little cousin Charlie's favorite. It had been too long since she'd seen the adorable seven-year-old. Too long since she'd seen his mother, June, and her sister, Isabel—Kat's first cousins. Not that they were close or ever had been. But even before Kat had become a baker by trade, she'd made an initial cake for every family dinner at the inn. Her way of . . . trying, she supposed.

Kat glanced at the clock and took off her flour-dusted, icing-smeared apron and tossed it in the wicker hamper. She had just under an hour until her cousins were due to arrive.

You okay? Oliver had texted twenty minutes ago. *I know you're worried about tonight. Call when you can. O*

He was right. She was worried. Her mother had summoned her nieces home. Years ago, when Isabel hadn't come for Christmas one year because no one had specifically invited her, Lolly had muttered, "Oh, for God's sake," and said from then on, the family would spend Thanksgiving and Christmas together, no matter what, no invitation would be issued, it was simply to be understood. And so every Thanksgiving and Christmas, Isabel and Edward would arrive from Connecticut in their black Mercedes, and June and Charlie would come from Portland in June's ancient forest-green Subaru Outback, and Kat would make her arrival by staircase, as she already lived at the inn. Always had.

But never had Lolly Weller called Kat's cousins home for any other reason. Her mother had mentioned it so casually that morning as she'd cracked eggs for the guests' breakfast. "Oh, Kat, you might want to make one of your initial cakes for tonight. The girls are coming for dinner. I asked them to come home for an announcement."

Bombshell. An *announcement*? Lolly Weller, with her long, graying braid, crab-dotted L.L. Bean flip-flops, and brown gauze skirt, wasn't the formal type. If she had something to say, which she rarely did, she tended to say it, no "song and dance" as she called making a big to-do out of something.

She's selling the inn . . . she's getting married . . . she's moving to Tahiti . . . Kat had tried to guess what her mother could possibly have to announce that would warrant calling "the girls" home when "the girls" both hated Boothbay Harbor and didn't much like each other, either. Or Kat. As Kat had gathered sunglasses from between sofa cushions and maps left in the breakfast room, and one iPhone from under a towel on a chaise longue and dropped them in the Lost and Found basket, then readied the Bluebird Room for today's new guests, she'd tried to imagine what her mother could be up to. Kat didn't think Lolly would ever sell the Three Captains' Inn, for any reason. Running off to Vegas with a sudden fiancé was out since her mother hadn't had a beau since Kat's father had died fifteen years ago. And forget moving to Tahiti or Canada. Lolly Weller had never left Boothbay Harbor, Maine—not even for her honeymoon.

Kat had tried to get something out of Pearl, her mother's elderly "helper," who came over a few times a week to fold bedding and towels and water the plants, by mentioning how surprised Kat was that her cousins were coming for dinner that night. When it wasn't Thanksgiving. Or Christmas. Just an ordinary Friday in August.

But all she got out of Pearl was "Isn't that lovely, dear. Perhaps we'll see you three gals for Movie Night tonight. Lolly said we're watching *The Bridges of Madison County.* Meryl Streep and Clint Eastwood."

Kat had let out the deep breath she'd been holding all day. If Lolly hadn't canceled her weekly Movie Night at the inn, the announcement couldn't be so earth-shattering. Then again, the happiest Kat had ever seen her quiet, somber mother was when she was watching movies in the parlor with the guests and Pearl. Kat's mother wouldn't cancel her movie club for any reason.

The oven timer dinged, and Kat checked on the lemon custard cupcakes she'd baked for Movie Night. They were done—and smelled divine. She took the trays from the oven and placed them on the cooling rack in front of the window, glancing out at the harbor in the distance. The Three Captains' Inn wasn't in the center of Boothbay Harbor, where the most popular hotels were, but rooms were always booked at the robin's-egg-blue Victorian on Harbor Hill Road, two long, twisty streets up from the harbor, but on a hill so that you could see the hustle and bustle in the summer, the long piers and myriad docks, the whale-watching boats and majestic sails, and shop after shop, restaurant after restaurant, without being right in the frantic middle of it. Inside, with its fishing-boat decor—ship wheels and buoys and nets—the Three Captains' Inn wasn't modern like some of the other area hotels, but guests seemed to love the place. They called it real New England with a real Maine proprietor who rarely smiled or made cheery small talk, but whose rooms were cozy and whose breakfasts were incredible. Kat's mother and father had inherited the Three Captains' Inn from Kat's mother's family (three sea-captain brothers had built it in the early 1800s), so generation after generation had grown up in the bed-and-breakfast.

A bell jangled above the swinging door to the kitchen. Her friend—client—Lizzie Hamm came in, her two-carat diamond ring glinting. "Hmm, that smells and looks amazing," Lizzie said, smiling at the cake the way people always did at Kat's creations, with their whimsical touches of tiny birds, shells, branches, or flowers that spelled out names or initials. Lizzie eyed the letters. "I can't wait to hear what your mom's big announcement is. Call me later to tell me, even if it's late. Oh, hey," she said, eyeing Kat. "You got your hair cut! It looks great shorter. And the bangs are hot."

Kat smiled. "Thanks. I needed a change." That was for sure. She'd gotten three inches chopped off her bra-strap-length, light blond hair so that it barely brushed her shoulders. And she'd gotten bangs for the first time ever, a fringe that made her feel . . . different. A feeling she'd been after lately. And older than twenty-five, which wasn't really that young.

Lizzie put her giant purse on a chair. "I'm dying to see my sketches!"

Kat led her to a little desk under another window that faced the huge backyard, where Lolly and Pearl were sitting at one of the picnic tables, playing what looked like poker and using small pieces of Kat's blondies as chips. It made Kat smile—and forget for a moment that in hours, the inn would feel the way it used to when Kat was growing up. Claustrophobic. Angry.

How had the four of them fit in this house, with guests coming and going through the halls and common rooms?

When the Nash sisters had moved in, Lolly turned the big attic room, with its romantic balcony, formerly her and Kat's father's bedroom, into a bedroom for the three girls, and Lolly had taken over Kat's little room across the hall. Sharing a bedroom with then thirteen-year-old June and sixteen-year-old Isabel had been an eye-opener for ten-year-old Kat. June and Isabel had been classic good-girl/bad-girl sisters, and between them Kat had turned out all right. Not too good and not too bad. Pretty much in the middle. On everything. Daring Isabel and smart June, with their strong personalities and loud lives, had made Kat go quiet, watching them from a short distance, yet unable to understand what she was seeing and hearing. Or feeling. Except for that bitter ache in her stomach reminding her that if it weren't for Isabel and June's parents, her father—her good, solid father who never drank, who never danced like a fool at family get-togethers, who never needed to borrow "a few bucks" until payday—would be alive. On the rare occasions Kat would be so overwhelmed by her cousins, by how they sucked the life out of a room, even kind June, she would scream at them, scream that she hated them, hated the sight of them, that she was sick of them, that it was their parents' fault that she didn't have a father, that they were stuck together.

Then quietly June would say, "At least you have your mother," before running away in tears. But the way Isabel, who'd always scared Kat, would stand there, unexpectedly staring at Kat with guilt, with sorrow, in her eyes, would make Kat feel worse.

Fifteen years of avoiding one another, and now her cousins were coming for An Announcement that could be anything.

Kat handed Lizzie the sketches and computer images she'd made for Lizzie's wedding cake. Lizzie was getting married next May and having 120 people. And she thankfully asked Kat, who'd baked her way through her every sad, bad, and glad time the two of them had had since they'd met in middle school, to make her wedding cake. And, no, Lizzie wouldn't hear of accepting the cake as a gift, which Kat extra-appreciated.

More of this and she could open her own bakery: Kat's Cakes & Confections, now just the name on her homemade label that graced her apricot-colored bakery boxes.

"Oooh, maybe I'll have one of those before I look at the sketches," Lizzie said, eyeing the tray of lemon custard cupcakes. "I don't care if I burst out of my gown. Gimme one."

Kat laughed. She loved her friend Lizzie. And wished she could be as sure about her own love life as Lizzie was about hers. Kat frosted one still-too-warm cupcake, and Lizzie inhaled it, then glanced down at the top sketch and gasped. "Oh, Kat, I don't even have to look past this first one. It's perfect."

Kat knew Lizzie would choose that one. Five-tiered in the shape of seashells, with delicate branches and baby's breath encircling the bottom tier. Perfect for a wedding at her family's summerhouse on Peaks Island.

"I'll take them with me and show the wedding crew," Lizzie said, sliding the sketches into her tote bag. "Okay, so tell me what's going on with Oliver." Lizzie loved Oliver, loved their "story," and wanted them married off. Everyone did.

Kat didn't know what she wanted where Oliver was concerned. Their "story" had taken over. Sometimes she thought their "story," which she could not think of without big honking quotes around it, was bigger than their feelings for each other.

Born just two months apart twenty-five years ago, Katherine Weller and Oliver Tate had grown up next door to each other, their homes separated by a stand of evergreens in which Kat and Oliver, as kids, would sit and talk, even when it was snowing. They'd been inseparable from toddlerhood, delighting their parents. "We can't wait to dance at your wedding!" they'd all say, making Kat and Oliver roll their eyes and run off. Kat remembered so clearly the moment Oliver had become *everything* to her: the cold New Year's morning she was ten years old and her mother had told her and her cousins that there had been an accident, that her cousins' parents, and Kat's father, were gone. Kat had shaken her head and started screaming and gone running barefoot in the snow through the thicket of trees, the branches scraping her, and pounded on the door of Oliver's house until Oliver's mother had let her in. Oliver had given her a pair of his boots and a jacket and mittens, and they'd rushed out under the trees, and he sat there with her in the bitter cold and rocked her back and forth and cried with her, saying over and over, "I'm sorry, Kat."

In the days and weeks and months afterward, when she'd felt so crowded out by her cousins, by her mother's grief, Kat had turned to Oliver even more. She had him. She was okay. Everything was okay. Oliver equaled okay.

One of the last things her father had said to her, that New Year's Eve she was ten years old, had been about Oliver. The first time he'd tucked her in that night he'd asked if she'd made any New Year's resolutions, and she'd said she had only one, to make a girl best friend too. Kat's only friend was Oliver, and Kat wasn't close to her mother the way she was to her dad. She longed for a girl best friend, as so many of her classmates had. Her dad had nodded and said that was a fine resolution, but that Oliver was true-blue, and if you had only one friend and that friend was true-blue, you had everything.

Oliver *was* true-blue. Was at five, when most boys were bratty. Was at ten, when most boys were horrid to girls. Was now at twenty-five, when most guys wanted to sleep with as many women as possible before settling down with the girl they'd practically been assigned to marry since birth.

"We're . . . dating," Kat told Lizzie. "Spending time together, but I don't know. Oliver is . . . my best friend. I think he should just stay that way." Sometimes, Kat felt very differently about Oliver. But just when she thought they should be together, a funny feeling would come over her, the way it always had. She couldn't put a name to it.

"I know you've always been ambivalent about Oliver," Lizzie said. "But he's *gold*, Kat. Don't let him get away because you're scared."

"I'm not scared," Kat insisted. "I've known Oliver my entire life. I'm not scared of him."

Or was she? She could still remember a singular moment, when she and Oliver had been thirteen, when everything had changed between them again—but this time in a way that separated them. One day, he was the same lanky Oliver, with his sandy-blond hair and dark blue eyes and dimple, and the next, she found herself staring at him. Differently. Thinking about what it would be like to kiss him. Her new feelings for him were the only thing she ever kept secret from him, and she was both terrified and exhilarated by that. At one of their first boy-girl parties on a Friday night, during spin the bottle, it was his turn, and when he spun that bottle, the opening landed right on her. She could remember the flush working its way along her body; she must have turned beet red. She wanted nothing more on earth than to kiss Oliver Tate.

But at the same time, that funny feeling gripped her and she'd blurted out, "I can't kiss you, Oliver. We're, like, *best friends.*"

He'd been watching her. Waiting to see what she'd do, she'd realized. And because she knew Oliver Tate, knew him the way she knew herself, she saw the flash of disappointment cross his face. She'd told him, in front of practically their entire eighth-grade class, that they were *just friends.* That she didn't want to kiss him. And Veronica Miller, with her long red hair and beautiful green eyes, had said, "I'll take the kiss for her, then," and grabbed Oliver's face. Veronica, who had so much of what Kat coveted, such as courage and the need for a real A-cup bra, had been just the first of Oliver's many girlfriends through school and college, and Kat had never had to worry about kissing Oliver again. The subject of kissing Oliver Tate had never come up again.

Until six months ago.

On a cold, snowy February morning, they'd been walking up Townsend Avenue to Oliver's cottage when he stopped in the middle of the sidewalk and looked at her and said, "I love you so much." Kat had laughed and said, "I think you're the bee's knees too," one of her mother's expressions, but Oliver turned serious and said, "No, Kat. I mean, I love you. *I love you, Kat,*" he shouted at the top of his lungs, and everyone turned to look at them. Two teenaged girls giggled and clapped. Then he took her face in his gloved hands and said, "I love you. I've always loved you."

Kat's response? That funny feeling started in her toes and worked its way up her every nerve ending until she stepped back from him and looked down at her feet, unable to speak.

"I know, I remember. You can't kiss me. 'We're, like, best friends,'" he'd said, his dark blue eyes full of tenderness and something else, something she'd never before seen in his expression when he looked at her. "But I'm serious, Kat. I've always loved you. Can you stand here and tell me we don't belong together?"

"I don't know," she'd said. Sometimes she thought she did. Other times she thought there was a man out there she hadn't met because she'd never left Boothbay Harbor. And still other times, she thought if she and Oliver Tate made love, she might explode.

Lizzie often said she didn't understand that last one. Explode? What? But Kat's cousins might get it. If anyone could,

Isabel and June could. But she couldn't talk to them; she'd never been able to.

And forget talking to her mother. Lolly Weller hadn't smiled more than a handful of times since she'd been widowed fifteen years ago and lost her sister and had raised three squabbling, grieving girls alone. Lolly didn't say much about matters of the heart at all. Lolly had had a great marriage to Kat's father until the accident. She'd been happy, well, *happier*, anyway. But then she'd gone quiet, leaving the girls to fend for themselves with their questions. But they hadn't turned to one another for answers.

And strangely, Kat had stayed. Right here in Boothbay Harbor, right here at the Three Captains' Inn, unable to even think of leaving. Her mother needed her, for one. And if she did ever leave, Kat feared she might never come back. She loved her life here. She didn't love cleaning the Three Captains' Inn, but she did love baking for the guests, both of which more than covered her beautiful attic room, which could command close to $200 a night in the summer, not that her mother would ever accept rent from her. And within a few months, six months at most, she'd have enough to finally lease a storefront and buy equipment and open Kat's Cakes & Confections. Even if she could only afford a tiny shop on a side street, it would be hers. Her savings had come from her wedding-cake business and her clients in town— gourmet food shops and coffeehouses that sold her muffins and scones. She was also the go-to baker for the town's birthday cakes. One mother of a four-year-old had frantically called last Saturday morning and paid her $100 to create a Max and Ruby cake by 4:00 p.m. One hundred dollars for a cake! Not only had she gotten the job done, she'd gotten five calls for children's birthday cakes the following week.

"Kat, if you let him go, he'll end up marrying someone else," Lizzie said, her diamond ring catching the late-afternoon sunlight. "The friendship you've been protecting all these years will change once he has a wife. You'll lose him. Which is exactly what you're scared of. So you might as well go for it."

"Lizzie, I . . ." Kat threw up her hands. She had no idea what she was where Oliver was concerned. Scared? Just not interested that way? Why didn't she know how she truly felt? "Anyway, I am going for it. We're dating."

Lizzie snorted. "You've been dating for six months and he hasn't seen you naked. That's not dating, Kat. That's *friendship.*" Lizzie stood up and slung her tote bag over her shoulder. "I just want you to be as happy as I am, sweetcakes. Cupcake for the road?"

Kat laughed, frosted one more cupcake, and kissed Lizzie good-bye. As Kat glanced at the clock, she realized she had only twenty minutes until Isabel and June were due to arrive. And until her mother made her announcement.

Kat took a deep breath, fortifying herself with the smell of cupcakes, which never failed her. Even when she was unsure what was about to happen. Kat's least favorite thing of all.

CHAPTER 4

Isabel

Isabel sat in the parlor of the Three Captains' Inn, staring straight ahead at a dour painting of her great-great-grand-father and his two brothers, the sea captains who built the inn back in the 1800s. She'd arrived ten minutes earlier and found her aunt Lolly in the kitchen, transferring steaming farfalle from a colander into a serving bowl. Lolly had touched Isabel's forearm in greeting, her version of a hug, said no to offers of help with dinner or setting the table, and told Isabel to make herself at home—relax in the parlor or backyard or out on the deck. That was it. No *How are you?* No *Where's Edward?* No *I'm so happy you're here.*

Just the usual standoffishness. Lolly had barely looked at Isabel.

Which was a good thing, since Isabel's eyes were red-rimmed from crying. Last night, after she'd learned that the anonymous note was not only meant for her but heartbreak-ingly accurate, she'd driven back home, filled two suitcases with clothes and toiletries, and then driven for hours until she'd had to pull over and let out the wrenching sobs that had dogged her through Rhode Island and Massachusetts and New Hampshire. She'd been somewhere in southern Maine, Ogunquit or Kennebunkport, found a motel, and had curled up in a ball on the bed and cried so loudly she was surprised no one had called the front desk.

She'd ignored the twenty-plus calls from Edward last night and all day today, listening to her iPhone chime over and over, oddly comforted that he'd cared, at least, to keep calling. To beg forgiveness.

Or so she'd thought, until she'd finally answered his call a half hour ago—almost twenty-four hours since she'd found him with that woman. She'd been on Route 27 just past Wiscasset, fifteen minutes from Boothbay Harbor. The familiar landmarks, the blueberry stands, the Chandler Farm, with its hilly acres of belted Galloways, their oblong black-and-white, furry bodies stark against the green backdrop of forest, made her feel less alone, and she'd pulled over alongside the white fence and answered the phone.

She'd listened to him, to what he'd said, and everything had gone so silent. Her ears felt stuffed with gauze and her mouth had gone dry and she'd started to cry again, when she'd thought she was all cried out. She'd tried to focus on the bulls beyond the fence, on the two geese that walked right past an orange barn cat, already busy stalking a leaf carried by the breeze. She'd dropped the phone in her lap, heard Edward say, "Isabel? Are you there?" And then she'd hit END CALL and sat there staring at the geese, at the cat, at the bulls, feeling so . . . shocked . . . until someone had knocked on her car window and asked if she was lost and needed directions, what with her Connecticut license plate.

From her car window she'd bought a pound of blueberries to have something from the comforting farm, and the middle-aged woman in green Wellies and overalls imprinted with the Chandler Farm logo had given Isabel some wildflowers and said, "With my compliments. I hope they brighten your day." People in Maine were like that. Kind.

"So where are you from?" a young woman sitting across

the parlor from Isabel asked. A guest. With a deep tan, huge, pearly-white sunglasses pushed atop her head, and a *People* magazine on her lap. She hadn't been sitting there a minute ago. Isabel was so lost in her thoughts she hadn't even noticed her walk in. Isabel envied the woman her ease, the cocoa-butter scent of sunblock, the ability to read a celebrity magazine.

"I'm not a guest here," Isabel said, staring harder at the painting. "I mean, I'm not from here, though I sort of am, but I don't live here now. I'm visiting." *I don't know what I am, clearly,* Isabel thought.

"I thought you said you weren't a guest here," the woman asked, wrinkling her freckled nose in confusion. "I'm from New York. The city. I'm going home tomorrow and wish I could stay here forever."

Isabel nodded. She couldn't handle small talk. And there was nowhere to go. A couple stood on the deck, sipping wine. Lolly was in the kitchen. And Kat was everywhere.

Naturally, Kat appeared in front of her with a plate of cheese and crackers and fruit and set it down, smiling at Isabel. "Help yourself," she said to Isabel and to the guest.

As the guest chatted with Kat about the number of lighthouses you could see from Boothbay Harbor—the guest "could only spot five and aren't there seven? I *have* to see all seven before I leave"—Isabel stared at the hunks of Gouda and Brie, at the plain and seeded crackers on the plate dotted with tiny flowers. *Do not cry. Stare at the little cheese knife. Stare at the painting. Focus on one of the great-great-uncles, on his wiry beard. Do not fall apart in this chintz-covered parlor.*

"Are you okay, Isabel?" Kat asked, peering at her.

She forced something of a smile. "I'm fine. It's nice to see you, Kat." She focused on Kat, tall and thin and so pretty, not a shred of makeup on her face. She'd cut her hair, Isabel thought, even though she hadn't seen Kat since last December. Kat was a low-slung-Levi's and hemp-fibered-

and-embroidered-tank-top kind of woman, exactly what she wore now, and the haircut, the poker-straight blond hair just grazing her shoulders, the fringe of bangs, made her look a bit older, more sophisticated.

"Edward with you?" Kat asked, glancing out the window for the familiar black Mercedes that Edward liked to use for long drives. But it wasn't there, of course. Just Isabel's silver Prius.

"He couldn't make it," Isabel said, looking away as the image of Edward, naked except for his open shirt, hit her again. *How could he? How could he?* she kept thinking over and over as though there were an answer.

We made a pact, Isabel . . .

And then he'd gone and broken the *ultimate* pact they'd made.

And with a woman who was a mother. The very thing Isabel wanted to be so badly. The very thing that had driven them apart, driven Edward away. It didn't make sense.

Kat nodded and then the guest peppered her with questions, leading Kat over to the hallway where an antique sideboard held maps and brochures. Isabel noticed Kat glance back at her, as though she wanted to say something else, stay with her, but Isabel looked out the window. She and Kat had never been able to talk to each other. They were six years apart, and when they'd become roommates when Kat was ten and Isabel sixteen, Kat's silence, the way she'd appear so suddenly, this thin, pale, always barefoot little girl, spooked Isabel, clammed her up.

Kat returned, holding a tray with a pitcher of iced tea, lemon slices floating, and two glasses. She poured a glass for Isabel and one for herself, then sat down on the love seat perpendicular to the chair Isabel was in. "June arrived a bit before you did, but she took Charlie over to Books Brothers so that Henry could watch him for a couple of hours." Kat leaned closer to Isabel. "Apparently, my mom told June that it would probably be best if Charlie not be here for the announcement."

The announcement. Isabel had forgotten all about it. "Not be here? Why not? What is she announcing?"

Kat picked up her glass and poked at the lemon wedge. "I have no idea. I've asked her three times in the past half hour, but she won't say and keeps telling me to set out appetizers."

"Do you think she's selling this place?"

"Why would she?"

Isabel could think of a number of reasons. But she could tell she'd offended Kat and she didn't have anything left inside her to deal with it. "I'm going to use the bathroom. Back in a minute."

She just needed somewhere to escape to with a door so she could take a breath. The bathroom on the first floor was occupied, so Isabel headed upstairs. She was about to go into the tiny powder room on the second floor when she saw that the door to the little room that had served as the Alone Closet was ajar. She pushed open the door and the Alone Closet was just as Isabel remembered. An old love seat, a faded, braided, round rug, an end table with an old lamp, and a small bookshelf filled with books and magazines. Isabel was struck with a flash of herself as a sixteen-year-old, of running up here that New Year's Eve after the fight with her mother, furiously moving the big, heavy vacuum cleaner against the door that had no lock.

The Alone Closet. Where she'd spent much of her time at the inn during the two years she'd lived at the Three Captains'. When the three girls had suddenly had to share one big room in the inn, Lolly had turned a utility closet on the second floor into the Alone Closet and put a sign on the door that you could flip over: OCCUPIED or VACANT. If one of the girls needed some space, somewhere to go inside the bustling house where she could be alone, she'd go to the Alone Closet.

She glanced into the round mirror on the wall. She was surprised she could look the same when her entire life had changed—shoulder-length, highlighted light brown hair falling right into perfect long-layered place, her light makeup, her usual slightly dressy outfit and high heels—except for her hazel eyes . . . sad was the only word to describe them. But they were less red-rimmed than when she'd glanced in the rearview mirror before she'd braced herself to get out of her car and walk up the steps to the inn.

Isabel braced herself again and headed downstairs. Now her sister, June, and Kat were in the parlor, Kat holding a cracker, and June holding a glass of iced tea and looking completely lost in thought.

"So Edward couldn't make it?" Kat asked as she reached for another cracker, clearly to have something to do. Isabel noticed Kat's cheeks redden as if she realized she'd asked that exact question ten minutes ago.

Isabel was about to say that he was away on business, but just shook her head and reached for a cube of cheddar cheese. Her sister, in her trademark outfit of jeans, white button-down shirt, and wine-colored Dansko clogs, a puzzle-piece pin that Charlie had made her only jewelry, sat on the sofa. She slid a pen from the loose bun at her nape and then gathered her wildly curly auburn hair back into a topknot.

"Hi, June," Isabel said, not even sure if her sister realized she'd come in.

June put her glass down and stood up. "I didn't even see you, sorry." She gave Isabel something of a hug, then sat back down. "Edward chatting up a guest about the Red Sox outside?" June asked with a bit of a smile.

Isabel squeezed the cube of cheese in her fingers. "He couldn't make it."

Lolly, who'd kept herself scarce for the past half hour, ap-

peared in the open doorway of the parlor. "Dinner's ready."
Saved, Isabel thought. For the moment, anyway.

"You look so nice, Aunt Lolly," June said, and her aunt
certainly did. Lolly had changed from her usual outfit of cotton tank top, gauze skirt, and flip-flops into a peach-colored
cotton dress and taupe ballet flats. Instead of her usual long
braid, her gray-blond hair was in a neat bun at the back of her
head. She also wore lipstick. Lolly never wore lipstick.

"Wow, what's the occasion?" Kat asked as they followed
Lolly across the hall into the big country kitchen, where Lolly,
who had declined continued offers of help, had everything set
out on the table—a tossed salad, pasta primavera in a pesto
sauce, a plate of cheese, a beautiful round loaf of Portuguese
bread, white wine, and the bouquet of wildflowers that Isabel
had brought.

"Oh, I forgot the Parmesan," Lolly said, walking to the
refrigerator and ignoring Kat's question. Then she forgot the
dressing. And the butter. She got up and down from her chair
at least ten times. *What* was this big announcement? Something that clearly had her rattled. And that she didn't want a
child around to hear.

When everyone was seated at the rectangular farmer's
table, napkins on laps, the serving bowl of farfalle making its
way around, Kat and June and Isabel had spent at least five
minutes glancing at one another with questioning looks and
shrugs. Finally Kat said, "So, Mom, what's the announcement?"

"Let's hold off on that until we've eaten," Lolly said, then
sipped her wine.

Isabel glanced at her aunt. Lolly's plate was empty; she
always waited until everyone else's plate was full before she
helped herself. But even as plates filled up, Lolly had taken
only a small piece of the bread and poured herself a quarter
glass of wine.

Dinner was a repeat of the parlor. Usually Lolly could be counted on to fill the silence, tell a dry story or two about a town referendum or a past guest, but she stayed quiet. June pushed pesto-coated farfalle on her plate. Kat slid worried glances at her mother. And Isabel tried not to let images of Edward enter her mind. But here at the inn, where he'd been such a vital part of her life, he was all she could think about.

"So how's Edward?" June asked, taking a sip of her wine.

"Great," Isabel said, stabbing a cherry tomato. She wondered if anyone would be surprised if she stood up and said, *You know what? He's not great. He's having an affair and I caught him in the act and I have no idea what my life is now. No idea who I am without Edward, just like you said, June.* No one sitting around this table liked Edward much. They had once, of course. But Isabel seemed to be the only one who hadn't noticed how much he'd changed. Or maybe she was the one who'd changed.

No one pushed Lolly about the big announcement. They'd learned growing up that when Lolly, the most secretive person on earth, was ready to say something, she would. When forks were finally rested on plates—after ten minutes, really, since no one ate much—Lolly stood up, seemed flustered, then sat back down.

"Mom?" Kat asked. "Are you all right?"

"No," Lolly said, glancing at her plate. She closed her eyes for a moment, then opened them, looking at each woman. "I have something to say. Something difficult. I . . . found out a few days ago that I have pancreatic cancer."

Kat bolted up, knocking over her wineglass. "What? *What?*"

Lolly righted the glass, then put her hand over Kat's. "I know this is shocking and is going to be tough to hear." She took a deep breath. "It doesn't look very good."

Acid burned Isabel's throat and sharp pricks of tears hit the backs of her eyes. This couldn't be.

"I'm going to fight it, of course, though it's advanced. Chemotherapy can manage the symptoms, slow the progression, but—" She glanced at Kat, then across the table at Isabel and June. "Sneaky bastard managed to get to stage four before I was diagnosed. There's no stage five."

Isabel felt a hollowness spread in her stomach. She wanted to get up, go to Lolly, go to Kat, who had covered her face with her hands. But Lolly stood up, said she'd be right back, and went into the kitchen.

"This can't be," Isabel whispered to Kat and June, who both sat there, looking stricken, their faces pale.

Lolly returned with the German chocolate initial cake and set it in the middle of the table. "I saw this cake cooling earlier in the kitchen, and I stood there looking at it and started crying—and you know I'm not a crier. So I doubly knew it was the right thing to ask you all to come tonight. I didn't want to tell you two over the phone," Lolly said to Isabel and June. "And, Kat, I didn't want to tell you without the four of us being together. We haven't been together in years. We've never really been together, have we?"

Together. Isabel used her napkin to wipe under her eyes. She glanced at her aunt, just fifty-two years old, looking so herself, so strong, so the way she always did. Her blue eyes sparkled, her cheeks were rosy. She looked healthy.

Isabel and June both fired questions at Lolly, but she held up her hand, and they went silent.

"Isabel and June," Lolly said, slicing the cake, "maybe you both could stay a bit, even just the weekend or the week. I'm going to be starting chemotherapy on Monday, and I'll need some help. I've long had the inn booked for Labor Day weekend and most of the fall."

"I can stay the week, longer if you'd like," Isabel said, clearly surprising everyone enough that they all turned to stare at her.

June shot her sister the same incredulous look that Kat did, then turned back to Lolly. "Me too."

Lolly nodded. "Good. Thank you. Though, I just realized I was so upset about the diagnosis that I wasn't paying attention and okayed reservations for this weekend and during the week and of course for Labor Day weekend, and now I don't have a room for one of you. I figured June and Charlie could stay in Kat's old room, and Isabel, if it's not too tiny, maybe we could bring a cot up to the Alone Closet."

"Or Isabel and June could stay in my room with me, and Charlie can have my old room across the hall," Kat said, then clamped her mouth shut as though even she couldn't believe she'd offered her sanctuary.

"Sure you don't mind?" June asked. "Charlie is a very light sleeper, so it would be great to give him your old little room."

"I don't mind," Kat said. "Okay with you, Isabel?"

Everyone stared at her, the one they all expected to say, *No way, it's not okay.* She nodded, unsure if it would be okay but finding herself a bit comforted by the idea of not being alone in a room with her thoughts.

"Good, it's settled then," Lolly said. "Oh, and tonight, at nine, Pearl and two of our guests are coming for Movie Night. It's Meryl Streep month. Maybe you three can join us. We're watching *The Bridges of Madison County*, one of my favorites. A movie to take me away is just what I need."

There were solemn nods around the table. Murmurs of "Of course we'll stay and of course we'll be there tonight for the movie and whatever else you need."

Out of the corner of her eye, Isabel saw June's hand reach out just slightly as if to take Isabel's, but Isabel didn't notice in time and June retreated. Isabel closed her eyes at the memory of the last time June had reached out her hand for Isabel's. On a day much like this one, when Lolly had sat the three girls down on the old red sofa in the parlor and told them there had been an accident, that their parents were gone, that Kat's father was gone. Then, Isabel had taken her sister's hand, and they'd sat there, clutching hands and not speaking, tears rolling down their faces, and Kat had started howling and run out the door. Lolly was all any of them had.

And now she might not be either.

With three nestled bowls in her hands, Isabel stood behind Kat at the stove, where Kat shook the big popcorn pot. Lolly didn't believe in microwave popcorn from a bag. For Movie Night, only hot oil, kernels from the farmers' market, a few shakes of the handle, and a generous sprinkle of salt would do.

Isabel hung on to the small details, finding the right oil for the popcorn in Lolly's huge pantry—canola, according to Kat—helping Kat frost the lemon custard cupcakes while June went to put Charlie to bed in Kat's old tiny room on the third floor, and bringing in extra padded folding chairs from the closet for the guests. Focusing on all this, on making sure each yellow cupcake was evenly frosted with Kat's lemon icing, on finding the three big ceramic bowls for the popcorn, on placing the chairs just so in the parlor, was all that stood between Isabel and her knees buckling.

Her husband. With another woman.

Her aunt. Stricken with cancer.

Isabel. Here.

Kat started to shake the pot with all her might, and Isabel expected her to fling it at the wall any second and howl. Isabel could tell from the subtle movements of Kat's narrow shoulders that she was crying. Isabel glanced at June, who came back into the kitchen, her own eyes glistening.

"Let me," Isabel said, taking the handle. Kat stepped back, tears streaming down her cheeks. Isabel shook the pot, tears welling. Aunt Lolly had always seemed as strong as the clichéd ox. She'd rarely had a cold. And now . . .

"She could have years," June said, her voice barely above a whisper. "She's strong."

"She is strong," Isabel agreed, turning around. "She always has been and she is now."

"What the hell do either of you know about my mother?" Kat said. "When's the last time you were here? Either of you? Last Christmas? It's *August*."

As Isabel stared at her sister in shock, Kat covered her face with her hands and she dropped to her knees in front of the stove. She was sobbing.

Isabel and June both knelt beside her.

"Kat, of course we care," Isabel said, pushing Kat's blond hair out of her face and behind her ear. "Your mother is all we have."

Kat bolted up and stormed out the back door.

"Oh, God," June said. "What do we do? Go after her? Leave her be?"

Isabel peered out the kitchen window to see if Kat was out there, sitting on a chaise or on the big rock at the far end of the huge yard. But she didn't see her. Isabel herself wanted to run. And stay. "I don't know. I shouldn't have said what I did. I always say the wrong thing to Kat."

"Lolly *is* all we have," June said. "I know how you meant it, Isabel. And so did Kat. She's just beside herself. We'll get through this. And Lolly will be okay."

Isabel let out the breath she didn't even realize she'd been holding. She nodded, unable to say anything.

The back door opened, and Kat came in, her eyes red-rimmed from crying. "Sorry. I'm just . . . freaked."

"We know," Isabel said, reaching out a hand to rub Kat's arm. At least Kat didn't shrink back.

Kat stared at the floor for a moment. "Is Charlie all set?"

she asked June. "I can bring in a fan if it's too hot in that little room."

"He's fine," June said, twisting her long hair into a side braid. "He was asleep before I even shut the door behind me. Henry took him clamming in the mudflats earlier and—"

"Girls, everyone's ready," Pearl called, poking her white-gray head through the swinging door of the kitchen. "I'll bring in the cupcakes." She came in and took the round tray, stopping to glance at the three of them. Clearly she knew about Lolly. "A movie can take you right out of yourself for a couple of hours. Movies are magic like that. Come, dears."

Isabel filled the three big bowls with the hot popcorn and handed one to Kat, one to June, and took one herself. "We'll talk more after the movie," she said to Kat. "Okay?"

Kat wouldn't look at Isabel, but she gave something of a nod and led the way to the parlor, where Lolly, looking as if everything were just fine, as if it were an ordinary Friday night, was placing a disc into the DVD player.

"Everyone ready for Meryl and Clint?" Lolly asked. "Doesn't get much better than those two."

No one questioned why Lolly Weller wanted to watch a movie, favorite actress or otherwise, on a night such as this, when she'd just told her daughter and nieces that she had cancer, that the prognosis wasn't good. Growing up, they'd heard the stories about how Lolly, just eighteen years old and heartbroken over a friend's death in a swimming accident, had gone to see *The Deer Hunter* because of an article she'd read in the newspaper about Meryl Streep—whose first name was really Mary Louise, just like Lolly's—and her fiancé, a celebrated actor who'd died young of cancer. And later, how Lolly had gotten through that first year as a widow rais-ing her daughter and orphaned nieces by losing herself in Meryl's weepiest dramas, and when she'd finally been able to watch a comedy, she'd rented *Defending Your Life* and smiled, laughed, even, for what seemed the first time since that tragic New Year's Eve.

Movie Night had been an inn tradition for decades. In the early nineties, a guest asked if Lolly had a VCR so she could rent the movie version of a book she'd just finished, *Sophie's Choice.* Lolly had seen the film and been so deeply moved that it was one of the few movies—and maybe the only Meryl Streep movie—that she was sure she could never bear to see again. She'd lent the woman her VCR, but then had bought a fancy one for the parlor, a large, cozy room that faced the harbor, replaced the ancient nineteen-inch with a thirty-two-inch, and stocked the cabinet with her favorite films, and she and Pearl had designated Friday nights as Movie Night. At first they each picked a movie, but then they decided on themes. Forties month. Robert De Niro month. Food month. Foreign month. Romantic-comedy month. Sissy Spacek month. Last month was John Travolta.

Meryl Streep month was just nine months ago, and Isabel, who occasionally came for Movie Night during holidays, had been riveted by *Julie & Julia* last Christmas. There was rarely discussion about the movies they watched; Pearl often fell asleep a half hour in. But Friday Movie Night was a tradition at the Three Captains' Inn, the back wall of the parlor devoted to black-and-white, glossy photos of Lolly's favorite actors and actresses in antique frames. There were three of Meryl Streep at various ages. Clint Eastwood. Al Pacino. Sissy Spacek, another favorite of Lolly's. Tommy Lee Jones. Cher. Brad Pitt. Susan Sarandon. Kate Winslet. Keanu Reeves, who Lolly thought was sexy. Rachel McAdams and Emma Stone, young actresses who Lolly thought "had something."

And now Isabel knew why her aunt had chosen to make it Meryl Streep month again. Lolly had always said that a Meryl Streep movie was as good as a chicken soup, a best friend, a therapist, and a stiff drink.

If only it could cure cancer too, Isabel thought as she sat on the cushy love seat with her sister, their backs against the many soft throw pillows, and placed the bowl of popcorn on the ottoman in front of them. Lolly and Pearl were on the white sofa, iced tea, wine, cupcakes, and popcorn on the old steamer trunk, supposedly found at the bottom of the Atlantic, that served as a coffee table. Kat, tying knots with the long red rope of Twizzlers that Isabel remembered was her favorite childhood movie snack, was on the big, flowered beanbag by Lolly's feet. And Carrie, a thirtyish guest at the inn—not the chatty one from earlier—who mentioned her husband was upstairs watching baseball, was on the high-backed, overstuffed chair, a cupcake and popcorn on a plate on her lap.

Kat bolted up and went running out, and Lolly put down the remote and went after her. Isabel shot a glance at June; her sister's eyes were teary like her own. In a few minutes, Lolly and Kat were back, Kat's expression grim, but she sat and started tying her Twizzlers in knots again.

Lolly turned out the lights and pressed PLAY on the remote control for the DVD player, which Lolly had upgraded years ago, along with the big-screen TV. At first, Isabel wanted to escape to her room, until she realized the rooms were booked and she was sharing Kat's bedroom. With June, as well. At least here in the parlor, she'd have a good two hours to sit in the dark, no one questioning her about Edward's absence.

Anyway, now, no one would have to wonder what was wrong. Her aunt had cancer.

As people filled the screen, Isabel was barely interested. When she realized she was watching the adult children of a mother who'd just died, tears welled up in her eyes. A brother and sister, in their early forties, going through their mother's things in an Iowa farmhouse. Via a letter their mother left for them, they discover there had been another man in her life.

Suddenly, they were back in the past with Meryl Streep, an Iowa housewife by way of Italy, with her beautiful face and long brown hair, her Italian accent, saying good-bye to her husband and teenaged children for four days while they attended a county fair. And there was Clint Eastwood, a photographer looking for a certain covered bridge, which Meryl would be happy to show him, since it was hard to find.

Then in the smallest gestures, in the most simple questions, Meryl's character fell deeply in love with the man who reminded her of the woman she might have been, a life she might have had. When Clint asked her to leave her husband and children and come with him, on the road, to not give up this once-in-a-lifetime love, her first reaction was yes.

Then it was no. She couldn't destroy her husband and children. Or the love between her and Clint. By going with him.

The test came on the day Clint was leaving. Behind his truck, at a red light, was Meryl and her husband in their old pickup. Meryl gripped the door's handle. If she was going to go with Clint, this was her chance. She'd have to do it *now*, when so presented with the chance to switch trucks, *lives*. She'd have to open that door and go. Isabel's breath caught as she watched Meryl Streep, in emotional agony, tighten her hand on the handle. *She won't go,* Isabel thought. *She won't.* When she didn't, Isabel let out her breath.

As the credits rolled, Pearl stood up and began gathering empty plates. "Wasn't that wonderful! I think I've seen it three times now, and each time it's like the first time, even though I know how it ends."

"Meryl Streep is a marvelous actress," the guest Carrie said. "I don't think she's ever looked more beautiful than in *The Bridges of Madison County.*"

"She's stunning," Kat agreed, and Isabel and June both nodded.

Lolly stood and pressed EJECT and put the DVD back in

the case. "It's one of my all-time favorites. I've seen it three times too, Pearl, and each time I see more and hear more." Lolly glanced at her daughter, then at Isabel and June. "I'm glad you girls came. It's been such a day that I think I'm just going to turn in. I'll see everyone bright and early in the morning—six thirty for our breakfast in the kitchen."

As Lolly and Pearl started to head out, June said, "No discussion? I can't even move I'm so shaken by Francesca's choice."

"Shaken by her choice? You mean to stay with her family?" Isabel asked as Lolly sat back down next to her.

They all bid good-bye to Pearl, whose husband was waiting outside in his car to pick her up.

June reached for a cupcake and took a bite. "She betrayed herself."

Isabel stared at her sister. "She betrayed herself? So if she'd left, she wouldn't have been betraying her husband and children? Her vows? It was bad enough that she gave in to her attraction for another man in the first place."

"Well, I totally understood why she did," Kat said, getting off the beanbag to stretch her legs. She sat down on the sofa. "Clint gave her back a piece of herself. And I like how she asked him to stay for dinner *only* after he said those very key words: 'I know exactly how you feel.' That's all anyone wants. Someone who understands them."

"That's what everyone wants, but sometimes it just can't be," Lolly said, glancing out the window, and Isabel wondered what she was thinking about, but Lolly didn't say anything else.

Isabel leaned her head back against the cushions. Edward obviously didn't think she understood him. Maybe she couldn't understand him since she'd changed. Just as he couldn't understand her.

But that was what working on your marriage meant. Mar-

riage was hard work. You didn't just give in to romance, to a
lack of responsibility. Meryl's character had fallen in love with
the traveling photographer the minute he said he knew where
she was from, that he'd been *there*. Because Bari was who she
was, deep inside.

Isabel felt the tears threaten again. Carolyn Chenowith
connected with Edward McNeal on a base level? How was
that possible? It was Isabel who was from where he was from.
Isabel who'd lost her parents as he had. Isabel who had cried
herself to sleep for months, as he had. Isabel who'd been by
his side for fifteen years, since they were sixteen years old.

How could Carolyn have trumped that? How?

"If it's what someone's looking for," Kat said. "What they
need, at a particular time. Don't you remember how Meryl
couldn't even remember how many years she'd been married when Clint asked? She was counting on her fingers and
couldn't even remember. Because she'd been married forever
and lost track of *herself*. And here Clint was, reminding her
she'd been someone. Someone else, once. And Clint was the
man who saw that woman she'd been."

Isabel felt herself tremble. What had Edward felt in Carolyn's presence? Someone he'd become? Someone who didn't
know who he once was? Maybe he wanted the opposite.

Isabel shook her head. "You know who else saw the
woman she'd been? Her *husband*. She met her husband in
Italy when he was a soldier. Her husband fell in love with her.
So he knew who she was too."

"But now—"

Isabel cut off June. "She slept with another man for four
days while her husband and children were away. She cheated.
Broke her vows. And then she says good-bye to her affair,
knowing it won't last anyway, and her life went on as though
she didn't do something awful—and almost left twice."

June stared at her. "Whoa. Did we watch the same movie?

Meryl gave herself up when she married the Iowa farmer. She was expecting something else when she married him and came to America. She wasn't expecting a farm in Iowa. Remember when she said, 'This is not what I dreamed of when I was a little girl'? In those four days with Clint, she found herself again. But she gave up her own happiness to do the right thing. Which was the wrong thing. I think."

"I know what you mean," Kat said, poking at the wrapper of her cupcake. "It's not like I wanted her to go off with Clint and leave her family. But I didn't want her to betray herself, either."

Isabel stared at Kat. "Betray *herself*? What about her *husband*?"

"I agree," Carrie said. "She married him knowing what she was getting, just like I chose what *I'm* getting. Guess who barely wanted to walk around town today? Guess who's upstairs watching the Red Sox on his iPad? She chose that life, just like I chose mine."

"She didn't know, not really," June said. "Remember she said that all she could think of was America? She wanted the adventure. Instead she got a rural farm in Iowa."

"I do think you know what you're getting, though," Lolly said, glancing out the window again. "How dashing could her husband have been when she met him? How exciting and adventurous could his personality have been? I think he just represented adventure to her. His very foreignness to her was enough then."

Kat's gaze was thoughtful on her mother. "And like Meryl said, 'We are the choices we've made.'" Kat let out a breath. "Make a mistake and . . ."

"I wonder if she did make a mistake," Carrie said. "She has her children, yes. And the farm is beautiful. But she was emotionally lonely. That's a high price to pay."

Everyone nodded at that. Isabel looked out the window, at

the harbor lights. She'd been emotionally lonely for months. Much longer, if she let herself really pinpoint it.

"My favorite part," June said, "was when Clint and Meryl were lying together on the floor in front of the fireplace after they slept together, and she's crying and she asks him to take her someplace he's been, someplace on the other side of the world—"

Kat nodded. "And he takes her to her hometown. A tiny town in Italy that he just happened to have gone to because he thought it was pretty."

"I think that's when Meryl fell completely in love," June said. "He gave her back herself, gave her back the woman she feels like inside, the one no one sees, not her husband or her children."

"And she made *him* need something again—her," Lolly said.

Isabel stared at Lolly. Carolyn had something that had trumped Isabel's sixteen years and everything those years were. Had she made him need her? What was that need?

Maybe just something different. Excitement. Hot new sex.

"It wouldn't have lasted, though," Isabel said, though she wasn't really sure of that. "Maybe it would have. But ninety-nine percent it wouldn't have, for exactly the reasons Meryl had said. She would have resented Clint for everything he took her away from. When he said that 'this kind of certainty comes but once in a lifetime,' Meryl knew he could have meant her certainty about everything—herself, her family's happiness—the world around them."

She wondered how long Edward's affair with Carolyn would last. A few weeks, now that he didn't have to skulk around at 6:00 p.m.? According to Edward on the phone today, Carolyn's husband had left her months ago for another woman. Isabel always thought the illicit quality of affairs was what sustained them, the drama of it, not any real feeling. But Meryl and Clint's affair was about *feeling*.

"I was kind of torn about one of the reasons she stays," Carrie said. "She's worried about what leaving will say to her daughter, who's sixteen and about to discover love and relationships for the first time. And what did her mother's life of quiet desperation say? The daughter ended up staying in a bad marriage for twenty years. So maybe staying *wasn't* the heroic thing."

"I do like what she writes in the letter to her children," Lolly said. " 'Do what you have to, to be happy in this life.' That has to be individual. I think Meryl's character was happy *and* miserable staying, just as she would have been happy and miserable leaving. She was trapped either way. She made the honorable choice for the right reasons."

Was this how Edward felt? Trapped? In love with another woman, but trapped by his wife, by the promises they'd made?

"I think she should have gone," Kat said, her voice quieter, sadder. "Life is too short, isn't that what everyone says? And isn't that so clear now?"

"Too short to hurt the people you claim to love," Isabel shot back. Kat glanced at her, surprised, and Isabel wanted to apologize, but Kat turned away, and Isabel didn't know quite what to say.

"There's no one answer," June said.

We are the choices we have made went through Isabel's head over and over.

It was true, Isabel knew. She'd chosen to change. She'd chosen to let the tiny glimmer of wanting a baby to blossom in her heart. She had chosen to share that with her husband instead of keeping it in the vault. She'd chosen to bust the pact.

"I think Meryl did the right thing," Lolly said, standing up and scooping up the empty cupcake wrappers and errant pieces of popcorn. "Why is her happiness more important than her husband's or her children's? Why is her happiness more important than what it will mean to her children, how it will color their lives?"

"I'm not sure I agree," June said, getting up to help collect glasses. "*Un*happiness colors lives too. The daughter is proof of that, isn't she? I'm not saying she could just run off with Clint and walk away from her life. But to betray yourself, to break your own heart like that . . ."

She shouldn't have had the affair at all, Isabel wanted to shout. If she hadn't let herself fall for Clint . . . But Isabel understood why she had. She burst into tears and sat there shaking.

"Isabel?" Lolly said.

"I caught Edward with another woman."

June gasped. "Edward?"

"I'm so sorry, Isabel," Kat said, laying her hand on Isabel's arm.

"Oh, no," Lolly said. "I don't believe it."

Isabel told them about yesterday. About the note. About the stupid, lumpy pasta dough and their anniversary. About walking up those white stairs. About the look on Edward's face. "And when I finally answered the phone today, he told me it wasn't just sex, it's not just an affair, that he's fallen in love with this woman, that he'd loved her for months before he even let himself—" Isabel couldn't say the rest.

"Oh, Izzy. I'm so sorry," June said. "I feel awful for defending the affair in the movie now."

Isabel looked at her sister. "But is it defendable? Because he's supposedly in love, it's okay? He didn't betray me and his vows? Everything's all good because he fell in love?"

I think it's important that you know that I love her, Isabel. It's not just sex, it's not just some torrid affair. I wouldn't do that to you.

Thoughtful. He'd done that to her for the real thing.

This kind of certainty comes but once in a lifetime. . . .

Obviously it didn't. Edward had been that certain about her once. Now he was certain about pushy Carolyn Chenowith. For now, anyway.

Isabel wrapped her arms around her legs and hugged her knees to her chest. She wasn't the same Isabel who'd fallen for Edward at sixteen. She wasn't that same scared girl anymore, that girl who thought she was terrible. She wasn't exactly sure who she was anymore. She wasn't going back to her house in Connecticut—except eventually to pack up her belongings and divvy up the contents of their big house. As if she wanted her soft and cozy down comforter that used to remind both her and Edward of Maine. Or paintings they'd picked out together on their honeymoon and vacations. What was she going to do now? Just stay at the inn with her aunt and help with whatever needed doing, she told herself, needing a solid plan to hang on to.

Lolly took her hand. "I'm glad you're with all of us."

Isabel let herself cry. Lolly tightened her grip, and for a moment Isabel felt her mother's hand on hers, more of a comfort than anything else could possibly be.

CHAPTER 5

June

The Movie Night dishes were washed, the parlor cleaned of every last trace of popcorn, and a quick google of *pancreatic cancer* both reassured and scared June, Isabel, and Kat from doing much more research on the subject tonight. June sat on the balcony of Kat's room, staring out at the harbor, at the lights on the boats, on the white and red lighthouse just visible. Pearl had been right about how a movie could transport you out of your life for a couple of hours; *The Bridges of Madison County* had touched June so deeply that she could talk about it for hours more. But it wasn't Meryl Streep dancing with Clint Eastwood to Italian opera in her farmhouse kitchen that she was thinking about right then. It was that rat bastard Edward.

At age thirteen, it had taken June only months to realize that her "dream boy," the one she'd taken quizzes over in *Seventeen* magazine, the one her prettier, sexier, worldlier older sister had won, was more nightmare boy and a jerk. *Edward says* had become sixteen-year-old Isabel's new way of beginning sentences. *Edward says cursing is totally uncivilized. Edward says sugary cereals like Lucky Charms will rot your teeth* and *lower your chances of getting into an Ivy. Edward says everyone grieves in his own way and you have to let them.*

That last one had been the only right thing Edward McNeal *had* ever said. He could talk about grief like no one else, make you feel so comforted, so wrapped in a cocoon of understanding that you almost forgot why you were in the Center for Grieving Children in the first place. For a few minutes, anyway. So, yeah, June had always gotten why Isabel had fallen so hard for him; June had too, for a few weeks until the *Edward says* began and Isabel began changing so drastically.

"She's changing for the good," Lolly would say when June had followed her aunt around the inn as Lolly dusted and polished, confused about what had happened to her loud, selfish, class-cutting, cigarette-sneaking, pot-trying, slutty older sister.

"But she's suddenly a Goody Two-shoes . . . like me," June had said. "She says *please* and *thank you!*"

"And that's a bad thing?" Lolly asked, the smell of lemon polish tickling June's nose.

"She's a weirdo robot now," June had explained, not wanting her mean sister back but not sure she liked this new one either. This controlled one—controlled by *Edward says.*

Not until much later, years later, did June realize Isabel wasn't controlled by Edward, but by her grief. And Edward was good at grief.

"Better she's going to school and eating healthfully and saying *please* than what she used to do," Lolly had said. "Cut her some slack, let her develop into who she needs to be right now. She's not hurting anyone. Remember that. She'll find herself, people always do."

That had stayed with June for a long time. The *people always do.* Did they? Had her aunt found herself after her husband and sister and brother-in-law were killed and she'd turned quiet, speaking only when spoken to? At least Lolly said a lot *when* spoken to. But unless you sought Lolly out, asked her something, she'd never engage you in conversation.

Not about if you had homework or if anyone had asked you to the dance at school or why you looked sad. Once, when June had screamed, "You don't even care that I'm sitting here looking like I'm about to cry!" Lolly had said, "I do care, June. But my way is to give you space to do that."

June hadn't been sure she wanted space in those days. Not that space was something she'd gotten much of, crowded into one big room with her air-sucking sister and quiet cousin who stared at them both. If June felt eyes on her, she knew Kat was around.

When the three of them had been in a room together, any room, one or two of them always left. It was no wonder why.

June stared up at the sky, just a few stars out, and focused on one, hoping it wouldn't turn out to be a plane. She needed that star to stay fixed. Isabel's news had shaken her. Edward might be an ass, but he'd been there—always. Once, a few years ago, after Edward had said something over Thanksgiving that had hurt June's feelings—she'd always cursed her sensitivity—something about giving Charlie American cheese in his grilled cheese instead of a healthy cheese such as Swiss or cheddar and didn't she care what she was putting into his growing brain and body, she'd whispered to Isabel, "God, I really dodged a bullet with Edward."

Isabel had winced, and June had felt sorry right away that she'd said it—to Isabel, anyway. But then Isabel had shot back, "Like you ever had a chance? And your one big romance lasted all of how long? Two days? Don't talk about what you know nothing about."

By the time the last of the stuffing and pumpkin pies had been gobbled up, Isabel and June wouldn't even look at each other. They'd politely avoided each other until the next get-together, Christmas. In between, they'd sent obligatory birthday cards. But then every year, Isabel and Edward would show up for Charlie's birthday party—a *five*-hour drive each way, every year, no matter if the party was held in a kiddie gym or at the playground or in her little apartment over the bookstore. Isabel was *there*, with a big wrapped gift, something amazing that June would never have been able to afford, such as a red PlasmaCar or an Indiana Jones LEGO City set, Charlie so excited he'd run around in circles clapping, and June would find all the anger going out of her. Five, ten minutes later, either Isabel or Edward would ruin it, say something awful about the public schools in Portland or how June was just scraping by, and the momentary magic was poof—gone.

June had always wished her relationship with her sister could be more like June's relationship with Kat. Polite. No slung comments—well, except for tonight, but June understood and then some. She and Kat had always spoken to each other like acquaintance coworkers at a company function. No depth, but no feelings got hurt, either.

"June? Help with the bed? I think it's stuck."

June ducked inside to find Kat wrestling with the trundle bed across the room, trying to pull out the lower, full-size bed. She yanked and then kicked it, dropping down onto the top bed.

June sat beside her. "Your mom can beat this. She *will* beat this."

Kat leaned her head back and let out a deep breath. "Let's get the bed out, okay?"

June peered at her cousin, wishing they were closer, wishing she knew just what to say. But she was scared about Lolly's diagnosis too, and being scared together was probably the best any of them could do.

It took a few minutes, but they finally wedged the bed out and it sprang up. June wheeled the bed by the balcony so that if she was on her stomach and kept her pillow at the near end, she could see the stars and the harbor. In minutes they made up both beds, spreading out the light summer quilts. Even though it was late August, it rarely got hot enough to warrant the noise the fan made, but Kat had the antique bronze one in the corner, just in case. June glanced at the bed where she'd spend the foreseeable future. The soft, faded shams and the old starfish quilt looked so inviting June could imagine falling asleep in two seconds.

The bathroom door opened with a cloud of steam, and Isabel appeared in a pink tank top and gray yoga pants, her long brown hair with its pretty gold highlights wet around her shoulders.

"Are you okay, Isabel?" June asked. Stupid question, she realized. Of course Isabel wasn't okay.

Isabel stared down at her feet, at her shimmery-pink toe-nails. "No."

June glanced at Kat. Clearly, neither had expected the honesty, even after the confession in the parlor.

"I'm so sorry, Isabel." Kat sat cross-legged on her bed, then pulled her knees up and wrapped her arms around them. Also clearly, Kat wanted to say something else but wasn't sure what.

June sat down on her bed. "What do you think's going to happen now? He'll get her out of his system and you two will work it out?"

Isabel walked over to the balcony and just stood there, staring out. June's gaze landed on Isabel's rings, the two-carat, round diamond that had long-ago replaced the tiny chip on her original engagement ring and the diamond-studded, gold wedding band.

"Is that how it works?" Kat asked. "I mean, how do you get past that?"

"That's exactly why the Meryl Streep character stayed in *The Bridges of Madison County*," Isabel said, still staring out at the night. "Because she knew her husband, her children, would never be able to get past it. I guess Edward just didn't care if I could or would or not." She broke into tears, and June and Kat glanced at each other again and jumped up, going over to the balcony. They stood on either side of Isabel, Kat touching her hand for a moment, and June letting out the breath she'd been holding for a half hour.

"This is crazy, but Edward's affair, how you found out about it, reminds me of how I felt when Lolly told us about the accident," June said. "When something happens that you never imagined, that you *can't* imagine, you're just so shocked for a while that you can't process it."

Unless it wasn't such a shock to Isabel. June knew that sometimes wives were blindsided, and sometimes they knew but managed to stay in denial. She had no idea what Isabel's marriage was really like.

"I was like that on the drive up here," Isabel said. "In total shock. It was how I was able to drive in the first place. But when it hit me, that it really happened, the anonymous note, finding Edward walking out of that woman's bedroom, his expression—and how things had been between us lately, more than lately, I guess . . . it all hit me and I broke down and stayed at some motel and just cried all night and most of the next day until I had to turn up here."

"And as if what you were going through wasn't enough, wham," Kat said. "My mom's announcement."

Isabel covered her face with her hands for a moment. "I don't even know what to focus on. Every time I think about Edward, I'm suddenly thinking about Lolly. And then I'm back to Edward, then Lolly." She took a deep breath and let it out, braiding and unbraiding her long hair over her shoulder. "He's not asking me to get past it, anyway. He said he loves this woman. I'm sure he would have told me he's going to file for divorce, but I hung up before he probably had the chance."

Kat sat back down on her bed. "I can't believe this. June

is right about what a complete shock it is. You and Edward have been together since I was ten years old."

"A week after we moved into the inn," June said.

"And now, Aunt Lolly . . . I know Lolly and I were never very close. But, Kat, your mother is—" Isabel took a deep breath. "She just means a lot to me."

"Me too," June said. "She looks so much like Mom, too, doesn't she, Iz?"

Isabel didn't say anything. Maybe mentioning their mother wasn't the thing to say right then. June always thought one of the reasons Isabel stayed away from the inn—from Lolly, June, and Kat—was because of what Isabel had said to her mother the last night they'd ever seen her. June knew Isabel had never forgiven herself. And that argument had happened here at the inn, in the first-floor hallway. June knew the way everything hung in the air here. Pain. Grief. Loss. Years of it.

Kat walked over to her desk and sat down on the chair, leaning back and staring up at the ceiling. "I can't believe any of this. Any of it."

They were silent for a few moments, the only sound from the front lawn, the crickets and cicadas, some people outside, heading back from the harbor.

"So tomorrow, we'll work out a schedule of taking over Lolly's duties," Isabel said, turning around and heading to the bed under the dormer window. "She may be very weak and sick from chemo and unable to do much."

June nodded. "It was amazing how talkative Lolly was after the movie. And just think, she almost left right after. I don't think I've ever heard her go on like that."

"I was surprised too," Kat said. "I mean, she can be opinionated, but watching the movie, talking about it, all the different points of view—and then what it led to," Kat added, glancing compassionately at Isabel. "She really opened up. I hope it continues."

"I'll bet it will," Isabel said. "Meryl Streep is her favorite actress and she's seen all these films before. They all must mean something to her—represent different times in her life. I got that feeling, anyway, from the way she'd look away or out the window sometimes."

"She's complicated, huh?" Kat said.

June smiled. "Complicated and tough." June glanced at Isabel. "Are you okay with taking over Lolly's duties? It'll be a big change for you."

Isabel stared at her. "Because I don't work?"

June felt her cheeks burn. Yes, that was exactly what she meant, but she hadn't meant to say it, hadn't meant to be unkind. Not now. "I just mean that none of us, Kat included, is used to running the inn and taking care of guests. Remember that obnoxious family from last Christmas? They rang bells! *More tea. Do you have softer hand towels? Can you do anything about the smell of the ocean? So fishy. It drifts up, you know.*"

Kat laughed. "The only reason I got through their visit is because they went nuts over my baking. The one who wouldn't take off her heels, even for a hike, told me I should start my own baking business and she'd make huge orders. I couldn't stand those ladies, but they did give me some confidence. Still, I wanted to take that little bell of theirs and flush it down the toilet."

June tried to picture Isabel Nash McNeal on her knees in front of a toilet with a scrubbing brush and Ajax. Her sister had a housekeeper who not only cleaned their four-thousand-plus-square-foot home twice weekly but cooked most of the meals and froze them with labels and reheating instructions.

"I'm sure I can do what's necessary," Isabel said, and June could tell her sister was stung by their perception of her. But Isabel wasn't exactly used to catering to others, including Edward, since he'd liked to pay people to do that. Then again, June knew that Isabel regularly volunteered as a grief counselor, and if Isabel's words and expression could soothe a woman who'd just lost her husband of thirty years, surely Isabel could handle a few vacationing guests. No matter how thoughtless or obnoxious.

"I guess you can take the little room when June and Charlie have to go back to Portland," Kat said to Isabel. "Or I can switch with you. I might like having that old childhood room of mine. Before everything changed, you know?"

"I might as well just tell you," June said, pulling out her own yoga pants and a T-shirt from her suitcase. "I'm staying a few weeks at least. The Portland Books Brothers is closing. And the lease on the apartment goes with it. Jobless and homeless." Jobless and homeless when she had a child to raise. Pathetic.

"You're not homeless, June," Kat said. "This is your home."

June got up and walked back over to the balcony and stared out at the harbor, following a midnight cruise boat as it moved through the dark water. The Three Captains' Inn wasn't home. June had lived at the inn, had this bedroom, for five years, and it hadn't felt like home. But she wasn't about to say that to Kat. "I'm quite the superstar, aren't I? This is the second time I've come running back here with my tail between my legs. I'll have to take Henry's offer of a job at Books Brothers. I'm exactly where I was seven years ago."

"Same place, maybe," Kat said. "But you can't possibly be the same person. You've been living in Portland. Raising a child on your own. And you're a superstar to Charlie."

June let out a sigh and stared at the stars. She'd never forget standing right here, twenty-one and pregnant, the father of the baby nowhere to be found, her beloved parents gone, her older sister hundreds of miles away. Not that she'd have turned to Isabel anyway.

"June, when you got pregnant, did you ever think of not keeping the baby?" Isabel asked.

June whirled around to face her sister. "What is *that* supposed to mean? That I shouldn't have had Charlie, that I should have given him up? That it was irresponsible of me then and shows even more so now that I don't have a job or a home of my own?"

Isabel's face turned red for a moment. "No, God, June, I didn't mean it that way at all. I just asked because . . ." Isabel bit her lip.

"Because?" June prompted, glaring at her sister.

"Forget it. We should all get some sleep."

"Because *why*," June repeated. Hard.

Isabel glanced down at her wedding ring and twisted it. "Because I always thought I wouldn't know how to be a mother, someone's mother. I just wondered if you worried about that too when you found out you were pregnant."

"Oh," June said, her anger and that same old sense of shame whooshing out of her. "Of course I did. I was only twenty-one and a senior in college. I went from caring only about my term paper on *Middlemarch* to being responsible for a baby. By myself. But, you know what? Even back then I didn't doubt I'd be a good mother. It's about love and taking care of the baby and doing what you have to. I knew I'd do all that. I was just scared."

And for a little while, anyway, she'd survived by living in something of a fantasy world—waiting for John Smith to come for her. Seven years ago, when she'd first returned to Boothbay Harbor, newly pregnant and carrying a baggie of saltines everywhere she went, she'd sit out here on the balcony and daydream about John walking up the cobblestone path, dropping down on one knee, and asking her to marry her as she stood bathed in moonlight. But he'd never come, of course. Wherever he'd been going, the independent, seeking, traveling guy hadn't wanted her to be a part of it, hadn't asked her along on his journey, as Clint Eastwood's character had to

Meryl Streep's. Because *The Bridges of Madison County* was a movie, a romantic movie, and not real life.

Except for the part about the four days. That was real to June. She'd fallen deeply in love with John in *two* days.

"I'm trying to imagine having a baby now, and I'm twenty-five, four years older than you were, June," Kat said. "There's no way I'm ready for all that responsibility. I have to hand it to you."

"Me too," Isabel said.

June glanced at both of them, touched by what they'd said. She reached into her tote bag for her body lotion, the scent of lilacs filling the room as she rubbed cream on her dry elbows and knees and slid under the soft quilt on her belly so she could look out at the harbor.

"I was just thinking how hard it must have been for you," Isabel said, slipping into her own bed. "I know, I know, you're probably going to say I'm sounding condescending. But I just mean that I realize now how alone you must have felt. I . . . know what that feels like now. Not that I'm comparing being a young single mother with— You know what I mean, right? I—I'm sorry I wasn't there for you at all, June."

June glanced at her sister, who was staring at the ceiling. She did usually accuse Isabel of being condescending. "I'm glad you're here now."

Isabel gave something of an awkward smile and turned out the lamp on her bedside table. "Well, good night."

"Good night," Kat said, turning out the main light.

"I'm just going to check on Charlie for a sec," June said, slipping back out of bed. Only once she was in the dimly lit hallway did she realize she'd been holding her breath again.

June, Charlie, Lolly, Isabel, and Kat sat around the big table in the kitchen, the early-morning sunshine lighting

the room. It was six thirty. Lolly had reminded June and
Isabel last night that the dining room was open for guests'
breakfasts from seven until eight thirty, so the family would
need to eat beforehand—and not to bring up the C-word in
front of Charlie until Lolly and June decided when and how
to tell him.

June bit a slice of bacon and buttered Charlie's freshly
baked corn muffin, her heart heavy. Her son had such little
family. And now he stood to lose his great-aunt.

"Guess what?" Charlie said, looking around the table, his
green eyes bright and happy. "My mom is going to find my
dad and my grandparents so I can fill in my family tree! It's
for my day camp project and due on Wednesday."

All eyes turned to June.

"Mom, are you even going to be able to find out anything
by Wednesday? That's in four days."

Her stomach knotted. "Well, sweets, I might not be able
to find out about your father's side of the family by Wednesday, but we can all help fill in my side of the family tree, and
we can write your counselor explaining that we're working on
the other side." And that Charlie wouldn't be finishing out
the remaining week of camp, after all. She'd talk to Charlie
about that over the weekend.

"Will I get an F on the project?" Charlie asked, hand
paused midway to his mouth with bacon.

June felt tears prick the backs of her eyes.

"First of all, there are no grades for camp," Isabel said.
"Camp is definitely not school. And second, all families are
different, Charlie," she added, her gaze soft on her nephew.
"Right? There's no wrong answer when it comes to a family
tree. Some families have lots of relatives and some just have a
few. But you're lucky because you have all of us in this room."

Thank you, Isabel, June beamed silently across the table as
she caught her sister's eye.

"That's right," Kat said. "You have all of us. And we all love you."

Charlie smiled and counted each person at the table. "I have Great-Aunt Lolly and Aunt Isabel and Cousin Kat—and my mom. That's four *different* kinds of relatives to put on the tree!" A dog barked and Charlie jumped up. "That's probably Elvis wanting me to play fetch. Can I go, Mom?"

Elvis was the neighbor's gentle yellow Lab. He'd been just a puppy when June had moved into the inn fifteen years ago. Now he was up there in dog years, sweeter than ever, and still loving to chase sticks.

"Make sure it's Elvis and not that stray who came into the backyard last night," Isabel said. "I went out to get some air, and a white mutt with black ears came over and put his chin on my foot. He looked friendly, but you never know."

Charlie ran over to the door and pushed aside the curtain. "No, it's Elvis."

"Go ahead, sweetie," June said. "Stay in the yard, though, okay? And remember, it's very early, so not too noisy."

When the door closed behind him, Lolly said, "He's getting so big." She said it so quickly that June knew she didn't want questions about her diagnosis. Or how she was feeling. Lolly looked more like herself today in a soft, black tank top, white gauze skirt down to her ankles, and her red, crab-dotted flip-flops, her silky, shoulder-length, gray-blond hair in its usual braid.

"And more handsome every day," Kat said, clearly picking up on it too. "He's such a good, sweet boy. What a doll."

"He looks just like his father." June stared at her plate, where she'd been pushing around eggs for the past five minutes, ever since Charlie had brought up his father. The family tree. "How am I going to find a man named John Smith after seven years when I couldn't find him then?"

"All you can do is try." Lolly took a sip of orange juice.

"Narrow down what you can. If you can't find him, it's just something Charlie will have to accept."

June felt herself bristle at Lolly's typical comment. Accept. Accept. Accept. "It's not fair. He has to accept never knowing his father, never meeting him, because I picked a guy looking for an easy mark."

"From what you told me about John Smith back then," Isabel said, pushing her own scrambled eggs around, "that doesn't describe him at all."

June wouldn't have thought so, either. It had amazed her that a guy with the most common name in the United States of America could be the most original she'd ever met. They'd had two incredible dates, the kind of dates where you feel there's no one else in the world but you and him, and you talk about everything, you laugh, you look into each other's eyes with the crazy surety that you'd found what all those love songs are about. They'd met in a bar on the Upper West Side of Manhattan near Columbia, where she'd been with two girlfriends, and he'd been sitting at the bar and overheard her mention Maine, where he was from, too—Bangor, a city two hours north of Portland—so they'd started talking and hadn't stopped. He was taking off a year from college (he'd been at Colby) to backpack around the country. He was beautiful, almost ethereal, so pale, with dark green eyes and dark brown hair. She'd never seen a guy as beautiful as John. He was supposed to leave for Pennsylvania and the Liberty Bell the next day, but he'd said he'd postpone it as long as she'd go out with him. On their second date, the next night, June, a virgin, had ripped off her own clothes and then his.

And as the cliché went, she never saw him again. They'd made romantic plans to meet for lunch—she'd bring the drinks, he'd bring the sandwiches—at the *Angel of the Waters* statue of the Bethesda Fountain in Central Park. As she sat there on that stone bench in her red peacoat and scarf with her two bottles of water and two chocolate chip cookies from her favorite bakery, she'd been thinking that she finally understood what everyone was talking about—what her sister, Isabel, had always been talking about when it came to Edward, who hadn't been so smug back then. June had never felt this way about a guy before, two dates or not. He'd been her first—in every sense of the word.

By one o'clock, when he still hadn't shown up, she gave him the old benefit of the doubt; he hadn't spent the past three years in New York as she had; maybe he'd gotten lost on the subway over, maybe he was lost in the park. But as she waited, biting her lip in the November wind, rubbing her gloved hands together because she was getting so cold, she began to realize he wasn't coming. He had one of those prepaid drugstore cell phones, but he could only make calls, not receive them. So she had no phone number to call and he hadn't called her. By three o'clock—two hours later—she'd finally gotten up. As she'd walked toward the beautiful steps, she thought she saw him at the top, but it wasn't him, and her heart sank so painfully that she burst into tears.

Valedictorian, ha. June had been a stupid twenty-one-year-old who'd believed everything he'd said, believed in that kind of falling in love. Idiot. She'd tried to track him down when she'd first found out she was pregnant, went back to that same bar they'd met at every night for two weeks. Walked around that *Angel of the Waters* statue so many times that cold January she could draw it from memory. But she'd never found him. He was a good-looking guy traveling the country and probably keeping some kind of log about screwing a girl in every state.

June Nash. The good Nash sister, knocked up at twenty-one, before her senior year of college. She'd dropped out, having too much morning sickness to continue, and she'd been such a mess then that she hadn't taken care of formally withdrawing from her classes the way her aunt Lolly had told her to, so she'd gotten incompletes for the semester and never did go back to finish her degree. When she'd come home, to Lolly's—"Well, what's done is done"—she'd driven up to Bangor, his hometown, and asked around about a John Smith, which was ridiculous, of course. Bangor was a city, not a small town. She'd been sent, albeit kindly, on a wild-goose chase where she'd met seven John Smiths, from a seventy-year-old barber to a young lawyer. None him, none related. She'd even gone to Bangor High School and asked to see yearbooks, but the year he graduated (if he really was twenty-one, as he'd said), there were two John Smiths, both blond and both not him. She'd sat in that high school office looking at yearbooks a few years before and a few years after his possible graduation year until the tears came and teenagers stared at her.

She'd told Henry Books the truth about why she was back, why she needed a job, and he'd hired her on the spot as a clerk at Books Brothers, even though he didn't need help. Henry, a loner with an intense girlfriend, had been a godsend those first months when Charlie was a newborn. Henry gave her as much time off as she needed, even letting her bring Charlie to work and rocking him when he started to fuss, which delighted female customers and brought in business that summer and early fall. But when living with Lolly at the Three Captains' Inn, living in Boothbay Harbor, period, became too unbearable, she transferred to the Portland store with her baby, the rest of her college fund, and Lolly's "You'll be fine, but you can always come home if you want. You know that."

Yes, she had known that. And that was the dichotomy of Lolly Weller. Ungiving. Giving. That people were complicated was one of the first lessons June had learned in life.

June wrapped her hands around her coffee mug. "He stood me up for our third date. After he got what he wanted."

There was no denying that, so everyone went back to eating. Pushing around their food, really.

"Of course, you might be opening a can of worms," Lolly said. "I'm not looking for trouble, but I'm just saying. You didn't know that boy then, obviously. You don't know what kind of person he really is."

A terrible combination of anger and shame slammed into June's stomach. Shame at being called out a fool. For being a fool. And anger at her aunt for not understanding. Never understanding. June *had* known John Smith for those two days. When she'd tried to explain to Lolly seven years ago that she'd fallen so deeply in love, the kind of love that now made her understand Meryl Streep's character in *The Bridges of Madison County*, Lolly had said you couldn't really love someone—let alone know someone—in two days. "And anyway," Lolly had added, "you found that out."

To say that her aunt Lolly had not been much of a comfort in those days, early in her pregnancy, would be the understatement of the century. But Lolly had been there. Had seen June through until she'd moved to Portland when Charlie was almost a year old. She owed her aunt for that and much more. Lolly wasn't the loving, motherly type with hugs and empathy. She was who she was, and June had accepted that long ago. Not that it made June come around much. But the thought of losing Lolly—

She wouldn't even go there.

"I'll help you track him down," Isabel said, covering June's hand with her own for a moment.

June looked at Isabel, surprised again.

"Me too," Kat said.

June waited for Lolly to say something, that she wished her the best, *something*, but she didn't.

. . .

With her big, black sunglasses and straw hat keeping her incognito from any old classmates, June wound her way through the throngs of tourists on Townsend Avenue and crossed over to Harbor Lane, the cobblestoned path that offered her favorite shops in Boothbay Harbor. The lovely, little Moon Tea Emporium with its five round tables and cheery yellow interior, a storefront palm reader/fortune-teller who was unusually perceptive if not exactly psychic, a gift shop that had been in its spot for generations, its one-of-a-kind wares, such as the lighthouse-shaped watering cans lining the steps, and of course, at the end of the lane, Books Brothers.

June pulled open the door with its red canoe handle and smiled as always at the interior. Books Brothers was like stepping into a magical living room lined with bookshelves and bamboo rugs. Comfortable, old chairs and throws invited sitting to read, and the artifacts on the walls and lining the tops of the shelves told of all kinds of sea adventures. Above one row of shelves was a battered, old red canoe. Above another, a local artist's photo essay on Boothbay Harbor. Teachers loved bringing kids on field trips for Henry to talk about where he'd gotten his finds.

She smiled at the clerk, a college student as June had been when she'd started at Books Brothers. "Henry in his office?"

The young woman shook her head. "Out on the boat. Docked, I mean."

June headed back past bestsellers and biographies and memoirs and Local Maine Interest, past the Kids' Corner, which Henry had built out of a lobster boat's facade. A little face appeared in the ship's round window and June smiled. At the back of the store, she pulled open the door marked EMPLOYEES ONLY and went through another door, which led directly onto the pier where Henry's houseboat was docked. Henry was kneeling at its starboard, a small can of something at his feet and a sander in his hand.

"Hey," she said, pushing her sunglasses atop her head. "She giving you trouble?"

He stood up and smiled at her, his pale brown eyes squinting like Clint Eastwood's. "This boat is never trouble."

On the outside, Henry's houseboat looked like a regular, albeit large, motorboat. But down the steps, it turned into a cozy home, with two bedrooms, a living room, a galley kitchen, and a bathroom. Many of Henry's artifacts decorated the walls and surfaces, as did his art collection. And a photograph of Vanessa Gull, his on-again, off-again girlfriend. Beautiful in a goth way, Vanessa was the least-friendly person on earth, which was likely why June suspected Henry liked her. She didn't believe in niceties. And Henry didn't like phonies. They'd been a couple on and off since June had first worked at the Boothbay Books Brothers. A long time. A few years ago, during a holiday visit, June had brought Charlie over to the boat to say hi to Henry, and Vanessa, who'd been there, had said to June, "Something about you bothers me," and stalked off in her shiny dress and Frye harness boots. Like Henry, Vanessa was ten years older than June and made her feel like an awkward kid. June was glad she wasn't around now.

"I've come to officially accept your offer," she said. Yesterday, before she'd driven up from Portland, she'd called Henry and was about to launch into her tale of woe, but he'd cut her off with an "I already know. You can start next weekend if that works. Manager, same salary."

She'd told him she wasn't sure what her plans were. If she could actually live in Boothbay Harbor again.

"It's been a long time since you left, June," he'd said. "You can let all that go. Job's yours if you want, but let me know this weekend—next weekend's Labor Day and I need to have someone in place for the rush. Don't make me hire Vanessa."

She'd laughed. Vanessa had once covered for her in the

store and scared away three customers who complained bitterly to June and Henry later. Vanessa was barred from working in the store ever since.

"Good," he said now. "To give you some time with your aunt, why don't you start Friday for the Labor Day weekend crush. It'll be just you most days, with Bean as salesclerk on the weekends and holidays. You and Charlie will stay at the inn, right?" She'd told Henry about Lolly's announcement when she'd picked up Charlie after dinner last night. The way he'd wrapped his arms around her, held her close, made the world go away for those fifteen beautiful seconds.

"For now," she said. "We'll see."

"Well, you know you're both welcome here anytime it gets too crowded."

God, she loved Henry Books. He was like a gift, the wise older brother she never had. She used to think about him a lot, about the way his driftwood-brown eyes did crinkle like Clint Eastwood's when he smiled. That his thick, dark, straight hair fell from a cowlick above his left eyebrow. How tall and rangy and muscular he was. The way he was a Mainer through and through, a man of the sea, but reminded her of a cowboy firmly rooted in land.

When they'd worked together, Henry had treated her like the scared twenty-one-year-old she was, like a kid who'd gotten herself in a situation, instead of like a woman, and she'd stopped thinking of him as any kind of romantic possibility. Anyway, she'd been very pregnant and then taking care of a newborn and infant in those days, and Henry had been out to sea or being mauled by Vanessa. The woman always reminded June of Angelina Jolie in her Billy Bob Thornton days, all long dark hair, kohl eyeliner, and ferocious sensuality. June Nash, in baby spit-up and Danskos, could hardly compete.

"Thanks again for last night, for watching Charlie for me,"

June said. "He's crazy about this boat and loved that you took him clam digging."

"He's a great kid," Henry said, and June knew he meant it. She felt her heart swell with a little bit of pride, a little bit of *I did something right.*

"Go be with your aunt and your family," he said. "I'll see you Friday and we can go over anything that's changed or is handled differently here. Be sure and tell Lolly if I can help in any way, to just call."

"Aye, aye," she said, slipping her sunglasses back on and heading up the pier. Six free days to spend with Charlie and helping out at the inn was perfect.

"Oh, and, June," he called out. She turned around. "You need anything, you know where to find me."

She nodded and smiled. She didn't have much, but she had Charlie and Henry Books. And from the way things had gone last night and today, she was starting to have her family again.

CHAPTER 6

Kat

Late Sunday afternoon, a bracing wind whipped through Kat's hair—still smelling faintly of the chocolate and icing she'd used to make a birthday cake earlier—as Oliver drove them "somewhere secret" in his convertible. They were heading around the far side of the peninsula. He had a surprise for her was all he would say. The wind felt so good, overtaking everything, especially thought. She watched the excursion boats in the gray-blue water, people pointing at a whale finally making an appearance. She was so numb that she was grateful to just sit, focus on the splash, on the sound of the car gears shifting.

She had blue icing under her thumbnail, she realized now. But there had been no time to shower or even wash her hands. She'd been working on the pirate-ship cake for five-year-old Captain Alex when she'd every now and then heard her mother training Isabel on the art of inn management. "If a guest calls for you, drop everything and see to him or her, even if you're in the middle of lunch or on the phone. If you see any type of mess, whether trailed sand or a dirty cup, take care of it immediately." In between, there were guests to greet and questions to answer about maps and how to get to the Botanical Gardens, and if they had only a day left, should they go to Portland or head up to Rockland and Camden? Her mother's voice was sure and strong and business as usual, and for a little while Kat was so absorbed in creating a perfect bridge for the top of the pirate cake that she forgot about words such as *cancer*. Until she heard it from the backyard, through the open window, two couples, guests, chatting over wine, Lolly's complimentary cocktail hour from five to six. "My sister had ovarian cancer," one of the women was coincidentally saying. "She fought for as long as she could, but she passed away two years ago." And then another voice: "My mother too. Breast cancer." Then: "I'm so sorry." And tears and a man's voice saying, "Come here, honey."

Kat had stood so still, her eyes closed, her hands, her lips, trembling. "Please don't take my mother," she'd whispered, her hands moving into prayer formation. And then her mother had come into the kitchen for another hunk of Gouda, saying something about the fog burning off, and when the door swung behind Lolly again, Kat burst into tears. She'd moved away from the window and over to the nook that was hidden from view and slid down and cried into her forearms. She couldn't lose her mother.

She'd sat there until a memory made her laugh. She and her parents in the backyard at the far end of the property, lying side by side, Kat between them, pointing out which clouds looked like what. Kat had a reindeer. Her mother had a car. Her father had a turkey, which made Lolly Weller howl with laughter.

But then the memory had faded and Kat had gotten up, sober and sad, grateful that Oliver had been due to pick her up any minute to "take you somewhere you need to go." She'd had to get out of the inn, away. He'd shown up, on time as always, looking so incredibly good, also as always, tall and muscular in worn jeans and a dark-green T-shirt, his thick, wavy, sandy-blond hair all tousled.

As the car headed down a side road to nowhere that she could think of, she reached into her purse, pulled out her little notebook and a pen, and wrote, *Where are we going?* Then held it up for him to see.

He glanced over and smiled. "Write for me, 'You'll soon see.'"

When Kat was little, she and Oliver would sit on the wide window ledges of their bedrooms, which faced each other across the side yard, and have conversations by holding up big pads of paper they'd write on. Their own text messaging, pre-cell-phone. Sometimes it was enough just to see him sitting there. When his parents or her mother would call one or both of them inside, Kat would feel the lack of him. Oliver's parents had long ago sold their house and now lived up in Camden, but sometimes, such as this past Friday night, Kat wished she could have gone to the ledge and held up her big pad with *I'm so scared* written across it, soothed by Oliver's *Anything you need, I'm here.*

This past Friday, after the movie, after she and her cousins had spent a couple of hours talking in the room they now shared, Kat had slipped out of bed, written a note, and quietly left to drive to Oliver's cottage. He'd taken one look at her stricken expression and seemed to know it was about more than her cousins' coming. She'd told him about her mother. Said words that got caught in her throat, such as *stage four. Metastatic. Chemotherapy.* He'd held her close against him and let her cry, as he had so many times before. They'd talked for a bit, but there was nothing to say; *I don't know* was the only response to all her questions, all his. They'd lain on his big leather sofa, his arms wrapped around her, and when she woke up a couple of hours later, she'd left him a note and driven back home, slipping back into her room, both startled and unsettled at the sight of Isabel and June fast asleep in the trundle beds. They were there *because* of Lolly, and the unfamiliar sight of her cousins in her room only reinforced how scary the situation was. The minute she'd lain down in her bed and pulled the quilt up around her chin, she'd felt scared again and wished she'd stayed with Oliver, his arms tight around her. She'd gone back over Saturday night after dinner, and they'd repeated much of Friday night. It was just what she needed. Little talking. Good soup. Strong arms. Someone who'd known her mother—and her—forever.

She wasn't much in the mood now for surprises or secrets. She wanted to tell Oliver to turn around, just take her to his house and draw her a bath and let her stare at the bubbles or the ceiling, but the words didn't come and she just let the car go. She *was* scared, scared in a way she hadn't been since her father died. Between her mother and her cousins, Kat couldn't take one more "surprise."

"We're here," Oliver said, pulling up alongside a gravel path, nothing but trees beyond. "Look out my window."

Kat realized how lost in thought she'd been. To their left was a meadow, a field of wildflowers. She could see pink and red sweet williams, her favorite. Foxgloves and black-eyed Susans and sweet yellow buttercups. She smiled. The flowers were better than a hot bath.

"Come." He took her hand and led her to a weathered wooden bench right in the center of the field.

Kat breathed in the scents of flowers, of sun and warmth and nature. For a moment she had an urge to spin around, her head back, and let the flowers and sunshine work their magic. Here, there was nothing but earth and sky. Possibilities. But she just lay down, her arms stretched high above her head. She plucked a buttercup, one of the first flowers Oliver had ever given her as a kid, and held it to her face. "This is beautiful and wonderful, Oliver," she said as he lay down next to her. "Just what I needed. It's like being transported to a fluffy cloud in a brilliant blue—"

But the fluffy cloud in a brilliant blue sky made her think of her parents again. Of the day they'd looked up at the clouds and spotted reindeer and turkeys and cars, her mother's laughter at the notion of a turkey-shaped cloud. A sound Kat hadn't heard in a long time. Not that same laughter, anyway.

"I knew you'd like it," Oliver said.

She felt the tears come and she couldn't stop crying. Her mother was dying. For as long as Kat could remember, her mother had been reserved, standoffish. And since Kat's father died, Lolly had retreated inward even more. Put some kind of thicker wall up between them, between her and everyone.

Kat would never forget what she'd screamed at her mother the day Lolly had told her that her father was gone. "He should have let me come with him, like I wanted to! Then I could be in heaven with him!" Over the years, as Kat thought about that, it shamed her to the point that she'd have to throw up. What a thing to say. To her mother. To someone who'd lost her husband, her sister, her brother-in-law. When Kat had been thirteen, she'd been consumed by it, what she'd said, and Oliver had told her to just go talk to her mother about it, say she didn't mean it, and Kat had worked up the courage, but her mother had shot her down, as always.

"Kat, we don't need to think about that." And then Lolly had gone back to her ledgers, leaving Kat alone with the shame, with the weight of something she couldn't dislodge from inside her chest.

But now, images of Lolly Weller's kind moments came over Kat. The way her mother had held her for hours that first night without her father as Kat sobbed and screamed. That she'd taken over Kat's father's nightly job of reading Kat her bedtime story, even when she was clearly so tired from running the inn, from taking on her grieving nieces, that she looked as if she might fall asleep herself. How she'd once driven sixty miles to a local bird healer when Kat had found an injured robin in the backyard. How she'd been there, all these years, steady, sturdy, going over figures in her ledger, taking care of guests, making the egg breakfasts.

How she seemed to be trying to do something now by bringing her nieces back to the inn. And by fighting the cancer. Kat wouldn't have been surprised if Lolly had said, "I'm not going to bother with that awful chemo and radiation. My time is coming and I'm going." That was more her mother. That she was fighting was both unusual and not; that was how complicated Kat's mother was. But no matter what, Lolly was her anchor. Even if they weren't close the way some mothers and daughters were, shopping together or sharing secrets while they peeled carrots, they were business partners, in a way. They shared the inn. And now . . .

Oliver sat up and pulled her to him and held her. He didn't say that everything would be all right. He didn't tell her to stop crying. He didn't say anything. Kat clung to him, gripping his T-shirt. When the tears finally stopped and she could breathe again, she looked out at the wildflowers, at the old bench right in the middle of the meadow.

"Some romantic must have put that here, just to sit and be among all this raw beauty," she said, gesturing at the bench. She took a deep breath and got up and put out her hand. Oliver took it and she led him over to sit.

Oliver nodded. "Yeah, me."

She glanced down and there it was, among the many scratched-in initials and names, OT carved into the second slat and KW in the third. Not in a heart of course, but marked. It had been their bench out by Frog Marsh, where they'd sit and talk away from their houses, watching the frogs and toads leap from lily pads. "What? How did you get this here?"

"I won the bid to design the new park. And they wanted this 'old thing' out, so I asked if I could have it, sentimental value and all. I passed this place a few weeks ago, and after I heard about your mom, I thought this would be a good place for you to come and think, come and breathe, to get away but feel rooted, you know?"

Yes, she knew. She knew exactly. She loved how sentimental he was. That a landscape architect who designed and built residential and commercial gardens and yards and walkways appreciated a meadow of wildflowers.

"Oh, Oliver." She reached for him. "You're beyond wonderful."

"Does that mean you'll marry me?" he asked, pulling a small box from his pocket.

That funny feeling started in her toes but didn't work its way up as it usually did. This was Oliver standing among the wildflowers and their saved bench in this field of possibilities and asking her to marry him. She wanted the world to feel right again, safe again. He held open the box and took out the antique gold ring with the glittering round diamond. He slipped it on her finger.

"I love you more than anything. And I know how scared you are right now, how worried you are about your mom. I want to be your family, Katherine Weller."

Damn him for saying exactly the right thing. In exactly the right place.

She hesitated, but only for a second. "Yes."

Then, shielded by old oaks and evergreens, Kat let Oliver lay her down on the wildflowers, lift up her sundress, and make love to her for the first time.

She didn't feel any different. After all these years, all these years of fantasizing about having sex with Oliver Tate, imagining it, but being so . . . afraid of it, she and Oliver had finally made love, the sun on her face, the breeze in her hair, and Oliver's eyes, full of love and tenderness and *I've waited for this my whole life*, intently focused on her.

But she didn't feel different. Or differently. *Why?* She certainly hadn't exploded into a million pieces the way she'd always thought she might.

She stood at the door to the inn and turned to wave at Oliver as he drove away, that funny feeling back in her toes. She knew she wouldn't tell anyone her news that night, and so she slid the beautiful ring off her finger and looked at it, then put it in her pocket. She took out her phone and texted Oliver, *Keep it to ourselves till the right time to tell Lolly, ok?*

A moment later, he texted back, *You got it.*

She braced herself at the door, sure that her mother would know something was different the moment she saw her. She and Oliver had made love. She and Oliver were engaged. Once again, in the space of a moment, her life was completely different.

Her mother had cancer.

Kat was engaged to be married. Married.

She sucked in a breath and opened the door, the smell of popcorn in the air.

"Oh, good, you're back," Lolly said as Kat closed the door. "I know it's not Friday, but since I'm starting chemo tomorrow and need something fun and light to take my mind off things, I declared it impromptu Movie Night. We're watching *The Devil Wears Prada*. It'll be us and your cousins, Pearl, and Tyler and Suzanne, our young guests." Though her mother was looking right at her, her eyes didn't light with *You finally said yes—to everything with Oliver. I can see it all over your face.* It had always surprised Kat as a child that people could have such big secrets inside them that didn't show.

Anyway, Kat wasn't in the mood for fun and light. Or a movie. She was nervous about the chemotherapy starting tomorrow. And she wanted to run up to the Alone Closet and take out the ring and stare at it. Had she said yes to Oliver's marriage proposal? She had. Without hesitation. Because of the gesture? The bench? The wildflowers? The thoughtfulness? Had he gotten her in a weak moment when she'd been scared?

She was still scared.

But now she could add *I told Oliver I'd marry him* to the list.

"Are you feeling all right?" Kat asked, peering at her mother. She'd been asking this practically every half hour since her mother had shared the news. And every time she got the same answer.

"Just fine," Lolly said, and Kat could tell her mother's mind was on a million other things—the inn, getting things set up for Isabel, Movie Night. Chemotherapy. "Let's not make it more of a thing than it already is, okay?"

Kat stared at her mother, but then felt her expression soften. This was her mother's diagnosis. Her mother's disease. And she had a right to handle it the way she wanted. "Okay," Kat said, squeezing Lolly's hands whether her mother liked it or not.

She told Lolly she'd be down in a minute, then ran upstairs and put the ring in the secret compartment under the bottom of her old jewelry box with its tiny ballerina dancing to "Moon River." Her father had given it to her for her ninth birthday with her first piece of jewelry inside, a gold necklace with a heart pendant with *K* on it. She glanced at the beautiful ring one last time, then slid the little drawer closed.

Back downstairs in the parlor, Kat took her usual spot on the beanbag by the sofa, where her mother and Pearl sat. Isabel and June were on the love seat. In the two hard-backed chairs were Suzanne and Tyler, twentysomething guests. Since they'd arrived, they'd never stopped holding hands. At check-in yesterday, when Kat and Lolly had been going over procedures with Isabel, Suzanne mentioned that they were

there to celebrate their one-month anniversary, and given the
lack of rings and their ages, Kat assumed that meant a month
of dating.

Kat hadn't had a chance to bake cupcakes for the impromptu Movie Night, but there was popcorn aplenty and
a big bowl of M&M's. Kat grabbed a few, but found herself
so struck by the opening of *The Devil Wears Prada*, of Anne
Hathaway zigzagging her way through the busy, crowded
streets of New York City, that the little candies slipped right
out of her hand. She wondered what it would be like to live
in a place like that, all that energy, all those lights, traffic,
people. Boothbay Harbor got crowded in the summer, very
crowded, and it was fun and exciting in a different way, but
it was still a small town.

The hot actor from the TV show *Entourage* played Anne
Hathaway's boyfriend. Kat liked them together; they looked
as if they belonged together—the same thing everyone said
about her and Oliver. Kat admired Anne's character, a recent
college graduate who'd moved to New York with her ideals
and dreams to become a hard-hitting journalist covering important issues. She had determination, but no job offers. So
when the most powerful editor in fashion-magazine publishing, Meryl Streep's character, Miranda Priestly, offers her the
position of second assistant, Anne accepts, despite how wrong
she is for the job.

Kat loved how wrong. With her long messy hair, lack of
makeup, lack of style, Anne was completely out of place at
a major fashion magazine. She didn't care about fashion at
all or how she looked, but she cared about the credentials
the job would give her. In the end, stylish and unexpectedly
indispensable to her dragon-lady boss, Anne is faced with
choosing her values—or her job.

Kat imagined herself working in a tony cake shop or
hotel or restaurant as pastry chef or pastry sous-chef, losing

her hemp tank tops and clunky Merrell sandals and dressing in sleek black, her apartment on the twentysomething floor, with views of the Empire State Building, the river, and thousands and thousands of lights.

Something stirred inside her as she watched Anne Hathaway's transformation from slouchy no-style to glamorous, confident, sleek. Maybe Kat needed a trip to New York, just to show her she could never live there, never breathe there. To put the fantasy out of her head.

Right. Suddenly you could imagine leaving Boothbay Harbor. Two hours after you get engaged to a man you're not entirely sure you should have said yes to forever to. But as the credits rolled at the end, Kat wished there were part two of the movie, so she could keep watching Anne Hathaway in New York, find out if her dream job really was, after all, and if things did work out with her boyfriend. Kat believed they would.

"Meryl was almost unrecognizable," Lolly said. "Isn't it amazing how much she made you sympathize with dragon-lady boss?"

Kat took a sip of wine. "I love how much Meryl humanized Miranda Priestly. Even when she was at her most awful, her most condescending, you understood her. I loved that scene when she explains how Anne Hathaway's choice of a simple blue sweater is based on what goes on inside the offices of the magazine."

"I knew fashion was serious business," Isabel said, "but, my God, that pressure, from all sides, just seemed so unbearable."

There were nods all around.

"Speaking of pressure," Suzanne, the young guest, said, "I sort of hated how Anne Hathaway's boyfriend wouldn't let her be this new person. Why don't people let you change and grow?"

"I would never hold you back from anything, Suze," her boyfriend, Tyler, said, his face in her hair.

"They get scared, I think," Isabel said. "You're out there doing your new thing, setting your world on fire, and they get left behind." She glanced down at her feet, and Kat wondered if she was thinking about Edward.

June reached for a handful of popcorn. "With that kind of job, though, it seemed like you couldn't have a personal life. It's either the job or a life. She and the boyfriend were what? Twenty-two? Twenty-three? This is the time to figure that out. Not be stymied."

"Still, she had to make choices," Suzanne said. "Her boss or her boyfriend's birthday party. She always chose the boss. I would never choose my job over Tyler."

You're probably not in a position to have to, though, Kat wanted to say. "You know what I think? I think she chose the boss, chose the job, because Meryl Streep's character was letting her become someone new, someone she didn't even know was inside her. An entire new facet of her came out at that job. The boyfriend didn't care about that at all—and he didn't like it. He liked her messy. Which is nice in itself. But not for Anne Hathaway's character. The boyfriend was kind of whiny to me."

"I didn't think he was whiny at all," Tyler said. "I think he was just keeping her in check, keeping her real, not letting her get away with treating him like shit." He glanced around. "Sorry."

Lolly stood up and began collecting plates and dishes, so they all got up too before Lolly could do too much. "Well, I do like that Anne Hathaway refused to let herself be compromised. She walked away from all that and went back to what she always wanted—to the person she wanted to be."

"But she did love her job at *Runway*," June said. "And she was good at it."

"Good at being someone's personal maid and conscience?" Suzanne asked. "That's not a role to aspire to."

"I'm not so sure going back to her boyfriend was so right either, though," June said. "I'm glad she took the job she always wanted. I mean, I understand that she realized she had to sacrifice too much, including her ideals, for her job, but it seemed like she became a new person and grew past the boyfriend. Does that make sense?"

Yes, it does, Kat thought, the ring in her jewelry box flashing in her mind. But Oliver wasn't some stick-in-the-mud, small-minded guy. If she wanted to travel, he'd probably be excited to plan a trip to Thailand or Austria or Spain. If she wanted to take a pie-baking class in the Deep South of the United States or a cannoli class in Rome, he'd encourage her. Well, to a point.

So why the cold feet, Kat? What was the problem? Was she so scared of Oliver, of losing the kind of love that came around once in a lifetime, that she kept herself at arm's length? Or in her heart of hearts, did she not love him that way, after all?

How did a person not know how she felt? Her friend Lizzie insisted Kat read too many women's magazines and let the mumbo jumbo sway her. She thought Kat should remember exactly how she'd felt the moment before that bottle spun to her when they were thirteen—secretly in love with Oliver, dreaming about kissing him, safe in the secret. Until the bottle opening did land on her. Exposure.

"I love that Anne Hathaway became her own person in the end," Isabel said. "Not the person she needs to be to fit into Meryl Streep's character's world. She becomes a more mature version of who she wants to be. The hard-hitting journalist."

June nodded. "You know what I was thinking of most while I was watching? That I love New York City, but I would not have lasted a minute at a place like that—*Runway* magazine. I wonder if all major magazines are run that way. Maybe I dodged a bullet, after all."

Kat *could* picture herself in that sleek black outfit, dashing to hail a cab to her trendy bakery-café in SoHo, sipping a chocolate martini, leaving her Merrells and mud boots in Maine. A day ago, she wasn't fantasizing about moving to New York and working in a posh bakery. But she wasn't leaving Boothbay Harbor. Her mother needed her more than ever. And once she was married, well, this was where Oliver wanted to be, where he wanted to spend the rest of his life, raise the four kids he always talked about having. Oliver did not want to live in New York City. Or Rome. Or Paris.

He would encourage her to a point.

If she married him, she'd stay right here—forever.

CHAPTER 7

Isabel

He was in the backyard. The guest, the good-looking one who'd checked in last night, just before the movie started. Griffin Dean was his name. He'd arrived, somewhat harried and wanting to hurry through check-in, with a little girl, two or three years old, asleep in his arms, and a teenaged girl with earphones and a scowl. The teenager had been upset to discover she wasn't getting her own room, but when Lolly explained about the alcove in the Osprey Room, how it was separated from the main part of the room by a wall that jutted out and had two twin beds and its own window, she'd calmed down with a "Fine." On the way upstairs, Isabel had chattered nonstop, about breakfast being served from seven until eight thirty, that if they needed anything, anything at all, to just let her know, and that if he was interested, it was Movie Night at the inn and they would be watching *The Devil Wears Prada*. He'd looked confused, as if wondering why on earth she'd think he'd want to watch that, then said thank you and waited politely for her to turn and go before he closed the door.

Isabel glanced at her watch. It wasn't yet six o'clock in the morning. Monday. She was up early for her first official day as proprietress of the inn. But still, a guest had beat her to it.

She wondered if that was okay. Another question she'd have to ask Lolly. But she'd also been unable to sleep much last night. It wasn't just her aunt's first chemotherapy appointment that afternoon, which she and Kat were taking her to while June and Charlie manned the inn, that had kept Isabel awake. She'd had a dream about Edward, an odd dream of the two them lying in the backyard under the oaks, but as adults, and Edward telling her that it was a good thing they'd made their pact because she'd be a terrible mother. She'd woken up in a cold sweat, her heart aching, and she'd whispered, "June," to see if her sister was awake, to talk, but June didn't answer, and Kat had been so quiet the past couple of days that Isabel figured she wouldn't be up for talking at 2:36 in the morning either.

At five, Isabel had finally gotten out of bed and sat on the balcony, trying to breathe, trying to remember it was just a dream, even though Edward had said as much more than once during their marriage. He'd said it with anger, during arguments that neither of them could win, and she was 75 percent sure he didn't mean it. She supposed it was that 25 percent of uncertainty why she'd let him win. As she'd stared out at the harbor, at the shimmering blue water and the boats of all sizes, watching the fishermen hauling over nets and cages, watching the joggers and bicyclists and a daddy longlegs make its way along the railing, the needs of the inn had begun pushing out her dream. She'd mentally gone over all Lolly had shown her the past two days, from signing in the guests, how to use the credit-card machine, handling the ledgers, checking up on their advertising with the B&B associations, making sure the rooms had an adequate supply of linens and toiletries. More went into the daily running of the inn than Isabel had realized; she'd discovered that just by helping Lolly check in the Deans last night, which seemingly involved greeting them and showing them to the large room. She'd assumed Mrs. Dean would appear any moment with a suitcase or two, but when she checked Lolly's records, the reservation was for one adult and two children. For an entire week, through Labor Day Monday.

He stood on the far side of the yard, beside the crabapple tree with his hands in the pockets of his army-green cargo pants, facing the house and the open view of the harbor down the slope.

She was about to say good morning when the stray dog scampered over from out of nowhere and lay down at her bare feet, resting his soft, little, white chin on her toes. Twice this weekend he'd come to find her. Yesterday, she'd been looking out the window when she saw the dog stop in the yard as though looking for her. He hadn't scampered up to June and Pearl, who were playing cards at the picnic table. But when Isabel had come out, exhausted, with her iced tea and dropped down on a chaise longue, she'd felt the familiar furry chin on her arm.

"Oh, fine," she said now as she had yesterday, petting the dog's adorable head. Which made him try to jump on her lap. The dog wasn't big, but he wasn't a terrier, either. And she was dressed typically, in a ruffled, pale-lavender silk tank top and white pants and her jeweled flat sandals. White pants, ruffled silk, and a jumping dog didn't mix. "Whoa there."

"What's his name?"

Isabel turned at the sound of the voice. Griffin Dean's. "I don't know, actually. He just sort of adopted me this weekend. And for some crazy reason, he seems to only like me."

He smiled. "Dogs have a sense about people. You must be one of the good ones."

"I think it's more that I gave him my nephew's leftover hot dog on Friday," she said, petting him under the chin. The dog put a paw on Isabel's arm. "I feel like he's adopted me. My aunt—you met her last night, she's the owner of the inn—is fine with keeping him if no one claims him. We put up a few flyers around town and alerted the police and animal control and—" And once again she was rambling. She glanced up at Griffin, unused to being unnerved, then quickly back down at the mutt.

Isabel had never had a dog, never had a pet, except for the goldfish her mother had allowed if she won one in a fair. She had enough on her plate, but she wanted something of her own to take care of. *I'm kind of a stray too,* she thought, giving the underside of the dog's chin a rub.

Griffin Dean smiled again, and for a second Isabel couldn't take her eyes off his face. Something world-weary but kind was in his expression. And he was attractive. Very, actually. Midthirties, she guessed. He had dark wavy hair and dark eyes and wore army-green cargo pants and a blue Henley T-shirt. And a wedding ring.

"I hope your room was comfortable," she said, remembering that she was standing proprietress. "If you or your daughters need anything, just let me know."

"Thanks. My fourteen-year-old slept in that little room across from ours—I hope that's all right. By the time I realized she'd sneaked out and I found her in there, she was out cold—her legs hanging over the arm of the love seat."

Isabel smiled. "That's fine. It's a room my sister and cousin and I used as teenagers when we wanted to be alone while we were growing up here. So I understand."

"You all grew up here together?"

She nodded and was about to ramble again—was it that he was so attractive?—when the dog started chewing on Lolly's tulips, and Isabel rushed over. "No, dog! No, no, no." But the dog wouldn't listen. He ripped off a tulip and brought it over to Isabel in his mouth, his tail wagging.

"He *does* like you," Griffin said with a laugh. "I could help you train him while I'm here. I'm a vet." He handed her his card.

GRIFFIN DEAN, DVM. BOOTHBAY HARBOR, MAINE.

"That would be great," she said. "Thanks. Boothbay Harbor? You're not very far from home." His office was right in the bustle of the harbor, just around the corner from Books Brothers.

"We needed to get away from the house, even though it's just a few miles out from here. This is one of the last places we—" He didn't finish the sentence and instead went over to the dog and knelt down and gave him a good rubbing all over. Which was when Isabel realized that the slim gold band he wore was on his *right* hand—not his left. "I'd better go check on my girls. Alexa will sleep till noon if I let her, but Emmy, the three-year-old, is probably coloring the walls. Kidding." He gave the dog another vigorous petting. "I'll work with him later."

He smiled at her, then went back inside. She wanted to follow him, ask him to finish his sentence. *One of the last places we* . . . But of course she couldn't.

The Coastal General Hospital smelled the way all hospitals did. Like antiseptic. Like hope and despair combined. Lolly had a private room in the oncology ward, where they were met by the resident on Lolly's team. Lolly's doctors had briefed her when she'd been diagnosed, so she knew what to expect, but Isabel and Kat didn't. Before they'd left for the hospital, Isabel and Kat had had a long talk in the kitchen about how little they knew about cancer, about chemotherapy. How it worked. Why. Kat had been on the verge of tears, and Isabel found herself drawing on her strength as a grief counselor; she'd been able to steady Kat, and they'd both been able to be strong (in other words, neither had broken down) for Lolly, who'd sat silently in the car, looking out the window, refusing to talk.

Kat asked the resident to overexplain, to speak to them as though they were twelve, and they were both grateful for his sympathetic tone and manner—especially as a nurse set up the IV for Lolly's chemotherapy. The treatment would take about four hours. Lolly would return every three weeks for six weeks, then her plan would be adjusted if need be.

Once Lolly was in the green recliner, the IV doing its job, the nurse let Lolly know to call for her if she needed anything, and the resident excused himself. Kat followed him, and Isabel had no doubt Kat had many more questions—questions she wasn't comfortable asking in front of her mother.

"Isabel, would you run and get me a cup of chamomile tea?" Lolly asked. The ten magazines Kat had brought, ranging from *People* to *Coastal Inn*, and the two novels June had bought from Books Brothers, rested on the end table with a pitcher of water. "I'll be fine."

"Sure," Isabel said, grateful for the chance to catch her breath. She took that deep breath the moment the door closed behind her. Up the hall a bit, Kat was deep in conversation with the oncology resident, a patient young man with a lovely Italian name that Isabel suddenly couldn't remember. She could hear him speaking gently but knowledgeably to Kat, his words banging against each other in Isabel's head. *Slow the progression. Inoperable. Metastasized. Standard chemotherapy drug is gemcitabine. Relieve symptoms . . .*

He was explaining how chemotherapy drugs couldn't tell good cells from cancer cells and so attacked all fast-growing cells, which was why chemo patients often started losing their hair, as cells in the hair root were among the fastest growing. Isabel thought of Lolly's silky gray-blond hair, her long eyelashes and arched eyebrows, and squeezed her eyes shut for a moment, then interrupted Kat and the doctor to stop the words she couldn't bear to hear as much as to ask if either wanted something from the café. Both declined with a thank-you, then resumed talking. Cells. White blood cells. Platelets. Cancer, cancer, cancer.

When the elevator doors opened on the third floor and someone got off, Isabel noticed the arrow sign LABOR AND DELIVERY AND NURSERY. She found herself getting off too and following the arrows until she stood in front of the glass wall of the nursery. It had been months since she'd let herself visit the newborns in the Connecticut hospital.

She stared down at her wedding ring. Last night, when she'd been unable to sleep at 3:00 a.m., she'd broken down and called Edward on the house phone, though she had no idea what she was going to say. Maybe to tell him about Lolly. She'd just needed to hear his voice, even still. He'd answered right away and then said, "Hang on a minute," and had picked up another extension, which told her that Carolyn Chenowith had been next to him in bed. She'd been about to hang up when he said, "I'm here." For a moment, she'd been unable to say anything.

"You're really doing this" was what had come out of her mouth.

"I'm sorry, Izzy." He was crying, she'd realized.

He hadn't said anything else. Seconds ticked by and finally Isabel hit END CALL and slipped her phone back inside her purse and sat out on the balcony, her heart squeezing in her chest to the point that she'd had to take deep, gulping breaths.

She let herself remember a moment in which a piece of her love for him had died. She'd worked so hard to bury it, but now welcomed the terrible memory. A few months ago, she and Edward had been at yet another law-firm dinner, the partners and their wives, the loud stories and expensive scotch and cigars making her want to run. One of the older partners had said to Edward, "So, when are you and the Mrs. going to start a family—if you're going to have three children, like everyone else, you'd better get started."

Edward had leaned in to whisper with fake gravitas, "We wish we could have four, but, unfortunately, Isabel isn't able."

The clichéd wind had been knocked out of her at the lie. She'd had to leave the table, which had apparently bolstered everyone's compassion for poor Isabel. Running off to cry for the four children she couldn't give her deserving husband.

It was the first time she'd felt anything like hatred for Edward. But he'd used his skill as a lawyer to talk his way out of it, to beat her over the head with a fifteen-year-old pact she'd made as a child in the throws of grief—and worse, self-loathing.

Let him go, she told herself. *Let it all go.*

She stared down at her beautiful rings, twisting them and quickly sliding off the diamond ring and then her wedding band before she could change her mind and leave them there, where they didn't belong. Was she supposed to put them in her purse? Or on her right hand, like Griffin Dean? She stared at her bare left hand and felt so strange without the sight of the rings that she put them on her right hand, where they didn't belong, either. Tomorrow was their ten-year anniversary. She forced her gaze up to the nursery, at the sleeping babies swaddled in the familiar white and blue little blankets.

A little voice inside her told her to come back tomorrow to see about volunteering in the nursery, and she took a deep breath. She could hold the babies that needed comforting. Could stroke the fingers of tiny newborns in the NICU. Bottle-feed. In all the years she'd volunteered back home at the hospital for the newly grief-stricken, she hadn't felt she could volunteer in the nursery, as if the pact she'd made somehow meant she could look but not touch.

When she returned with her aunt's tea and a blueberry muffin, Lolly's favorite kind, though it would be tasteless compared to Kat's, Kat was still talking to the resident. Isabel poked her head into Lolly's room, and Lolly gestured at her to come in.

Lolly sipped the tea. "Perfect, thank you, Isabel." As Isabel sat down in the chair across from her aunt, Lolly said, "Before I forget to mention it, Isabel, I'd like you to do something for me later."

"Of course, anything." Isabel was feeling much more confident about running the inn, had a notebook full of little things that needed seeing to.

"Your mother kept a journal, did you know that?"

Isabel stiffened. "No."

"When I packed up your mother's bedroom all those years ago, I found them, just two of them, from the last year of her life. She was taking a journal-writing class at the rec center. I used to read them over and over when we first lost her, just so I could feel her with me, hear her voice. She'd write about what she would make for dinner, that June got a sunburn, that you looked so pretty, so grown-up in your dress for the dance, just real everyday family stuff, and I'd feel her right there with me."

Isabel stared at Lolly for a moment, surprised to hear her talk about her sister, Isabel's mother. And so warmly. Lolly had never been one for reminiscing.

Maybe Lolly was now because she wasn't sure how much time she had left, Isabel realized with a wallop to the stomach.

She walked over to the window to have something besides Lolly to look at. She couldn't bear it if her aunt started to cry.

And she didn't want to know there were journals. Her mother's words. Especially from that final year. Their worst year.

"Would you find them for me?" Lolly asked. "I know it's a mess down there in the basement, but they'll be in one of her trunks—you know how she loved those old-fashioned trunks and kept buying them from flea markets."

That brought a smile from Isabel and she turned around to face Lolly. "She loved the ones with stickers best." Her mother would come home with another trunk, making Isabel's father roll his eyes and say, "Now, Allie, where are you going to put that?" And she'd smile and say, "But, look, this trunk has been to Indonesia! Bali! And Australia too!" Isabel remembered how her mother had closed her eyes and said, "God, I'd love to see a kangaroo. Wouldn't you, Isabel?" And Isabel, even in her gloom and doom, headphones in her ears that she'd uncharacteristically turned down, had said, "Yes, actually. That's something I would like to see." Her mother had turned triumphantly to her father and said, "See. Even Isabel is charmed by the thought of a hopping kangaroo." That had stung her, the "even Isabel," but she'd deserved it, sulking about the house, complaining about her curfew, which she always broke, and the house rules, which she rarely paid attention to.

They'd never gotten to Australia, had never seen a kangaroo, but on her sixteenth birthday, her mother had given her a silver bracelet with a tiny silver kangaroo charm, and she'd worn it for years, never taking it off, even at her wedding. "That goes beautifully with your gown," Edward had whispered, quite reverently, at the altar. "It's like she's here."

Isabel closed her eyes against both memories. And another, of the day two years ago when she'd been about to take a sip of a cappuccino at Starbucks and realized the bracelet was gone. Gone. In a panic, she'd retraced her steps, had the barista unlock the garbage so she could tear through it for the bracelet, but she'd never found it. Not in the parking lot or her car or anywhere she'd been that day. She'd posted signs, offering a reward, but no one had ever turned it in.

"I'd love to read the journals again," Lolly was saying. She took a sip of her tea, then a nibble of the muffin. "Have my sister with me, hear her voice, you know?"

"I'll find them today," she promised, though Isabel wouldn't read them herself. In between writing about lobster bakes and flea-market finds, her mother must have written about how miserable Isabel had made her and her father. "You're destroying us," her mother had said to Isabel a few months before she died. Isabel didn't need to go back there.

"I know there was friction between you and your mother," Lolly said, glancing at Isabel. "But you might want to read those journals too. It's important to know the truth about things instead of what you think you know. I don't know how long I have here, Isabel. Weeks? Months? I don't know. And now it all seems so dumb, all that tension and estrangement, family not speaking, treating one another like strangers. I've been guilty of that too. But it's wrong."

Isabel stood in front of the window and glanced out at the trees against the brilliant blue sky. "I don't want to remember who I used to be."

"Reading her journals won't tell you who you used to be. It'll tell you who your mother was, what she thought. Really thought. Not what you think she thought. Not who you think you were through her eyes. There's a lot you didn't know about your mother."

Isabel let out a deep breath. She didn't want to read her mother's diaries and she knew she wouldn't, couldn't. A lot was going on right now, and even seeing her mother's handwriting could push Isabel over the edge. But her aunt was sitting there with a needle of poison in her arm and tears in her eyes, so Isabel just took her hand and held it tight and assured her again she'd find the diaries.

It had taken Isabel hours to bring herself to open the basement door in the short hallway between the kitchen doorway and the back stairs and walk down the creaky wooden steps.

The basement was full of old furniture that Lolly had planned to refinish or sell and the furniture from Isabel and June's old apartment in the two-family house their parents had rented. Isabel had kept her old dresser, which was antique with a beautiful oval mirror, and had it refinished so that it barely resembled the junky thing it used to be. Her parents' old headboard and footboard were against a wall lined with shelves containing every possible supply, from potting soil to paint thinner. And over by the row of short, narrow windows were her mother's old trunks.

There were seven of them, stacked up on top of each other in two rows on a faded, old rug. Isabel grabbed one and sat down cross-legged on the rug and opened the thin wood top. Clothing. Shirts and sweaters, neatly folded. Years ago Lolly had told Isabel and June to go through them and take what they wanted, that perhaps she'd donate the rest to Goodwill, but clearly Lolly hadn't been able to get rid of anything. Isabel slipped her hands underneath sweaters and shirts, feeling for the journals. Lolly had said there were two, hard-backed, red-fabric books with the outline of an angel embroidered on each. If they were here, she'd feel them, but as she went through, there was only clothing. She felt a bit guilty for being relieved.

She went through two more trunks, but the diaries weren't in either. Lolly had said she'd last read them right after Isabel's mother had died—fifteen years ago. Perhaps she'd forgotten where she'd put them. Or maybe the diaries would be in the last trunk Isabel checked. Murphy's Law said they would be.

At the bottom of the third trunk she saw one of her mother's favorite sweaters, a dusty-pink cashmere with a V-neck. A few weeks before the accident, her mother had been wearing that sweater when she'd been yelling at Isabel for cutting her last two classes and being caught (by the mother of one of June's friends) skinny-dipping with two guys, both of whom she was dating. Isabel had screamed something like "It's not a huge deal," and her mother had grabbed her arm, hard, and Isabel had been shocked, but her mother pulled her against her, wrapping her arms around her tight, even though Isabel's arms hung at her sides. "The huge deal is that I love you so much, Isabel. I care about everything you do, everything you are. That's what the huge deal is." For a moment she let her mother hold her, hoping she wouldn't say another word and make Isabel run off, but she went on, "I wish I knew how to reach you. Make you care about yourself." Isabel had squirmed and tried to get away, but her mother had tightened her grip. "I love you whether you want me to or not," she'd said, then abruptly released her.

I want you to, Isabel had thought, running to her room and slamming the door, which had gotten her into more trouble for bothering June, who'd been studying for a test.

Isabel pulled out the sweater and brought it to her nose. It faintly smelled of the perfume her mother always wore, Coco by Chanel. She could remember the weeks when she'd been fourteen and she'd started to change, when she'd been so impressed by a trio of wild girls who didn't care what anyone thought of them. She hadn't realized then, of course, that they hadn't cared about themselves, as her mother had always said of them and Isabel, that they had no self-esteem. They were popular for their antics when Isabel was invisible for being herself. She'd passed some test without even meaning to in front of the school one afternoon when one of the girls handed her two cigarettes and said her mother would search her, so would Isabel hide them for her until tomorrow? Just like that, Isabel was in. The next day, she had a borrowed shirt—tight and sexy. Then a borrowed pair of cool jeans to go with it. Borrowed knee-high black leather boots. By the following week, she wore black eyeliner and big hoop earrings. "It's just a phase, leave her be," her mother would say to her father, who'd made his feelings about her new look quite clear. But the phase lasted until a week after the accident. When Edward told her she had such beautiful eyes, if only he could see them. She'd washed off her makeup, and he said, "Much better. You are so pretty." In days she was choosing clothes from the back of her closet, the clothes her mother had insisted on buying her in hopes of her dressing like a normal teenager. Her "friends" had been so freaked out by the accident, by what to say to her, as so many people had been, that they'd disappeared on her. They hadn't even come to the funeral.

"I'm sorry I was so awful," Isabel whispered to the sweater. And instead of *feeling* awful, the way she always did when she remembered these times, she felt . . . okay. Almost as if apologizing to her mother's favorite sweater, which still smelled so much like her, was like saying *I'm sorry* to her mother. To herself too.

She stood up, the sweater in hand, unable to go through another trunk, at least not today. She'd let her aunt know that she did look for the diaries, show her the sweater as proof, and promise to look through the rest tomorrow.

She took one last glance around at her parents' things, then went back upstairs and closed the door. She was heading up the main stairs when she heard the front door open and raised voices.

"Stop treating me like I'm Emmy!" a girl was shouting. Griffin Dean's teenaged daughter. "*I'm fourteen!* It's just a walk!"

Griffin closed the door behind him. "Alexa, you're not going off with a strange boy. Period. But especially not at"— he glanced at his watch—"eight twenty at night."

"Then why'd you make me come here if I can't do anything?" Alexa screamed, tears running down her cheeks. She turned and ran upstairs past Isabel, almost knocking into her. A door slammed.

Isabel hadn't meant to be right in the middle of the Dean family drama, but there she was.

She expected Griffin to sheepishly smile and say, *Teenagers,* but he closed his eyes and just stood there, very still, and Isabel thought he might cry too.

"I used to be just like that," she said as she came back down the stairs and stood at the landing. "In fact, I think I said that exact thing to my father and he said that exact thing back."

He glanced at her. "And did you go screaming and crying upstairs and slam doors?"

She nodded. "Oh, yeah. Lots of that."

"But everything turned out okay, right? Everything *will* be okay, right?" he asked, with a hint of a smile for the first time.

"I guess it did. But I wish I could go back and change things."

A door opened on the second floor and a little voice said, "Daddy?"

"She must have woken Emmy." He shook his head and headed upstairs. "She rarely wakes up once she's down for the night," he said over his shoulder. "Unless Alexa slams a door. She does that a lot these days."

"Daddy," Emmy said at the landing. She clutched a stuffed, yellow bunny rabbit. "I'm thirsty. Can I have hot chocolate milk?"

He turned toward Isabel. "Kitchen open?"

"Of course." She waited for Griffin to go up and scoop Emmy in his arms and carry her downstairs, then led the way to the kitchen.

"Can I sit there?" Emmy asked, pointing at Kat's papasan chair with its overstuffed, round, pink cushion.

"Sure can," Isabel said, watching the toddler amble over. She was such a pretty girl. Her hair was a burnished dark brown with copper highlights, and her eyes were almost the same color.

As Isabel made the hot chocolate and offered Griffin something to drink, which he declined, he scooped Emmy up in his arms, sat down on the big, pink chair and started whispering the story of "Goldilocks and the Three Bears." When he finished, he kissed Emmy on the head.

Isabel handed the girl a not-too-hot hot chocolate in a little plastic pink cup with polka dots.

Emmy stared at Isabel as she took a sip, then another. "You're pretty."

Isabel felt herself blush. "Thank you. I think you're pretty too."

"I like when my mommy brushes my hair. Before bed-time. Now Lexa does it."

Was Griffin widowed? Divorced?

"Would you like me to brush your hair, Emmy?" Isabel asked.

The girl stared at Isabel, then shook her head and buried her face in her father's chest.

Griffin handed the pink cup back to Isabel. "Sweets, let's get you back to bed. Good night," he said to Isabel, then was gone.

She waited for him to come back down, to offer him a beer or a glass of wine or coffee, but once she'd polished every possible wood surface and ran the sweeper over the rugs in the hallways and in the parlor, she realized over an hour had gone by and he never did come back. Never had she so badly wanted to sit outside with someone in the breezy August air and say nothing at all.

CHAPTER 8

June

In June's first three hours as manager of the Boothbay Harbor Books Brothers, she'd hand-sold four novels, two biographies, a travel guide to northern New England, special-ordered five books, rung up more than $300 in various purchases, and sold over $200 of children's books to a Mommy and Me group that had wandered in after their coffee hour across the street.

A great morning, even for the Friday of Labor Day weekend. And great personally too. Boothbay Harbor or not, a bookstore—Books Brothers, in particular, of course—was June's territory and probably the place she felt most comfortable, most herself. She sat behind the counter of the checkout desk on her director's chair, working on a list of "Bring in New Business" initiatives. She'd already talked to Henry about a weekly book club and children's story hour, and she was thinking about a Coffee Klatch—general talk about books, life, come-hang-out-with-good-coffee-and-conversation kind of thing in the early evenings, a drop-in type of event where people could relax—and then go book shopping.

The bell over the door jangled, and June was about to look up from jotting down her new idea when a woman said, "Juney Nash? Is it you?"

Oh, no. That couldn't be good.

She put her pen down on the Books Brothers stationery pad to glance into the cold blue eyes of Pauline Altman. Twice in one summer. And with her two old friends, Marley Something and Carrie Fish. The trio had been quadruple threats: smart, pretty, popular—and not so nice.

"I always wondered what happened to you since I saw you last!" Pauline said, adjusting the white bathing-suit straps that peeked out of her sundress. "Last time I saw you, you were so pregnant."

Carrie's big diamond ring glinted on her finger. "Oh, that's right, Pauline, you said June had gotten pregnant and dropped out of college. So you've been working here all this time?"

"I was living in Portland for the last seven years." June kicked herself for feeling the need to explain herself at all. "But my aunt is sick, so I've moved back to help out."

They all nodded with fake sympathy. Well, except for Marley Something, who was too busy flipping through *Vogue* at the magazine rack.

"Well, I guess you'll be at the all-years reunion in October, then," Pauline said. "Everyone wondered why you weren't at our five-year, and I discreetly explained your . . . *situation*," she added in a whisper, as though June had had a communicable disease.

The reunion. Ha. There was no way June was going to that, even if Kat and Isabel were attending. Labor Day weekend brought half their classmates back to town as it was. "It all depends how my aunt is feeling in late October."

"Of course," Carrie said, admiring her ring. "Oh, did you hear that Pauline is now associate editor of *New York City* magazine? She had the most amazing party to celebrate the promotion. Oh, God, you should see her apartment. Terrace with a view of the Empire State Building and a million lights."

"That's great, Pauline," June said, an unwelcome twinge spiraling into her stomach. And it was great, really. It was exactly the life June had wanted.

As the three women browsed among the shelves and displays, Pauline worked in a mention of her boyfriend, a senior producer at ABC News, her summer share in the Hamptons, and the new boat her parents, who lived in one of the most gorgeous waterfront houses in Boothbay Harbor, had bought this summer. "Too bad I'm only visiting for Labor Day weekend. It's glorious here." Pauline and Carrie stood in front of the checkout with armloads of books. "You're so lucky you get to live here year-round again, Juney. The city is *so* hot in the summer."

"I remember," June said as she rang up their purchases. Pauline bought a literary bestseller, a memoir, a travel guide to Machu Picchu, and a complete hardback set of *Harry Potter*—for her "gifted eight-year-old niece." Carrie bought two celebrity cookbooks. And Marley Something bought nothing. Between Pauline and Carrie, they spent a small fortune. So there was that.

Pauline put her gold credit card back in her wallet and took her shopping bag. "The other day I was visiting my sister while her husband was traveling, and, oh my God, Juney, I totally tip my hat to you single mothers. We had to do *everything* ourselves without a break! I really don't know how you do it. It must be *so* hard."

June could almost see the condescension falling out of Pauline's glossed mouth.

"What's worse for single mothers," Carrie added, "is that no one has your back at all. You do everything alone, and then there's no husband to call on his business trip to complain to. That must be so hard and lonely."

God, June hated these two.

"June, when you get a minute, I need your help in the

office" came the voice of Henry Books from the back of the store. Saved. Thank you, Henry.

The women all turned to see Henry heading into his office. "Damn, he's hot," Carrie whispered. "Single?"

Marley Something, who June had always thought looked like an angel with her huge blue eyes, heart-shaped face, and petite figure, put the magazine away and came to stand behind her friends. "He's a total catch." At least the first thing that had come out of her mouth was nice. And accurate.

"God, Marley, this is why you're so single," Pauline said. "He's hardly a catch. He owns a *bookstore.* Please."

"Meaning?" June asked, staring at Pauline. How obnoxious.

Pauline rolled her eyes. "Oh, come on, you know what I mean."

"Yes, I absolutely do." *And I feel sorry for you. Thanks for making me realize you're nothing but a snotty, shallow bitch. And I don't care what snotty, shallow bitches think.*

June did hope that Henry hadn't heard what Pauline had said, though she doubted he'd give two figs in the slightest. Henry was the most self-assured person June had ever met. He was who he was, and if you didn't like it, oh, well.

June was about to leave the three witches and go see what Henry wanted when Marley slammed the *Vogue* magazine back on the rack and walked back up to Pauline and stuck her finger in her face. "You know what, Pauline? I'm so sick and tired of you and your snotty I'm-better-than-everyone attitude. You're not. And I've *had* it."

Whoa. Go, Marley.

Pauline's eyes widened, but she quickly recovered. "Find your own way back to your little shack, then." She turned to leave, Carrie, openmouthed, trailing after her. "Told you she's been a freak lately, Carrie. Ew. Oh, and Marley Mathers? You're *out.*" With that, Pauline pulled open the door, and Carrie shoved a rack of postcards by the door so they'd fall out.

You could take the girls out of high school . . .

"Immature bitches," Marley said, going over to pick up the postcards. June went over to help, kneeling down beside Marley. Which was when June noticed she was crying.

"They're not worth it," June said.

"It's not them," Marley whispered, wiping under her eyes, which were the strangest combination of scared, upset, and, oddly enough, happy. She collected the postcards and put them in June's hands, then darted to the nonfiction section. In moments she was standing in front of the checkout counter with a book pressed up against her stomach and her arms crisscrossed against it as though she didn't want anyone to see what it was.

But June knew what it was. She'd know that book, off-size and familiar, anywhere.

June went behind the counter to ring up the book. But Marley didn't hand it over. "Marley?" June prompted, gently as she could.

"I—" Marley started to say, her chin-length brown bob falling in her face, her lower lip trembling again.

To give Marley some privacy, June slipped the book into a Books Brothers bag. "Come sit," she said, gesturing at the little round café table facing the magazine rack. June poured a cup of lemon water for Marley and sat down across from her. And waited.

Marley's hands were shaking on the cup of water. "I just found out that—" She leaned close to June and whispered, "That I'm—" She glanced around the store, as if to make sure no one she knew was around. Then she took a sip of her water. Anything, it seemed, not to say the word.

As "So Single" Marley bit her lip and stared at her hands, which were indeed ringless, June waited, giving her a chance to say what she needed to say. But her face crumpled and she closed her eyes.

"It's a good book that you chose," June whispered, giving Marley's hand a compassionate squeeze. She remembered taking *What to Expect When You're Expecting* out of the library and reading it week by week, afraid to move ahead, not ready to learn more than she needed to know at any given moment. "And it's on me. But if there's anything I can help you with, you just let me know, okay? Even if you just want to talk."

June had a feeling that what Marley needed to know most, what she could expect, would not be found in the pages of any book.

The bell jangled and a few people came in.

"I need to go," Marley said, bolting up. "Don't tell anyone, please? No one knows yet."

"Of course I won't."

Marley eyed June as though debating something. "So, I could give you a call, if I have a question?"

June wrote her cell phone number on the back of a Books Brothers card. "Anyone who tells off Pauline Altman is okay by me." She smiled, and Marley gave her a wobbly smile back, but then she sobered again. "Seriously, Marley, anytime. I know how it feels to be pregnant and alone," she added in a whisper.

"I know. That's why I— Thank you for the book," Marley whispered, then ran out.

June went after her, but when she opened the door and looked both ways, the streets were so crowded that she couldn't spot Marley. She headed to the stockroom to get Bean to watch the store while she finally went to see Henry. A few minutes with Mr. Books could always fix just about anything.

Henry was sitting at his desk going over orders on the Mac, a folded white bag that smelled amazing next to it. "There you are. Hope it hasn't gone cold on you." He held out the bag. "Come out to the pier with me?"

She smiled and went to tell Bean she'd be away for lunch for the next twenty minutes or so, then headed out with Henry into the brilliant sunshine. He was as hot as Carrie had noted. Even just standing next to him, walking beside him, June was so aware of him, of his height, of his lanky, muscular body in worn jeans and a white, button-down shirt, the sleeves rolled to his elbows. The way his brown hair blew in the breeze against his neck, across his forehead.

She was glad she'd dressed up some today. She usually wore jeans and white, button-down shirts herself, the ever-present wine-colored Dansko clogs on her feet. But today she wore a pretty cotton dress that was just professional enough, just casual enough, for the manager of a bookstore on the second-busiest weekend of the summer tourist season. Henry had told her she looked nice when she'd arrived that morning, and the way he looked at her, the way his gaze lingered on her, made her think that maybe Henry Books had finally stopped seeing her as a twenty-one-year-old kid in trouble.

They walked down the pier near his boat. Henry took off his shoes, rolled up his pants, and eased his long legs into the blue water. June kicked off her sandals and did the same, the early-September sun a soothing balm on her shoulders. Henry unwrapped two fried haddock sandwiches with tartar sauce and lettuce, the most delicious greasy fries, a little cup of ketchup, and two bottles of Boothbay's Own lemonade next to him.

"You got this for me?" she asked.

"Actually, I got it for Vanessa, but she slammed the phone down in my ear and told me to feed it to my 'precious fucking swordfish.' In those exact words."

June glanced at him. "Trouble in paradise?"

"There's always trouble," he said, shaking his head "We used to make up faster, but lately—and I mean the past *year*—we just argue all the time. Something's changed, you know?"

"Actually I don't know. Or maybe I do. My one great love lasted for all of two days. I wouldn't think that's enough time for anything to change. I guess something just wasn't there to start with. For him, I mean."

He glanced at her, the corners of his deep, brown eyes crinkling from the sun. "What about since then?"

"Well, when Charlie was real little, I didn't bother dating at all. And then there were some fix-ups once I moved to Portland. A few of your brother's friends. A couple of customers. The electrician who came to fix some faulty wiring. Jasper's lawyer. My romantic life has consisted of one date to two and a half months of an almost-relationship."

"Maybe you just haven't fallen in love. I'd like to know the guy who wins June Nash's heart. I'd think he'd have to be one pretty cool dude."

She smiled. Henry always made her feel that she was something special. The opposite of how Pauline Altman had made her feel five minutes ago. "I'm looking for Charlie's dad. I don't know what I'm going to find."

He took a long swig of his lemonade. "Charlie mentioned the family-tree project when I took him clamming."

She let out the sigh that had been dogging her since last night. "Once I explained that we were staying here for a while, that he wouldn't be going back to camp, he was relieved that he didn't have to hand in the sparsely filled-in tree. He taped it to the wall above his headboard," she said, her heart clenching in her chest. "And last night, when I was tucking him in, he asked with such hope in his eyes if I've found out anything about his father yet."

"Have you?"

She shook her head. "My research has gotten me absolutely nowhere."

It had been an entire week since she and Charlie had arrived at the inn, and she knew no more about John Smith than when she'd started her search seven years ago. She'd gotten so nostalgic and wistful the other night while watching *The Devil Wears Prada*—the shots of New York City, of places she'd been, especially that November when she'd met John and that early January when she'd gone back to school, newly pregnant and desperate to find him. After the discussion of the movie, she'd gone upstairs and spent over an hour online, looking at photographs of Central Park, of the *Angel of the Waters* statue, where they were supposed to meet. All that feeling came rushing back, how she'd felt about John, how full of hope and yearning she'd been.

Then she'd checked on Charlie and was reminded of her promise to find his father. She'd chastised herself for reminiscing, for living in the past, in a fantasy world, and had researched Bangor, Maine, prep schools, looking up alumni photos, but the several John Smiths she'd come across weren't her John Smith. Either they were fair blonds or bright redheads or with features not even close to the beautiful face of Charlie's father. His intense green eyes, the shock of dark hair. She'd know him the minute she saw him. And he wasn't on any of the pages she'd gone through. Yesterday, Isabel had brought up the possibility that he'd been homeschooled. And Kat had reminded her that boarding school was also possible. They'd been trying to assure her she'd find him, that she couldn't give up hope just because he wasn't in any of the Bangor yearbooks.

June put her sandwich down, her appetite gone. "Last night, Charlie was telling me all the things he and his dad could do together. Fishing and clamming and overnight camping trips. The scary big-kid rides at carnivals. And he had the dreamiest expression before he started drifting off to sleep. But then his eyes opened and he said, 'Mommy, what if my dad doesn't want to be my dad because he has another family already and other kids?'"

Henry took her hand and held it. "And you said, 'Charlie boy, I don't want you to worry about anything. Especially because there's no way anyone who meets you could not adore you.'"

June stared at Henry, wishing she could throw herself into his arms and just let him hold her. "That's exactly what I said. God, Henry, you're going to make a great dad someday."

He smiled. "Me? Maybe. One day."

Henry with a kid or two? Yeah. She could easily see it. Fishing and clamming and hunting for periwinkles and shells. Roaming through the woods with his boy and girl. But June couldn't picture John Smith married with children. In her mind he'd always be traveling, backpack and map in hand. The kind who didn't settle down.

She'd been wrong about so many things that she might as well accept that he *could* be married. With children. And uninterested in the seven-year-old son he never knew about from a two-night stand in New York City.

A chill made its way up her spine to her neck. What if she found John Smith and he didn't want to be found? What if it hurt Charlie more than not knowing his father at all?

You might be opening a can of worms. . . .

Aunt Lolly might be right. But she didn't want to teach Charlie that what-ifs and mysteries and fear were meant to be catered to. She would seek out his father and what would happen would be . . . life. Maybe John Smith would take one look at her, run to her in slow motion, say he'd been looking for her every day for the past seven years, and then rejoice in having a child, a son.

It could happen.

"At some point, I might just have to let it go," she told Henry. "*Accept* like my aunt Lolly said I'd have to. Accepting *is* important, even if it sucks."

"Well, you're not there yet, June. Right now you're looking, and for good reason. If I can help you, I will." He put his hand on top of hers and shot her one of his trademark reassuring smiles, and for a moment she was transported back seven years ago, when she would find herself staring at him as he spoke and missed half of what he said. "You said he went to Colby, right? We could take a drive up. See if we can get his parents' address. There were probably a hundred John Smiths at Colby at that time—but I doubt more than one, possibly two, is from Bangor, Maine."

She explained how she'd gotten nowhere on the phone with Colby College years ago ("We cannot, under any circumstances, give out personal information about our students, past or present, unless they sign alumni documents granting . . . I'm sorry, however . . ."). "And I tried typing *John Smith* and *Colby* and *Bangor* into Google and got over 329,000 hits."

"Maybe there's something, the smallest detail, you're not remembering that might help set you off in a new direction." Henry took a bite of his sandwich and waved away a beautiful dragonfly.

A few nights ago, Isabel and Kat had said the same thing. That perhaps there was something June hadn't thought of. Isabel had suggested June share every detail of those two nights with them, that maybe June would say something that would spark something for them.

So they'd sat around the kitchen table, sipping their iced tea and taking bites of their scones to the music of the cicadas, and June recounted every detail. How she'd felt when she realized this beautiful guy was staring at her—sweetly, intently, interested. How they'd talked about Maine. About how he'd once gotten to shake Stephen King's hand at a local reading. How he'd told her she was startling beautiful, the only man who'd ever said that to her. She'd described his face, his body, long and lean, like a baseball player's, and noticed Isabel had jotted that down. But as June spoke, she'd realized she couldn't visualize John so clearly anymore. For the longest time, she could remember the exact shade of green of his eyes, like emeralds, the number of beauty marks she'd counted on his right thigh, in the shape of the Big Dipper. But now when she thought of him, the details blurred with Charlie's sweet face. Charlie's emerald-green eyes. Charlie's beauty marks. Charlie's same dark, straight hair that fell over his forehead.

The *thought* of John was so clear, but the specifics of his face had begun to fade. June was gripped by a hollow sense of loss again, a loss of . . . nothing.

Maybe he had a family now. Maybe he wouldn't welcome a blast from the past. Maybe this, maybe that. But she would find John Smith for Charlie. She'd given up on herself and love a long time ago. But she wasn't giving up on her son's dream.

Bean came rushing out. "Guys, I hate to bug you during lunch, but a tour bus of people just came in, and there are like thirty people in the store."

As she and Henry collected their wrappers and bottles and walked back up the pier toward the back entrance to Books Brothers, Henry slung an arm around her shoulder, the best kind of comfort there was.

The moment June stepped through the doors of the inn at eight thirty that night, she smelled popcorn. The bookstore had been so busy all day that she'd forgotten it was Movie Night.

"Oh, there you are, June," Lolly said, holding some fresh-cut flowers in a vase. She set it down on the hall table. "I wasn't sure if you were back from your first day. How was it?"

"Very busy. Everyone came in for their beach books." And Marley Mathers told Pauline Altman to shove it and made my day. The thought made June smile. Until she remembered that Marley was probably sitting home alone right then, worrying herself or reading *What to Expect When You're Expecting* with no one to talk to about any of it. She'd have to track down Marley's number.

"Come chat with me in my office for a moment, will you?"

Uh-oh. June hoped this wasn't bad news. June knew that Lolly had been feeling tired the past couple of days—from the chemotherapy. That morning, Isabel had found strands of Lolly's hair on her pillows when she went to change her bedding. Lolly's blue eyes were clear and bright, but with uncharacteristic dark circles underneath, and her cheeks did seem flushed.

June followed Lolly inside the small, square office. Photographs of the inn, beautiful shots in black and white and color from over the years, since the inn was built in the 1800s, graced the walls, along with shots of the family. Generations of Nashes and Wellers. Lolly, young and healthy. June stared at one photo of Lolly in a bikini, her hair in a seventies-era shag. What was that adage? *Days pass in years, but years pass in minutes.*

"Lolly, are you feeling all right? Did you hear something from your doctor?"

Lolly shut the door behind June. "No, no, it's nothing about that. I just thought I'd better ask. . . . Pearl chose *Mamma Mia!* for tonight's Movie Night because it's so uplifting and fun, but if you think it hits too close to home right now, we can just pick something else. *It's Complicated*, perhaps."

Mamma Mia!? June hadn't seen it, but she remembered hearing about it. Meryl Streep played a single mother who lived in a beautiful old villa in Greece with her twenty-year-old daughter—who just got engaged to her young beau. The daughter has never known the identity of her father, so she secretly invites three possibilities, whom she read about in her mother's diary, to her wedding, hoping the truth will come out.

June couldn't remember if it did or not.

"Thanks for being concerned about my feelings, Aunt Lolly," June said, kissing her aunt on the cheek. "But it's really okay. Maybe I'll learn some detective work or something about how to track down *one* guy." She'd planned to spend the evening online, researching John Smiths, hoping to find something, anything, that would link back to the guy she'd known, but a movie to shut out the world right then sounded pretty good.

Lolly gripped June's hand, as if to keep the warmth of the moment, of their closeness. But then Kat called for Lolly, and Lolly headed for the door. June took a last look at her aunt in the bikini with the shag hairstyle. People seemed to live so many lifetimes. Phases.

"Let this just be a phase," June whispered to herself. The phase with cancer. *Remember when Lolly was being treated for cancer?* she would say to Isabel years from now as Lolly served one of her fabulous, traditional Thanksgiving dinners. *I didn't think any of us would get through that time,* Isabel would say back, and they'd give thanks for one another, the way families did on TV and in movies . . . well, sometimes.

Isabel, Kat, and Pearl, and one set of guests, a pair of elderly, widowed sisters-in-law whom Lolly introduced as Frances Mayweather and Lena Haywood, were arranged around the parlor, the elderly pair delighting in the fancy swirl of icing on Kat's cupcakes.

June took a chocolate cupcake with white icing, poured a glass of iced tea, and settled next to Isabel on the love seat. *Their spot,* she realized. June wasn't sure she'd ever had a "spot" in this inn before. Especially one she shared with her sister.

"Everyone ready?" Lolly asked, sliding the disc into the DVD player. She sat down next to Pearl on the sofa, remote control at the ready.

Kat got up and shut the lights. "Looks like everyone's ready."

"Where is this, Italy? Greece?" Pearl asked as the movie opened, the beautiful blue Aegean Sea and whitewashed villa on the cliffs above the beach.

"Greece," Lolly said, taking a handful of popcorn into a napkin on her lap. "That's another thing I love so much about movies—you can travel to so many beautiful, interesting locations without leaving your living room."

"Wait a minute—Meryl can sing too?" June asked while Meryl started belting out a strong, fun song about not having enough money as she moved about the villa. "That's almost wrong. How talented is this woman?"

"You just reminded me that we'll have to see *Postcards from the Edge,*" Lolly said. "She sings a song at the end of that movie that is so good I was sure it was a famous country singer."

"And wait till you hear Pierce Brosnan sing," Kat said, laughing. "It's been a while since I've seen this movie, but I remember he sort of sounds like he's underwater."

The movie was as uplifting as Lolly had said. How had June missed seeing this? Well, she knew how. Getting a sitter to see a movie when a trip to the theater cost a fortune, and popcorn and soda and Junior Mints topped the ticket price, meant waiting for movies she wanted to see to come to cable. Not that June had ever had cable.

She was surprised to find out that Meryl Streep wasn't actually sure which of the three men her daughter had secretly invited to her wedding festivities *was* her father. Apparently, she'd told friends and family that one was the father—but withheld that she couldn't be sure. Because after Pierce Brosnan had broken her heart, she'd taken up with another man. And then another.

"Three lovers in the same week!" one of the elderly sisters-in-law muttered, shaking her head.

June and Isabel glanced at each other and smiled. June was more focused on the bond between Meryl Streep and beautiful Amanda Seyfried, who played Meryl's daughter and who had a voice to match her angelic face. Even though Amanda had grown up without a father, she seemed confident and happy and had found a wonderful young man to marry. It was just a movie, but it made June feel good. Charlie would grow up confident and happy and also find a wonderful young woman to marry. Though at twenty, June realized, they were awfully young to be getting married.

One of the possible fathers, Pierce Brosnan, whom June had always thought one of the world's most handsome men, was questioning Amanda Seyfried about her life plans once she married, which involved staying at the villa to help her mother. Didn't she want to leave the island and see the world? Pursue her talent as an artist?

June glanced over at Kat, wondering if she ever thought about leaving the Three Captains'. Surely if she and Oliver got married, which June figured was in the cards, they'd live in their own house. Or maybe they'd take over the big attic room and the duties of the inn. Well, Kat, anyway. As Amanda Seyfried responded that she was staying at the villa because her mother needed her, June noticed something shift in Kat's expression.

Perhaps that was why Kat had never left. Maybe Kat did want to open her own bakery—maybe she already had the money saved up. But that would mean leaving Lolly and the inn. And perhaps now, given her mother's diagnosis, she felt she'd have to stay forever.

Aha—June saw Kat stiffen as Pierce Brosnan told Meryl Streep that her daughter was only getting married and settling down on the island because it was unthinkable for her to leave Meryl Streep there on her own. Kat was biting her lip and poking at a cupcake, still in its wrapper. June glanced over at Lolly, who was laughing at something Pearl had whispered in her ear.

"I love this song!" Isabel said when they started singing "S.O.S." Isabel started singing low along with it, and Lolly surprised everyone by singing along too, making everyone clap—well, except for the elderly sisters-in-law, who shushed her. June was humming along, but her mood changed when Amanda Seyfried said something about how it "sucked" not to know who your father was. She had no father; now she had three.

"It's a birthright for God's sake," Frances Mayweather shouted.

Isabel shot the woman a grimace. "I like what the fiancé just said to Amanda Seyfried. That 'finding herself' won't come from finding her father. It'll come from finding out who *she* is."

"I think he's right about that," Lolly whispered back.

Frances Mayweather munched her popcorn loudly, perhaps in protest. She made a *humph* sound as Amanda Seyfried happily announced she didn't need to know who her father was; all three men were her father. And instead of marrying, the young couple were finally breaking free of their island and seeing the world.

But the planned wedding wasn't going to waste. Because Meryl was marrying Pierce Brosnan in their place. They made one gorgeous couple.

"Now that's a happy ending," June said. "She ends up with her first love. Makes me think there's hope for me." She laughed, though she was dead serious.

"Cavorting with three different men," Frances said, taking a bite of her cupcake. "Not knowing the father of your own child—that's what's celebrated in this movie? Frankly, I find it appalling."

"Oh, Francy, please. It's a movie," the other one said.

Lolly sipped her iced tea and put the glass down a bit forcefully, June noticed. "Well, I like how you get the perspective of the child involved. And she fared quite well without knowing her father. Meryl Streep's character clearly raised her very well on her own."

Thank you, Lolly.

"Still, in *my* day," Frances said, "you didn't sleep with a man unless he was your husband. So you knew who your child's father was. These days, women are so desperate for a man's attention that they give themselves away. And then a poor kid is born and gets stuck without a father."

June almost choked on her iced tea.

"The daughter seemed perfectly well adjusted to me," Kat said, teeth gritted. June had a feeling that if Frances Mayweather wasn't seventysomething years old, Kat would give it to her good.

"So well-adjusted that she got engaged at twenty because, growing up with that hippie-dippy mother, she needed a man's guiding hand," Frances countered.

"Hardly," Lolly said, as politely as she could. The woman was her guest, after all. "Amanda Seyfried's character got engaged because she fell in love. And when you're that in love, you celebrate it."

Thank you again, Aunt Lolly, June sent telepathically again. Huh. She liked this new, supportive Lolly Weller. She just hated what might be underlying it.

Frances Mayweather snorted. "She's *twenty*. She knows nothing of love. I married at thirty, relatively late, I'll grant you, but I loved my Paul, Lena's brother, God rest his soul, because he was a good man, a good provider, and had manners. He worked for IBM for forty-one years. Rose every time I entered or left a room. I knew what love was."

"I fell in love with a guy at twenty-one," June said, staring at her cupcake, which she'd lost all appetite for. "He also had manners. I fell in love with him in an hour. Sometimes you just *know*."

Frances stared down her pointy nose at her. "Dear, you can't fall in love in an hour. That's called romance. Lust. Men will go to bed with anyone they find attractive and new. It's what keeps men going to prostitutes. All these politicians getting caught with high-priced call girls? That's what it's about. It's hardly love. It's why their wives don't leave them, either. They know the difference."

This time June did choke on her iced tea.

Isabel stood up, her gold bangles clinking. "You know what I think? I think there are a million different reasons for why people do what they do when they do them. And judging others when you don't know a thing about their lives or stories or situation is just wrong."

"Said by a fancy-dressed gal without a worry in her life," Frances muttered to her sister-in-law, who clearly was the henpecked listener of the traveling pair.

"Actually, I just found out weeks ago my husband was having an affair," Isabel said, hands on her hips. "I caught him in bed with another woman."

"All of this airing of dirty laundry is inappropriate," Frances said, standing up. "We'll be checking out a day early tomorrow. And I expect not to be charged a fee."

"Oh, no," Lolly said, crossing her arms over her chest. "We'll be glad to see you go."

Frances's beady eyes widened as much as they could, then she grabbed her sister-in-law's arm and led her out of the room. "I still expect my special-ordered breakfast at seven forty-five. Poached eggs on lightly toasted wheat bread and a fruit salad. Same for Lena, but the toast doesn't have to be light."

"Good night," Lolly said, rolling her eyes as the pair shuffled out and up the stairs.

Everyone was staring in awed shock at Lolly.

"Good for you, Mom," Kat said, high-fiving Lolly, who seemed quite pleased at the praise. But then Kat's expression changed, and June had a feeling she knew what was bothering Kat. The same thing that had been bothering June a few minutes ago.

Lolly had uncharacteristically told a guest to shove it, not in those words of course, because she was likely on last hurrahs.

"Don't listen to that old witch, June," Pearl said—also uncharacteristically. "If you and John had something special between you, even after an hour, that's all you need to know."

June plunked her lemon wedge off the rim of her glass and watched it plop in the tea. "Thanks, Pearl. But she's right, though, in a way. It isn't fair that Charlie has never known his dad. Because of a choice I made."

"June Jennifer Nash," Isabel said, "stop that right now. *Circumstance* led to Charlie not knowing his father."

June was so surprised at Isabel's using June's full name the way their mother used to when she wanted her full attention, at the way her sister was sticking up for her, that she just squeezed Isabel's hand and mouthed, *Thank you*.

Maybe her story with John would end the same way it had for Meryl and Pierce Brosnan. Separated by circumstance and finding their way to each other. It was possible. Last week June had read a newspaper article about a couple who'd been separated by World War II, only to reunite after divorces and widowhood forty-two years later.

"If we did have something special," June said, "if I was more than just a girl he found 'attractive and new,' then why did he leave me like that?" Tears stung her eyes. "Why did he make me believe in all that beautiful stuff, and then just disappear like it hadn't meant anything, hadn't mattered?"

Because it had mattered to her. It had mattered in so many ways. And the most important one was Charlie.

Lolly sat down beside June and pulled her into a hug. "He missed out on a great person."

June was so touched that she couldn't speak for a moment. "Thanks, Aunt Lolly," she finally whispered. She couldn't remember her aunt saying anything like that seven years ago. She leaned her head back against the sofa. "I've always thought he'd seek me out. Wonder about me, where I was, and come find me. And I'm easy to find. Even back then, I stayed at school for two months after I found out I was pregnant. And I even left a note for my file to say that if anyone wanted to get in touch with me, they could reach me at my aunt's inn. I left an e-mail address, phone, everything. I was an idiot like Frances Mayweather, or whatever her name is, said."

"Ignore that shrew," Isabel told her. "You'll encounter people like that your whole life. You have to brush them off. Why should you care what a stranger thinks of you, anyway?"

"Good point," June said. "I beat myself up enough over it anyway. Who needs mean old ladies?"

Isabel gave a firm nod of her head. "That's right. I'm sorry for what you went through, June. Sorry that John hurt you. Sorry that he missed out on Charlie."

June glanced at Isabel and could see that her sister seemed to mean it. "I can't tell you all how much this means to me. You all being supportive."

"We have your back," Kat said. "Definitely."

June did feel stronger, sitting here among these women. Her sister, who suddenly felt like a sister. Her aunt, who seemed motherly. Her cousin, who was beginning to be a true friend. She took a good, cleansing breath and felt very, very grateful. And because she was feeling grateful, she sent out a wish to the universe that somewhere tonight Marley, with her secret and her book, had someone to talk to also.

CHAPTER 9

Kat

Early Saturday morning, after Kat scrubbed the bathroom on the top floor (her least favorite task) and pulled off her yellow rubber gloves, she took a long, hot shower and headed to the kitchen to bake the muffins (six dozen—cranberry, blueberry, chocolate chip, and corn) and scones (four dozen mixed berry, and white chocolate and raspberry) for her clients around the harbor. Even after all that scrubbing, a few hours of baking would be as good as a restorative nap. The feel of flour sifting through her fingers, of dough, warm and pliant and sweet-smelling in her hands, of chocolate chips and fruit, always lifted her heart in the way movies did for her aunt. The way playing with the stray dog Isabel had taken in did for her cousin. And the way June looked when her son sat on her lap at meals, unable to get close enough to her.

Kat checked her production schedule and realized she also had a child's birthday cake (train tracks with choo-choos for three-year-old Max) due for a 2:00 p.m. delivery. As she set out her big silver mixing bowls and reached for the sack of flour, Kat saw she was short. Enough for the cake, but way too short for the dozens of muffins and scones she needed to make this morning. She'd been a bit scattered lately, she knew. Between her mother and Oliver and her cousins and the holiday weekend, she'd forgotten to add flour to her list. And chocolate chips, she saw.

She got her bike from the shed and took the long route to the market, to avoid Oliver's office. After the discussion of *Mamma Mia!* last night, she'd called Oliver to say she wouldn't be coming over; it had been late and she was exhausted, plus she had a full day of baking ahead. He'd asked her straight out if she was avoiding him; she'd barely had time for him all week—and they had something pretty spectacular to celebrate, to talk about, unless she'd forgotten all about that. Hardly, she'd told him. As if she *could*.

She *was* avoiding him, she supposed, but she hadn't admitted it. She just wanted—needed—some time to herself to figure out how she truly felt. But how could she say that to Oliver without hurting him even more? He'd told her to get a piece of paper and a pen, that he'd scoped out three more potential storefronts for her bakery and had addresses and leasing information for her, and Kat reminded him she wasn't ready for that, which led to a bit of an argument about foot-dragging.

"Why am I arguing with you about my own business?" she'd snapped. There was dead silence, which meant she'd offended him. "I mean my *bakery* business. I don't want to be pushed, Oliver."

"I'm not pushing, Kat. I'm *helping*."

She'd almost wished he'd been over last night, watching *Mamma Mia!* with them, so that he could see the young couple had chosen *not* to get married on their wedding day, after all. They were still together, but were giving each other time to grow up, as individuals and as a couple.

Was that what she wanted? Needed? More time?

She'd felt eyes on her during *Mamma Mia!* Her cousins'. And worse, her mother's. If Lolly Weller had wondered if Kat, like Amanda Seyfried, had always felt she needed to stay in Boothbay Harbor, needed to stay at the inn, because her mother needed her, Lolly hadn't come out and asked. She wouldn't; it wasn't her way. Lolly took people at their word. At their actions, really. If Kat had never left Boothbay Harbor, it was because she didn't want to.

Sometimes she wished her mother were one of those nosy, prying busybodies. Wished she'd ask the question. Probe for possible truths. Kat had been raised to say what she meant, but so much went unsaid. Surely her mother had to know that.

Then again, her mother was feeling like hell. Tired. Nauseated on and off. Losing her hair. If Kat had something to say, if she wanted her mother to know something, she'd have to say it and not expect her mother to be a mind reader. A heart reader.

Kat swerved her bike to avoid a gray cat that darted across the street, her heart skipping a beat when she neared the little storefront on Violet Place with its FOR LEASE sign in the picture window. Only four businesses were on the side street, a cobbler, a masseuse who specialized in Reiki and reading auras, and a law office. But there were beautiful trees and big planters of impatiens, and each shop had an old-fashioned, sweet quality to it, as the awnings had to be similar, based on an old ordinance. Even the law office looked inviting. She *could* imagine Kat's Cakes & Confections in that space.

She got off her bike and leaned it against a streetlamp, then peered into the vacant shop. It was small; there would be just enough room for a counter and display case, but the back room, visible through a gorgeous exposed-brick archway, was large enough for a comfortable working kitchen. She liked that the long wall of the shop was all brick and the others a pale apricot, the floors a warm tile. She envisioned Kat's Cakes & Confections painted across the huge window.

Oliver had pointed out the empty shop—months ago.

From the moment they'd started dating six months ago he'd been encouraging her to open her bakery, assuring her he'd lend her start-up costs, that he knew she'd be a success. But start-up money wasn't what was holding her back; she was close to having the ideal figure she'd gotten from the Start Your Local Business seminar she'd attended last summer. She was holding back and wasn't sure why. Maybe because opening the bakery would take her away from the inn—especially now when her mother *did* need her. Kat wasn't clinging to that as a reason to stay; she couldn't leave Lolly now even if she wanted to.

Maybe one day, she thought with one last look at the storefront. Just not *now*. She got back on her bike and rode to the grocery store. She was heading back, the flour and chocolate chips in the bike's basket, when she saw Dr. Viola, her mother's oncology resident, lying out on a pier beside an old lobster boat. Matteo Viola. Such a beautiful name. He wore aviator sunglasses, but she was sure it was him; his hair, dark and wavy and slightly long, especially for a doctor, was unmistakable. As were his green scrub pants, rolled up to his knees, his olive skin, and the hard lines of his long, tall body. His bare chest was a revelation, though. She couldn't take her eyes off him. He lay at the end of the pier, his head on a backpack, one knee up, reading a book.

She walked up behind him and read the title of the book. *Handbook of Evidence-Based Radiation Oncology.* "Light beach read?" she asked with a smile.

He sat up and turned around, pushing the sunglasses up on his head. "Oh, hey. Kat Weller, right?"

She was too pleased that he remembered her name.

He glanced at her bike, at the ten-pound bag of flour in the basket. "That's quite a lot of flour."

"All out. Not good for a baker. I make lots of extras just because it calms me. My family lucks out on those sessions.

Yesterday I baked four pies. Even the sulking teenage guest at my mother's inn smiled."

He did too. "I've been the beneficiary of those kinds of pies and cakes my entire life. My parents own a bakery in town, did you know that? The Italian Bakery on Townsend, next to the flower shop."

She gasped. Alonzo and Francesca—of course. She realized she'd never known their last names because they were on a first-name basis with everyone. Warm and friendly and always handing out cookies to the kids. Sometimes you'd open your box of cookies from the Italian Bakery and find a decadent cannoli slipped in. They specialized in breads and Italian pastries. No one bought bread from anyone else. Even her nephew, Charlie, had been salivating at the window over the cannoli.

"I had no idea Alonzo and Francesca were your parents. I love their place. Sometimes I buy from there just to take the incredible pastries home and re-create the magic. I've never had an éclair like from the Italian Bakery."

"So you're a baker too? What's your specialty?"

"I started my own baking business out of the Three Captains' Inn, where I live. Kat's Cakes and Confections, I call it. I bake for the inn, but I specialize in wedding cakes and do cakes and cupcakes of all kinds. And I'm getting kind of famous for my muffins too."

They both turned to watch a whale that jumped out of the water; a cruise boat of people standing on deck clapped and cheered.

"I'd love to try one sometime," he said. "So tell me, how is your mother feeling?"

"She says she feels okay, but I can see she's slowed down considerably. She holds the rail very tightly as she comes downstairs. She's never done that before. And I've been finding hairs on her pillows and in the shower."

He nodded, sympathy in his eyes. "That's all the chemo. How are her spirits?"

"She's in pretty good spirits, actually. I think she likes having her nieces and grand-nephew back at the inn. Her family—what's left of it—is back together again. I think it means more to her than any of us ever realized."

"Family has restorative properties. And what about you, Kat? How are you doing?"

"I've been better. Holding up. Worried." She shrugged.

She knew he'd have something to say to comfort her. She thought of the way he'd reached for her hand when she'd started crying that first time they'd met in the hospital, outside her mother's chemotherapy room, and had said, "What am I supposed to do?"

"There's no right response from you or from anyone," he'd said, looking at her so intently. "You can cry, you can rage, you can hold in your fear, you can do any damn thing you need to."

She'd felt such a freedom in that moment that she'd burst out crying and he'd squeezed her hand until she stopped. She found herself thinking about him, often, since.

"Could I ask you some questions, Dr. Viola? Real questions about how long my mother has? It's so hard to get a straight answer."

He sat up and tapped the peeling wood of the pier beside him. "Call me Matteo. And come sit."

She slipped off her sandals and sat with her knees up and bent her arms around them. *Matteo.* "Dr. Samuels said she could have weeks, months, even a year, that it was impossible to say, that the chemo might prolong her life. But it's also making her weaker."

He nodded. "Chemo is that way. It gives and takes. And we can't say, can't give you a definitive time period, Kat. We can only try to make your mother's life as comfortable as we can."

"I know you can only tell us what you know, know for sure, I mean, but I wish you could tell me what to do with the worry. And fear."

"Actually, I can tell you. At least what I did."

She stared at him. "Someone in your family?"

"*Mio padre.* My father. I wanted to focus on oncology because of him. His cancer—of the prostate—was caught relatively early because I kept on him about testing. But just to be safe. When he was diagnosed, I was scared out of my mind. Especially because of how much I know."

She often peeked in the windows of the Italian Bakery to see what they were offering, or to pick up some breads for breakfast or as a treat for her mother, who loved dipping good bread into olive oil. Alonzo was often chatting with a customer, telling stories about Italy. She had no idea he'd been sick.

"He's a survivor, but I worry about him every day. It's why I'd hoped to do my residency here. I'm lucky we have a great teaching hospital right in Boothbay."

"You seem so focused and calm. I would never have known you had so much as a hangnail."

He smiled. "People are like that, aren't they? Facades. Professional demeanors. You really never know what's going on with someone."

She nodded. "I've been finding that out about my cousins. You met one of them, Isabel, the other day. I've kind of had them pegged all wrong."

"It's the great thing about life. How surprising people are. Good and bad."

"I prefer the good."

He smiled. "Me too."

"So what did you do with all your worry when your dad was first diagnosed?"

"I reminded myself that he was there. Standing. Alive.

That I had to focus on that—and on treatment. Not on possibilities or on fear. I focused on having him with me. And I made the best of that. We bought season tickets for the Red Sox. We took long drives. We built a go-cart with my little niece. I don't want to sound like a greeting card, but we celebrated life—instead of anticipating the opposite. That's not only good for you, and your cousins, but for your mother, as well."

Kat took a deep breath, letting his words, the warm, fresh air, seep through her. She could sit here all day. Talking to Matteo. Feeling the breeze in her hair.

When he leaned back, his arms behind him, their hands touched, and for a moment neither of them moved, until they pulled away at exactly the same time.

"I'd better go," she said. *Before I fling myself on top of you and kiss you the way they do in movies.* "Thanks for talking to me. It helped very much."

"I'm glad. And if you ever need to talk more, just call. Anytime."

She smiled and headed back up the pier, and when she turned to take one last look, he was watching her.

Kat lay against Oliver's chest in the bathtub, the hot, bubbly water soothing her tired muscles. After spending a couple of hours baking and making her cake delivery, she'd helped Isabel with general cleanup, including the tracked sand (they both guessed a certain fourteen-year-old guest was responsible) and wet, dirty footprints. The inn was booked for the holiday weekend, which meant cleaning rooms and hallways and common spaces by the hour for poor Isabel. Wet footprints, crumbs from that morning's breakfast blondies, tissues, spilled this and that—all taken care of by Lolly's "green" cleaners and sweeper vac. All day long. Kat had been impressed by Isabel. Her cousin had either been busy handling guests or cleaning all day, and when Isabel had finally had a chance to relax, she'd made fresh lemonade and handed it out to guests in the backyard.

Oliver had picked up Kat at seven and driven her back to the cottage he was renting on Townsend. The carriage house was separated from the main house by a stone wall and evergreens, and every time Kat visited, she felt as if she were entering a fairy-tale cottage in the woods. She loved the place.

Waiting for her at the fairy-tale cottage was a grill ready to go with steaks and asparagus and baked sweet potatoes, her favorite. Over dinner he got a little pushy about the available storefronts for lease, but when she explained she was back-burnering the idea of opening her own bakery while Lolly was undergoing treatment, he seemed to understand and backed off with an "Okay, I get it." He'd led her upstairs to his bedroom, to the king-size bed with its soft down pillows, peeled off her clothes, and given her a massage over every inch of her tired body, then made love to her with exactly the right touch.

But she'd done something terrible while they'd been in bed, something that made her feel ashamed. She'd thought of Matteo. Of his dark eyes. His hard-as-rock abs. The way those green scrubs inched down his stomach. His face, so handsome, exotic. He made her think of Italy, of Europe, of her teenage dreams to be a baker's apprentice in Rome or Paris. Of riding around with her cakes in her Vespa's basket.

She'd tried to focus on Oliver's handsome, sweet face. But over and over it was Matteo's face, Matteo's body, she thought of.

"So do you think it's time to tell your family our news?" Oliver asked, his strong, wet arms across her chest.

"I . . ." Just can't. "I don't think it's right to force my

mother—or my cousins—to pay attention to something so big," she said—and meant it. "Last night, she was tired from just watching a movie. She's worried about so much, Oliver. If I spring the engagement on her, she'll feel forced to be all cheerful and happy and maybe even plan the wedding, not to mention pay for it, and how can I do that to her? The focus should be on taking care of her. Not me and my wedding."

Oliver massaged her shoulders, his soapy hands untightening knots. "I get what you're saying, but I'd think the news would do wonders for her. Cheer her up. She'd be so happy to know you're settling down, taken care of."

Taken care of. Kat didn't want to be taken care of, though. And the word *settle* scared her. She'd once wanted Oliver so badly, so much, but then the years of repressing that (as her best friend Lizzie's fiancé—a therapist—insisted) had done a number on her head. She'd had a chance with Oliver years ago and hadn't taken it. Now, she was being offered forever with him and was too scared to take it. (That was the therapist's take, anyway.)

"You just don't want to belong to any club that would have someone like you for a member," Lizzie's fiancé had said via Lizzie. So you'll date this guy and that. Have hot, months-long romances that fizzle or explode. Because you're afraid of who you really are, what you really want.

"Which is?" she'd asked.

"Maybe to be right where you are. Maybe the reason you've never left Boothbay Harbor, left the inn, isn't because your mother would be alone. Because you feel this burning need to give back to her. But because you love it here. Love the inn. Love your mother. And Oliver. But if you say yes to him, to this life here, you dare accept what you cherish most in life and you're scared to death of losing it."

She'd written it off as psychobabble. Therapist-speak. But

it had so many kernels of truth that Kat tried not to think too hard about it.

"Kat," Oliver said, scooping up the lavender bubbles and caressing her breasts, her stomach, her inner thighs, "until you tell your family, I can't tell anyone, either. And I want to scream it from the rooftops."

"I know," she said, trying to focus on the sensation, on the rhythm of his hands. "I'm just letting everyone adjust to Lolly's news before I spring something everyone has to be happy about."

"Have you told Lizzie we're engaged?"

Sigh. "No," she whispered.

"So maybe the reason you're not telling your family and your best friend is because you're not sure," he said, his voice edged with anger. Or frustration. "Maybe that's really why you've been so scarce all week, Kat."

She stared down at the bubbles. "I'm not sure if I'm not sure, Oliver." She shook her head. "God, listen to me. I'm ridiculous. Not sure if I'm not sure."

He took her hands. "I know things are very rocky right now, Kat. Between your mom and your cousins—it's one of the reasons I proposed now instead of waiting. To support you, make sure you know someone seriously has your back."

And she appreciated that. But— But, but, but. What was the but? That she didn't need someone to have her back? That she needed to find her way through this herself? That she felt she was supposed to experience something else before she settled down forever in this one place? Now that her mother was— It meant the inn would fall to Kat. Isabel and June would go back to their lives eventually. The inn and Oliver would be her life, just as they'd always been.

"Kat, I want to be here for you. I want to spend my life with you. But if you said yes in a weak moment and you meant 'I don't know' or if you meant no, say so. Don't play with me." His voice had become hard.

"I just . . . I just don't know exactly right now."

He turned her shoulders so that she would face him. "Do you want to marry me or not, Kat?"

"I don't know," she said honestly. "Can you give me a little time to process everything?"

"I care about you very much. And of course I'll give you time. But I believe a person knows how they feel, Kat. In the deepest parts of themselves, they know. I think you know, and the fact that I'm not sure which way you feel worries me. A lot."

"Just give me some time, okay?"

He got out of the tub and left the bathroom, and she suddenly felt cold.

CHAPTER 10

Isabel

Not long ago, Isabel lived in a fancy Connecticut house, cleaned by a housekeeper twice a week. Now Isabel was in the Osprey Room in a borrowed pair of Kat's old jeans, with her sweeper and yellow rubber gloves and cleaning supplies. She'd already taken care of the Bluebird and Seashell rooms, saving Griffin's for last. Given her secret little crush on him, she felt a bit funny being in here. As though she were spying.

But she was indeed here to clean. She was out of practice, certainly, but over the past week she found she actually liked stacking the dirty plates in the dishwasher, scrubbing down the counters and sweeping the floors and giving them a once-over with the lemony-scented mop, picking up after guests, and straightening the rooms. She liked stripping beds and making them up new again, smoothing down quilts and fluffing pillows. Carrying the sheets and pillowcases and towels in the wicker basket down to the laundry closet off the kitchen made her feel purposeful. For the first time in a long time. It wasn't that she loved cleaning so much as she liked taking care of the inn. More than she ever imagined she would.

At least she was better at cleaning than she was at cooking the family dinners. Last night, no one had taken seconds of her chicken cacciatore or her Caesar salad. Nor the night before of her lasagna, one of Charlie's favorites, though the garlic bread she'd made was okay. She wasn't a good cook, clearly, but she enjoyed cooking, following the steps in Lolly's Julia Child cookbook. She'd had no idea how good it felt to make dinner every night for people she cared about. She and Edward had often picked up dinner at their favorite gourmet takeout or gone out to dinner or to dinner parties at clients' and firm partners'. Or she'd been alone for dinner with the housekeeper's labeled frozen meals, especially the past few months. She'd try to become a better cook. Maybe take a class. She'd always wanted to do that.

Griffin was neat, she noticed. Alexa wasn't. Her clothes were in a jumble in the open drawers, as though the girl couldn't decide what to wear and had half pulled out everything. Alexa's face came to mind, that sweet heart-shaped face with the angry dark-blue eyes. *I understand you, my girl,* she said to the tangle of clothes. *All too well.* She had an urge to tidy everything, fold it all neatly, but according to Lolly, if guests left dresser or closet doors open, you could close them, but not touch anything inside them. Isabel closed the drawers, shaking them a bit to let the tumble of shorts and tanks and jeans fall in.

She collected the sheets and pillowcases and tossed them into her laundry basket, then grabbed the fresh bedding and made both kids' beds, turning over the starfish quilts and fluffing the pillows.

She saved Griffin's bed for last. As she slowly stripped the pale blue sheets off the bed, she imagined him lying there, naked. She imagined herself lying with him, on top of him, under him.

"Oh, sorry to interrupt. I didn't realize you'd be cleaning in here. I'll come back in a bit."

She turned to find Griffin standing in the open doorway

with his room key. She wondered if her cheeks were as red as they felt. He was staring at her. Almost as though he knew what she'd just been thinking. Which made her blush again. "No, no worries. Just get what you need and don't mind me." She dropped the sheets in the basket, then grabbed the pillows. They smelled like him. Masculine. Fresh, like his shampoo.

"To tell you the truth, Isabel, I have been minding you since I checked in."

She glanced up at him, so surprised that she dropped the pillow on the floor. He moved closer and picked it up, taking off the case and dropping it in the basket.

"I think you're beautiful, for one. And for another, I've liked spending time with you and working with Happy."

Griffin had spent the past few afternoons working with Isabel's dog, Happy (aptly named by Charlie), giving Isabel lessons on the basics of dog training while Alexa watched Emmy on the deck. Often Isabel would be so mesmerized by his face, by his eyes, his voice, that she'd realize she'd missed a full minute of what he'd said. That she was attracted to another man, that she had this . . . crush, amazed her. She wouldn't have thought it possible, that she'd have room inside her head, inside her heart, that she'd be capable of thinking of Griffin Dean naked. And now here he was, saying that he had similar thoughts.

She was so surprised, so . . . delighted and suddenly shy like a teenager that she couldn't speak for a moment. "Um, it's Movie Night at the inn tonight. Well, it's Sunday and not our regularly scheduled Movie Night, that's Friday Night. But my aunt, Lolly Weller, you've met her, of course, she sometimes decides it's Movie Night just because. So we're watching *Heartburn*. Meryl Streep. Jack Nicholson. It's a classic. Funny. I mean, as funny as a movie about an affair could possibly be." Oh, God, had she just said that?

"I know all about how unfunny affairs are," he said, and she sobered. Instantly.

Had he had an affair? Is that what all the family strife was about? The angry teenager? The vacation at an inn in the same town?

"What time?" he asked.

"Nine o'clock. There'll be popcorn. And Kat's amazing Movie Night cupcakes. Wine and beer, if you're interested." *Stop rambling, Isabel.*

"I'll be there." He gave her a smile of sorts, then headed toward the door. He stepped into the alcove and appeared again with Alexa's iPod and Emmy's pink sun hat. He looked at her again, then was gone.

After dinner—Isabel's Julia Child meat loaf and garlic mashed potatoes were a hit, especially with Charlie, who had seconds—Isabel went back down to the basement for a third time. When Isabel had reported to Lolly the other day that she hadn't found the diaries in any of the trunks, Lolly said she was *sure* she'd put the two red journal books in one of the trunks with stickers. Isabel conceded—to herself—that she might have looked through most of the trunks quickly, hoping not to find the diaries, which made her feel awful. Her aunt wanted them, needed them to feel better—the chemo was doing quite a number on her stomach and making her so fatigued. And Isabel was being selfish by not trying harder to find them. She wouldn't leave this stale, airless room without them.

In one of the trunks she found her old school records. Isabel flipped through the report cards and occasional tests or papers with an A that her mother had saved. There was a letter, a copy, from her mother to the guidance counselor dated fifteen years ago, in October.

*I want to assure you that at heart, Isabel is a wonderful
girl, with much compassion. I think she's going through
a difficult and unfortunately long phase of testing,
herself and others, but I have no doubt my daughter
will come out of it a stronger person for her experiences.
Isabel is a gem, and once she's able to sparkle, watch out,
world. . . .*

Isabel read the letter again, tears slipping down her cheeks.
Her mother would give speeches sometimes, insist she believed in Isabel, knew she was capable of better, but Isabel
had written it off as lies to get her to behave. Her mother
had been her champion. Isabel folded the letter and put it in
her pocket, then resumed the search for the diaries with less
worry. Maybe what her mother wrote wouldn't be so bad,
after all.

But after forty-five minutes, no diaries. She carried up
some treasures she'd found, a few dresses and a hat she was
sure June would love, a painting Kat had done as a seven-
year-old for Isabel's parents, Kat's aunt Allie and uncle Gabriel, that Isabel would like to put on her desk. The diaries
weren't in those trunks, Isabel was sure of it. But she was glad
she'd looked harder for them, for Lolly and for herself.

Isabel had chosen *Heartburn*. Another affair movie, yes,
but a very different take. One she could relate to. Meryl
Streep, a New York food writer for a magazine, and Jack
Nicholson, a Washington, DC, columnist, marry, despite
how cynical both were about their first marriages. Meryl
gave up her life in New York and moved to DC, only to
discover Jack was having an affair with a socialite while she
was pregnant with their second child—and that she was
one of the last to know.

She wondered if Griffin would relate—too well. Given the big age difference between his children, there had to be a story there. She glanced at her watch. Just before nine. Rain sluiced against the windows, the kind of downpour that meant Griffin wouldn't decide to take a walk instead.

"I love this movie," Pearl said as she sat down on the sofa next to Lolly. "You wouldn't think a movie about infidelity could be so funny and poignant."

Lolly slid the DVD into the player. "That's thanks to Nora Ephron. She wrote the screenplay based on her book. It's supposed to be *very* autobiographical. The husband is the one who Dustin Hoffman played in—what's that movie? About Watergate?"

"*All the President's Men.* And also based on a true story," Kat said, coming in with her gorgeous red velvet cupcakes. June was behind her with a tray of two big bowls of popcorn. "I'm the weirdo who actually likes to read the book after I see the movie version. I'm going to read *Heartburn* after we see this. I've never seen it or read it."

Pearl set a cupcake on the coffee table. "I can lend it to you. I'm such a fan of Nora Ephron. And every time I see this movie, I totally get why Jack Nicholson was such a movie star. He's so incredibly charming—for a while, anyway."

"Oh, I forgot the iced tea," Isabel said, heading into the kitchen for the pitcher and glasses. She took a peek up the stairs, hoping to see Griffin coming down. No sign of him. But just as she was coming back, Griffin was halfway down, looking so . . . *sexy* was the word. The classic tall, dark—and slightly disheveled. Even his hair was sexy.

"I'm not late, am I?" he asked. "Emmy woke up and it took me a while to get her back to sleep. I had to fumble my way through a song from *The Little Mermaid* twice before Alexa couldn't bear another off-key moment and took over. Emmy was asleep halfway through her first go-around."

Isabel smiled. How she would love to sing a small child to sleep. She led the way to the parlor. "I wish you could have a video of that—daddy singing his off-key lullaby to his baby girl. It's just so sweet."

"I sing like Pierce Brosnan in *Mamma Mia!* Have you ever seen that? I wouldn't have, but Alexa was watching it one night and said I had to come watch with her. That doesn't happen often."

Isabel laughed. "Just a few days ago, actually. It's Meryl Streep month at the Three Captains'. All Meryl all the time. I'm glad you're joining us."

"Me too. It's been a while since I've seen a movie that didn't star singing woodland creatures," he said as they sat down next to each other in the high-backed chairs.

June smiled. "I know just what you mean."

There were hellos and small talk and the passing of cupcakes and popcorn, and Kat ran to get herself and Griffin two bottles of beer.

"Is everyone here who's coming?" Lolly asked with the remote control in her hand.

"I think so," Kat said, handing Griffin a Shipyard beer. Another guest was sitting in Kat's usual spot on the beanbag, a chatty twentysomething named Jillian who had checked in with her boyfriend, who was apparently playing *Warcraft* something or other on his laptop in the Bluebird Room.

Griffin was so close. Maybe an inch from Isabel. As the movie started, she was so aware of him, the side of his arm. The side of his thigh. His profile, strong and masculine. That hair. He smelled like soap. Ivory.

"Wow, I really love Meryl with brown hair," June said. "She's so beautiful. I just love her face."

"Me too," Kat said. "Her bones are so elegant. Even with that funny eighties-era hair and shoulder pads."

Some serious shoulder pads, indeed, were on Meryl

Streep's fancy dress. She was at a wedding—and carrying on a staring type of flirtation with total stranger Jack Nicholson. Yadda yadda yadda, they were suddenly in bed, sharing a postmidnight snack of the spaghetti carbonara she'd whipped up for him. As they ate, sheets wrapped around them, Jack Nicholson said that when they got married, he wanted her to make spaghetti carbonara once a week.

Which reminded Isabel of Edward. When they were sixteen, just weeks after they met, Edward had said, "When we're married, I'll make you spaghetti every day." They'd eaten a lot of spaghetti in those weeks and months after her parents died. It was the one thing Edward knew how to make, besides sandwiches. So he'd make her bowls of spaghetti with homemade sauce and they'd sit and swirl their spaghetti and talk about how things would be when they were married. Not only wouldn't there be children, but there wouldn't be any heartache at all, according to Edward. She didn't hold out much hope for Meryl and Jack's future.

"Whoa," Griffin said. "When Meryl says she's never getting married again, that marriage doesn't work, that she doesn't believe in it, and Jack says, 'Me too,' they should have just stopped right there. End of the movie. Cut."

All eyes were on Griffin. Including Isabel's.

"Sorry," he said. "Couldn't help myself."

"I think everyone in this room agrees with you," Lolly said.

Isabel wondered if she'd ever believe in marriage again.

"That can't be right," Kat said. "Forty percent of all second marriages end in divorce? I'd think people would choose so carefully the second time around that the percentage would be much lower."

June reached for a handful of popcorn. "Or maybe they expect even more. Stomped on or whatever the first time, so they won't take crap the next time. Or they get out quicker."

Meryl and Jack's marriage, second for them both, was going great, though. And they'd just had a baby.

A baby. Tears pricked the backs of Isabel's eyes when Meryl told her editor at the magazine she wrote for, "You get born too. It's almost like you expand." Isabel imagined that was exactly how it was. She'd ask June about that later.

Kat was shaking her head. "How crazy is it that everyone's talking about the fact that this Thelma socialite is having an affair with somebody's husband, and no one knows who, and it turns out to be Jack Nicholson?"

"It's hard to even imagine that he did cheat on Meryl," Isabel said. "They seemed so truly happy. I just don't get this at all."

June licked some icing off her cupcake. "I wish I understood what led people to cheat. I mean, I get it, sometimes. But in this case, in so many cases, it just makes no sense."

Kat nodded. "Do you believe he's reading off this list of words that define him in this stupid dinner-party game even after his affair walks by? How can he not add *cheating liar*? How can he not feel guilty?"

"Maybe some people compartmentalize," Isabel said. "To make it okay for themselves. So they can go on living in their house with their spouse like everything is status quo or whatever." Like Edward had done for months until he got caught. "But I still think a woman in Jack's situation, a woman cheating, would throw down her list and run off crying."

"My wife didn't," Griffin said. "Ex-wife."

All eyes swung to Griffin.

"She didn't feel guilty, I mean," he said. "She felt *right*. Entitled to happiness. She fell in love and that overrode other feelings, loyalty to her marriage, family."

Oh. He hadn't cheated. He'd been cheated on. She wanted to watch him instead of the movie, but of course she couldn't.

"It's funny how she—Meryl Streep, I mean—just *knew*," Griffin said, clearly wanting to change the subject back to the movie, "the minute the hairstylists started talking about an affair in their circle."

Pearl shook her head—in agreement. "I have a feeling it's like that a lot. My sister, God rest her soul, she just walked in the door one day and just *knew*, including that she was the *last* to know in her neighborhood. Do you think it works like that? That everyone knows but the wife?"

"I didn't know," Isabel whispered.

"Me either," Griffin whispered back.

They glanced at each other, and Isabel was aware of everyone staring at them.

"Oh, God, I hate this part," Lolly said. "When she finds the receipts from hotels and gifts, she *knows*, and she confronts him and asks him, 'Do you love her?' and he says he can't do this right now." She was looking out the dark window, and Isabel wondered what Lolly was thinking about, what she was remembering. Isabel doubted her uncle Ted had ever had an affair. He'd doted on Lolly—as much as Lolly would allow such a thing.

"Yeah, like it's just all too much for poor him." June rolled her eyes. "I liked his character so much until that—well, until you know he's having an affair."

"What's so scary to me is how your life just changes. Just like that"—Kat snapped her fingers—"your life changes."

Isabel nodded. "It is just like that. Your life completely changes. Hey, look, Meryl went home to the house she grew up in just like I did." Well, sort of.

"What I can't believe," the guest said, "is that she's actually waiting for that ass to call, to come for her. After the way he treated her? You're not waiting for your ex to come for you, are you, Isabel?"

A little personal, lady, Isabel thought, aware that Griffin was half watching her. Waiting for the answer. She wasn't waiting for Edward to call or come for her. But she wanted something from him. An explanation that would make sense. Maybe no explanation ever would.

"Good Lord, did her father just say that?" June asked fast, saving Isabel from having to respond at all. Isabel sent her sister a look of thanks. " 'You want monogamy, marry a swan.' I wonder if that's what Nora Ephron's father was really like or if this is made up."

Isabel and June were both quiet when Meryl told her father that she missed her mother, who had died years ago, even after she added that her mother "wasn't good at a time like this."

Isabel wondered how *her* mom would have been at a time like this. Maybe their adult relationship would have been different. Then again, if her parents hadn't died, if she hadn't met Edward, if she hadn't changed so abruptly, who knows what her relationship with her mother—or anyone—would be like. She might have married a completely different man. Or perhaps she and Edward would have found their way to each other differently. It was impossible to know.

Isabel thought her mother would be wonderful at a time like this. For herself and for June.

"Is she really going to go back with him?" Kat asked when Jack Nicholson showed up with his "I want you to come back. I love you."

"Isabel, would you go back to your husband if he arrived at the inn and said that?" the guest asked as she blew a bubble.

Isabel glanced at June and could tell that her sister wanted to smash the bubble right in the woman's face.

Edward hadn't called. Hadn't come after her. Hadn't said the words that Isabel admitted in the deepest part of her she did want to hear, just to know that she'd mattered, that their marriage had mattered. She had no idea if she could ever trust him again. But to know that he was sorry, that he knew he'd made a mistake and was begging her to come back—she did want that, if she was honest with herself.

"How about those Red Sox?" Kat said, widening her eyes at the nosy guest until the woman seemed to get the message.

"Oh, right, Jack Nicholson won't see his affair again." The guest made some weird snorting noise. "How can she be so stupid to believe him? I hope Nora Ephron didn't do that in real life."

"You really can't judge unless you're right in someone's shoes," Lolly said.

The guest blew another bubble. "I'm just saying that once a cheater, always a cheater. What's to stop them, especially when they have you back?"

"Dear, I can't hear the movie," Pearl said, and Isabel could have kissed her—even though they'd all been talking through the whole thing.

Isabel mentally shook her head as Meryl Streep, now back in Washington, DC, with Jack Nicholson, was wide-awake in the middle of the night, staring up at the ceiling in emotional turmoil while he slept, oblivious and happy. How many nights had Isabel lain in bed just like that, Edward fast asleep beside her?

"Ha, see," the guest said. "She doesn't trust him. She gave it a shot, but she wasn't stupid, thank God."

"You know what I don't get?" Griffin said. "How it's possible to live with someone and not know something so big is going on inside them that has nothing to do with you. Makes you feel like one hell of an idiot."

Isabel reached for his hand, and he glanced at her in surprise, but held her hand for a moment until she slipped it away.

The guest snorted again. "People see what they want."

"Ah, there it is," Kat said, eyes on the screen. " 'You know things are wrong, but it's a distant bell.'"

June sighed. "I like what Meryl just said about how to

handle your spouse's affair. 'You can stick with it, which is unbearable, or dream another dream.'"

Dream another dream. Isabel wanted to do just that.

The guest started clapping. "Awesome! Meryl throws a pie right in Jack Nicholson's lying, cheating face and flies back home to New York."

As the credits rolled, Isabel wondered what she'd do with herself. Maybe Lolly would be just fine. Her cancer could go into remission. And maybe Isabel would stay close or maybe she'd think about what she might have done if she hadn't met Edward at sixteen and let him direct her life. She must have had dreams back then—more than not to be invisible. The only dream she had now was to have a child. Which meant she *had* dreamed another dream, she realized with a smile.

"Take a walk with me around the harbor?" Griffin whispered. "The rain stopped."

"I'd love to," she said.

Isabel went upstairs to get her purse and make sure she didn't have popcorn in her teeth, and she wasn't surprised that June and Kat, grinning goofily, appeared a moment later.

"Are you going to wear that?" June asked, eyeing Isabel's movie-watching clothes: yoga pants and a ruffly cotton tunic and ballet slippers.

Isabel was comfortable, but she glanced in the antique floor mirror in the corner. "Should I change?"

Kat shook her head. "You look great. A little lip gloss and you're good to go."

"Or a sexy sundress and strappy sandals," June said. "It's your first second date ever."

Isabel was bursting with a goofy smile herself, but she said, "It's not a date. It's a *walk*. I'm not exactly ready to date anyone, even—"

"A gorgeous veterinarian?" June supplied.

Isabel couldn't help her smile. "He is very attractive."

"Very," Kat agreed.

"Maybe if we develop more of a friendship and we do go on an official date, I'll dress up a bit," Isabel assured June. "But tonight, it's just a walk."

And so after June assured Griffin that she'd keep an ear out for the girls, off Isabel and Griffin went. As they walked, Isabel found out he was born and bred in Boston but had followed his ex-wife to Camden, Maine, where she was from, and since Alexa had been conceived on a vacation to Boothbay Harbor, they'd decided to move there. His ex-wife liked fine things, and though he did okay as a vet, he didn't do as okay as her investment-banker boss with the multimillion-dollar house.

"I was blindsided like you were," Griffin said as they turned onto Townsend Avenue, still crowded with tourists despite how late it was. "I came home a day early from a conference to find my wife in bed with her boss. In our bed. After two years of convincing me that we should have another child, that Alexa needed a sister. Emmy wasn't even a year old when our family fell apart."

Isabel shook her head. "I wish I could get the image of Edward and what's-her-face out of my mind. How long did it take you?"

"A while. Too long. But it started fading. Now I don't think of either of them much at all. My ex and I are cordial enough for the girls' sakes, but I lost all feeling for her, even as a person. I make sure I speak kindly about her around the girls, though. Alexa's still furious at her mother for breaking up the family. She claims to hate her mom, but I know she doesn't really. It's all just anger. And hurt."

Isabel sighed with remembrance. "Fourteen is such a tough age. And I know what you mean about losing feeling.

I was with Edward for so long that even though I'd started to lose feeling for him, I repressed it, stomped it down, anything to avoid it. And even when he betrayed me in little ways—and some big ways—I still looked the other way, trying so hard to fight my way back to him."

"Until he made that impossible." Griffin took her arm and wrapped it around his. Her entire body tingled. "Like my ex."

A coffee shop was open late for the holiday weekend, so they stopped in for iced coffees to go and walked down to the harbor to the footbridge. They stood in the center of the bridge under a crescent moon and so few stars that Isabel could count them. Seven. Seven lucky twinkles.

Griffin sipped his coffee. "When I let Alexa know I was going out for a bit, just for a walk down to the harbor, she said, 'Alone?' When I mentioned that you were joining me, she slammed a pillow over her head."

"It has to be rough on a girl her age, dealing with all that. Her mother remarrying, her father dating. Even if it's just a walk."

"I told her it was just a walk, and I got a 'Right. Just a walk.'"

They looked at each other then, and he took her hand. Goose bumps skittered up Isabel's spine, her neck. A group was coming up the bridge, so he wrapped her arm around his arm again and they headed to the far end of the bridge and watched the midnight excursion boats.

"I'm glad I met you, Isabel. Even if meeting someone was the last thing I expected when I booked a room at the Three Captains'."

"I'm glad I met you too, Griffin." She wanted to stop and kiss him under the seven stars. She wanted to ask him a million questions. "Speaking of the Three Captains', you said you stayed there before?"

"The three of us—me, Alexa, and Emmy, when my ex first left. I needed to get us out of that house—it just suddenly changed on us, you know? So I booked us a room at the Three Captains' because of the name, and because I thought the girls would like the house and the gardens, and we stayed for a weekend. Emmy was too young to understand what was going on, but Alexa was a mess. She spent a lot of time in that Alone Closet. Your aunt said it was okay. But I don't think she remembers us."

"She's preoccupied. She's been diagnosed with stage four pancreatic cancer. It's why I'm here. Why we're all here."

"I'm very sorry to hear that. I'm glad I'm helping then in my own way, by training Happy as the official Three Captains' Inn dog."

Isabel smiled and they looked at each other long enough that Griffin leaned over and kissed her.

For a second, she felt herself pulled into it, aware of his soft, strong lips, the Ivory scent and broad chest, the strange maleness of him. But then the very strangeness of him, of this man she hadn't known a week and a half ago, took over and she stepped back.

"I'm sorry," she said. "This feels . . . stranger than I thought. It was barely two weeks ago that I found out about the affair. And I really was blindsided. I mean, I knew we were having problems, that there was a big issue between us, but I never thought he—" She clamped her mouth shut and sighed. "I'm not supposed to be talking about this, am I?"

"No supposed-to's. No rules. And I know how you feel. Exactly."

She started to cry and he pulled her into a hug. They stood like that at the end of the bridge until a group of teenagers passed them and a boy shouted, "Get a room." Giggles and footsteps later, she and Griffin both laughed.

"I actually have a room," he said, "but I'm sharing it with an angry fourteen-year-old and a snoring three-year-old."

"And I'm sharing with my sister and my cousin."

"Probably a good thing," he said, his dark eyes on her.

"Yeah," she whispered. And they walked back, hand in hand.

CHAPTER 11

June

How did I get here? June wondered at six o'clock in the morning on Labor Day as she sat behind the wheel of her trusty Subaru, which had somehow become Marley Mathers's getaway car—just in case. Marley sat squirming in the passenger seat, staring at the windows above Boothbay Flowers, where her former high school sweetheart, a baseball star whom June remembered as particularly good-looking, and current off and on summer fling (now off), lived. Apparently, they'd had a huge argument weeks ago and Marley announced it was over between them, and Kip (short for Christopher, June learned last night) began dating someone else immediately. He lived in Boothbay year-round, coaching varsity and recreational programs. The former flames had hooked up early in the summer, but like old times, Kip wasn't interested in dating only Marley.

And now she was about to tell him she was ten weeks pregnant with his child. Six a.m. didn't seem like the best time, but when was? Marley had called him last night and said she had something important to talk to him about, and before his workout was his only free time. Marley had explained all this to June when she called late last night, in tears, asking for advice. How did Charlie's father take the news? she wanted to know. How did June tell him?

And so over a glass of wine at midnight in the parlor, June told Marley the very short story. Despite June's lack of experience in sharing the news with the father of her baby, Marley asked if she'd come with her to tell Kip, to just be there, before and after. June wondered what it would have been like to have found John when she discovered she was pregnant. If she'd told him and he'd taken off on her, she'd have been alone in New York City with that kind of rejection, that kind of abandonment. She might not know Marley Mathers well, but she'd be her getaway person.

"Okay," Marley said, reaching for the car-door handle for the third time in the past five minutes. "I'm going."

"I'll be here," June said.

After a minute, Marley did finally get out and walk to the door between the flower shop entrance and the paint-your-own-pottery shop. With her hand on the doorknob, she turned for one last commiserating smile, then disappeared inside.

June had no idea what Kip was going to say, how he'd react, but she envied Marley the access to him. At least Kip would know. *Please be ecstatic,* June prayed. *Grab her into your arms, swing her around in celebration, tell her you were meant to be together and now you'd be a family.* She wanted it for Marley; she wanted it for herself. It didn't have to be a fantasy, and Marley could prove it right now.

Not five minutes later, Marley came running out, crying, and shouted at June to drive, to get her away from there.

June's envy was replaced by dread.

Over breakfast at the inn, which Isabel kindly made and served in the kitchen, Marley told June about her dream response from Kip, a proposal, and his real response, which was his saying "What?" over and over as though one broken condom wasn't enough to result in a pregnancy. He'd been in shock and said he needed to think and couldn't damned well do it with her standing there looking at him like that. So she'd run out.

Jesus. June's stomach churned at the thought of John's reaction being similar. Seven years ago and now.

When Charlie came into the kitchen in his Spider-Man pajamas and rumpled hair, flinging himself into June's lap for a hug, Marley's expression changed.

"Oh my God," Marley said, her eyes full of something like shining wonder.

"Yeah," June whispered. "No matter what, this is what you get."

Marley bit her lip and touched her hand to her stomach, and June knew her new friend would be okay.

The guy standing in the Local Maine Interest aisle, holding *Off the Beaten Path: Coastal Maine*, looked so much like John Smith that June gasped at the sight of him until she realized, a second later, a heartbeat later, that it wasn't him. He was tall and lanky with that same shock of dark, straight hair against fair skin—and he was no older than twenty-one. Which reminded June just how much she was living in the past. A pretty young woman with two hardcovers from the New Fiction table joined him, and June felt a pang so sharp in her heart that she'd had to sit down on her director's chair behind the checkout desk and take a breath.

She missed love. She missed arms wrapped around her. She missed sex. She had to accept that John Smith wasn't going to walk in the doors of Books Brothers, wasn't going to appear on the cobblestone path of the Three Captains' Inn, wasn't going to track her down after seven years and say he'd never stopped thinking about her.

He *had* stopped. After two nights. She needed to let him go, even as she looked for him for Charlie. That was the key here. She was finding him for Charlie, not herself. Marley's experience that morning hit that home for June more than anything else. And these past few weeks of drifting off to sleep with fantasies and dreams of something that wasn't going to happen were doing a number on her, setting her up for a letdown that would crush her again, and she had no time or energy to be crushed. Especially by her own stupidity.

Let him go, she told herself for the seventieth time.

She glanced at the big pirate-ship clock on the children's wall: 9:45 p.m. Fifteen minutes till closing. For Labor Day weekend, Books Brothers had extended hours, 8 a.m. until 10 p.m., to take advantage of those heading out to the beach and in need of a book and those walking off dinner or coming off the excursion boats and happy to come in and browse— and buy a book or three or four. She'd been up so late last night talking to Marley and then up so early this morning on their mission, but she felt energized, as though Marley's . . . epiphany at the sight of Charlie reiterated—reinforced—for June just how much she had to be grateful for. She'd barely had time to think about anything other than the store today: hand-selling, helping customers, working the register, arranging her special displays. The shop had been packed all weekend, and now that it was Monday night, the unofficial end of summer and the tourist season, she was looking forward to the celebratory clink of champagne on Henry's boat at closing time.

Right before locking up, June called Kat to check in on Charlie; she and Oliver had taken him to a clambake and fireworks celebration, and he fell asleep clutching his lobster-shaped horn blower. She loved how surrounded Charlie was by family. She found herself smiling as she and Bean headed down the pier to the houseboat—more so when Henry handed them each a glass of champagne and a thank-you bonus check that would more than pay for Charlie's two hours of aftercare at school for the year. They clinked and sipped their champagne and ate Henry's specially good home-made salsa on blue-corn tortilla chips, Van Morrison singing low from the ancient stereo system.

Five minutes later, Bean's boyfriend came to pick her up, and again June was struck by how much she wanted that for herself. Someone to come pick her up. Someone there for her. Someone to love her, care about her. She'd been on her own for so long that she'd grown used to handling everything—despair and joy, a leaky faucet, putting her child to bed every night, the occasional mouse. She wanted someone to lean on. To love. To make love to.

"I couldn't have done half the business we did this week-end without you, June," Henry said, leaning against the galley kitchen's counter. "The way you hand-sell books is really something. And people can tell you mean what you say, that you really loved a book, that you're passionate about a subject or the author's voice."

She liked the compliment. "One of the bonuses of spending Saturday nights alone is all the good books I have time to read."

He put down his full champagne flute and cracked open a beer, more his style. She watched him, watched him raise the bottle at her in a toast, watched him take a drink, tip back his head so that his slightly long, chestnut-brown hair, tinged with gold, brushed his neck. He was so good-looking. So lone-wolf. So . . . sexy. But when she imagined kissing Henry Books, he morphed into a pale twenty-one-year-old with dark hair and green eyes.

If even Henry Books couldn't shut down John inside her, maybe she'd never be free. Her heart was still with a guy who hadn't wanted it, who'd walked away. But who remained every moment in her son. How was she supposed to let him go?

Henry put down the bottle and looked at her, those crinkled-at-the-corners, Clint Eastwood brown eyes intense on her. *Help me let him go,* she thought, looking back at him. *Here we are, alone. Years of . . . unspoken attraction between us.* Unless she was crazy. Unless he'd never looked at her that way. But something in his expression told her he was working out something, contemplating something. Grabbing her into a passionate kiss and carrying her to his bed?

What are you thinking, Henry Books? That they could make love right here, right on this boat, right now?

Or that she was just plain old June, same as she ever was, and he wasn't the slightest bit attracted to her? She wished she knew. She wished she had the courage to get up off this stool she was half swiveling on and go up to him and kiss him right on the lips.

"Oh, isn't this fucking cozy."

June whirled around and there was Vanessa Gull. As usual, June had blocked out reality and forgotten The Girlfriend. For a moment June was so shocked that Vanessa was standing there that June couldn't move. Vanessa stood glaring from June to Henry in her summer uniform of sundress and Chuck Taylors.

"We're just having a clink of the glass to a great holiday weekend of business," June rushed to say.

"Right," Vanessa said, her dark eyes spitting mad. "Henry, why don't you just admit it already. Save me the trouble of waiting a few more years for some kind of marriage proposal, not that I'm even sure I want to marry you anyway. Just say it, so we both know—so the three of us know. You're in love with June and always have been."

June stared from Vanessa to Henry. *What?*

Vanessa glared at her. "Oh, for fuck's sake, quit the 'Who,

me?' act, June. It might have worked when you were eighteen and knocked up or however old you were, but it's boring now. Trust me. You're past the ingenue stage."

June stared at Vanessa, and Vanessa stared at Henry.

"I don't like being pushed into corners, Vanessa" was what he finally said.

Vanessa stuck her pointer finger at his chest. "And I don't like having to compete with someone whether she's in town or not. I'm sick of this, Henry. Consider yourself free. I've started seeing Beck Harglow anyway. He hasn't been carrying a torch for someone else for years." She picked up the champagne flute Bean had left behind and threw it against the wall next to where Henry stood. June watched it shatter to the ground. Then Vanessa turned and walked up the steps and a door slammed.

"Go after her," June said, unsure what had just happened. Beck Harglow—the ace mechanic whom everyone raved about—or not, Vanessa had been upset enough to throw stuff.

"Not this time," he said. "Except for the drama, she's not wrong."

June glanced up at him, holding her breath.

He looked at her, those Clint Eastwood eyes intense on hers. "I *have* always loved you, June."

She stiffened, froze, every cell in her body stopping.

He came closer, stood in front of her, and tipped up her chin, then he kissed her, full on the mouth as she used to fantasize about when Charlie was tiny. He leaned back from her, his eyes on her. "I've wanted to do that forever. All weekend, all day, but forever. For years."

She was speechless, she realized. She wanted this. She'd always wanted this. But . . . now that someone—and not just someone, but Henry Books, the only other man she'd dreamed about—was offering her everything she claimed to miss, she couldn't let go of finding John, of the possibilities there, no matter how slim. She carried this crazy notion that she'd find him and get the answers that had lulled her to sleep all these years, that he *had* been looking for her all this time too. Maybe she'd never even told him her last name. They'd spent all of seven or eight hours together in total, a few of those hours under the hazy effect of beer and gin and tonics.

He could be looking for me right now, she thought.

"June?"

"I—" She turned and sat down on the leather desk chair. "I'm—"

"You're waiting for someone else," he said. "I know you are."

She felt tears prick her eyes. "Am I an idiot? Right now, while I'm so actively looking for him, for Charlie, I just keep thinking— I keep hoping. Maybe it's stupid and pointless, but I can't seem to help it." *I have always loved you. . . .*

He leaned back against a post. "Who says it's pointless and stupid? There are a lot of what-ifs you need to get answered, June. Right now, this is what you're doing, where your head and heart are. That's not pointless. You're settling something. Maybe in time, depending on what happens, you'll be free and clear."

She let out a deep breath, grateful that he understood. *I love you too, Henry,* she wanted to say. And she did. Even if she was scared of what she felt for him. "You've always understood me. You're the only one who ever has. You make me feel okay."

He smiled. "Good."

She got up and picked up her champagne and took a sip. "You and Vanessa have been fighting and getting back together for years. Clearly there's some very real passion between you two."

Between *them* too. That kiss, all of five seconds long, had made her knees turn to Jell-O.

He shook his head. "I used to mistake drama for passion. And habit for something real. Vanessa and I haven't had much of a real relationship in a very long time. And to be very honest, we both served some kind of purpose for the other."

Like John Smith does for you, she knew he was thinking.

She turned away, confused. Until she noticed a picture of her and Charlie, taken two or three Christmases ago, on his desk. She remembered that day. She'd had to escape the inn and her sister and Edward. Henry had come to the rescue, building a snowman with Charlie and then having a snowball fight. He'd taken the picture of her and Charlie making snow angels, their smiles as bright as Charlie's orange down jacket and snowpants. No matter what, Henry had always been her "person," the one she turned to first when she needed something. Someone.

"We've had some very good moments, the three of us," Henry said, standing behind her.

The three of us. He never forgot Charlie. Ever. She turned around and looked at him. She had no idea what she would do without him. Even as she and her family got closer, Henry remained as vital as air to her. He was her *person.*

He looked at her, and a montage of moments flitted through her mind. Henry rubbing her back when she was nine months pregnant. Henry rocking Charlie as an infant. Changing his diaper and getting squirted. Henry holding her as she cried over the absence of John Smith, the weight of her life, the uncertain future. Henry.

"Do what you need to do, June," Henry said.

I'm very lucky to have you, she wanted to say, but she found she couldn't speak.

· · ·

The next morning, as June was in the kitchen, preparing Charlie's snack and lunch for school, Lolly slipped one of Kat's famous chocolate-chunk cookies into the Spider-Man lunchbox and eyed her niece. "You look happy, June. Being back here, your job—even if it's not the same store—must make you happy."

June almost laughed. Happy here in Boothbay Harbor? Granted, she was happy that *Charlie* was happy, and boy was he. He loved living with family. Having a dog, even if it was really Isabel's. He took his job of walking and brushing Happy—for which Isabel paid him $2 a week—seriously. He was so excited about school, which started up today. But with his hopeful expression, he continued to ask if she'd made any progress with finding his father. He'd asked five minutes ago.

"I'm going to do some more research this morning at the library," she'd told him, and instead of the shimmer of disappointment that usually crossed his sweet face, he'd said, "Okay, maybe you'll find out something today," then rushed outside to play with Happy in his final minutes before they'd have to leave for the bus stop.

He *was* happy here. Surrounded by relatives who adored him, who sneaked cookies in his lunchbox. Who wrapped him in impromptu hugs in the hallways and bought him Red Sox T-shirts with his favorite player's name on the back. He had family here.

It was nice to wake up to people. To not have to be so responsible for every little thing. Like replacing toilet paper. Fixing flat tires. Stopping a bloody nose at 2:00 a.m. Last night, she'd already been wide-awake when Charlie had called out that his nose was bleeding all over the place; she'd been thinking about Henry, about what he'd said. *I have always loved you, June.* Her Henry. That someone she loved so much, admired so fiercely, could have such feelings for her boosted her inside in a way she couldn't remember ever feeling.

You look so happy this morning. . . .

Because of Henry? Even though she did hold out hope for John?

Or because she *was* happy here? Here with her family, which would always include Henry. Last night, as she'd been holding tissue after tissue to Charlie's poor nose, Isabel had gone to his dresser to pull out a new pajama top and get some wet wipes for the blood on his cheek and collarbone. And Kat had changed Charlie's bloodstained pillowcase. To one with little blue and red robots.

For the first time really, she and Charlie had family in the full sense of the word. They were among people who cared about them. Somehow, in these weeks of being here, of worrying late at night about Lolly, of bearing witness to the small and big things that made up their days, their lives, the four of them had gotten closer when June hadn't been looking.

June moved over to the screen door. Charlie was tossing Happy's favorite little rag toy in a game of fetch. "Ready, sweets?" she called.

"Ready. Bye, Happy!" he said, giving the dog a vigorous rubbing all over.

Lolly and June walked Charlie to the bus stop just a half block away, and June thought her heart would burst as Charlie bounded on the school bus after a hug for his great-aunt and mother. On the way back, Lolly told June stories of how she used to tear up when she'd put Kat on the big yellow school bus and watch her baby go off into the world alone. They walked back arm in arm, June too aware that her aunt was walking much slower than usual. After two bracing cups of coffee and Lolly assuring June she was just fine and "go do your research," June headed to the blessedly cool, quiet library to use the communal computers.

As if the different environment, the library opposed to Lolly's office or Kat's laptop, would bring forth something new. But she didn't know what else to try that she hadn't already. Aside from a private investigator.

Perhaps that was what she had to do. She'd never gone that route because she'd never had the several hundred extra dollars it would cost. She had once consulted with a PI, who'd told her if she didn't have anything, such as a Social Security number or a birthday, it would be difficult to track down a commonly named man. And that she could do what he could do online and save the initial $250 "look-see" fee.

She heard kids' voices singing and followed the happy sound to the children's room. A group of ten or so toddlers sat in a circle on their caretakers' laps, a librarian leading the way in "Itsy Bitsy Spider." June smiled, remembering singing the song to Charlie as a toddler, making the hand movements.

She got a computer pass and headed upstairs to the community computers. As she passed the nonfiction section, she spotted Marley, in dark sunglasses and a floppy sun hat, on an overstuffed chair, a stack of books wedged spine-side-in beside her. June's heart lurched at how she used to feel the need to hide, disguise herself in town. Not anymore.

She went over to say hi to Marley, who was reading *What Your Baby Really Needs* and making a list of essentials.

"Have you heard from Kip?" June whispered.

Marley shook her head. "I told my mom, though, and she wants me to stay in Boothbay and look for a teaching job here. She said she'll be my free nanny. My ganny." She smiled. "I don't feel as desperate anymore."

"And it's nice that you'll be here—Kip'll come around, surely. Even if it's not till the baby is born."

"I hope so. I guess this is just a stupid fantasy, but I keep thinking he's being offered this amazing gift, a family—a woman who's madly in love with him, a child—and he couldn't be less interested."

"We'll see," June said. "With time. Once it sinks it." After making plans to meet for dinner this week and go over what June thought every new mother should have and what was nonsense (such as baby-wipe warmers, in her opinion), she left Marley to finish her list and headed to the one open computer.

She went through the usual searches. A half hour later, she realized the few sites she was reading through were ones she'd already pored over. Another half hour later, she was going through hit after hit, mention after mention. Nothing jumping out.

But then she came across something promising. Very promising. When she typed *John Smith, Colby College, 2003, 2004, 2005* into Google Blogs, a short piece—and a grainy photo—came up about a college jazz band, a foursome called the Jazz Experience, in 2005. Her John Smith had talked about loving jazz, but he hadn't mentioned being in a band. Still, the caption noted John Smith as second from the left, and that guy, the one on bass guitar, did have that straight, floppy dark hair. He was looking down at the guitar, his hair hanging over his eyes.

It *could* be him. The year was right.

But now what? Contact the three other guys and ask, *Uh, you went to college with a John Smith with dark, floppy hair. He played guitar with you in the Jazz Experience. Do you know if he dropped out in his senior year to travel?*

At least she had someone—three someones—to ask. It was a start.

"I'm sorry, but your time was up ten minutes ago, and someone else is waiting for the use of the computer," a library clerk said.

June leapt up. "Sorry! All yours," she said, then rushed toward the stairs. She finally had something to follow up on.

I'm going to find him. This was it. She felt it. She would finally know what happened, why he hadn't shown up, despite what they'd shared the nights before, despite how he'd looked at her, held her, made her feel that he was as in love with her as she was with him. And maybe, no matter how much of a sliver of maybe it was, there was a chance for her and Charlie's family of two to become three.

After dinner, June googled the guy in the blog post with the most unusual name. Only one Theodore Theronowki was listed. One! *Thank you, Theodore Theronowki, for having that name!* She typed the name and the words *white pages* into the search engine, and an address and telephone number came right up. He lived in Illinois.

Her heart beating like mad, she grabbed her phone and dialed.

"John Smith, John Smith," Theodore Theronowki said after she explained why she was calling. "From the Jazz Experience? I don't remem— Oh, wait, yes. When Parker got mono or something like that, his friend John filled in for him on bass for a couple of months. I transferred to BU at the end of that year, so I didn't get to know John too well."

He remembered him. June closed her eyes in silent thanks. She was close.

"So you don't have an address for him? Even an old one or an old number? Something that I could use to maybe link back to him?"

"Nope, sorry. I do remember that he lived on Haywood Street or Place or whatever, though. Haywood's my middle name and some buddies call me that, and I remember him once saying he grew up on Haywood something. Don't know where, though."

Haywood Something. In Bangor. It was all she needed.

That would lead to his parents. Which would lead to him. *Thank you, Theodore Theronowki. Thank you.*

After she and Theodore hung up, she typed *Haywood, Bangor, Maine* into Google Maps and there it was, Haywood Circle, a cul-de-sac. Of course, his parents might not still live there. But a quick search of *Smith, Haywood Circle, Bangor, Maine,* brought up Eleanor and Steven Smith, 22 Haywood Circle.

Tears sprang to her eyes and she covered her mouth with her hand, shocked that she'd finally found him—or almost—after all this time, all this looking. She had her way back to him. But now what? Did she call his parents? Say she was an old friend and would love to get in touch with John? What if they didn't forward the message? What if they were estranged? What if John was engaged or married and his parents didn't want to give his contact information to an old friend? An old girlfriend. How much should she say to get the ball rolling? How little?

Hello, Mrs. Smith. My name is June Nash, and I knew your son, John, seven years ago when he was traveling in New York. I lost touch with him, and I'd love to have his contact information.

That sounded reasonable.

She'd talk it over with Isabel and Kat, get their opinions on her opening. For the hundredth time she was grateful they were right here, available for important talks at all hours of the day and night.

CHAPTER 12

Kat

Her mother looked so frail. Instead of recovering from the first infusion of chemotherapy—her next would be in another week and a half—Lolly's body seemed in constant revolt. She was often nauseated and fatigued, so tired at times, such as right then, that she could barely lift her arm. Lolly lay propped up on the special hospital bed that Kat had ordered for Lolly's bedroom, and Kat cringed at the effort it took her mother to flip the pages of her *Good Housekeeping* magazine.

Kat sat on the edge of the bed, the late-afternoon sunshine dappling the yellow quilt, embroidered with faded sea stars, that had belonged to Lolly's sister, Kat's aunt Allie. The sight of the quilt sometimes took Kat's breath. With loss. With strong women taken before their time. Kat remembered her beautiful aunt, how she'd wished she'd had Allie Nash's long, thick, wavy auburn hair, lit with golden highlights. Isabel had gotten the gold and June the auburn. When Lolly would send Kat over to her aunt and uncle's to watch her during a busy Saturday or Sunday at the inn, her aunt Allie would sit and brush Kat's long, light blond hair, so light it seemed colorless to Kat, and murmur that her hair was beautiful, which used to make Kat proud. Her aunt had been so kind, and Kat had loved being sent over to their apartment. On the way there, Kat would peer in the fortune-teller's window a couple of blocks away. The fortune-teller's name was Madame Esmeralda, and Aunt Allie had told Kat that though she and Kat's cousins didn't believe Madame Esmeralda could really see into the future, the woman was able to make a good living just by reading people's expressions, that everyone pretty much walked around with their fears and wishes right on their face. Once, on a slow winter weekday, when Madame Esmeralda turned town seamstress to make up work, she'd told Kat's fortune for the price of Kat's making three deliveries to her customers. She'd sat her down in the little shop with its rich, red draperies and candelabra and told her a bunch of obvious things, except for one line that had always stayed with her: "You will surprise yourself in the end." But days after the accident, Kat had seen Madame Esmeralda in the grocery store and had run up to her and screamed that she was a fake, that she didn't know what she was talking about, that Madame Esmeralda should have warned her father not to pick up Kat's aunt and uncle, that a man way drunker than the Nashes would ram his car into Kat's father's Subaru Outback just minutes away from their home. Minutes from their all being safe. Alive.

Madame Esmeralda had looked so shocked, so sad, that day in the grocery store that Kat had gone still for a moment and blurted that she was sorry before running away. She'd written off the line of Madame Esmeralda's that she'd liked, that she would surprise herself in the end, since she didn't believe a word Madame Esmeralda said anymore. And of course she'd surprise herself. Life was full of damned surprises.

Kat looked away from the faded sea star that had brought on the memory and focused on cutting bite-size pieces of the strawberry shortcake she'd made for her mother. Kat wasn't crazy about strawberry shortcake, but it was one of Lolly's favorites.

"Mmm, this just melts on my tongue," her mother said as Kat forked small bites into Lolly's mouth. Her mother sighed, then stared at her. For the third time in the past fifteen minutes.

"Mom, c'mon. Something is obviously bothering you."

Lolly eyed her. Clamped her lips tight. Finally she said, "I was hoping you might have something to tell me."

"About what?" Kat asked, fork poised in midair.

"About a diamond ring?"

Oh, no.

"Earlier, I was about to come into the kitchen, but I saw you through the little window on the door, standing by the stove, holding what looked like a diamond ring. I didn't want to seem like I was spying, so I pushed at the door to come in and you looked over and shoved the ring in your pocket."

"Oliver gave it to me," Kat whispered, so low she wasn't sure her mother heard her. *Almost two weeks ago and it still feels as strange as the day he slid it on my finger.*

"Did a question come with it?"

Kat nodded.

"And?"

"And I said yes, but I . . . I just don't feel right being engaged and making a fuss over it when you're going through all this, the chemo, and having a full house. I've . . . just kept it quiet."

Lolly stared at her for a moment, so hard that Kat had to look away. "Kat, you know I don't like to poke my nose in anyone's business, including my own daughter's, but I need to say things now that I normally wouldn't."

Uh-oh.

"Nothing would make me happier—nothing—than to see you and Oliver married and settled."

Kat turned back to Lolly. "Why?" *So you don't have to*

worry about me? Because you think I want to get married? Because you and Dad had Oliver picked out for me at age five?

"Because you love each other. Plain and simple."

Love is plain and simple? Kat wanted to say. But she couldn't. She couldn't talk to her mother. Not ever and not even now.

Kat cut another piece of shortcake to have something to do with her hands. "I just don't want the focus taken off you, Mom. How can I think about headpieces and guest lists when my mom is . . ."

As the words came out of her mouth, Kat realized they were true. Ambivalence about Oliver aside, she didn't think she could give a fig about a wedding gown when her mother was dying.

Her mother was dying. The truth of it clawed into Kat's stomach. *I never really had you and now . . .* An image slammed into Kat's mind, of Lolly finding Kat crying about something that had happened in school, mean girls calling her an orphan. She'd been picked on before, and when she'd dared confide in June, June had told her it was because she was so pretty and nice, and some mean girls wouldn't like that, and since those idiot girls clearly were too dumb to know what an orphan was, Kat should surely ignore them but tell her guidance counselor on them. That had made Kat feel a little bit better. But these were things she'd always talked to her father about, bullies and slights and C's on tests that she'd studied for, and her father always knew what to say. Lolly would only tell her to buck up and add a "For goodness' sake" for extra salt in the wound, and once her father was gone, Kat hadn't turned to Lolly to talk. In fact, when Lolly did ask her what was wrong, Kat would mutter, "Nothing," and run away. Sometimes she'd talk to June, who was three years older and smart. But mostly Kat stuck with Oliver.

She'd never realized how much she'd pushed her mother

away. Maybe she hadn't given Lolly enough of a chance once her dad was gone.

Lolly sat up, with an effort that drained Kat's blood. "Kat, you know what I was thinking during the chemo infusion with that IV in my arm? You. Leaving you here alone. Remember in *Mamma Mia!* how the daughter was worried about leaving her mother alone? It's the opposite with us. I'm worried about leaving *you* alone."

"Mom, I—"

"Kat, I know you and your cousins are getting closer, but I'm not sure if Isabel will go back to Connecticut and June will go back to Portland or not. It scares me to think of you being alone. I'm not saying you're not perfectly capable of running this inn or your own life, but I can't leave you here alone, Kat. It would make me so happy to see you married off to Oliver. To know you were safe and sound. You know what I mean."

Tears pricked at Kat's eyes. Now that her mother was talking, really saying how she felt for once, Kat wished she could blurt out how confused she was, how ambivalent. But how could she, given what Lolly *was* saying?

"I was also thinking about how much Oliver loves you. And how wonderful he is, how wonderful he's been," Lolly continued. "Do you remember how when Dad died, you two would sit under those evergreens between our houses? Oliver would sit with you there for hours, bundled up in your snowsuits and mittens, and he'd run into his house and come back with thermoses of soup and hot chocolate. You didn't want to be anywhere else but under those trees for a long time, and he'd sit out there with you for hours in the freezing cold. He was just ten. Just like you."

"I remember," Kat said.

"I'll never leave you," Oliver would say then. "I promise. Want to make a blood oath?" And they did, several times.

Lolly seemed lost in thought for a moment. "And when we both had strep throat—five, six years ago, and Pearl had been sick too, Oliver took care of the inn and brought us meals on trays and that amazing soup from Chowhounds."

"And that hot chocolate from Harbor Lights Coffee. With the big fat marshmallow," Kat said, remembering how Oliver had changed the linens on their beds. Brought them fresh flowers and *People* magazine.

"He was a keeper at ten years old," Lolly said. "And he's a keeper now. You're so lucky, Kat. So lucky to have found him so young, to have that kind of love always."

I am *lucky to have Oliver,* she knew, thinking of his handsome face, his beautiful actions. She was being an idiot. Of course she was lucky. Who said she couldn't travel? That was what honeymoons to Paris were for. Vacations to Rome and Sydney and Moscow.

And her attraction to Dr. Matteo Viola just meant she was a normal red-blooded American woman. It didn't mean she didn't love Oliver.

"To spend these weeks planning your wedding," Lolly said, "looking through photos of bridal magazines and making guest lists—I'd much rather do that than worry. I'm telling you, even the thought of what type of wedding gown you'd like, what kind of food for the reception, makes me feel stronger right now. What kind of dress are you thinking? Something big and white and elaborate? Or something more simple?"

Kat couldn't remember the last time she felt this close to her mother. And she'd let Lolly have this, let her do this. Kat and Oliver belonged together; everyone seemed to know that, to understand that. She needed to trust in all that.

"I was thinking something simple," she heard herself say. "Not too much pouf or lace."

Lolly's excited smile lit up her entire face. "How about

the wedding and reception in the backyard? Wouldn't that be just perfect!"

"It would be, Mom."

Maybe this was how it was supposed to be, Kat thought. The decision taken out of her hands, twice. Maybe that was what she needed, someone to take hold and say, *Now listen here, Oliver is the best guy on earth, there'll never be another guy as great as him, and you're marrying him.*

"Let me see that ring on your finger."

Kat pulled it from her pocket and slipped it on. The heirloom ring, handed down from Oliver's great-grandmother, was so beautiful with its thin band of gold and round, glittering diamond with tiny baguettes on either side.

"Now everything looks right with this picture," Lolly said, admiring the ring.

So why did Kat still feel that she was the one who didn't belong?

On Friday, the engagement ring sparkling on her finger for two days, two days of congratulations from everyone at the inn and from calls and e-mails from Oliver's family and their mutual friends, Kat was ready for a quiet night in with her family, just the four of them watching a movie, talking about the movie—and not about the engagement or wedding plans or the future. Or asking Kat a million questions about where she and Oliver would live and did they know there was an old Victorian for sale two blocks over that Kat would just love. Lizzie was beside herself with joy at the news and had dropped off at least thirty bridal magazines with color-coded Post-it notes for her favorite gowns, headpieces, shoes, undergarments, jewelry, and hairstyles. Kat's dear friend also had lists of venues and caterers, ideas for wedding-party gifts, and honeymoon destinations. Lizzie and her groom-to-be were headed to Hawaii. Kat was headed for a headache. It was all much too much.

She stood looking through the DVDs in the parlor. Her mother had charged her with picking out something fun from the Meryl Streep collection for Friday Movie Night. They were going to watch in Lolly's bedroom since she'd been feeling so tired for the past couple of days and would likely fall asleep during the movie. The films were arranged by theme and indexed. In the Meryl Streep section, notations on the labels indicated every other major actor in the films. Clint Eastwood. Shirley MacLaine. Tommy Lee Jones. Nicole Kidman. Robert De Niro. Cher. Jack Nicholson. Uma Thurman. Robert Redford. Albert Brooks.

Defending Your Life. Now there was a title. Kat picked it up and read the back. After fatally crashing his fancy new car on his birthday, Albert Brooks had to defend his life—particularly the moments of fear that had held him back—in a Judgment City courtroom in order to ascend to heaven with his new love, Meryl Streep, whose life was beyond reproach. "Hilarious and heartfelt," a critic said.

Moments of fear. Kat had many of those. She set the DVD on top of the player and headed into the kitchen to bake a miniature wedding cake for Movie Night—just to see what it felt like. Kat was always fearless in the kitchen. *Let's see how fearless I am baking my own wedding cake.*

"It's been a while since I've seen *Defending Your Life*," Lolly said, remote control on her lap in bed. "I remember that it's very funny but really makes you think about what in your own life you might have to defend. And not be able to."

A slice of miniature wedding cake—Lolly, Isabel, and June had all oohed and aahed—on the tray between her and her mother in the big hospital bed, Kat took a deep breath.

She'd actually enjoyed making her own miniature wedding cake—with tiny chickadees and rugosa roses—but she hadn't been thinking of herself or Oliver or a wedding while she'd worked on it; she only thought about the cake. Making it perfect.

Yet as she took her first bite—and it did come out perfect—the sweet cake turned bitter on her tongue. She *did* need some help defending her feelings—both in wanting to marry Oliver and not. In being attracted to Matteo Viola whether she wanted to be or not. In wanting to stay, wanting to go.

Isabel and June were on the padded folding chairs to the right of the bed, a bowl of popcorn on June's lap. Pearl was at an anniversary party, so it was just the four of them. Kat was grateful that no opinionated guests would be running off at the mouth.

"Even Albert Brooks's face makes me laugh," Lolly said as the movie opened with Albert Brooks giving a funny speech at work. "I mean his expressions, the way he uses his voice— he's just so funny."

Kat watched as Albert Brooks, playing a lovable, funny advertising guy, bought himself a BMW convertible for his birthday and then accidentally crashed it into a bus while looking for a dropped CD (good thing no one used those anymore). He ended up in Judgment City, which looked a bit like Las Vegas, where he had to defend his life on earth, in a trial with a defense attorney and a prosecutor, before he could move on to heaven with Meryl Streep, who had done wonderful things on earth, such as adopt children and save cats from fires. If he lost his case, he'd be sent back to earth to try again.

June cut into her slice of wedding cake and took a bite. "Oh my God, can you imagine if every second of your life really was recorded and would be used against you to decide if you could go to heaven. I'd be sent back to earth over and over."

Me too. For the moment I said yes to Oliver's marriage proposal because I was scared of everything—including saying no. Like the moment I thought of Matteo's face and body while in bed with Oliver . . .

"Middle school alone would keep me out of heaven forever," Isabel said, shaking her head.

"Ha, people on earth only use three percent of their brains," Kat said, repeating Albert Brooks's lawyer's words, "which accounts for their problems in life. That's probably true."

The movie was warm and funny and interesting, as hilarious and heartfelt as the DVD proclaimed, and Kat found herself relaxing, enjoying her bites of miniature wedding cake. Until one line made her think. Just as Lolly said it would.

"Do you think that's true?" Kat asked. "That fear is a fog that prevents people from real happiness?"

"Probably," June said. "I know I've been afraid to act at certain times because I didn't know the outcome. Or just because I was plain afraid. That's only human."

Isabel nodded. "Fear of not hearing what I wanted kept me from asking Edward about our problems more than a few times."

Kat adjusted her pillow, trying to get comfortable, then realized her discomfort was coming from inside. Fear was keeping her from saying—and doing—quite a bit. Maybe she did know what she wanted and was just afraid to go for it.

"Albert Brooks has to defend nine days of life?" June said. "I'd have to defend a lot more."

"Me too," Lolly said quietly.

Kat glanced at her mother, but Lolly had reached for her

iced tea, which was her way of saying, *Don't ask.* Maybe if Kat weren't so afraid of pushing past boundaries, she *would* ask.

Me three, Kat thought.

"Ooh, there's Meryl," Isabel said. "It's hilarious that they meet in a comedy club with a bad comic performing."

Kat was glad that Meryl Streep had finally appeared; her face, that silky blond hair, her expressions and joyful laugh, had become so familiar to Kat that she realized she was comforted by the sight of her.

"Now *that* is a good question," Isabel said as Albert Brooks's trial began and an incident from his childhood was flashed on a movie screen in the courtroom. "About the difference between fear and restraint. Fine line sometimes."

Lolly nodded on a yawn. Her third since the movie began. "Too much self-control can keep you from doing what you actually should. But sometimes, people should show more restraint. It's hard to know when to use which sometimes."

June put her empty cake plate on the bedside table. "Ha, this is good too—now showing moments from his misjudgments—fear- and stupidity-based. I've made plenty of those."

"Me too," Isabel said. "Though not lately, Aunt Lolly, promise."

Kat was relieved when her mother laughed. Lolly had gotten quiet, her expression somber, and she seemed to be lost in thought. Kat wondered what the movie was reminding her of.

"Albert Brooks is a total revelation to me," Isabel said. "He's so funny and self-deprecating, but there's something so true in his expression, the way he looks at her, how he speaks. I can totally see why Meryl falls in love."

June nodded. "Me too. And I get what he means about being tired of being judged. But you know what's weird? Lately I've been thinking that I'm my worst critic."

"I think we all are," Isabel said.

Kat was riveted when Albert Brooks told Meryl Streep that he didn't want to go up to her room and have sex because he was afraid of ruining how wonderful and perfect things were between them. He wanted to preserve the fantasy. He was making the wrong choice; but she understood it. Too well.

"Awww, he has to go back to earth," June said. "And try again."

Kat sighed. "That's the key to life, isn't it? What his lawyer just said—that when Albert Brooks goes back to earth, he should take the opportunities that come. He held himself back and now he can't go to heaven."

Marry Oliver. Don't. Marry Oliver. Don't. I do. I don't. What was she supposed to do? What was the opportunity she was supposed to reach for and why didn't she know?

Kat watched as Albert Brooks was in a trolley car with the others who had to go back to earth—and suddenly there was Meryl Streep in her trolley car for those headed to heaven. Meryl screamed his name, and he busted out to get to her.

Taking his opportunity. Not being afraid of the reality of love. And he got to go to heaven with her.

"What a great movie," June said as the credits rolled.

Kat turned on the light on the bedside table. "Mom?" she said, looking closely at Lolly. "Are you crying?"

Lolly wiped under her eyes. "This movie always makes me think that—" Lolly began, her expression sad, wistful. "I'm not sure I'll get past Judgment City." She turned away, looking out the dark window.

"Mom, of course you will," Kat said, wondering what her mother was referring to. "And then some."

"Okay, hit pause," Isabel said. "Aunt Lolly, you took in your two orphaned nieces. That alone gets you to heaven."

Kat's mother gave Isabel something of a smile, but didn't hit pause, her attention back on the television, on the rolling credits. Kat could tell by her mother's expression, that particular locked look in her eyes, on her lips, that Lolly wouldn't say a word more. Kat often wondered about her mother's personal life; in the fifteen years that Lolly Weller had been widowed, she hadn't dated at all. Kat had once asked her if she ever thought about a "beau," a word Lolly liked for "boyfriend," but her mother told her, "Don't be ridiculous," that she was done with all that.

Done with love? Her mother was a hard-to-read mystery most of the time. But she had her inn, she had her clubs, she had her dear friend Pearl, who'd always been like a wise aunt to Lolly. Kat had never known her mother to be particularly joyful; perhaps some people just weren't.

Of course, every time Kat thought that, she dismissed it. Lack of joy was a symptom of something.

As Kat collected the plates and glasses, she realized her mother was either sleeping—or pretending to sleep. Lolly had yawned several times throughout the film, so she might not be faking, but this definitely wasn't a discussion her mother wanted to continue. Kat was so curious what Lolly had been thinking about. "Mom?" she whispered.

No answer.

"Let's move into the parlor," Isabel whispered. "Or upstairs."

"Upstairs," Kat said, putting the mini-wedding-cake leftovers on a tray with their drinks. "More privacy."

They quickly cleaned up stray popcorn from the floor and straightened up, then turned off the light and gently closed Lolly's door. They headed up the back stairs, tiptoeing past Charlie's room. June poked her head in and smiled. "Could he be any cuter when he sleeps?"

Kat and Isabel poked their heads in too. "So sweet!" Isabel

said. Happy was curled up in his usual spot next to Charlie, and Charlie's arm was flung over the dog's paw.

In their bedroom, Kat set down the tray on her desk and noticed a bunch of crumpled pieces of paper on June's bed. "Working on something?"

June blew a curl away from the side of her face as she dropped down on her bed, the crumpled balls of paper bouncing. "A letter to John's parents. It's been three days since I left a message on their answering machine. No call yet. I've been checking obsessively, so there's no way I missed it."

Those three days ago, the three of them had sat up late into the night talking about what June might say if one of John's parents answered the phone and what to say if she got voice mail. With Kat and Isabel as her audience, June had rehearsed what to say at least ten times until she was satisfied that the squeak and nerves were out of her voice, so that his parents would have no problem giving a nice-sounding gal such as her their son's telephone number—or at the least, assuring her they'd give him her number.

"He's probably married," June said, her face falling. "They're not going to give his number to some woman who calls. I figured I should write a letter, saying I met him in New York City seven years ago and that there was something very important I want to tell him. And leave it at that. But how exactly to say that without coming off as crazy is what's not working."

"I think you can just say that, keep it short, but friendly," Isabel said, sitting cross-legged on her bed with her half slice of cake. "The 'something important' should at least get them to give him the letter and tell him about your call."

June leaned back against the wall and wrapped her arms around her legs. "I can't help but wonder what would have happened if he *had* met me that day by the fountain in Central Park. Would he have stayed in New York with me until I graduated? Would he have convinced me to travel the country with him and take a year off from school? Would we still be together right now?"

"It's so impossible to know," Isabel said. "While watching *Defending Your Life*, I kept thinking about those moments I would have to defend, when I acted out of pure fear, or whatever. And then I started thinking, what if I hadn't met Edward that day at the center? What if it had been a different teenaged mentor? Who would I *be* now?"

Kat turned onto her stomach, her hands folded under her chin. "Do you think you're that different? I mean, at heart? Deep down?"

"I was pretty wild," Isabel said.

June smiled. "I can vouch for that."

"Yeah, I remember that too," Kat said, "but isn't that because you were drawn to be? Drawn to those wild girls? Just like after the accident you were drawn to Edward. That was about *you* and what pulled you in or away."

Isabel seemed thoughtful for a moment. "I suppose so. I do like the idea of having more control over my own self than I thought I had. Like it was me reacting to circumstances rather than circumstances controlling me."

Kat nodded. That was what she was worried about now. Circumstances controlling her. There was a difference, but it seemed such a fine line that she had one foot on either side, but couldn't find the line itself.

"You know what I wonder?" Kat said. "I wonder if my father hadn't died, if my aunt and uncle hadn't died, if my mother's whole world hadn't changed with a phone call from the police, if I would have gone to college. If I would have gone to cooking school or taken a year abroad in France. If I would have ended up with Oliver."

"Destiny would say so," June said. "If you believe in that sort of thing."

"Yeah, I was thinking that maybe I would have met Edward anyway," Isabel said. "If not at the Boothbay Regional Center for Grieving Children, then somewhere else."

They were quiet for a moment.

"I guess we can always defend our lives," Isabel said. "Why we made certain choices. Not that we'd necessarily get into heaven. But I think the movie's point was so important. That if you're afraid of something, find out why and then act without fear. Make a decision you really mean."

Kat turned over on her bed and stared up at the ceiling fan. "What if you're afraid you'll make the wrong decision, though? Like, just saying, what if marrying Oliver isn't what I'm supposed to be doing? What if I'm meant to be doing something else?"

"I'd think you'd know," June said. "You do, don't you, Kat?"

Kat sat up, hugging her knees to her chest. She nodded. But she didn't know.

"You've known Oliver your whole life," Isabel said. "I love that you're marrying him after knowing him all this time. It's like the opposite of what I did with Edward. Met him at sixteen and married him at twenty-one. You know exactly what you're getting. You know who you are."

"Do I?" Kat asked—and then was surprised to discover she'd said it aloud. "I mean, I know who Oliver is. As much as you can absolutely know someone. But I'm not so sure of the 'I know who I am' thing."

"Really?" June stared thoughtfully at Kat. "I always think of you as being lucky for having your life on such a great set path now. Baking. Oliver. The inn. There's such security."

"Sometimes I want to take off for Paris and just walk around tasting cakes in every neighborhood. Kiss every cute guy I see. Sleep with a few too. Is that crazy?"

"You're asking the wrong two people," June said. "I mean,

here we are, our lives totally up in the air. Security and a bright, shiny future handed to us sounds pretty good."

"Are you having second thoughts about getting married?" Isabel asked. "If you are, don't do it, Kat."

But it's my mom's dream to see me married. To see me pronounced husband and wife with the man my father adored and declared I'd marry at five. How can I take that away from her when it's the only thing kicking my ambivalence in the tush?

"I'm not having second thoughts," Kat said, but they were both staring at her.

"Kat," June said, eyeing Isabel, "let's say, hypothetically speaking, that Isabel and I were throwing you a small, surprise engagement party tomorrow afternoon here at the inn. And let's say we invited Oliver's parents and his brother, and some friends of yours from town. You'd be okay with this?"

Kat could jump up and say, *No, cancel it, cancel the whole thing.* If there was an engagement party, it was real.

But she looked at her ring and thought of her mother, asleep on that hospital bed, and said, "Of course I'm okay with it. And thank you." Isabel was staring at her, so Kat changed the subject. "Do you think my mom's okay? Is she just worried about . . ." Kat couldn't even say it.

"I think so," June said. "I'm sure all that talk of heaven and judgment and defending your choices just got her thinking about her own life."

"Sure got me thinking about mine," Kat said.

On Saturday, Kat acted all surprised when she and Oliver walked into the backyard of the Three Captains' Inn and found a small engagement party in their honor. Oliver's parents had come down from Camden, along with his brother and his girlfriend, and some old friends from childhood also mingled in the yard, sipping mimosas and sampling hors d'oeuvres. Kat smiled as Lizzie had Lolly rapt at the picnic table, Lizzie's bridal magazines spread out as she explained her color-coding system.

Kat stood with a trio of friends she knew all the way back to preschool and watched Oliver being hugged by his brother, a younger version of himself, and then by his pretty girlfriend. Oliver's parents, Fred and Freya, stood chatting with the Nutleys, who'd bought their house next door years ago. *This will be my family,* Kat thought as she sipped her mimosa. She'd known these lovely people forever, been the recipient of Freya Tate's kindness many times over the years. But as she tried to imagine spending holidays and birthdays and special occasions with the Tates, she found herself watching Lolly and Isabel and June with a fierce protectiveness. They'd never felt like hers, even her mother, yet now she wanted to run off with the three of them to the parlor and watch *Silkwood* or *The French Lieutenant's Woman.*

"You know what would be wonderful?" Oliver was saying to Lolly. "A Thanksgiving wedding, right here. I know Thanksgiving is your favorite holiday, Lol."

And just two months away, Kat realized, her stomach tightening. Oliver was being kind and practical, wanting to ensure Lolly would watch her daughter walk down the aisle. Over the past few days, he'd text things like *Paris=Honeymoon. Taste our way through patisseries, though none could match your pastries.*

Had he forgotten she was unsure? That she might have accepted his marriage proposal in a weak moment when she'd been so upset about her mother's diagnosis?

Then again, he knew it had always been her dream to go to Paris. To taste her way through those patisseries. To learn from master bakers. Was he taking advantage of the moment—again? Or just hoping to break through her thick head?

This would be one of the moments she'd have to defend in Judgment City. She knew it.

Paris is perfect, she'd texted back. And it was. Just everything else wasn't. Like the part about the honeymoon.

As Oliver's brother's girlfriend told her in detail what kind of gown she herself would want, a sleeveless version of Kate Middleton's, if, say, Declan Tate, proposed to her, Kat's cell rang. Matteo. Concerned that his call had something to do with her mother's recent round of tests, she excused herself into the house and went into the first-floor powder room.

"Matteo, please tell me everything is okay."

"Yes," he said quickly. "I'm so sorry to alarm you, Kat. Her results aren't in yet, won't be until Monday morning, but we're not expecting changes. Try not to worry. The reason I'm calling is just to check up on how Lolly's doing. She wasn't feeling well at all when I saw her. How is she holding up?"

Kat's shoulders sagged with relief. "That's very thoughtful of you, Matteo. She's doing much better."

As he spoke of what to expect from the second round of chemo coming up and its effects on the body and how Lolly might react, she was struck by how much she wanted to just reach out, feel his knowledge and words of wisdom and let them seep into her.

"I need to get back to rounds, Kat. But if you ever need to ask a question, if you ever need help with all this, just page me. Oh, and I almost forgot. I told my father about you and he'd like to teach you how to make his famous cannoli in exchange for you teaching him to make your famous muffins. Muffins are not his thing, but he'd like to learn. He tried your muffins at Harbor Lights Coffee and said they melted on his tongue."

Kat's smile started in her toes and worked its way up. "I would be honored to show the incomparable Alonzo Viola how I make muffins. And a cannoli lesson—I'd love that. It would almost feel like I was in Italy, learning from a master."

"Someplace you've always wanted to go?"

"Italy. France. Spain. England. Russia. Sweden. I used to dream of traveling all over the world, learning to bake in each country. But I've always been needed here, so it's been put off."

"Well, spend a few hours baking with my father and you'll feel like you've been to Italy for sure."

They made arrangements for next week, and Kat realized she'd better leave the bathroom just in case anyone else was waiting. "So you'll call Monday if there's news about her results?" she said, opening the door. She glanced at Isabel, who was waiting just outside the door, a mimosa in her hand. "Okay. Thanks again."

"Was that Dr. Viola?" Isabel asked as Kat slipped her phone into her purse.

Dr. Viola. He'd become Matteo to Kat. "He was checking up on my mom. Seeing how she's holding up."

"That was very nice of him."

"His father is going to teach me how to make cannoli," Kat added, staring down at her sandals, at her pink-red toenails. "His father is Alonzo of the Italian Bakery. I had no idea."

"Have you always wanted to learn to make cannoli?" Isabel asked, her sharp hazel eyes on Kat's. And asking much more, Kat knew.

"I didn't know that I wanted to learn until it was offered," Kat whispered. "And then the moment it was, there's nothing I wanted to learn more. Does that make any sense?"

"Yes," Isabel said, squeezing Kat's hand for a moment. "I know just what you mean."

Kat wanted to drag Isabel upstairs and ask how she could be so attracted to another man if she loved Oliver, if it *did* mean she didn't love him, shouldn't marry him, or if this was normal, if women were attracted to other men here and there and it meant nothing. Or did it always mean something? This was an emotional affair. An affair of the heart. Wasn't that more intimate than sex?

Until she figured out something, she'd keep her feelings to herself.

CHAPTER 13

Isabel

On Monday morning, Isabel began her first official day as a volunteer in the Coastal General Hospital neonatal intensive care unit. She was assigned to two babies who had jaundice and needed to be under the bilirubin lights for at least six days. Her job was to sit between their incubators and, if they were awake, to reach inside the two armholes and gently stroke what she could reach. At their feeding times, she could bottle-feed and change diapers under the supervision of a nurse. She'd gone through an orientation and three training sessions on everything from proper hand-washing before entering the NICU to proper procedure and how to hold a newborn. Now that Labor Day weekend had come and gone, and with it the summer rush, Isabel felt okay taking a little time away from the inn to volunteer. Although it was a Monday, a week after Labor Day, two of the three guest rooms were booked, and Kat had offered to relieve her for Isabel's first official day.

She sat with three-day-old, six-pound-two-ounce Chloe Martel in her arms, her white-cotton-capped head a beautiful, soft weight against Isabel's arm. She held the tiny bottle, three ounces of the baby's mother's expressed breast milk, and fed Chloe, her heart swelling so much Isabel thought it might truly burst. *I'm meant to be doing this,* she thought. *Whether with my own child or through being right here.*

She thought about what life might have been like if Edward *had* said okay to having a baby. They'd have a newborn, a toddler, a preschooler—and one day she'd get the anonymous note or see him skulking through backyards herself. She was grateful now that she'd been unable to budge him.

A couple walked through the nursery and spoke quietly with the nurse. They were the parents of two-months-premature twins, one of whom wasn't doing well. Isabel saw tears in the father's eyes; he swiped them away, then the couple embraced and Isabel could hear the mother crying.

I'm so sorry you're going through this, she said silently to them, and said a silent prayer in the direction of their twins, little fighters. The nurse had explained to Isabel during orientation that things could change in an instant, from so-so to bad or bad to worse or worse to better and then fine. Isabel knew all about that.

Emmy Dean had been six weeks premature, Griffin had told her on the phone last night. He'd called every night since checking out of the inn last Monday, sometimes just to say good-night, sometimes to talk. She liked that he respected her need to get to know him, slowly, before she could even think about kisses on long walks by the water. She hadn't been with another man since she was sixteen, and as attracted as she was to Griffin, she was hardly ready to feel another man's hands on her. But she anticipated his nightly phone calls, almost holding her breath when her cell phone would ring. She'd told him that she was starting her first day as a NICU volunteer, and he'd said that was incredibly kind of her, that Emmy had been in the NICU for over two weeks before she was strong enough to come home. He'd come see her three times a day, morning, noon, and night, and every day at noon, the same sweet volunteer, a grandmotherly type named Ernabelle, would be rocking Emmy. It was how she'd gotten her middle name, Belle, because the woman had been such an angel.

As he'd told Isabel this story, she realized that, ready or not, she was falling for him in a no-turning-back kind of way. He was coming over later that afternoon to work with Happy. "Okay, I'm really coming to see *you* again," he'd added, and she'd gone warm all over.

After Chloe finished her bottle, Isabel gently burped her the way the nurse had taught her, burp cloth on her shoulder. Then she settled the baby back in her arms and rocked her, the wooden rocking chair slightly creaking. Isabel hummed a lullaby she'd heard June singing to Charlie one night, but she couldn't remember the words. Chloe's little eyes closed, then opened a crack, then closed again.

"You're a beautiful, strong girl," Isabel whispered before she put the baby back in the incubator.

While she waited for four-day-old Eva Rutledge to wake up, Isabel straightened the diapers, then the nurse came over and told her she could rock a newborn boy whose parents couldn't come until three o'clock. Isabel leapt up and headed across the NICU, where impossibly tiny preemie Logan Paul lay with his wires. The nurse took him from the bassinet and placed him carefully in Isabel's arms. She sat back in the rocking chair and rocked back and forth, humming the lullaby, more at peace than she'd ever before been in her life.

It was almost four o'clock, Griffin was due to arrive any minute, and the inn was in order. Isabel had updated the Three Captains' website, spoken with two of the local travel agents to introduce herself, and hit up Home Depot for a new doorknob for the Bluebird Room. The books were up-to-date, her calendars synced with guest arrival and departure dates, and the inn's many plants were watered. *There's happiness in being on top of your life,* Isabel thought. She'd never had much of a life to be on top of, and this purpose, this direction, felt good.

Happy lay on his back in a patch of sunlight, his favorite toy, a squeaky, comical rubber rat, half in his mouth. Griffin had worked magic with the dog over the week he'd been a guest, turning him into a well-behaved, if mischievous, pet. Even Lolly liked Happy and enjoyed having him curl up next to her while she read at night. Isabel took Happy for walks every day and played and cuddled with him as much as she could, but her sweet nephew had commandeered the dog for his own, and that was fine with Isabel. They could share him.

When she spotted Griffin and his girls walking up the front path, Isabel's excitement started in her toes and worked its way up to her stomach. Happy-nervous butterflies. She was so attracted to him, Isabel almost couldn't believe it. She'd found men attractive before, of course, noticed a good-looking man, swooned over a movie star or two, but she'd never been attracted-attracted. As in *I would like to kiss you and I can kiss you because I'm available for the first time since I was sixteen.*

Alexa had her ubiquitous iPod clipped to her white shorts and earphones in her ears. She didn't say hello. She lay on a chaise, turned her face up to the sun, and moved slightly to the music. Emmy stared up at Isabel as usual and had one hand behind her back.

"This is for you," Emmy said, and pulled out a pink flower.

Isabel, her smile wide, knelt down in front of her. "I love it. Thank you. How about if I tuck it behind my ear?" Isabel shifted her hair behind her ear and slid the flower in. "How do I look, Emmy?"

The girl beamed. "You look nice."

Emmy ran over to Happy and started rubbing his belly.

He moved his comical head from side to side in joy, which made Emmy laugh that huge laugh of hers.

"You look *beautiful,*" Griffin whispered, right in her ear, sending goose bumps up her spine. *He* looked hot in his army-green cargo pants and a black T-shirt. "Okay, girls, I'm going to work with Isabel and Happy. Lex, you're in charge of keeping an eye on Emmy."

Silence.

He walked over to his daughter and removed an earbud. "I need you to keep an eye on Emmy while I'm training Happy. Earphones out."

"What am I supposed to do, then?"

"Enjoy the sun. Play with your sister. Skim a magazine." He pointed to the array in a wicker basket. "Build a sand castle with Emmy in the sandbox," he added, as Emmy plopped down in the sandbox by the fence, filling an orange bucket with sand.

"I'm wearing white shorts. They'll get totally ruined."

Griffin's restraint from rolling his eyes was impressive, Isabel thought. "Then sit here, enjoy the sun, and just keep an eye on her. Got it?"

"Got it, got it."

Isabel led Griffin over to the far side of the yard for Happy's training. "I was *so* much like Alexa when I was fourteen. So much it's scary."

"There are times, not often, when she's incredibly sweet, like the wonderful little girl she used to be, that I try to focus on that so I can get through this patch. The sullenness and sarcasm. Do you know that every weekend I have her and Emmy, *she* puts Emmy to bed? I come in when she's done tucking her in, but she puts her to bed. She reads her a story, she attempts to comb out her tangles, she kisses her on the forehead, she turns out the light. Every time."

"Wow," Isabel said, glancing over at Alexa, her big, black

sunglasses practically covering her entire face as she read a magazine. "She loves her little sister. I'm glad Emmy will grow up with that. My own sister and I didn't get along very well, ever."

"Really? I got the impression you and your sister and cousin were thick as thieves, as they say. The way you three talked after the movie, you all really opened up, really seemed to care about one another."

Huh. They did open to one another in their movie discussions. They had from the start, when discussing their very different views on *The Bridges of Madison County*—and when Isabel had blurted out that Edward had cheated on her, that she'd caught him coming out of a woman's bedroom with just an unbuttoned shirt on. The three of them, the four of them, Lolly included, had gotten so naturally closer these past weeks, from the movie talks, from sharing a home, a room, from working together, from uniting over their concern for Lolly.

Happy started digging, which got a "Whoa, boy," out of Griffin and began the training session. Griffin stuck to basics, showing Isabel how to handle naughty behavior, like the digging. How to reward Happy when he followed commands. How to get him to heel, which was vital on walks in a busy downtown such as Boothbay Harbor's. Griffin was going over reward systems when his cell phone rang.

"That's my emergency ringtone," he said, taking the call. He spoke briefly, then pocketed the phone. "I've got an emergency situation not too far away, an old sheepdog I'm crazy about. I'll go pack up the girls quick. If I can work it timewise, we'll come back and continue Happy's session." He started toward the deck.

"I'll watch the girls—you go take care of that sheepdog. No worries."

He glanced at Isabel. "You sure? I don't want—"

"I'm sure. No problem at all." She'd love the chance to spend some time alone with the Dean daughters, get to know them a little better. Be a mom of sorts for an hour.

He squeezed her hand. "I appreciate it." He went up to Alexa, slid her sunglasses up on top of her head, and told her he'd be back in about forty-five minutes to an hour and that Isabel was in charge and would be keeping an eye on them both. She watched Alexa slide a glance over at her, then drop down the sunglasses. Griffin let Emmy know he'd be back soon, that Isabel would be watching her and Alexa, kissed the top of her head, and raced up the path to the front.

"How about I bring out some freshly made lemonade and some cookies," Isabel said too brightly—for the fourteen-year-old, anyway.

Emmy clapped. "Yes!"

"I just got an even better idea," Isabel said. "What if I bring out a pitcher of cold water, some ice, sugar, and lemons, and we can make our own lemonade? You can have your own lemonade stand out here and offer it free to guests."

"Yes!" Emmy said again.

"What's your favorite cookie, Alexa? My cousin Kat is a master baker and has all different kinds today."

Alexa eyed her. "Does she have peanut-butter chocolate chip?"

Isabel smiled. "Of course she does. It's her favorite. I'll be back in three minutes tops with everything. You'll keep an eye on Emmy?"

Alexa nodded and went back to her magazine. Excited to spend some time with the Dean girls, to . . . be responsible for them, Isabel hurried inside, grabbing a large, sturdy tray and setting it on the table. She filled a pitcher with water, threw ice in an ice bucket, got the sugar bowl and a bowl of lemons, plus a plate of three kinds of cookies, peanut-butter chocolate chip included, and picked up the heavy tray and went back outside. Alexa wasn't in the chaise anymore. Isabel glanced over at the sandbox. No Emmy.

Okay, very funny, Alexa. Hide-and-seek to scare her? "Alexa," she called.

No answer.

She glanced around the yard, looking through low tree branches. Around the large rock at the end of the property. No sign of the girls. "Alexa. Emmy," she shouted. "Please come out. I've got everything ready for our lemonade stand."

No answer.

Her heart starting to beat fast, Isabel raced around the yard, looking behind trees, along both sides of the inn, then ran inside. She checked the bathroom—empty. She checked the Alone Closet and every common room of the inn, every nook and cranny. Panic set in deeper with each place she checked. She ran around front. No one but Pearl watering the roses.

"Pearl, did you see Alexa and Emmy? You know, Griffin Dean's two girls? Teenager and a three-year-old?"

"I did see the older one just a few minutes ago. She was practically jogging down toward the harbor. When she passed me, she was laughing while on her cell phone."

Isabel sucked in a breath. Okay. "What about the three-year-old?"

"No, Alexa was alone."

Then where was Emmy?

Isabel quickly told Pearl what had happened, then raced into the backyard, checking again, calling out for Emmy. Over and over and over. Nothing.

Alexa's cell phone. Isabel had no idea what the number was. She'd have to call Griffin for it. Explain that Alexa had skipped out on her. And that Emmy was nowhere to be found.

Oh, God.

She called out for Emmy over and over as she punched in Griffin's emergency number. No response from Emmy, but Griffin picked up right away. "Isabel? What's wrong?"

She explained, her voice rising hysterically. She stood alone in the yard, looking around frantically, rushing behind trees, racing to the front yard to see if she could spot Emmy. Maybe she'd followed a squirrel. Isabel scoured every bit of area to the left and right. Nothing. Empty. *Emmy, where are you?*

"Pearl is sure Emmy wasn't with Alexa?"

"She's sure. She said Alexa rushed past her alone, laughing on her cell phone. I don't have the number. Oh, God, oh, God. Griffin, I'm so sorry."

"Damn it. Maybe Pearl just didn't notice Emmy walking in front of Alexa or something." Isabel could hear worry settling into his voice. "I'll call Alexa, then call you back. Keep looking for Emmy. Check little hiding places. If you don't find her by the time I call back, I'll call the police."

Isabel closed her eyes as her stomach fell. She put her phone in her pocket and rushed in and out of the inn again, calling out Emmy's name, checking every possible spot. Nothing. Nothing. Nothing.

Five minutes later, her phone rang. Griffin. "I've got Alexa. She left Emmy in the yard and snuck away. Alexa's with me now in the car. We'll be there in a minute."

Isabel could hear Alexa crying and saying, "I'm sorry, Dad. I thought Isabel was coming right back, so I left."

I did come right back, Isabel thought numbly. *It was just a few minutes.*

Just a few minutes. Anything can change in an instant.

Anything can change in an instant.

"Emmy!" Isabel called as loudly as she could. "Emmy!"

She strained to hear. But there was nothing but the usual sounds of summer. And Isabel's racing heartbeat.

Emmy, where are you?

• • •

The police had just arrived, along with June, whom Pearl had called in a panic, when Isabel heard Happy bark, which was unusual. Isabel trailed behind Griffin to the yard next door, narrowly accessible where the fence ended and the stand of evergreens began. Happy was rolling on his back in front of the Walsh's doghouse at the head of their old yellow Lab, Elvis, who was lying down half-asleep.

"Happy," Griffin said, rushing over to him. "Help us find Emmy." He put Emmy's little sweater at Happy's nose, and Happy started barking like crazy. "Happy, find Emmy. Go."

But Happy wouldn't budge, just kept barking and then started moving in circles in front of the doghouse. Elvis stayed put, watching Happy with lazy eyes.

"Griffin, I'm so sorry," Isabel said. "I—"

C'mon, Isabel, it's not like you have that maternal instinct, Edward had said more than once.

"I'm so sorry," she said again, her voice breaking.

Alexa was staring at her feet, her toenails polished metallic blue and green. She wouldn't look at Isabel.

Griffin got down on his knees and peered inside the doghouse. "She's in there! She's fast asleep. C'mon, Elvis, come on out so I can get my girl, okay?" But the dog wouldn't move. Eric Walsh helped lure the dog out with a dog biscuit, and Griffin tugged on Emmy's arm.

"Daddy?" came the little voice.

Griffin scooted her out and collected her in his arms. He glanced at Isabel, his dark eyes flashing anger and frustration and relief. But mostly anger, she thought. "Home *now*," he said to Alexa.

With Emmy in his arms and Alexa sulking at his side, he headed along the side yard to the driveway where his car was parked. Without a word to Isabel or a backward glance.

CHAPTER 14

June

Early Tuesday morning, the seagulls woke June, but it was worth it for the pink sunrise over the bay. She moved to the balcony and breathed in the salty air, the fresh scent of flowers and cut grass, which all combined to make her think of Henry. So many times over the past week she'd longed to talk to him, but what was burning inside her these days had to do with another man, and so she'd avoided Henry. And because Henry was Henry and so great, he'd let her be.

She looked out over the harbor, the fishermen already out in their crafts. *Maybe today will be the day,* she thought. It had been exactly a week since she'd left a message for the Smiths, short and simple, that she was an old friend of John's and would love to have his contact information. Every morning since, she'd woken up and sat out here, sure that day she'd hear back from them.

She wasn't so sure today would be the day, though. If they were going to call back, they would have already. One phone call she did get every day was from Marley, checking in to see if she had heard from the Smiths, which made June feel better. Or at least understood. Marley had swung into mama mode since the day she'd met Charlie, making lists of what she needed, scoping out the best day-care center, reading her

What to Expect book. June had made a real friend in Marley, and when she thought about how unexpected that was, she realized anything *could* happen. Such as hearing from the Smiths. Finding John. Becoming a family.

She went to check on Charlie, more to see his sweet face, his rising and falling narrow chest, than anything else. Her gaze landed on the family-tree poster that he'd taped up above his headboard. No changes made, yet.

When she headed back into her bedroom, she noticed Isabel wasn't in her bed. Had she gotten up during the two minutes June had slipped out, or had she been gone when June had gotten up? Kat was fast asleep, so close to the edge of her bed that her pretty blond hair hung over the side. June had an urge to move her over a bit, the way she used to with Charlie when she'd find him precariously close to the edge. She'd heard many a thud in the middle of the night. But Kat was a grown-up, and June was pretty sure you didn't have to worry about grown-ups falling out of bed in the middle of the night.

She glanced at Isabel's empty bed. The pale blue sheets dotted with buoys were rumpled, as if her sister had tossed and turned all night. Isabel had been so quiet the night before. She'd made dinner for the family, three different specialty pizzas with interesting toppings, as though she'd needed lots of vegetables to chop, the comfort of a long recipe to follow, with its steps and directions. She'd refused all offers of help, and nothing anyone said seemed to make Isabel feel better—the assurances that it could have happened to anyone, that it probably *had* happened several times to Griffin over the years: Alexa promising to keep an eye on her little sister for a moment and then not. Emmy wandering off. But Isabel had been equally sad and stone-faced and said she just needed to be alone for a while. She'd called everyone to dinner but had gone up to the bedroom without eating. When June and Kat had come up with a plate for her, she'd pretended to be sleeping. June had no doubt her sister hadn't slept a wink all night.

She glanced out the front window to see if she could spot Isabel walking Happy, but Isabel wasn't among the dog walkers and joggers. June moved to the small window facing the backyard, and there was Isabel, sitting on top of the flat-topped big rock that children loved to climb and play on. She sat with her knees drawn up to her chest, her arms wrapped around them, a mug beside her. Happy lay gnawing on a rawhide bone beside the rock, then went chasing after a huge white butterfly.

June didn't bother changing; she headed downstairs in her T-shirt and yoga pants. She stopped in the kitchen to pour herself a cup of the coffee Isabel had made and grabbed two muffins from the canister Kat had marked YUMMY MUFFINS—TAKE ONE!

"Hey," June said, placing the mug and muffins on the rock before climbing up beside Isabel.

Isabel glanced over with red-rimmed eyes, then stared ahead at the trees. "Hi."

"What happened yesterday doesn't say anything about you, Isabel. I hope you know that."

"It does say something about me. Edward once told me—during a fight, granted—that I didn't have any maternal instincts, that I didn't have that natural protective force inside me. It's true. Maybe I would be a bad mother."

"Edward has proven himself to be a king ass, Izzy. He's dead wrong. I can list twenty-five ways that you have shown in the short weeks you've been here that you *do* have maternal instincts. That you'd be a great mother."

"Name two," Isabel said, her voice glum.

"One, the way you've treated Charlie since the day we showed up here. How you told him that first day he was talking about the family tree that he had everyone sitting around that table to add. Two, how you raced to get him fresh pajamas when he had a bloody nose and then changed his sheets. Three, how patient you've been with Griffin's fourteen-year-old when anyone else would have snapped at her many times. Four, how kindly you've treated Pearl, who needs to feel useful. Five, how lovingly you've treated Lolly and the inn. I could go on."

Isabel started to cry and covered her face with her hands. "I thought I was doing okay. Letting my marriage go even though it's the only thing I've known for the past fifteen years. Waking up every day on my own, doing something important here—helping with Lolly and the inn. Letting myself fall for someone—and someone with kids. But then I lost Emmy and I thought about what Edward said and—" Isabel let out a deep breath. "What happened with Emmy could have been so much worse, June. She could have run into the street and been hit by a car. Elvis could have freaked out and bitten her. Someone could have snatched her—"

"It can *always* be so much worse. You can't live that way, Izzy. You just have to . . . have faith, I guess. In yourself, in other people. In things working out because you give a damn and because you *try*. That's all we can do. Otherwise, you just give up and let worry win. You can't do that."

"How do you not worry, though?"

"You have to trust yourself. And you should."

Isabel took a deep breath and broke off a piece of the muffin—cinnamon chip with white chocolate. June knew right then that she'd gotten through, even if just a little.

That night, June, Isabel, Kat, and Lolly gathered in Lolly's room for an impromptu Movie Night. Everyone was so glum that Lolly had put June in charge of selecting a Meryl Streep movie that was poignant and affecting, something that stuck to the heart. June flipped through the DVD collection in the parlor, hoping Lolly had the one she wanted. Yup, there it was.

Kramer vs. Kramer.

June had seen it a long time ago, and then again when she had the flu and it was on network TV. Meryl Streep leaves Dustin Hoffman and their five-year-old son—or maybe he's six—because Dustin is a selfish workaholic and she's sick of it, so he has to take care of the boy on his own and discovers what being a parent truly means. But just when he finds out, when he realizes that being his son's father is more important than anything else in the world—his job, himself—Meryl comes back and wants the boy, but Dustin won't give him up. He's fought to be the father he's become, and he fights Meryl for custody. But she wins. Even she can see how Dustin has changed, how reliant her son is on him, how much he loves and needs his father, and she lets them stay together.

Maybe the movie would help Isabel see why Griffin was upset and unable to return her calls. Which had less to do with her and more to do with his own fear. And maybe Isabel would see why she would make a damned good mother—because her instincts, her capacity for love, the person she was, had already proved it.

Isabel came in with a tray of popcorn in bowls. "Everyone's here, right?"

It was just the four of them tonight. Pearl's husband had a cold, so she'd stayed home to see to him, and since Lolly wasn't feeling so hot, she'd wanted to have Movie Night in her room with just family.

Kat lay on the hospital bed with her mother, a cashmere throw she'd received as an engagement gift covering most of her. Looking sad, Isabel handed Kat a big bowl of popcorn for her and Lolly to share, then shut the lights off and sat down next to June on a padded wooden folding chair. She put her legs up on the ottoman next to June's.

"Still haven't heard from Griffin?" she whispered, taking a handful of popcorn from the bowl on Isabel's lap.

Isabel shook her head. "I guess I won't. I called him twice last night and once this morning."

"I'm sure he'll call," June said. "He's just freaked. It has nothing to do with you."

"The whole thing wouldn't have happened if I hadn't left the girls alone. Even for two minutes."

"Alexa is fourteen, Isabel," Kat said. "Not that I'm eavesdropping. Okay, I am. Anyone would have done what you did—asked a fourteen-year-old to watch her little sister for a couple of minutes while you grabbed lemonade fixings inside. Including Griffin. This wasn't your fault."

"Then why do I feel like absolute hell over it? Why hasn't Griffin called me back?"

June did understand, but she'd give Griffin only one more day to get over it. To make Isabel feel this way—and it was clear how upset she was yesterday—bothered June.

Lolly sat up a bit. "As June said, Emmy going missing like that scared him to death. But the person he's likely maddest at is himself, Isabel. When that settles inside him, he'll call."

Isabel took a handful of popcorn, another good sign. "I hope so."

Lolly pressed PLAY on the remote control. "I think June picked a *very* good movie for tonight."

"Look how young Meryl is," June said as Meryl Streep told Dustin Hoffman that she was leaving him and their son. "What year was this made? Seventysomething?"

Lolly switched on the lamp on her bedside table and scanned the DVD box. "Nineteen seventy-nine, actually."

"She won an Oscar for this, right?" June asked.

Lolly nodded. "For this and *Sophie's Choice* and *The Iron Lady.*"

"Wow, I totally get why Meryl was so fed up," June said.

"But to just walk out on her own child? I'm not sure I get that at all."

Kat reached for a handful of popcorn from the bowl between her and Lolly. "It's amazing how Meryl Streep actually makes you sympathetic towards her, though. She's crazy talented to be able to pull that off."

"She really is," Lolly said. "It's why I can watch her movies over and over. And she was so young when she made this film."

They all settled down with their treats and drinks, quiet as Dustin Hoffman both slowly and quickly transformed from selfish workaholic to actually seeing his son as a little person who needs him, truly needs him.

"Dustin Hoffman is an amazing actor too," June said. "You really see how he changed, how he discovered his child was more important than any work project could ever be."

Lolly took some popcorn too. "And how cutthroat the advertising world is—or was, then, anyway. That his boss fired him actually goes to show him how no one cares about anybody in that world."

"Whoa—Meryl Streep comes back *fifteen months* later?" Isabel said, her eyes wide. "Fifteen months and she suddenly wants her son back?"

June shook her head. "I can't imagine a day going by without seeing Charlie, hugging him, making sure he knows I love him."

"I can't believe this custody battle," Kat said. "The way it's presented, because the lawyers, the judges, weren't there, they can't know what happened, how it happened. Like the son's accident on the playground."

"But Meryl *does*," Isabel said. "Because she knows Dustin Hoffman, knows her son."

June nodded. "Oh, God, I knew this was coming, but I still can't believe custody is awarded to Meryl. He loves his son so much. He just found him, really found him, became a father in the truest sense of the word, and now he's being taken away."

There was not a dry eye in the room.

Lolly dabbed under her eyes with a tissue. "I love that. Meryl comes to get her son, then says she knows Billy is already home."

"At least I'm crying happy tears now," Isabel said, wiping under her eyes. "Omigod, that was emotional."

"Call Griffin again," Kat said. "Just talk into voice mail. Just tell him you understand why he's not returning your calls and you just want him to know you understand."

Isabel shook her head. "I've called three times. He hasn't called back at all. For the past week, we've spoken on the phone every night."

"I think he's being unfair by not returning your calls," June said. "I get why he's upset, but to make you feel so rotten is wrong. He could at least call you back to say he just needs some time or something."

"You could shoot him an e-mail," Kat said. "Tell him we watched *Kramer vs. Kramer* for Movie Night, and how it affected you, that you got a very emotional glimpse into the life of a single dad, that how terrified Dustin Hoffman was when his son got hurt on the playground, for example, helped you understand how terrified he must have felt yesterday."

"What if he thinks I'm an idiot for comparing real life to a movie?" Isabel asked.

"The movie got inside you and made you see things from a single father's perspective," Lolly said. "I think you can mention it. In any case, you'll get to say your piece." Lolly started to say something else, but yawned, her eyes beginning to close.

"We'd better let you get to sleep," Kat said, kissing Lolly on the hand.

Isabel and June did the same. Then Isabel went upstairs to e-mail Griffin, and Kat went to Oliver's. June was suddenly alone downstairs in the quiet inn until the Bluebird Room guests came in and asked for coffee, if June didn't mind, which she didn't. In the kitchen she brewed them a pot of coffee and put leftover chocolate chip cookies on a plate. Her phone rang and she lunged for it. Maybe it was the Smiths.

It was Henry.

"Hey, June. There's something I need to talk to you about. It's important. Can you come over?"

Was he firing her? No, that was silly. Of course he wasn't firing her. He wanted to talk to her about what had happened on the houseboat on Labor Day. June was sure of it. He wanted to let her know he understood that she needed to do this, see it through no matter what, and that things didn't have to be awkward between them, as they'd been. Tuesdays and Wednesdays were June's days off, so she hadn't seen him right after Labor Day, when he'd told her he'd always loved her. He'd made himself scarce all week, then he'd taken off for the weekend, on his motorcycle. The one time she'd had to talk to him about an order that had gotten messed up, she'd knocked on his office door but had gotten no answer. When she peered out the back window, she saw him working on the boat, but he stopped and just looked out at the water, then down at the dock. *He doesn't know what to do,* she'd thought. About this, about her. About them.

She had something to tell him too. After he confessed his feelings for her, she hadn't wanted to share the news about finding John's parents—their telephone number and address, anyway. But maybe she'd better tell him so he'd know she was close, that she wasn't just grasping at air anymore.

Unless, of course, she never *did* hear back. But she would; she just needed to word the letter she was working on in such a way so that she wouldn't sound like a stalking "girl he briefly dated." She couldn't just come out and tell them why she wanted to track down their son. She needed to tell John first, let him tell them. She'd work on the letter tonight, and then if she didn't hear from them by noon tomorrow, she'd send it.

"I can come now," she told Henry, pouring the coffee into two mugs and putting the cream and sugar next to the cookies on a silver tray. "Let me just ask Isabel to keep an ear out for Charlie. Be there in twentyish minutes."

"I'll wait for you on my dock," he said, and she could swear she heard his heart beating in the seconds before he hung up.

When June opened the door to head out to Henry's, Marley and Kip stood on the porch, about to ring the bell. Kip was the same as June remembered—good-looking and tall, in his coach-wear of gray basketball pants and a black, long-sleeved T-shirt. God, they would have a gorgeous baby.

Marley looked like a different woman. Her big blue eyes were bright and shining. And a smile was on her face. "June, I hope it's all right that we just dropped by," Marley said. "Are we catching you at a bad time? Were you going out?"

We, June thought, looking from Marley to Kip. Had he come around? Kip stood there, looking so serious that June wasn't sure.

"I'm on my way to the bookstore to meet Henry," she said, noticing Marley and Kip hadn't come by car. "Want to walk down to the harbor with me?"

Kip put his arm around Marley as they started walking. Eyes widening, June glanced at Marley. Marley was beaming. Glowing.

"I wanted to thank you for being there for Marls, June," Kip said. "She told me you were like a rock for her, something I couldn't be when I first found out. So I appreciate that. I'm still getting used to everything. But I know I love Marley, and that's all I need to know."

June smiled. She liked when love wasn't complicated.

"I was shocked when he knocked on my door last night," Marley said. "We talked for hours. We even came up with a list of boy and girl names." Kip and Marley shot each other giddy smiles. "I can't thank you enough, June. I keep thinking how you were on your own at twenty-one. I hope you had someone there for you the way you were there for me."

"I did," she said, the image of Henry coming fast into her mind, refusing to let her lift a shipment of books. Bringing her five boxes of saltines when she'd been so nauseated from morning sickness that she'd been stuck in the tiny Books Brothers bathroom for two hours. He'd been the first to know she'd gone into labor, since she'd been at work. He'd been the one who'd called Lolly. He'd been the one who'd waited outside her delivery room, pacing like a nervous father. He'd been the first to tell her, "Charlie is absolutely perfect, just like you, June."

Tears welled up in her eyes and she blinked them away. He'd told her he loved her, and here she was, chasing a dream she couldn't let go of.

Because proof was standing in front of her. The happy couple.

John's parents will get back to me with John's contact info, and I'll get my chance too, she told herself, watching Marley and Kip make googly eyes at each other.

Down in the harbor, June hugged Marley and Kip good-bye, reminded Marley that they had plans to test out baby strollers next week, and watched them walk away hand in hand. *Possibility* was June's favorite word, and there it was in tangible form. A happy calm built inside her as she approached Books

Brothers and headed down the side alley to the pier. If Marley and Kip had found their way back to each other, so could she and John.

It was one of those beautiful September nights when Maine was in its glory, when the warm air wrapped around you with the scent of flowers and the hint of fall, and it was just cool enough to make you glad you'd grabbed a light, airy cardigan to put on over your tank top. Henry was standing on the dock as he said he'd be, near his houseboat, his hands in his jean's pockets, looking out at the water.

"Hi," she said as she approached. "I'm glad you called. I have something to tell you too."

He turned and looked at her for a long moment, and something was different in his expression, something that she couldn't remember ever seeing before.

Was he firing her? He couldn't bear to work with her?

"Henry?"

"Let's go inside and sit down." He extended his hand to help her onto the boat. "So you said you had something to tell me too. You first."

She headed down the three steps into the living area and turned to face him. "I found him."

He stared at her, then finally said, "Found Charlie's father?"

She sat down on the tall director's chair. "I found an old college photo of him in a band and tracked down one of the guys—thank heavens he had a very unusual name. Turns out his middle name was the same as the street John grew up on, so the guy remembered that. I was able to find his parents, well, their address and telephone number."

Again he stared at her, as if he were waiting for her to say something he expected.

"I called and left a message, just saying I was a friend of their son's and met him in New York City seven years ago while he was traveling and would love to get in touch with him. They haven't called back, but I'm working on a letter. I can't just come out and—"

"June."

She stopped and looked at Henry. He held her gaze for a second, then closed his eyes for another second and sucked in a breath.

She stood up. "Henry, what's wrong?"

He turned and reached for a folded piece of paper on his desk. He held it, but didn't look at it or hand it to her. "The thought occurred to me to check, just check, just to see, and, oh, God, June, I'm so sorry to have to show you this."

He unfolded the piece of paper and handed it to her. It was a printout of an obituary from the *Bangor Daily News*. Dated November, seven years ago. The day she and John were supposed to meet at the *Angel of the Waters* statue of the Bethesda Fountain in Central Park.

John Smith, 21, of Bangor, Maine, died of leukemia on November 10th in New York City. Very ill, John chose to live out his remaining months fulfilling his dream to travel the country, from the biggest cities to the smallest towns. He leaves behind his parents, Eleanor and Steven Smith of Bangor, Maine, his maternal grandparents . . .

There was a photo. There he was, the face of the beautiful guy she'd had imprinted in her memory for seven years, the features she saw in her son's face every day.

The unmistakable image of John Smith smiling. June gasped and staggered backward, letting herself find the edge of the chair before her legs gave out. "While I was calling him a user and stalking New York City for him, he was lying dead in a hospital a mile away." She burst into tears.

"I'm so sorry, June. He didn't leave you," Henry whispered. "He was taken from you."

June cried, wrenching sobs that came from somewhere deep inside her, and when Henry knelt in front of her chair and took her hand, she pulled away from him.

"Why would you even look in the obituaries?" she screamed at him. "This is what you wanted? For him to be dead?" It wasn't fair of her; she knew it the moment she said it, but all thought went out of her head again. John Smith was dead. He'd been gone all this time.

"No, June," Henry said, his voice gentle, almost broken. "I looked because there was only one explanation that made sense for why a man would leave you."

Her heart broke and she ran.

When she got back to the inn and raced upstairs, tears streaming down her face, Isabel was tiptoeing out of Charlie's room.

"Fast aslee—" Isabel started to say, then stared at June. "What happened? June, what's wrong?"

She couldn't speak, could only cry, so Isabel gently shut Charlie's door, then led her by the hand into their bedroom. The moment the door closed behind them, June slid down against the back of it, sobbing.

Isabel dropped down on her knees in front of her, pushing away the curls sticking to June's wet face. "What happened?"

June was still clutching the obituary. She hadn't even realized it was still in her hand. She thrust it at Isabel, who scanned it and gasped.

"Oh, no. No, no, no," Isabel said, then started to cry too and pulled June into a hug.

June grabbed on to her sister, crying so loud she was afraid Charlie would wake up.

CHAPTER 15

Kat

The Italian Bakery looked and smelled magical, as if you'd been transported to Rome and stepped inside a *pasticceria*. The shop specialized in Italian pastries—cannoli with ricotta cheese, yellow and chocolate cream, dotted with chocolate chips, small pies sprinkled with powdered sugar, cream puffs, lobster tails, and napoleons. Parmesan soda breads, focaccia, long loaves of Italian bread, flatbreads, ciabatta, and jars of homemade olive oils. Kat could stand in the doorway and just breathe in the delicious aromas all day.

The sight of Matteo, in a dark green T-shirt and jeans, sitting at one of the round café tables with a cup of espresso and a small plate of cookies, made her too happy. As she opened the door, the little bell above jangled, and Matteo smiled at her and stood. His father, Alonzo, was behind the counter. He was tall like his son, but heavier set, his dark, thinning hair peppered with gray. "So this is my lovely competition," Alonzo said as he came around the counter and grasped both of her hands with a smile on his warm face. "It's my pleasure to meet you and learn from you."

How kind he was. "I'm honored you think my muffins are good, Mr. Viola. My whole family loves your cannoli. They usually don't buy baked goods from anyone but me, but for your cannoli and tiramisú, they make exceptions. My young cousin thought he was betraying me by bringing in his dog-walking money to buy one of your cannoli. He raved about it for days."

The mention of Charlie made Kat worry for June, who hadn't gotten out of bed that morning. When Kat had come home from Oliver's last night, she'd found June and Isabel sitting on June's bed, June's eyes red-rimmed from crying. Isabel had shown Kat the obituary. This morning, Kat had heard June crying, but she lay facing the wall and wouldn't turn around. When Kat heard Charlie's door open and his usual morning greeting—"Ahoy, mateys!"—she'd told June she'd see Charlie to school this morning and would tell him that his mom had a headache and would be fine in a few hours. Isabel had called Books Brothers to report in that June wasn't feeling well and wouldn't be in that day. When Kat had come back from dropping off Charlie at school, June was still in bed, still facing the wall.

Kat had lain next to her and rubbed her back, offered her her favorite cinnamon-chip, white-chocolate scone that Kat had baked early that morning, but June could barely even shake her head.

"I just need some time alone," June had said, and so Kat had reported in to Isabel, who had also been up to the bedroom many times since the morning. Isabel had said she'd take over June-watch, so Kat had left for her appointment at the Italian Bakery.

"I'm sorry you can't meet my wife, Matteo's mother. She's taking care of a sick little niece today, but I'm sure you'll have the chance to meet her soon." Alonzo turned to Matteo. "Why don't you give the young lady an espresso while I make sure everything is set up in the kitchen."

For a moment, though, Matteo didn't move. He was staring at her ring. "It looks like congratulations are in order."

She glanced at the ring, the beautiful diamond glittering on her finger in its lovely antique setting, and offered something of a thank-you smile. "I can't wait to get into that kitchen. It smells amazing in here. It's wonderful of your father to take this time to teach me," she added, realizing she was rambling.

She felt Matteo watching her, waiting for her to say something, but what could she say about the ring? *I said yes, but I'm not sure? I'm not sure why I'm not sure? My mother is sure and made me feel surer, but I look at you, I look around me at this place, my dream, and I wonder . . .*

"Would you like that espresso?" he asked, his dark eyes on hers. She wondered what he was thinking, but she didn't know him well enough to read his expression. At her "No, thank you," he said, "To the kitchen, then."

In the large kitchen, Alonzo stood behind an old wood farmer's table, a ball of dough, wrapped in plastic, bowls, and supplies laid out. Matteo stood in the doorway, leaning against the side, sipping his espresso and watching her.

"Tell me how you decided to become a baker, open your own *pasticceria*," she said as she stood next to Alonzo, taking in all the ingredients in front of her. Bowls of various sizes contained everything from flour to sugar to ricotta cheese. Today, she would have her lesson, and next week Alonzo and Francesca would come to the inn to study how she made her muffins.

"Decide?" Alonzo said as she dusted flour on a large, flat wooden board. "It's something that chooses us, no? You're drawn to the kitchen, to the oven. I used to bake as a kid and sell my pastries and breads in the village. Now, on vacations, my wife and I travel, searching for breads and pastries that will—how do you say?—knock us out. Teach us something."

Her heart soared at the idea. "That sounds wonderful. I'd love to travel the world, tasting every cake until I found one that made me swoon and apprenticing myself to that master."

"Exactly. You're young, you can go. Take your new husband on your honeymoon, perhaps," he said, nodding at her ring.

Again she glanced at the ring, then at Matteo, who leaned silently against the wall, then returned to the front room. He was disappointed, she realized. Perhaps he'd planned to ask her out after the cannoli lesson? The notion sent goose bumps skittering up her spine. She tried to imagine what a date with Matteo would be like, with a guy who'd grown up with immigrant parents and would have so many stories to tell about his family and relatives, a guy who'd gone to medical school in New York City, come home for his residency to be closer to his parents while his father was undergoing chemotherapy, a guy who'd traveled to over fifteen countries. A guy who could whisper all sorts of romantic things in her ear in Italian.

It's just outward stuff, she reminded herself. *I'm romanticizing him. I don't even really know him.* Her first real boyfriend, whom she'd thought so smart and cool and seemingly worldly at sixteen, ended up being small-minded in ways that had surprised Kat until she'd finally realized that true compatibility and chemistry and love come from a place far different than a list of accomplishments. Another boyfriend who called everyone *dude,* followed U2 around the country, and had a lawn-mowing business in the summer and operated a beat-up snowplow in the winter, knew more about politics and history than anyone else she'd ever met. People could surprise you. So she would not let herself be dazzled by a beautiful Italian name and hospital scrubs. Or amazing abs and an exotically handsome face. She already was, of course, but she'd keep an eye on it. Oliver deserved better.

"I've already let this dough rest for the one hour required," Alonzo said. "I wasn't sure how long you'd have, so I didn't want to spend too much time on waiting." He had his recipe handwritten for her and explained how he'd formed the stiff dough. Then he showed her step-by-step how to use the mold, how to fry the cannoli shells until golden brown, just a couple of minutes, and how to fill them with the mixture of cream, ricotta, and sugar. They made several different kinds of fillings, dipped the ends of some of the cannoli into melted chocolate, added chocolate chips.

She was having such a good time, she'd forgotten all about her ring. And Matteo. Until he returned to the kitchen to sample her work. Alonzo had excused himself to take care of customers, and suddenly the large kitchen felt small with Matteo standing so close to her. She could smell his soap. She watched as he bit into a cannoli with that too sensual mouth.

"Perfetto," he said. "Perfect."

She smiled and took a bite of her own. It was good. Not Alonzo Viola good, but good nonetheless.

"You have a bit of cream and powdered sugar on your lip," he whispered, his eyes on her mouth, his expression . . . telling. "I would take care of it for you, but the ring prevents that."

Something inside her fell away, a flimsy barrier that wasn't going to hold no matter how much she told herself he was just a hot guy in scrubs whose father could teach her how to make the real-deal cannoli. She liked that he respected the ring. Even if she was guilty that very minute, via her thoughts, of not doing the same.

He took another bite. "I admire how completely focused on the lesson you were. I can see how passionate, how serious, you are about baking. You'll have your own bakery one day, I have no doubt."

"It's my dream," she said, glancing around. "That oven, these silver bowls, this dusting of flour. This *place.* One day." She put down the cannoli. "Right now, everything is so . . . tenuous."

"Except that," he said, his gaze on the ring.

"Even that," she whispered so low she wasn't sure she'd even said it aloud.

"Oh?" he asked, his expression serious.

She stared at the dusting of flour. "I'm just so confused about everything right now. My mother— She's . . . You know what she is. I can't think. I can't— I don't know how I feel about anything. I just feel so . . ."

"You feel what?" he asked, covering her hand with his own. His hand was strong, warm.

"Like I'm on a one-way track, I guess." She threw up her hands, missing the contact of his skin immediately.

"A one-way track to where? Do you mean to the life you're already living?"

She turned to him. "Yes, that's exactly what I mean. The life I'm already living. The life that won't change. Nothing will change. I'll marry the boy I met at five years old. I'll bake my one-hundred-millionth scone and muffin for the inn. Once a year I'll vacation in Paris or Rome or somewhere I've always wanted to go. And then I'll come home, to the life that's been set up for me forever."

"Set up for you? By whom?"

She stopped pacing and turned to face him. "By—" Huh. *By whom* was right. "By . . . circumstances. I thought about college, but I knew I wanted to open my own bakery, so I figured I'd work at my craft by baking for the inn. So I've been doing that. And since my mother's always been alone here, my staying and helping out always felt like the right thing to do."

"So this life you're not so sure feels completely right anymore was set up by you. You know that you can change your life, right? You're the captain of your own ship, as they say."

"But now my mother is dying, Matteo. And her greatest wish is to see me settled and happy, married to the boy that my father loved like his own son. And I'm not sure I *don't* want to marry Oliver. He's gold, like my friend Lizzie says. He really is. I'm just not sure I'm ready to settle down yet. I want to see Paris. I want to eat tapas in Spain. I want to see the land where Isak Dinesen had her farm in Africa. I want to taste every pastry in Paris and learn from the masters, like your father. But that's not reality."

"Who says? You're twenty-five years old, Kat. If you're not going to travel the world and meet new people and live an adventure now, when will you? Now is the time."

"Now my mother is dying. And Oliver proposed to me and I accepted. Watching me marry him in the backyard of the Three Captains' Inn will put her heart at peace."

He looked at her thoughtfully. "I would think that *you happy* would put her heart at peace. But no matter what and where your life takes you, Kat, I'm glad I met you."

She was so close to tears that she turned around and willed herself not to cry.

"I assume you have a wedding date in the not-too-far future."

She turned to him, almost shocked that he'd gone there. But it meant that he understood.

"We've set the date for November, around Thanksgiving. It's my mother's favorite holiday. She's been busy planning the details—when she's up for it. Will that be too much for her—running around to bridal salons and caterers to sample prime rib?"

"She'll need to be the judge of what she can handle. If she feels weak, she simply needs to rest. But if she wants to plan your wedding, it sounds as though it might be just what she needs, a happy purpose, the beautiful cycle of life, of new beginnings. If it's for the right reasons."

The right reasons. Right and not right had gotten so confused inside her that she didn't know the difference. And new beginnings? Why did the idea of marrying Oliver, of living in Boothbay Harbor forever, of managing the inn and even opening her bakery downtown, feel the opposite? Her stomach started to churn.

"I'd better get back to the inn." She needed air. "Thank you for arranging this, Matteo. It was a very special morning. I'll never forget it." She began collecting bowls to carry to the sink, but Matteo stopped her, his dark eyes intense on her. "You're our guest."

"Thank you. For everything."

He smiled and she hurried past him out the door, away from that face, that body, that voice that mesmerized her. She spent a few minutes thanking his father and was swept into a crushing hug and given a box of pastry for the family, including something "extraspecial" for Lolly.

She wanted to stay and leave at the same time.

In the afternoon, Kat took her mother to the hospital for tests to check her blood cell counts. Isabel was staying close to June, who'd gotten out of bed for Charlie's sake, but was still so shaken she could barely speak. Kat had offered to meet Charlie at the school bus, but June said she'd go, that she hadn't seen Charlie's sweet face since the evening before. Kat had gone with her and let June have the silence, the lack of questions, the lack of statements, on the brief walk. When they'd returned to the house, June disappeared to her bedroom. Kat filled in Lolly, who slowly made her way upstairs to the attic room, spending at least a half hour with June before Kat saw, through the little kitchen window, June helping Lolly down the back stairs. June looked a bit better, Kat had thought. Whatever Lolly had said had clearly helped.

As a nurse came in and out of Lolly's room to take her vitals, Kat's mother lay reclined on the padded chair, slowly flipping through a bridal magazine, and even turning the pages seemed to take her energy. "Oh, Kat, look at this."

Kat pulled her chair closer to her mother and looked at the photo. A bride in a beautiful, simple wedding dress, exactly the kind of dress that would have stopped Kat in her tracks in front of the windows of a bridal salon. It was white satin, sleeveless, and tea length and had a subtle fifties quality, the palest of blue ribbon running along an Empire waist. The dress was meant for an outdoor wedding in Maine. She could see herself in that dress. She could.

"It's just perfect, Mom. You always did know my style, didn't you."

"You're easy. You like simple. No muss or fuss."

Yet she was complicating her life.

Lolly's eyes got glassy and she brought her hand up to her mouth and gestured for Kat to get the "throw-up bowl," as she called it. Kat hated to see her mother so sickened from what was supposed to help her. How would she tolerate the second round of chemo next week when she was still so sick from the first?

When Lolly finished, she lay back, her face glistening with sweat. Kat rushed into the bathroom across the hall for a cool washcloth and blotted her mother's forehead and cheeks, running her hand over the top of her head to smooth away the escaping, sweaty strands of hair from her braid. A clump of gray-blond hair came out in Kat's hand and she burst into tears.

"It's okay, Kat," Lolly said. "This is what happens. What's expected. It's the surprises that I hate."

Kat stared at the hair in her hand. "I love you, Mom," Kat said, surprising herself. Clearly surprising her mother too. Lolly reached for Kat's hand and held it.

Kat was about to lose it. She needed to go somewhere, somewhere private and just cry, let it out, all the fear and uncertainty. But she couldn't cry in the bathroom and upset her mother.

Lolly pulled her baggie of Wheat Thins out of her tote bag. Her favorite antidote to the nausea. "Kat, could you get me an iced tea? With two lemons. And one sugar."

"Be right back," Kat said, grateful for the task. She'd stop in the hallway restroom and cry there, then dash down to the cafeteria.

But as she rushed down the hall, she saw Matteo outside a patient's room, looking over a clipboard. Kat stopped in front of him, unable to stop the flow of tears.

"Kat? Is your mother all right?"

"She's so frail and pale and nauseated. Her hair came out in a clump in my hand." Kat realized she was still holding the hair and uncurled her palm. "I hate this. I hate it." She started to cry and he held out his hand and led her over to a group of chairs by the wall. *And she's picking out dresses and shoes and thinking up hors d'oeuvres and it's the only thing making her happy through all this.*

He gestured for her to sit down, then sat beside her, still holding her hand. "Try to remember that the effects of the chemo are temporary, that it's what your mother needs right now."

"I just didn't realize it would be like this. I thought the chemo would make her feel better, not worse. It's so backward. I hate it."

He leaned closer and took the hairs from her hand, wrapping them in a tissue from his pocket. "This is a side effect." He got up and tossed the tissue into the little wastebasket at the end of their row of chairs. "But it's helping to prolong her life."

"Miserably, though."

His dark eyes were so compassionate, so full of empathy, that Kat just wanted to throw herself against him and let him hold her. "I know how you feel, Kat. I remember going through this with my dad. The only way to get through it when you watch someone you love so much feel so sick, when you feel so helpless, is to lean on your friends, your family, anyone who gives you strength."

"Is it okay that I'm leaning on you?"

"More than okay." His phone vibrated and he checked it. "Look, today we'll find out how we need to adjust the infusion for next week. That'll be very helpful." The phone vibrated again. "I have to go, Kat. But call me anytime, day or night. Got it?"

"Got it," she said, surprised to discover she did feel stronger. She could go get her mother that iced tea, be there for her, instead of falling apart and making her mother feel worse.

She watched Matteo walk away until he rounded a corner.

"I didn't realize you and your mother's doctor were so close."

Kat glanced up, and there was Oliver, his expression one of angry confusion. She bolted up, her cheeks hot.

He was staring at her, in his blue eyes a combination of anger and hurt. "I came because you said last night that you were worried about the testing today, that you needed to be strong for your mother, especially when you had June on your mind too. I came to support you. But it looks like you found someone else to turn to."

Oh, no. "Oliver, I've gotten to know Matteo—Dr. Viola—over the past few weeks, and when I came out of my mother's room just before, I burst into tears and he led me over to these chairs to talk. He was holding my hand because—" She stopped, realizing that what she was about to say was not a lie. Not at all.

"Because?"

"Because he's become a good friend."

"Well, Kat, I was standing over there watching you from

the moment your 'good friend' Matteo led you over here—by the hand. I saw the way you looked at him. The way he looked at you. So don't lie to my face."

"Oliver, I'm not—"

"Are you sleeping with him?"

"Oliver!"

"Are you sleeping with him?" he repeated. Slowly. Angrily.

"No."

"Tell me right now, Kat. Do you want to give me the ring back? I'm asking you for the truth."

She dropped her head to her knees for a moment, willing her brain, her heart, to tell her how she felt.

"No" was what she said. And she'd have to trust that it was the truth, that deep down, no matter what, she did want to marry Oliver Tate. She just didn't know.

She saw the relief cross his face. "I don't want to make life harder for you right now, Kat. I know you're going through something very painful. I know I have to give you serious leeway. But if you tell me something, I'm going to believe it. Okay? That's how love and trust work."

She nodded. "I need to get my mom her iced tea. I'll come over tonight, okay? We'll talk more."

He nodded too and collected her into a hug, and she felt his eyes on her back as she rushed down the hall to the bank of elevators.

The next morning, Kat and Lolly headed into Beautiful Brides, an elegant little shop downtown, for their appointment with the owner, Claire Wignall. Lolly had called when they'd returned from the hospital and told Claire about the photo they'd seen in *Coastal Brides,* which Claire had in the shop. She didn't have that exact dress, but she did have two close to it.

Dress up. Make-believe. Fairy tale. Those were the thoughts that hit Kat as she walked into the store. Photographs of real brides in their Beautiful Brides gowns lined one wall. Mannequins in dresses and veils dotted the shop. Claire greeted them and congratulated Kat and oohed and aahed over her ring, then led them to a dressing area with a love seat. On the door to the dressing room, two gowns hung from a hook.

"Lolly, you just sit down right there," Claire said, gesturing for Lolly to sit on the plush apricot-colored love seat facing the door. "Kat, you go in and try one on and come out when you're ready. You'll find a nice pair of satin pumps in your size already in there."

Lolly smiled and sat. "I can't wait to see you in a wedding gown."

Kat smiled back at her mother, but her heart was starting to pound. As she stood there, fingering the plastic overlay of the first dress, she knew with certainty she didn't want to try it on. Or the second one. Or any one. This wasn't how you were supposed to feel when you were in a bridal salon for the first time. A few months ago when Lizzie first got engaged, she made Kat watch two back-to-back episodes of *Say Yes to the Dress,* a reality TV show about a famed bridal salon in New York City. She was supposed to feel the way those brides felt. Excited. Hopeful to find the right gown. This was supposed to be a big, magical moment in her life.

Last night, she'd gone over to Oliver's house as she'd promised, but instead of pressing her about her feelings, about holding hands with a resident on her mother's team, he pulled a classic Oliver: kindness. He hadn't demanded she explain herself. He'd simply opened the door for her, taken her into his arms, and held her tight, which was just what she'd needed: a hug from her best and oldest friend. They'd walked downtown for ice cream and took licks of each other's sherbet, then they'd gone back to his house and he'd made love to her as passionately as always.

This morning, when Lolly told her about the appointment she'd made at the bridal salon, her mother's blue eyes glowing, her cheeks more rosy than they'd been yesterday, Kat had felt that same sense of peace over her engagement as she had several times before. It was the antidote to Lolly's cancer; where the chemo made Lolly weak, Kat's engagement made her strong.

But now, as she stood in the middle of all this white, all these dresses symbolizing forever, the future, *vows,* she wasn't so sure she should be making any decisions about dress length, let alone the rest of her life.

Fake a migraine, she thought. *Suddenly feel faint and brace against the door. Just get out of this store.*

Except there was her mother, sitting on that apricot love seat, twenty pounds thinner than she'd been in mid-August. Lolly Weller, no romantic, had a look of pure happiness on her pale, gaunt face.

Lolly gasped, and Kat whirled around, hand on the doorknob. "Oh, Kat, look at that veil," her mother said, getting up slowly, gingerly, and walking over to a bust on an antique table. The veil was short, its headpiece a lovely combination of tiny, white sea stars and rosebuds. "This is so perfect. Kat, do you see the sea stars?"

Her father had collected sea stars. All manner. From heavy silver paperweights to the papier-mâché ones Kat made in elementary school every Father's Day. "It's beautiful," Kat said, remembering the little gold-filigree starfish earrings he'd bought her for "someday, when you get your ears pierced." Kat had begged her mother to let her get them pierced that day, and Lolly had relented. Kat wore those earrings all the time and had them on now.

Are you trying to tell me something, universe? Kat directed at the ceiling.

Claire nodded at her mother, and Lolly removed the headpiece from the bust and walked over to Kat. Kat tucked her chin down so Lolly could place the veil on her head. The head-piece was actually comfortable instead of tight or scratchy.

Lolly covered her mouth with her hand. "Oh, Kat. Look at you." She stood behind Kat at the mirror on the wall above the table.

It was pretty. And it did make Kat feel very bridal.

Lolly squeezed Kat's shoulders. "Go try on the dresses with this."

"Let me know if you need help," Claire said. "These two dresses are easy on—and *off*."

Kat slipped inside the elegant dressing room, so large it was almost the size of the Bluebird Room at the inn. She hung the two dresses on the high hook, took off the headpiece and put it on the padded bench, then peeled off her shirt and skirt. She stepped into the first white satin dress and reached behind her to zip it up. Pretty. It did look like the one in the picture. Kat put the headpiece back on and examined herself in the three-way mirror. She still felt that this was dress-up, make-believe. That she wasn't really going to be the bride.

"Kat, do you need help?"

She came out and faced her mother.

"It's so pretty," Lolly said.

"Just beautiful," Clair seconded. "But what do you think, Kat?"

"Well, I do like it," she said, moving in front of the three-way mirror in the corner of the shop. "But I'm not sure it's *the one*."

"Try the other. And remember, this is your first day, your first five minutes in the store. It may take trying ten, twenty dresses to find the one. You'll know it the minute you have it on."

Ten or twenty dresses? Kat didn't think she could bear to try on *two*.

Back in the dressing room, she took off Dress #1 and hung it up, then stepped into Dress #2. The moment she looked in the mirror, something shifted inside her.

This was the dress.

She knew it more clearly than she knew anything else lately. It was perfect and beautiful and breathtaking. Her skin seemed luminous. She put the headpiece back on and gasped at herself.

It's just a pretty dress, she reminded herself. *It doesn't mean anything. The universe isn't telling you anything. It's just a dress that happens to make you look like you were meant to wear it, that it was only meant for you.*

"Kat, ready?"

She sucked in a breath. The moment her mother saw her in this dress, with this headpiece, she'd burst out crying, Kat knew it. Her mother wasn't sentimental, but if the dress had moved Kat, had made her gasp, it would affect her mother doubly so.

She opened the door. And wasn't wrong.

Lolly stood up, her hand over her heart. Both hands flew to cover her face, the tears coming. Her mother loved her, Kat knew, in a way Kat had never before known.

"It's the one," Kat said.

"You'll barely need alterations." Claire smiled. "I need to take it in a bit at the waist and lengthen the hem just a half inch, but otherwise, it's as if the dress was made for you."

"Is it a fortune?" Kat asked.

"The dress of your dreams, whichever it is and no matter its cost, is covered by Anonymous," Claire said, a twinkle in her eyes. "I'll tell you, I don't get a lot of that."

Oliver. Kat knew it.

Lolly beamed. "Well, then, if you're sure of it, Kat, we'll take it."

Kat looked in the mirror again. Oliver had arranged for

the dress of her dreams so that her mother wouldn't have to worry about the cost. So Kat wouldn't have to worry about her mother worrying.

Lolly stood next to her, openly admiring her daughter's reflection. "If the last thing I do is see you walk down the aisle in the backyard of the Three Captains' to Oliver in this dress, I'll go a happy person."

Kat stared at her mother. *The last thing I do . . .*

"But if you're not sure, Kat," Lolly said, "we can keep looking. I see at least three other gowns on the mannequins that would look stunning on you."

If you're not sure, if you're not sure, if you're not sure. The words knocked inside Kat's head until she had to turn away from the mirror. She was only sure of one thing: wanting to make her mother happy for however long she had left.

"I'm sure," Kat said.

CHAPTER 16

Isabel

"Remember this?" June asked, holding up a photo album.

Isabel rested the album she was looking at on her criss-crossed legs and glanced over. Isabel, June, and their parents smiling with Donald Duck at Walt Disney World when Isabel was seven and June just four. Their father wore a Mickey Mouse hat complete with ears, and their mother looked so pretty in her white cotton sundress, a straw hat on her head, and a Cinderella sticker on her upper arm, plastered there by June.

Isabel and June had come downstairs to the basement of the Three Captains' to root through the old trunks for their mother's journals. Together they'd gone through every trunk, but the journals weren't there. In two of the trunks, they'd found twelve photo albums and had, for the past half hour, been captivated by them. Over the years, Lolly had reminded Isabel of the albums, but Isabel had taken a few favorites in the weeks after her parents' deaths and always feared looking through the rest, especially as the years passed. Afraid of memories. Of sorrow. Regrets.

An hour ago, when Isabel had come up to the attic bedroom to find a sweater for a guest to borrow, she'd found June sitting on the balcony, staring out at the harbor, her expression so sad that Isabel almost cried. It had been two days since June learned that Charlie's father had died on the day they were to meet in Central Park, and though she was up and moving around and putting on a good front for Charlie, June was devastated. Isabel had suggested that June help her look for the journals, unsure if it would help June in some way or remind her of more loss, but June had nodded and followed her down into the basement.

Their parents' possessions, their mother's favorite dress, their father's old, wire-rimmed John Lennon eyeglasses, seemed to make June wistful in a healing way. She'd held the glasses up and laughed, lost in a memory she didn't share, then buried her face in the scarf their father had worn the night he died, a dark blue wool their mother had knitted. She'd cried, and Isabel had pulled her into a hug and June let it all out again, her anguished "Everyone dies. Everyone dies," over and over, breaking Isabel's heart.

Just when Isabel had been afraid June would run off, Isabel had noticed the bundled letters from the final year she and June had gone to sleepaway camp when Isabel had been fourteen and June eleven. Isabel had loved every minute of being away from home, even if her counselor and the director had threatened to send her home if she broke one more rule. But June had been terribly homesick. Isabel had pulled out the top letter and started reading it aloud, noticing that June had scooted closer to read it too.

My darling June Bug,

I hear that you're feeling a little overwhelmed at camp and want to come home. I understand that you're experiencing lots of new things and that can be tough stuff. But you're such a smart, strong girl with a huge heart, interested in so many things, and I know if you give camp a chance, you'll find your place and your friends and you'll suddenly never want camp to end. Let's give it one more week, June. If you absolutely hate it then, Dad and I will come get you. But go show Camp Acadia who you are—fun, smart, sensitive, creative, imaginative, a great dancer and a great friend, and strong of body and mind. You can do anything, June.

All my love, Mom

"She really loved us," June had said, holding the letter against her heart. She folded it and slipped it into her back pocket, then reached for another letter.

She did love us—even me, Isabel had thought. *Coming down here—for both of us—was the right thing to do.*

June smiled at the Disney World photo and turned the pages, even laughing at one point, a beautiful sound coming from her grieving sister. Isabel glanced over to see a photo of their dad trying to put toddler June on a snowman's "shoulders" as Isabel, maybe five or six, stuck a carrot in the snowman's face to make a nose. They looked through the rest of the album together, then June set it down and pulled another letter from the bundle. "This one's to you, Iz," she said and began to read aloud.

Dear Isabel,

Dad and I miss you so much, Izzy-biz. The place sure is quiet without you. I know we weren't getting along too well in the weeks before you left for camp, but I know that when you come home, we'll spend lots of time together. I'll even see the new Scream movie.

I heard from your counselor that you were really shaken up about Flop dying. I know he's been the camp bunny for three years and has lived a good, happy life, surrounded by adoring kids who delighted in touching his soft long ears and sweet fur. Your counselor said

one girl was so homesick until she was put in charge of
feeding Flop his morning carrots, and just the sight of
Flop and his twitching pink nose started making her so
happy that she forgot all about wanting to come home.
That's a special bunny, and when we lose something,
someone, very special to us, we need to remember the
good things, the happy times, and let that stay in our
hearts. That's how I deal with loss. Like when Pappy
passed on, remember? You were just five and probably
don't, but I was so sad until I started remembering how
special Pappy made me feel, what a great father he was,
how glad I was to have had him in my life. I focused on
that and my heart felt healed instead of broken.

I hope that helps, Isabel, my brave girl.

All my love, Mom

As tears fell down Isabel's cheeks, she stared at June in disbelief.

"Read it to me again," June said.

Isabel read the letter. She'd forgotten all about Flop. And she didn't remember her grandfather, or his death, at all. Or this letter.

"She's right," June said, taking the letter from Isabel and scanning it. "I need to remember how special John made me feel, how lucky I was to have known him, even for that short time." She looked around the basement at their parents' things, then up toward the ceiling. "Thank you, Mom."

Isabel reached over and squeezed June's hand. "You keep that letter." Coming down here over the past few days had done Isabel a world of good too. She'd let go of expecting Griffin to call back. The incident, three days ago now, had spooked him away—maybe not necessarily from her, as Kat had suggested last night, but from dating, period. Isabel wasn't so ready to date herself, so perhaps it was best that Griffin stay in her fantasies, where all sorts of wonderful things happened, such as slow kisses and his hands all over her. Such as bits of conversations that made her feel all the things she'd stopped feeling in her marriage. Sexy. Interesting. Wanted.

Nothing bad happened in her fantasies. Children didn't go missing in doghouses. Teenagers didn't scowl at her. And men she'd just begun allowing herself to like didn't pull away and make her shrink back inside herself.

That way of thinking had kept Albert Brooks from getting into heaven in *Defending Your Life,* though.

As they rooted through more letters, Isabel found an entire packet of photocopies of letters that Lolly had sent to Isabel's, June's, and Kat's schools, teachers, and principals over the years.

> *Dear Ms. Patterson, thank you for alerting me to Isabel's refusal to participate in English class or turn in essays due on the assigned text. As you know, she lost her parents less than a month ago and is slowly finding her way back to everyday life. Perhaps you could show some understanding and compassion, particularly as the text deals with a happy, intact family. Thank you, Mrs. Lolly Weller.*

Isabel gasped. "I had no idea she had my back like that in those days. She was always so no-nonsense. 'Just do what you're supposed to and things will work out.' Remember how she always used to say that? I hated that."

"Me too. Especially because most of the time it was true. It's funny—she's still like that, and still so guarded, even though she's opening up more, but I guess I find myself appreciating it more. Nothing is sugarcoated, you know?" June scanned another letter in Lolly's packet. "Listen to this one. 'Dear Principal Thicket, My daughter, Kat, has indicated

on several occasions that two particular girls in her class are
teasing her relentlessly by calling her an orphan and making
fun of her clothes. Twice, I have brought this to the attention
of her teacher and to you. If I hear of this one more time,
I'll be down at the school with News Channel 8 to ask why
the school isn't protecting my child from bullies. Thank you,
Mrs. Lolly Weller.'"

"Wow," Isabel said. "We'll have to show that to Kat. Lolly
acted like she couldn't be bothered three-quarters of the
time with what was going on with any of us. But behind the
scenes, there she was, raising hell with Principal Thicket."

The inn's phone rang upstairs, and Kat called, "Isabel,
telephone for you."

Isabel dashed upstairs to the office and picked up the
receiver Kat had left on the desk. Kat had also left inn mail
on the desk, including a small card addressed to her with a
teenaged girl's handwriting. Isabel flipped it over—no return
address. "Hello, Isabel speaking."

"I'd like to book the Osprey Room, if it's available for
Saturday night. One adult, two children."

"Griffin?" she asked, but there was no question that the
strong, deep voice at the other end of the phone, the first
connection they'd had since Monday, was his.

"I'm sorry I haven't called back. I've been— Anyway, we can
talk about that this weekend—if the room's available, that is."

"We had a cancellation for the Osprey Room just yesterday."

"Then the girls and I will see you Saturday. Oh, and Isabel,
maybe we can go for a walk on Saturday night, after I get
Emmy to bed."

Her heart leapt. "I'd like that."

She wanted to ask him so many questions. But he and his
girls were coming. Which said something was being offered.

She opened the card. It was from Alexa Dean.

To Isabel,
    I'm sorry for what happened on Monday. I shouldn't
have said I'd keep an eye on Emmy while you went
inside if that's not what I planned to do. I was wrong.
Sorry for all the trouble I caused.

                                                    Alexa D.

Isabel raised an eyebrow and smiled. She could just imagine Griffin standing behind Alexa, her earphones in and scowl on, insisting she write a letter of apology with exactly the sentiments Alexa drily noted.

She couldn't wait to see them all. Alexa D. included.

When Isabel brought the popcorn into Lolly's room for Movie Night on Friday, Lolly was looking through one of the photo albums that June had brought up, an old family album of Lolly and her sister, Allie, as kids.

"I love looking at these pictures," Lolly said, laughing at a photograph of Isabel's mother, no older than ten, holding up two fingers behind Lolly's head while making a funny face.

Isabel smiled. She still got a kick out of seeing her stoic aunt Lolly as a mischievous eight-year-old, sticking out her tongue. "June and I have been looking through the albums too. We found such amazing stuff in those old trunks. Old letters, little mementos that you wouldn't think would stir up such great memories, but they do. I still can't find the journal books, though. Maybe they got misplaced?"

"Maybe," Lolly said without hesitation, flipping another page.

Isabel eyed her aunt. She had a feeling she'd been played. "Lolly Weller, do those journals even exist?" she asked with a smile.

"I was sure they did, but maybe I was mistaken?" Lolly yawned, letting Isabel know not to press too hard.

Isabel sat down on the edge of Lolly's bed and took her aunt's hand. "Thank you for making me look. I found a lot of unexpected treasures." *You weren't who I thought you were.*

"I was sure you would."

"Those trunks helped June too," Isabel whispered. "We found some letters our mom wrote us at camp that were just what the doctor ordered for her. And some copies of letters that you'd sent to teachers and principals. Thank you."

Lolly smiled and gave Isabel's hand a gentle squeeze.

Just then June came in with tonight's DVD—*Postcards from the Edge,* which no one had seen except for Lolly, twice, but a while ago—and Kat was behind her with four chocolate cupcakes with white icing. It was a wonder none of them had gained twenty-five pounds since the first Movie Night. Lolly, of course, had lost too much weight.

"Oh, I almost forgot," Lolly said. "Pearl and I went to the bridal salon where we found Kat's gown, and I took pictures." She reached for her camera in the drawer of her bedside table, pressed a few buttons, and handed Isabel the camera.

"It's beautiful!" Isabel said, passing the camera to June.

"Gorgeous," June agreed.

Kat wasn't rushing over to gape at her own wedding gown, the way an excited bride-to-be might. She didn't ooh over the delicate beading or aah over the lovely neckline. She didn't say anything. She only smiled her thanks. Isabel put the camera back in the drawer.

"Everyone ready?" Kat said, her hand on the light. She clearly wanted to change the subject. *Was* she unsure she wanted to get married? Problems with Oliver? Interested in Dr. Viola? Worried about her mother? Maybe she and June would try to talk to Kat that night, after the movie. They'd tried before, but Kat always got cagey or insisted everything was just fine.

Lolly pressed PLAY on *Postcards from the Edge*. "I think you'll all love this one. Such great acting. Meryl and Shirley MacLaine. And Dennis Quaid is in it too, and, oh my, he's quite attractive."

Meryl played an actress—the daughter of famous former film star Shirley MacLaine—with a drug problem. Fresh out of detox, the insurance company on her new film wouldn't cover Meryl unless someone was responsible for her at all times during filming. Which meant she had to live with her outrageous mother, with whom she barely got along.

"Shirley MacLaine is so insufferable—the role she's playing, I mean," Kat said. "Her daughter just got out of detox, she's trying so hard, and Shirley MacLaine just has to put her down and one-up her."

"Oh my God, did she just say she might not live much longer because they found fibroid tumors?" June asked, shaking her head with a smile. "You can't help but love her, even as you hate her for being so melodramatic."

Lolly was laughing, even if Kat wasn't. Especially when Shirley told Meryl that she wanted Meryl to be prepared for her death.

"Is the whole thing like this?" Kat said. "I'm not sure I can watch this. I know it's supposed to be funny but—"

Lolly peeled away the edge of her cupcake. "One of the things I love about this movie, Kat, is how Meryl and Shirley start out so far apart—in every way—and find their way back to each other. But you've got to start with the bad to get to the good. It's all worth it, I swear."

Kat stared at Lolly. "I'll shut up and watch," she said, shooting her mother a warm smile and taking a bite of her own cupcake.

Isabel burst out laughing when Dennis Quaid, who was

absolutely gorgeous and sexy in this movie, just professed his love for Meryl with "I think I love you." Meryl's response: "When will you know for sure?"

"Good Lord, I hope she doesn't fall for that line," Kat said. "Dennis Quaid telling her she's the 'realest person he ever met in the abstract,' that she was his fantasy and he wanted to make her real. Do you think people do that? Have relationships with people that are built on fantasy?"

"To start, maybe," Lolly said. "The fantasy goes pretty fast. Then you have reality."

It struck Isabel how Griffin Dean was fantasy and reality rolled into one.

"Wow, is that Annette Bening?" June asked. "She's stunning. It's no surprise she became a huge actress. And there's the answer to your question, Kat, since Dennis Quaid is cheating on everyone, even her."

As the movie neared the end, Kat grabbed a tissue and dabbed under her eyes. "You were right, Mom. I love that Meryl and Shirley discovered what was really important in their relationship—each other, having each other, being there for each other. They both have a ways to go, but you really believe that they're going to have a fresh start."

"I wish my mom and I had before— I hate that I treated her that way," Isabel said. "Like she had nothing to tell me, like she was trying to run my life. I wished I listened more."

"But Mom saw through all that, Izzy. Those letters we found in the basement, that's what it was all about."

"You're right," Isabel said. "It's helped me so much to know that. To know now that she saw through my stupidity and bravado. But if I'd listened more to her, I might not have made that stupid pact. I might have been stronger, had more self-esteem, believed in myself more."

"What pact?" June asked.

Isabel glanced around at the faces. She'd never told anyone

about the pact. She'd just shrugged when anyone used to ask if she and Edward were thinking of babies, starting a family. "When I was sixteen. With Edward. We made a pact not to have kids so they'd never have to suffer a similar loss."

"Oh, Isabel," Lolly said.

"Edward once said I probably wouldn't be a very good mother. It was so hard not to believe him, even though deep down, I *did* think I'd be a good mother. I used to defer to him in everything because of how he helped me when Mom and Dad died. I always thought he was so right about everything. But he wasn't. He was so angry that I'd changed my mind, that I wanted a baby."

"Bastard. I hate that," June said. "*He* was the stuck one, Isabel. He was stuck and couldn't move forward, and he put you in place and kept you there until you started getting uncomfortable."

Kat was shaking her head. "I'm surprised it only took you fifteen years. God, no wonder you were so broken up about what happened with Emmy running off. You thought it was reinforcing what Edward said."

Isabel leaned back. She could feel the cool breeze on her face as though she were in the backyard with Edward that night they'd made the pact. She understood why she'd made that pact. Why she'd fallen so deeply in love with Edward. Why she'd stayed with him long after his slights and jabs and small betrayals made her realize she wasn't the same scared girl of twenty-one he'd married. That young woman who'd felt so alone in the world, despite having a sister, a cousin, an aunt. She'd let Edward tell her who she was for a long time. But she was done with that. Never again would she let anyone tell her who she was or what she was capable of.

"I wished I'd talked to you about it then, Aunt Lolly," Isabel said, but when she glanced over, Lolly was asleep, her hand on the remote control.

"'Night, Mom," Kat whispered, moving the remote and pulling the quilt up to Lolly's chest. She turned out the light as Isabel and June collected the popcorn bowls and glasses.

They headed into the kitchen, and June started the kettle for tea.

"Things we feel as teenagers shouldn't get to define us," Kat said, storing the extra cupcakes. "Sometimes I . . . wonder if that's why I'm with Oliver in the first place. I'm supposed to be."

June added loose Earl Grey tea to the strainer of the teapot. "Are you having second thoughts about getting married?"

"Maybe?" Kat said, dropping down into a chair. "Yes. No. I don't know. I don't know anything. Ignore me."

"Impossible," Isabel said, putting a hand on Kat's shoulder before pouring the boiling water over the tea leaves. "I just hope you'll do what you really want. Not what anyone else thinks you should do. Capisce?"

Kat smiled. "Capisce."

"One thing I've learned," June said, "is that when you're not sure about something, there are two things you can do. Take a step back or stay still—but not move forward. Something will give you clarity. You'll wake one morning and realize that you understand something you didn't the day before."

Kat filled three cups with the fragrant tea. "I hope so. I'm waiting for that morning. At least Isabel knows how she feels." Kat grinned. "You have a date with Griffin tomorrow night, right?"

"It's not a date. It's just another walk. Maybe he wants to make a truce. And then let me know it's over before it started."

June dropped a sugar cube into her tea. "I don't think he'd spend a hundred and fifty bucks on the Osprey Room for that."

Isabel smiled.

• • •

Isabel had seen the Deans coming and going throughout Saturday afternoon. When they'd arrived, Alexa barely looked at Isabel, and Emmy asked if she could visit nice Elvis, the dog she'd curled up around the last time she'd been to the inn, which elicited an almost comical death-stare jaw-drop from Alexa. The way Griffin had looked at Isabel when he'd come through the door—with utter *feeling*—had sent goose bumps up her arms, and she'd wanted nothing more than to grab him into the office, shut the door, and pull him into a long, hot kiss. But Emmy had been asking for a Popsicle, and the phone was ringing, and Alexa was charging up the stairs, so any thought of a kiss would have to wait until that night.

If there would be a kiss at all. Isabel had been unable to sleep last night, thinking about their date. About walking, maybe hand in hand, with Griffin down to the harbor, along a moonlit pier, the way he might tilt up her chin for that slow, deep kiss.

Isabel had been going over the books in the office when she caught the Deans leaving; a few hours later, when she'd been dusting the parlor, they'd returned with Emmy holding a chocolate, lobster-shaped lollipop and Alexa with a blue slush drink and her earbuds in. Griffin had smiled and asked if eight thirty would work for their walk.

At seven, Isabel raced up to the attic bedroom and took a shower, imagining that kiss, the feel of Griffin's hands on her, on her soapy body in the shower. On her unsoapy body in bed. That her thoughts turned so X-rated about Griffin thrilled her. Like that old Carly Simon song from *Heartburn,* it meant to her that she was coming around again.

She put on her favorite casual dress, a new one she'd bought in the harbor a few weeks ago. It was the palest yellow cotton and had embroidered tiny flowers at the straps and an Empire waist. It made her feel pretty and carefree. She added a light spritz of Coco, her favorite perfume, a few swipes of mascara, and a berry-stain lip gloss, gave her hair another once-over, and headed downstairs. At the second-floor landing, she could hear someone crying. She stopped, listening for where it was coming from. The Alone Closet. Was it June? She knocked gently and something was thrown against the door. Like a book.

Alexa.

"Alexa, it's me, Isabel. Let me in."

"No."

Isabel stood in front of the door. "I really want to talk, honey."

"What's the point? You hate me and now you're my father's girlfriend. My life is great. What could possibly be *wrong.*"

Father's girlfriend? They'd barely taken one walk together. But to a teenaged girl with a divorced father, that was enough. "I don't hate you, Alexa. Not one bit. I'm not angry at you."

There was silence for a moment, then the sounds of crying. "I don't believe you. But whatever. Aren't you late for your *date*?"

Ah. This wasn't her place, to talk to Alexa about her father's love life. Not that there was a love life between her and Griffin. Yet. Or maybe not ever.

Isabel turned the doorknob, wanting to talk to Alexa face-to-face. The knob turned, but the door wouldn't budge. Alexa had moved something heavy in front of it. "Your dad and I are going for a walk. With Happy."

"You're going on a *date*. Just like my mother went on a date with her boss and broke up the family. And now my father is going on dates. I hate my mother. I hate her, I hate her, *I hate her*," Alexa shouted. "If she hadn't ruined everything, everything would be great. I hate her and I'm glad I told her so."

Good Lord, this was heavy stuff. Isabel wasn't sure if she should go get Griffin and let him handle this or if she should follow her instincts. She leaned closer to the door. "I really want to talk to you, Alexa. There's some stuff I think would help you to know about me."

"I don't want to know *anything* about you."

Isabel touched the necklace she wore, one of her mother's delicate gold chains with a small heart locket. "Well, I do want to share one thing with you." She took a breath; she hadn't told anyone this story in a long time, since she was sixteen and had opened up to Edward. "The last thing I ever said to my mother was that I wished she was dead. We had a terrible, stupid fight. And when I woke up the next morning, I found out she *was* dead. She'd been killed in a car crash on New Year's Eve. With my dad and my uncle—Kat Weller's father."

Silence.

Isabel took a deep breath. "I didn't mean it. I loved her, really loved her, even if sometimes I didn't know it. I was mad at her for setting my curfew at twelve thirty for New Year's Eve, for getting mad at me all the time, grounding me, telling me I was running wild, that one day I'd do something I'd regret. And you know, she was right. I never had the chance to tell her I didn't mean it, that I was sorry."

Isabel could hear crying and some books being shoved onto the floor.

"She didn't cheat on your father, though," Alexa shouted. "She didn't break up your family and ruin your life."

"No, but she's gone, honey. Gone forever. I'll never be able to fix things. She'll never have a chance to fix things with me. Alexa, you never know what's going to happen in life. Painful things happen all the time. But if you walk around all mad at everyone, you'll just feel worse and worse. Making things right with your mom will change your entire life."

"So I'm just supposed to forgive her? Right."

God, Alexa was tough. "You can try to forgive her. And you can still love her even if you're mad at her. You can let her love you. You can let her try to make things as right as they can be for you two. She's your mother, Alexa. My mom died when I was sixteen. She's gone forever."

There was silence, then a few moments later, Isabel heard the sounds of something being pushed away from the door, then the latch sliding open. She waited a moment, but the door didn't open. Isabel slowly turned the knob, and Alexa sat on the love seat, which was now sideways in the middle of the small room, her eyeliner and mascara running down her face.

"I didn't mean all the stuff I said to my mother," Alexa said, tears streaming. "But I'm still so mad at her."

Isabel sat down next to the girl. "My mom isn't here for me to talk to, for me to tell her I didn't mean half, a quarter, of what I said—especially the last thing. But your mom lives just two towns over. She's a fifteen-minute drive away."

"But I do hate her. Even if I really don't," Alexa said, and started to sob again.

Isabel understood this girl so well and from a place so deep inside her that she wished she could come up with just the right thing to say. But that would take time. Trust. And Alexa to mature some.

So Isabel put her arms around Alexa, who went ramrod stiff, and held her. Isabel told her about the letter she and June had found the other day. About the bunny who'd died, about much more than that between the lines, and how the letter, their mother's words, ended up soothing both of them in different ways all these years later. As Isabel talked, it didn't

take as long as Isabel thought it would for Alexa to go all
Jell-O–like against her.

It was after nine when Isabel told Alexa she'd better go let her
dad know what had happened to her and their eight thirty
date, and that she'd be back.

"You don't have to come back," Alexa said, her voice low
and shaky. "You should go on the walk. With my dad and
Happy."

Isabel smiled at her. "Let me talk to your dad."

Downstairs, in the hallway, Isabel ran into June. "He's
in the parlor," June said. "About twenty minutes ago, I told
him I'd go see what was keeping you and reported back that
you and Alexa were deep in conversation. He glanced up the
stairs as though deciding whether or not to intervene, but
then went into the parlor with a sigh and the beer I gave
him."

Isabel squeezed her sister's hand. "Thanks, June."

She went into the parlor, where Griffin sat staring straight
ahead at the painting of the original three captains, his elbows
on his thighs. The beer sat untouched on the end table.

He stood up when he saw her come in. "What happened
up there? Or shouldn't I ask?"

"Alexa opened up to me. Took a while, but she opened
up. I can't tell you how good it made me feel to help her feel
better about things, about herself."

Griffin's look of shock made her smile. "Whatever you
said must have really broken through. Thank you, Isabel."

"I'll bet if you go up and talk to her now, she'll be open to
it. We can go for that walk once she falls asleep. Or another
night. Go to your daughter."

This was what having children in your life meant, Isabel
knew. Complications, interruptions. Drama. It was all give-

and-take. And for every bit of sacrifice, every bit of heartrending, there was something magical and beautiful.

Isabel watched from the doorway as Griffin headed upstairs.

June appeared from the office and leaned close to Isabel. "And you were worried that you wouldn't be a good mother."

CHAPTER 17

June

June stood in front of a dusty, old wooden floor mirror in the basement of the inn and put on the red wool car coat. The collar still smelled faintly of her mother's perfume—or that may have been June's wishful thinking. She'd found the coat hanging in a garment bag on a rack of old coats. Her mother's L.L. Bean orange down parka. Her dad's brown leather bomber jacket. A few other wool coats that June didn't remember. Maybe they were Lolly's.

Her mother had been four inches taller than June's five feet four, so the coat was a bit big; it would probably fit tall Isabel perfectly. But June loved the coat, loved how it felt, how it comforted her and reminded her of her mother. With her auburn hair and "spring" coloring, June never thought she could wear a true orange like this coat was, but it seemed to bring out a glow in her complexion, in her hazel-green eyes. Then again, maybe that was just wishful thinking too. In any case, the coat made her feel happy. Just a couple of months from now, the weather would turn November cool and she'd use it as her everyday coat.

She took it off and hung it back up, sliding it to the left toward her pile of treasures growing by the side of the rack. June picked up one of the photo albums in her pile, full of old photos of the Miller sisters, June's mother and Lolly as children, growing up in Wiscasset, a beautiful town not too far from Boothbay Harbor. June sat down cross-legged on an old, round braided rug and flipped through the album. June found herself focusing on her aunt Lolly. She stopped at a photograph of teenaged Lolly standing in front of her family's yellow Cape Cod in a lavender prom dress with a corsage pinned to her chest, a handsome guy at her side.

Harrison? June wondered, thinking of the mystery man her aunt had spoken of the day after June had found out John Smith had died. Lolly had come upstairs to the attic bedroom and found June curled up in the fetal position and facing the wall, tears running down her cheeks. June had been unable to stop crying. Unable to stop thinking about what-ifs. About the loss of her dream. About loss, period. The one constant. But she'd been so humbled by Lolly's climbing the stairs all the way to the third floor, when it was so difficult for her, that she'd bolted up, apologizing to Lolly for making her worry, making her come all the way upstairs.

"I would do anything for you girls," Lolly had said, sitting down on the edge of June's bed. "When your heart is broken, so is mine, even if you'd never know it." She glanced at June for a moment, then looked away. "I think I know just how you feel, even if what I went through was different."

"Uncle Ted."

Lolly had shaken her head. "No. Not him. Harrison. A man I once loved. While I was married."

June caught her gasp and waited for Lolly to continue. Lolly Weller had had an affair?

"Do you remember how it was between Meryl Streep and Clint Eastwood in *The Bridges of Madison County*? I once had something like that. It was a love like that. But it couldn't be and that was that. I grieved the end a very long time. And sometimes, when I think of him, my heart aches like I just said that final good-bye. But do you know what saved me?"

June had so many questions, but they'd have to wait. "What?"

"This may sound a little backwards, but—a man who I thought was so amazing, so special, loved *me* like crazy. *That* saved me. Gave me what I needed to go on. It's what I tucked inside my heart and soul and moved on with."

That was exactly how Henry's admission of love had made June feel. She had so many questions for Lolly.

"Aunt Lolly, when—"

"I'm not feeling very well and think I need to get back down to bed," Lolly had interrupted in a voice June knew well. That voice said, *Don't talk back, don't ask questions. Just do what I say.* June would respect her aunt's need for privacy and do just that.

What Lolly had said had helped immeasurably. Because she'd never believed that John had cared, June hadn't thought of her feelings for John, his for her, in that way: that the guy she'd thought was so amazing and special and beautiful had felt that exact way about her, and that was a gift.

In the days that had followed, over breakfast, over dinner, when she'd drop in on Lolly to bring her tea or one of Kat's creations, June wanted to ask about the man, this Harrison, and she'd tried once, but Lolly had cut her off and changed the subject to Kat's wedding reception dinner choices. June had understood that Lolly must be trying to be protective of Kat's feelings about love and marriage, especially concerning Lolly and her late husband, Kat's father. So June tucked away the nugget Lolly had shared and let it stay at that.

Between Lolly's story and reading her mother's letter to Isabel, June had found the strength, the words, to write the letter she'd started and stopped so many times since she'd seen that obituary. But she wrote it, addressed it to Eleanor and Steven Smith, and sent it three days ago, along with a photo of Charlie as a baby and Charlie now. Every time June's phone rang, she jumped.

Her phone didn't ring often. Marley called with sweet updates about Kip, who was true to his word about commitment and was building a sleigh crib with his own hands. Henry had called once, the night after she'd run crying from his houseboat, and left a message. Letting her know he understood if she didn't want to come in to work for a while, or ever, just to take her time and know her job would be open when and if she wanted to come back. She hadn't called him back or gone in.

She owed him an apology for how she'd acted. For not coming in to work the entire week. For taking his generosity for granted. She'd say all that. There was more she wanted to say, she could feel it welling up inside her, but she had no idea what it was, exactly. She just knew that a pressure was building underneath her heart, that it involved Henry somehow.

She took her cell phone from her back pocket and was about to call Henry, to say *something*, but the phone rang: 207-555-2501.

John's parents.

June stared at it, her mouth falling open. For a moment she couldn't move, then realized she'd better answer it before it went to voice mail.

"June? This is Eleanor Smith. John's mother."

June felt her legs go rubbery and was glad she was sitting down.

"We're stunned," Eleanor said. "John's father and I. We've been away for most of the summer and just came back yesterday. Your telephone message and your letter were waiting for us, but it took us a day to let your letter, news of a child, a grandchild, settle. I hope it's okay that we took some time."

June could barely speak around the lump in her throat. Eleanor Smith sounded warm and lovely. "Of course."

"The moment we saw the photograph you enclosed of your boy, we knew it was definitely John's son. They look so much alike—" Eleanor broke on a sob just then.

"I know," June said. "The same beautiful green eyes and dark hair."

"And something in the expression."

Yes, June thought. *Something in the expression.*

"You know," Eleanor said, "you've helped us solve a bit of mystery on our end. One of the nurses told us that John had slipped in and out of consciousness a few times before he passed and had said just one thing: 'June.' We couldn't figure out what he meant, since it was November then."

June gasped. She started to cry.

Eleanor Smith gave her a moment. "I'm so glad you wrote to us. We're so happy you finally found your way to us."

"Me too," June whispered.

They'd both agreed that there was much to discuss—and see, such as Charlie—in person, so they made arrangements for the next day. At least it would give June little time to be nervous.

As she drove up I-95 to Bangor on Friday morning, June glanced in the rearview mirror at Charlie. Once again, he was admiring his family-tree poster, which was carefully placed on his lap. Yesterday, after the long talk she and Charlie had had in the backyard of the inn, about his father, what she'd learned of his death, and that his grandparents had invited them over, Charlie had jumped up and said he had to update his family tree and gone racing into the inn. He'd come running out a minute later with the poster and his lucky green pencil, then carefully added the word *heaven* inside a circle next to his father's name and then two new names: *Grandparents: Eleanor and Steven Smith.*

Now they were on their way to meet those grandparents. After all the searching June had done over the past seven years, particularly when she'd first discovered she was pregnant and again these past few weeks, it seemed almost wrong to so easily pull into the driveway of John Smith's parents' home. Their white clapboard New Englander, with its neat rows of flowers and blooming window boxes, looked friendly and welcoming and helped calm her nerves.

As June and Charlie got out of the car, the front door opened and a couple came out onto the porch and waved. When she and Charlie stepped up to the porch, both Smiths reacted the same way—they burst into tears, covering their mouths with their hands and then falling into each other's arms.

"You don't like us?" Charlie asked.

Eleanor Smith knelt down in front of Charlie. "Oh, we like you. We like you very much, Charlie." She stared at him, every bit of him, drinking in the sight of her grandchild, this walking, breathing connection, continuation, of her child. "You look so much like your daddy, Charlie. I can't wait to show you photos of him when he was seven. Wait till you see." She stood, and Steven Smith, tears in his eyes, wrapped Charlie in a hug, shaking his head with "He's the spitting image. The spitting image."

She could see John in their features too. In Eleanor's green eyes and fair skin and Steven Smith's strong jawline and dark hair. She saw so many emotions in their faces as they watched Charlie kneel down on the lawn to pet their orange cat, who rubbed against his leg. Wonder. Joy.

"Charlie, would you like some fresh-baked chocolate chip cookies and milk?" Eleanor asked.

"Yes!" Charlie said. "Oh, wait, we brought a box of cookies that my cousin Kat made. She's a baker." He ran to the car and took the box Kat had made up and carried it over to

Eleanor, who burst into tears. Charlie opened the box and held it up. "Kat always says you can't cry and eat cookies at the same time, so you might as well have a cookie."

That made Eleanor laugh and she knelt down and pulled Charlie into a hug. "I'm not sad, Charlie. I'm just so incredibly happy to know you. It means the world to me that you're here."

"So can you tell me about my dad?" Charlie asked, holding out a cookie for the cat, who sniffed it and walked away.

Steven Smith put his arm around Charlie. "Let's go in and talk and see those pictures. You won't believe how much you look like your dad."

The moment June stepped inside the Smiths' house, she saw the painting, hanging over an upright wooden piano— of John, just as she remembered him. He was sitting on the porch of this house, his feet covered in fall leaves of vivid yellows and burnished oranges and bright reds. She'd stopped in the middle of the hallway, and Charlie followed her gaze.

"Is that him? Is that my dad?"

June held Charlie's hand. "That's him."

"I look just like him!" Charlie said.

"You sure do," June whispered, unable to say anything else. She still couldn't quite believe she was here.

They sat on the sofa, the Smiths flanking her and Charlie, a photo album open on June's lap. Eleanor and Steven went through the pictures, of John as a baby, a toddler, on a two-wheeler bike and skateboard, at school dances, in all kinds of boats. She'd known him just two days out of the life depicted in these albums. Two days.

She thought of Albert Brooks's lawyer in *Defending Your Life,* telling him to take the opportunities given him on earth. June had taken the opportunity presented in John Smith. And she'd been given her memories and a beautiful child.

While Charlie played with the cat, whose name was Miles,

Eleanor told June that John had been diagnosed with leukemia when he was nineteen, a year and a half before he died. He'd wanted to travel the country and see amazing things, such as David Bowie's Ziggy Stardust jumpsuit and platform shoes in the Rock and Roll Hall of Fame and Museum in Cleveland, Ohio, and J. D. Salinger's hideaway house in New Hampshire. He'd been in New York to walk in Strawberry Fields in Central Park and see Greenwich Village and buy a book, any book, in the Strand bookstore. He'd made a deal to call his parents every day around dinnertime, to check in, no matter what. And every night, he called, for the three weeks he'd been traveling. Sometimes he'd leave a message. Sometimes he'd tell them a funny story about something he saw.

"When he didn't call by dinnertime on November tenth, I knew," Eleanor said, her fingers touching a photograph of John in a 5K-race T-shirt. "I remember taking out the roast from the oven around five fifteen, and realizing very suddenly that he hadn't called, and he usually called between four and five, since we always eat at five thirty. I remember staring at the clock, and when it ticked past six, I knew. I called the hostel where he was staying, and the manager told me that the maid had found him unconscious on the floor at just before one o'clock, right by the door, as though he'd either been about to leave or had just come in."

One o'clock. Exactly when she and John were supposed to meet in Central Park.

"There was a mix-up in notifying us," Steven said. "The hostel manager had been told by the EMTs that the hospital would notify the parents, and the hospital was under the impression that the manager had alerted us and that we were on our way. If we hadn't called the hostel at six, I'm not sure when we would have been called. But he passed away within an hour of being found in his room."

"He was just fine the day before. Just fine," Eleanor said,

her voice cracking. "He'd been in New Jersey for a few days, wanting to see that famous little club where Bruce Springsteen played before he got famous. He was just fine. And his first two days in New York, he sounded so happy, his voice strong. But that's how cancer can be. One minute you're standing and the next, an infection you didn't even know you had is slowly atta—" She covered her face with her hands for a moment, her husband rubbing her back.

June had had no idea he'd been sick. No idea. And he'd been terminally ill. Dying. It scared her even more for Lolly. She closed her eyes for a second, unable to process any of this.

"And now we know what 'June' meant," Eleanor added. "He was thinking of you with his last breath. You must have been very special to him."

June took Eleanor's hand, and his mother smiled at her. And for the next hour, while Charlie and his grandfather played badminton outside, June told Eleanor all about her son's last two days, how she'd fallen in love at first glance, what they'd talked about for hours. By the time Steven and Charlie returned, both women were crying, and June assured Charlie that once again they were happy tears.

"Guess what?" Charlie said to June. "There's more names to add to the family tree. I have an uncle! He lives in California, but he'll be coming to Maine for Christmas and I can meet him. And there are great-aunts and -uncles and cousins too. Grandpa Steven is going to write down all the names for me."

Grandpa Steven. June's heart almost burst. Charlie had never had anyone to refer to as grandpa before.

The Smiths invited them to stay for lunch, and they spent another hour around the dining room table, June and Charlie sharing stories about the inn and their family. By the time June and Charlie got back into June's car at four o'clock, a beautiful bond had been formed. As June drove off, Charlie waving good-bye, she felt very, very lucky.

• • •

At dinner, Charlie had told everyone about meeting his grandparents and Miles the cat and about all the new relatives he'd be adding to his family tree. Over barbecued chicken and corn on the cob, his favorite, which he'd barely eaten because he'd been too excited, he'd asked Lolly if his new grandparents could come visit, and Lolly had said she couldn't wait to meet them and would give them the best room on the house. Great-Aunt Lolly had gotten a fierce hug from a happy little boy for that.

Everyone was excited for tonight's film for Friday Movie Night: *It's Complicated.* No one had seen it, except for Lolly, when it first came out, and everyone was in the mood for light and fun. Yet another "affair movie," as Isabel had called it, but one that kind of turned the tables since the affair was between a divorced couple. Alec Baldwin was cheating on his hot young wife with his ex, Meryl Streep.

"Okay, so once again, I only sort of get it," Kat said, looking over the back of the DVD case. "The hot young wife stole Alec from Meryl, so we shouldn't care that he's cheating on her with Meryl?"

"I think that's why the movie is called *It's Complicated,* dear," sweet Pearl said. "Not that I condone affairs, of course, but it is an interesting situation."

Kat shrugged in her good-natured way and peeled the wrapper off the cupcake she balanced on a napkin on her lap. Chocolate with chocolate icing.

They had gathered in the parlor since Lolly was feeling better, had felt strong all day, according to Isabel, and June loved seeing her back on the sofa in her usual spot next to Pearl, munching popcorn, talking about how handsome Alec Baldwin was.

"Another reason I'm glad Edward and I don't have children," Isabel said as Meryl Streep and Alec Baldwin found themselves staying in the same New York City hotel for their youngest son's college graduation, having drinks and dinner—and lots of happily sloshed dancing. "We'll never have to see each other again. No ballet recitals or parent-teacher conferences or graduations or weddings."

June raised her glass of iced tea and clinked Isabel's. "That must be awkward for divorced couples—and their new spouses. Meryl and Alec seem friendly and all, but it must be weird."

"Guess that's how the affair starts," Isabel said. "Remind me not to have a glass of wine around Edward."

"Oh my God, Meryl and Alec are dancing to Tom Petty's 'Don't Do Me Like That,'" Kat said. "There's your sign, Meryl. Don't do it!"

June laughed. "Too late," she added as Meryl and Alec were naked in bed together. Meryl looked appalled. Alec looked quite pleased with himself.

Isabel sipped her iced tea. "Wait a minute, did Meryl just tell Alec it took her *years* to feel normal after he left her? Years? I don't have years to feel normal!"

"Can you even imagine you and Edward having dinner and drinks and laughs ten years from now?" June asked.

"No way," Isabel said. "Even if I'm totally over the divorce—and the divorce papers were forwarded here a few days ago—I can't imagine laughing with him that way."

"So now Meryl Streep is all back into her ex-husband who left her for another woman?" Kat said. "Okay, fine. She said there's still feeling between them, and, yeah, she's being cautious, but still, I don't get how she could go there. He cheated on her, broke up their family, upended her whole life, which she said took her years to put back together, and now she's sleeping with him again—as he cheats on his new wife? He's not a scumbag anymore? I don't get this."

"I'm glad you don't," Isabel said. "It means you're idealistic—a good thing when you're about to get married."

"Does idealistic mean naive?" Kat asked.

"No, it means idealistic," June said. "Ideals are good."

"Ooh, here comes Steve Martin into the picture," Pearl said. "I just love him. So funny and handsome. I hope Meryl ends up with him and not that cad Alec Baldwin."

"I love that Steve Martin is the architect designing the renovations for her dream house," June said. "Talk about a good metaphor." Henry flashed into her mind. Tall, strong, and silent Henry holding infant Charlie while June sobbed in the storeroom for two minutes because she'd been overwhelmed. Henry teaching three-year-old Charlie to fish. Henry sending Charlie kites and books and hilarious Halloween costumes for gifts over the past seven years.

Henry telling her he loved her and always had. June running away. Hurt and afraid.

"I hate how likable Alec Baldwin is," Isabel said. "I can totally understand why Meryl is so drawn back to him."

Kat reached for some popcorn. "I can't get over how absolutely stunning Meryl Streep is in this movie. She must have been sixty or close to it when this first came out—and it's been two or three years, I think."

Lolly read the back of the DVD case. "*It's Complicated* came out in 2009, and Meryl was born in 1949—so you're right, she was sixty. She has great bones and a great face. She radiates joy."

"This is exactly how I was hoping this movie would end," June said as Meryl realized what she wanted. She loved the movie so much she could watch it again right now.

"You know what line really stuck with me?" Isabel said. "Remember when Alec Baldwin is trying to convince Meryl to give them a shot, and she's explaining why they shouldn't and says something like 'We both grew into the people we wanted to be.' I love that. Maybe you really can't go back after that."

"I think that's probably true," Lolly said quietly, her voice almost breaking.

June glanced over at her aunt. Was she thinking of Harrison? The man she'd told June about? But a moment later, Lolly put a smile on her face and said, "I loved when Rita Wilson or Mary Kay Place—one of Meryl's friends—tells her, 'Don't let him talk you into saving him.' I think that might be the most important line of the whole movie." Her smile faded and she glanced out the window. Just what had happened between Lolly and this man?

"I think so too," Pearl said, nodding. If Pearl knew about Lolly and Harrison, nothing in her expression or the way she looked at Lolly gave it away.

"You know what stuck with me?" Kat said. "When Meryl was telling Steve Martin that she'd gone to Paris in her early twenties for a six-day pastry class and ended up staying for a year as a baker's apprentice. I would love to do something like that." She seemed to notice her mother eyeing her and went quiet.

"Maybe you can find a class to take during your honeymoon," June said, "Unless that would be weird—since it's your honeymoon."

Kat poked at the wrapper of her cupcake. "I'll actually talk to Oliver about that."

A short honk sounded outside—Pearl's husband in his white Subaru. Pearl stood. "I loved that scene in Meryl's bakery when she and Steve Martin are making chocolate croissants. You ever do that with Oliver, Kat?" she asked as she tied her crocheted sweater around her neck and headed toward the door.

Kat laughed. "Well, no, but I had the most amazing morning last week with Matteo and his father—he owns the

Italian Bakery. Alonzo taught me how to make cannoli." She smiled, lost in memory for a moment. "It's not like I hung croissant cutouts as pasties like Meryl did, though. God, I love her. That looked totally unrehearsed, like they really were having fun as actors."

Lolly was staring at Kat. "Kat, is there something between you and Dr. Viola?"

"No," Kat said, her face flushed. "Of course not." But she was looking down at her feet and then suddenly collecting glasses and dirty plates.

"One of my favorite parts of the movie was when Meryl explains to Alec Baldwin that she knew the divorce wasn't all his fault," Isabel said quickly, as though she sensed Kat needed someone to change the subject. Now. "That she thinks she gave up on them too. I thought I was trying to save me and Edward, but I think in here"—she touched her heart—"I gave up. I wanted something he refused to give me. Which was complicated in itself, I guess."

June nodded. "It is all complicated. And I love how the movie really shows you why. Alec Baldwin ends up disappointing her again—for complicated reasons. What amazed me most about the movie, though, was how incredibly close the family was. Sibings saying 'Yeah!' over the sight of one another, hugging and cheering. They're always so thrilled to be together."

"I kinda think we're like that now," Kat said. "I have that yeah feeling whenever I see you two. And I see you two a lot."

Isabel and June laughed.

"To family," Lolly said, raising her glass of iced tea, but her gaze was on her daughter. June noticed that Kat wouldn't look at her mother. *Was* Kat seeing Dr. Viola—Matteo? They all raised and clinked.

Kat looked so miserable, like she wanted to flee, so June got up and began picking up popcorn from under her feet.

"Why can't I ever eat popcorn without it ending up down my shirt and on the floor?"

"I can feel a piece of popcorn in my bra," Isabel said, digging it out.

Lolly smiled. "Didn't you all love that scene when Alec Baldwin is staying over with Meryl and their kids and says they'll have movie night like old times, that he'll make the popcorn?"

Then there was reminiscing about how many movies they'd watched already, June sure it was seven, but Kat, who looked grateful for the complete change in subject, thought it might be eight and did a count. *The Bridges of Madison County. The Devil Wears Prada. Mamma Mia! Heartburn. Defending Your Life. Kramer vs. Kramer. Postcards from the Edge.* And now, *It's Complicated.*

"Eight Meryl Streep movies in just a few weeks," Isabel said. "I'll never get tired of looking at her face, watching her extraordinary talent. Her range is incredible. From the most serious dramas to more lighthearted comedy."

June nodded. "And the comedies still manage to really make you think, probably because she's so good. I think what I loved most about *It's Complicated* is that Meryl got a second chance to see. That any what-ifs she might have had got answered." June would never get that chance. The dream she'd been holding on to, hiding behind, perhaps, all these years, was gone.

"Sometimes, you shouldn't even ask what-if," Kat said, her tone serious, her gaze on her ring.

"No," Lolly whispered, her voice cracking.

"What do you mean?" Kat asked.

"What-ifs can kill you either way," Lolly said. "I know because . . . I—" She looked at Kat, then turned away. "I had an affair once. And lately, I guess because of the cancer, the what-ifs have been coming fast and furious." She took a deep breath and sat down heavily, her eyes on the floor.

"An affair?" Kat repeated, her expression incredulous. "When you were with Dad?"

Lolly didn't look up. She nodded.

Kat glanced at Isabel and June, then sat down next to Lolly. "What happened?"

"It started as just an emotional affair—as they call it now," Lolly said. "An affair of the heart. He was a guest at the inn. He came alone to get over a relationship that had ended, and we just got to talking and . . ."

"What was so special about him?" Kat asked, her voice emotional, but not angry.

Lolly seemed lost in her memories for a moment. "I felt like a different woman around him, like the person I'd always wished I was—smarter, funnier, prettier, sexier, more interesting. I'm not totally sure what about him brought that out in me. Maybe the way he listened so intently to me, the way he looked at me as though he couldn't take his eyes off me. He came back every weekend, staying in a different inn, of course. And over the summer, the affair blossomed. We even talked about my leaving your father, Kat. All that fall, and the long, cold December that followed, I thought about it."

"You almost left Dad," Kat whispered. "I can't believe it."

"And then the accident happened," Lolly said. "It was my fault."

Kat gasped. June and Isabel stared at each other.

"Your fault?" Kat asked. "How could it be your fault?"

"That night, that New Year's Eve, when my sister called to ask for one of us to pick up her and Gabriel, I woke up your father and asked him to go." Lolly's voice broke and she let out a terrible, guttural sound that felt wrenched from somewhere deep inside her. "I asked him to go because I'd get to spend fifteen minutes of New Year's with Harrison—

by telephone." Her hands flew to her face and she sobbed.

June reached for Isabel's hand. Kat stared at her mother in shock.

"I had an affair, was thinking of leaving. And because of that, I lost my husband, my child's father, and my sister and her husband. My two young nieces were left orphaned." Lolly took a deep breath and didn't say anything for a moment, then looked at Kat. "I asked your father to go. So I could talk to my lover in private. If *I'd* gone, I might have taken a different route, might have swerved—everything might have been different."

"Aunt Lolly, you can't do that to yourself," June said. "You can't play what-ifs with history. It was a terrible accident. An *accident.*"

"Did you love my father?" Kat whispered.

"I loved him more than I ever knew," Lolly said. "When he died, I was devastated. I realized just how much I did love him. How I'd kept him at arm's length because I was so damned scared of losing him. And then I did anyway."

"Oh, Aunt Lolly," Isabel said.

June sat, stunned, tears rolling down her cheeks. She'd pushed Henry away in much the same way.

"Like maybe I'm doing with Oliver," Kat said.

Lolly held Kat's gaze. "All I know is that telling the truth here is very important. More important than the consequences themselves."

June knew what Lolly meant. That the truth had to be told, even if it broke someone's heart. Even her daughter's. Because in the end, the truth might end up saving her daughter's happiness.

"I was scared to death about being a good mother to you two," Lolly said to June and Isabel. "And I was brokenhearted for Kat." She finally looked at her daughter. "You were so close to your dad. And I was so ashamed of everything that

I sent Harrison away." Lolly stared down at the floor. "I told him I never wanted to see him again. And I never did. He was a great man, though. At the time, I thought he was everything I'd ever dreamed of."

"What do you think now?" Kat asked.

"I think I did a terrible thing that night."

Kat looked so pale and her hands were trembling. "You know what, Mom?" she said, and June's heart started pounding. If Kat said something cruel, June didn't think she could bear it. "I think if I were in that same position that night, if I had Oliver next to me and Matteo a phone call away on New Year's Eve, I probably would have done the same thing you did. Because you can't know. You can't know what's ahead. What will happen. You just have to do what you think is right at the time. Or what feels right."

Lolly grabbed Kat and held her, and they stood, their arms wrapped tight around each other. "I did love your father, deeply. I didn't realize how much I loved him until he was irrevocably gone. But I'd been lucky to know Harrison. I was in love with him. And I've never forgotten him. Never stopped wondering." She glanced around the room. "Living with regrets is the worst. I just wanted to tell you that, but I didn't know how without telling you how I know."

"You've been through so much, Aunt Lolly," June said, her heart squeezing for her aunt. Losing her parents when she was barely twenty to a car accident. A husband—and a sister—gone to a drunk driver. A great love sent away. Cancer. "So much sorrow."

Lolly's eyes filled with tears. "I wanted to tell you all before. But when I saw firsthand what Edward's affair did to Isabel, how could I talk about an affair of my own?"

Isabel moved over beside Lolly too and took her hand. "Kat is right, Lolly. People do the best they can at the time. Maybe something that's wrong, or that's supposed to be wrong, feels right at the time. It's how I made sense of what Edward did to me."

"But what Edward did *was* wrong," Lolly said. "What I did was wrong."

"But giving up the man you loved was wrong," Isabel said. "I remember not thinking so when we watched *The Bridges of Madison County*. I thought Meryl Streep did the right thing by giving up Clint Eastwood, even if she broke her own heart. I still do. Because it was the right thing for her, really. But, Lolly, you were free to love Harrison and you punished yourself instead."

"I think people do punish themselves—maybe unknowingly—in the guise of 'doing the right thing,'" Kat said. "Sometimes the wrong thing can be right. If I'm making any sense."

Lolly looked at her daughter and nodded. "You are. But—you're okay with knowing all this, Kat? You don't hate me?"

June could see the hope behind the usual guarded expression in Lolly's eyes, in her entire face.

"I could never hate you, Mom. Never. I just want you to be happy."

Lolly and Kat hugged again, then Lolly put the DVD of *It's Complicated* back into its case. She rested her arm on top of the TV as though she needed the support, then put her hand to her forehead. She swayed for a moment, bracing her arm against the TV.

"Mom? Are you okay?" Kat asked.

"I feel so funny," Lolly said. "In my head and—"

Lolly slumped over and fell to the floor.

CHAPTER 18

Kat

Kat decided that something in the stars or maybe something shimmering on the bay had made Matteo call to check in about Lolly, about Kat, just when she needed him, when the fear that had gripped her the past few days had subsided with Lolly's recovery from the infection that had done a number on her. Lolly had been in the hospital since Friday night, and all Kat could think about was her mother. Now she craved Matteo—his knowledge, his personal experience of having gone through this with his father. The sound of his voice, despite its lack of an Italian accent like his father's, still took her away, far, far away, even for just a few moments.

He'd come by to check on Lolly quite a few times in the hospital, once when Oliver was there, which made for a tense moment that even Lolly had picked up on. Matteo had called Kat each day to check in, to let her know her mother was fighting the infection—common to the weakened immune systems of chemotherapy patients—and that she'd make it through this. Those calls had kept Kat standing up.

On Monday, when Lolly was discharged and came home, Isabel, June, and Kat settled Lolly in her hospital bed in her room, the trusty day nurse they'd hired at the ready. Then they spent some time in the kitchen with a pot of strong coffee, making schedules of "Lolly care" so that she'd have one of them at her beck and call round the clock. The day nurse would be available to Lolly from nine to five, Monday through Friday, and Kat and her cousins would take the night shifts and early mornings.

When Kat went to check on her mother, the nurse was reading to her from a biography of Margaret Thatcher. The Iron Lady. Kat used to think of her mother that way. Iron. Not a soft bone in her body. Kat had been wrong, of course. Her even-keeled, impassive mother had been deeply in love with a man named Harrison. And had given him up. Maybe she *was* the iron lady.

Kat was so confused about the revelation. Her mother had had an affair. But she'd had her great love and she'd given him up—because of guilt or shame or just recrimination. Or had Lolly realized that her husband had been her great love and that was why she'd sent Harrison away? What was Kat supposed to take from this? To find out if her feelings for Matteo did mean she shouldn't marry Oliver? To give them a chance? Is that why her mother had told her about the affair in the first place? Kat thought so, but as her mother had been fighting the infection, she'd been so weak and tired that Kat had been afraid to bring up the past. Or the present. Or future. When she had finally asked her mother about Harrison that morning, Lolly had waved her off with an "I'm so tired, Kat," code-speak for *I don't want to talk about it.* Because it was too painful? Because Lolly was afraid Kat would read something into it? Why couldn't Lolly just say what was on her mind? And why couldn't Kat just come out and ask?

Her cell phone buzzed. A text from Matteo. *Lunch today?*

She excused herself and called him. They spoke for just a few minutes—about Lolly and the new nurse. How Lolly was feeling. About the next round of chemotherapy and the potential for the infection to reoccur.

Yes. *Lunch today* sounded just like what the doctor ordered. Especially at his house, where they could talk more freely. Where he could comfort her, if need be, without anyone getting the wrong idea. Or wrong-ish idea. Where she could . . . examine how she felt about him.

On the way over to his house, Isabel's words from the discussion of *It's Complicated* were tumbling over and over in Kat's mind, about the way people went with what they needed at a particular time, sometimes throwing the ole caution to the wind. Sometimes it was right and sometimes it was wrong. Sometimes for the right reasons; sometimes for the wrong.

But it didn't make Kat feel less guilty that it was Matteo she was drawn to. It wasn't Oliver's fault that he couldn't discuss white blood cell counts and neutropenia. It wasn't Oliver's fault that the very sight of him reminded her of The Wedding, of the dress awaiting a fitting. Of the shoes Lolly was clipping out of bridal magazines with Charlie's child-friendly plastic scissors because the regular scissors had gotten too heavy for her fingers. And it wasn't Oliver's fault that Kat wanted to run away and that Matteo made her picture herself rolling out cannoli in the kitchen of an Italian *pasticceria.*

She and Oliver hadn't spent a lot of time together the past week. Two nights ago, when Lolly was still in the hospital and Kat had been bone-tired and mind-numb, he'd told her light stories over the phone that had managed to make her laugh. About a client, a wealthy man with a multimillion-dollar property, who wanted to hire a landscape architect to design and create a walled children's garden in his backyard, complete with topiaries in the shapes of famed storybook characters, such as Winnie-the-Pooh and Alice. He'd told her about his brother's girlfriend, who kept forwarding him links he instantly deleted, to wedding gowns and photographs of lavish backyard weddings, even though he'd told her Kat had found her dress and that they were planning a simple outdoor wedding. Talk of the wedding had Kat hurrying off the phone.

As she neared Matteo's house, she made a promise to herself. No matter what, she wouldn't cheat on Oliver. There was no right-wrong there. Just wrong. If she needed to make a decision about Oliver, about their future, she could do that with her heart, mind, and soul. She didn't need lust to factor in and foolishly tip the scales.

A teenaged boy was mowing the bit of lawn when she arrived at Matteo's house. She walked up the short stone path and knocked on the door. And then there he was, filling the doorway with that gorgeous olive complexion and those intense black eyes, with that smile, which held so much: kindness, possibilities . . . *different.* She was staring at his lips, she realized, and quickly glanced away at the living room behind him.

The house Matteo was renting was very different from Oliver's. Where Oliver's cottage looked like Maine with its soft-blue couches and whitewashed furniture, Matteo's was high-tech and leather, except for a painting of a weathered canoe.

"It came furnished," he said as he closed the door behind her. "But I like it."

"I suddenly feel like I shouldn't be here. Like something is starting between us and . . ." She trailed off, feeling stupid. For all she knew, he didn't have romantic feelings for her. Sexual feelings, even.

He sat down on the black leather sofa and gestured for her to sit beside him. On the glass coffee table were two bottles of Shipyard beer, two BLTs, a bowl of tossed salad, and another of cut fruit. Matteo took a couple of blueberries and popped them into his mouth, mesmerizing her again. "So maybe that means you *should* be here, Kat. I believe in being honest—with others and perhaps even more importantly, with yourself. If you're having some second thoughts about getting married because you have feelings for me, I think you should consider how you feel. Not run from it."

"I guess I'm just not sure how I feel. Exactly," she said, staring at the BLTs, at the romaine lettuce and edge of red tomato.

"So you don't know if you want to get married? Or you do want to marry this guy and I've just thrown a monkey wrench into the works."

"I felt this way before I ever laid eyes on you. And then when we did meet, when you held my hand in the hospital that first day . . ."

"I complicated things."

She nodded and picked up a strawberry. He fixed her a plate and handed it to her. She took a bite of the BLT, but couldn't eat. "I've known Oliver since I was five years old." She put the plate on the coffee table. "Once, I was so in love with him that I couldn't breathe around him."

"And now?"

"And now I know that I love him. I know he loves me. I know I'll have a happy life with Oliver, that he'll be a great father. That's why I'm so confused. How could I love him and not be sure about marrying him?"

"Maybe you're not ready to get married, Kat. You're only twenty-five."

"Maybe. Maybe I'm meant to go to France. Or Australia. Or Japan. Or maybe that's running away. Maybe I'm supposed to be right here, helping with the inn." She threw up her hands and leaned back against the leather.

"Maybe you should move to New York City and work as a pastry chef in a top restaurant or bakery," he said. "And then we can explore what's between us."

She turned to face him. "You're moving to New York?"

"I've accepted a fellowship at Mount Sinai Hospital. And you know what I keep thinking about? Not seeing you every day. Not running into you around town or on the footbridge or around the bend in the hospital. I hate what-might-have-beens, Kat."

What-might-have-beens. She thought of her mother, tears streaming down Lolly's face, as she told her what-might-have-been good-bye.

"All I can say, Kat, is that I'd like the chance to get to know you."

"When are you leaving?"

"Mid-November. I can move into my new apartment on the Upper West Side on the fourteenth. It's a studio and pretty small, but it's on the twenty-third floor, and I have a slight view of Central Park."

Her wedding was the fifteenth. She would say good-bye to Matteo on the fourteenth, watch him drive off to New York City, and then marry Oliver the next day.

She wasn't sure she could do any of it.

He reached his hand over and moved a tendril of her hair away from her face. His hand lingered on her cheek, her chin. Then he moved closer to kiss her, but Kat put her hand between them.

"I can't."

"Can't right now. But perhaps you will in the near future. Or maybe not."

"Was that a test?"

He shook his head. "It was completely impulsive. I've been wanting to kiss you for a long time, Kat. But just then, it was overpowering."

"I want to, but I can't," she said, getting up. "Thank you for this lunch. But I have to go, Matteo."

She was out the door in seconds and ran until she couldn't breathe.

• • •

Kat went straight for the kitchen when she got back to the inn. A classic apple pie for her mother. Those big, crumbly chocolate-drop cookies that Charlie loved. A few hours of baking, *the do this, then that* comfort of following recipes, would surely set her straight again, clear her head. But she'd added too much sugar to the cookie batter. Then forgot if she'd added the vanilla or not.

Something niggled at her, wouldn't let her go. Not Oliver. Or Matteo.

Harrison. A man named Harrison who'd been sent away fifteen years ago for the wrong reasons.

Kat took off her apron and washed her sticky hands, then headed to her mother's bedroom before she could change her mind. Or think. She gently opened her mother's door and peered inside. Lolly was sleeping. *Perfect.* The day nurse was reading a *People* magazine and smiled at Kat; Kat smiled back and pointed at the bedside table to the photo album there, then quietly came in to take it.

Album in hand, Kat headed back into the kitchen and sat down at the desk, mentally crossing her fingers that she'd find what she was looking for. The album was her mother's most treasured, full of her favorite family photos throughout the years. Lolly liked to label the backs of photos. *Allie and Isabel, 1993: Izzy's ear piercing. Dad and Kat, 1995: Kat rides a two wheeler.*

Kat looked under the back of every photo, and finally, on the last page, hidden behind a photo of Lolly standing in front of a tree in her navy blue down coat, snow falling in her hair (*Me, December 1996: first snow*), her expression full of wonder and joy and secrets, Kat found what she was looking for.

Harrison Ferry, September 1997: Pier 10.

Harrison Ferry.

You have to do what feels right to you because all you have to go on is self-trust. Kat went upstairs to her bedroom and awakened her laptop. Harrison Ferry was easy to find. One simple Google search and there he was, a distinguished professor of astronomy at Bowdoin College in Brunswick. He was forty-five minutes away. She easily found his e-mail address at the college, hit COMPOSE MESSAGE, and typed *Lolly Weller* into the subject box.

> *Dear Mr. Ferry,*
>   *You knew my mother, Lolly Weller, some fifteen years ago. My mother is dying of cancer. She recently told me that she'd once loved and lost a man, a love she deeply regretting giving up, for very complicated reasons. I don't know how much longer she has, but I do know that some things don't have to be complicated. I think it would ease my mother's heart to see you once again, to hold your hand or simply to look into your eyes and tell you of her regrets. I think it would mean a lot to her.*
>   *Please forgive me for intruding, Mr. Ferry. I will understand if you can't respond.*
>   *Sincerely, Kat Weller*

With tears in her eyes, Kat hit SEND, unsure if she'd hear back. But absolutely sure it was the right thing to do to ask.

Sometimes, asking was all you could do.

"Kat, I'm going to throw your phone out the window," Oliver said, glaring at her.

She stood in his kitchen, where she'd gone to get spicy mustard for their hot pastrami sandwiches, her iPhone in hand as it had been for the past four days. It was Friday night, but Lolly was feeling so sick that they'd postponed Movie Night indefinitely, until she was up for it.

Kat was waiting for an answer from Harrison Ferry. And checking her e-mail a bit obsessively.

"Maybe he's passed on," June had said yesterday when Kat mentioned he still hadn't responded. "It's going around, unfortunately."

"Always has been," Isabel added in a whisper.

The brief conversation, in the moments after Kat had turned off the light and they'd all pulled up their quilts, had left Kat heavyhearted. Something would have come up about his death when she'd researched him online. And there was no indication of that.

"I'm just waiting to hear back from someone," Kat said, slipping the phone into her pocket and grabbing the mustard.

He crossed his arms over his chest. "From who? *Matteo?*"

"Oliver."

"Well?"

"No. Not him. I—"

She didn't want to tell him. She hadn't told him about any of it. Lolly's confession about the affair and the aftermath. She wasn't sure why, exactly. Maybe because it would put ideas in his head about ideas in *her* head. About Matteo.

"You check your phone *all* the time, Kat."

"Oliver, let's just eat before the pastrami gets cold."

"It'll be fine cold. I'd rather talk right now."

She lost her appetite. "I wouldn't. Please, just let it go."

"No, Kat. I want to know who you're waiting to hear from."

"It has to do with Lolly, and that's all I want to say about it, okay?"

"What about Lolly?"

"I just said I didn't want to talk about it."

"So now there are secrets between us, Kat?"

"Oliver, come on. You're being . . ."

"Being what? Ridiculous? Overbearing?"

"Yeah."

"Who are you waiting to hear from?"

Leave me alone! she wanted to scream at him, but then she realized it wasn't really a name he wanted so much as her absolute trust. He wanted to know she loved him above all else. Above complications and secrets. He wanted to be Her Person. And she hadn't let him be that lately.

Because her cousins were. Isabel and June had become Her Person. Whom she turned to when everything fell apart. Whom she shared everything with. Whom she needed now like air.

Oliver, I'm sorry, but I just don't want to tell you.

But she would give him something, to get through dinner. "I e-mailed an old friend of Lolly's. Someone she knew before the accident. I let him know she was . . . very sick and that if he wanted to stop over for a visit, I thought she'd like that."

He stared at her. "And you couldn't just tell me this because?" He stepped closer, putting his arms around her neck.

She shrugged. "I'm crazy lately, Oliver. That's all I can say."

They sat down to pastrami and sour pickles, which Kat had thought would cheer her up some. But the pickle just sat sour in her throat. She couldn't let herself obsess over this. She wasn't going to let hearing from this man—this man she wasn't even sure she wanted to meet—become the most important thing in her life at the moment.

But he was. Because Lolly's heart depended on it.

CHAPTER 19

Isabel

Isabel wheeled the wagon full of pink, white, and red peonies in their plastic pots from the little greenhouse business down the road, imagining the colorful big bursts lining the white porch. Lolly loved peonies, loved coming out to the porch swing with her morning tea, when she was up to it, and just sitting among her flowers. Many mornings, the two of them did just that, arm wrapped around arm, Isabel filling her aunt in on what was happening at the inn, the guests, the orders, funny stories from the breakfast room. These past few days that Lolly had been back from the hospital, she'd barely gotten outside, but that morning, she'd come out with Isabel and told her she was so proud of the job Isabel was doing at the inn, that it was as if she were meant to be back here, running the Three Captains'. When Isabel had said that she felt that way too, her aunt's eyes filled with tears and they hugged with an emotion that had never before been there. Then Lolly started talking about peonies, how she'd love it if Isabel would plant some, with such wistfulness—a memory?—that Isabel had called the greenhouse the moment she'd gone back inside. Anything that made her aunt smile, done.

Isabel pulled the wagon along the sidewalk, pushing escaping tendrils of her hair back into her ponytail, and breathed in the make-you-stop-and-smell-the-roses fresh air, the lingering scent of cut grass, the breeze carrying the scent of flowers, the bay. As she approached the Three Captains' Inn, she could see a man in sunglasses sitting on the porch swing. Had she forgotten a guest was checking in today? Kat was handling the inn that morning, and it was still early for check-in, but perhaps she'd—

He stood up and walked over to the steps. Oh, God, it was Edward.

"Wow," he said, taking off his dark sunglasses. "You look beautiful. Tan and relaxed. It's good to see you." He was studying her, she saw. Taking in the ponytail. The wagon she held on to. Her embroidered cotton shirt and faded jeans, the red, flat Mary Janes. Nothing the old Isabel would have worn.

Edward. For a moment, she had a rush of memories. Of being sixteen. Of being able to look at his face, into his eyes, as dark as chocolate bark, for hours, sometimes without saying a word. They'd sit on this porch, on the swing or against the white wooden rails, holding hands, united in a way that had made her feel so safe and protected. She'd always been so afraid to remember that girl, afraid to conjure her up inside herself, but now Isabel had compassion for who she once was.

"Why are you here?" No anger was in her voice, she realized.

"Why didn't you tell me about Lolly? I had no idea she was so sick."

She walked up the porch steps and sat down on the swing. He leaned against the railing, his head so close to a hanging pot of African violets that a purple petal looked as if it were growing from his ear. "How did you hear?"

"It's a small world up here. My brother heard from someone and called me. I'm sorry, Izzy."

"You drove all the way up here to say you're sorry?" Isabel

leaned down to straighten the Boothbay-region brochures on the wicker table next to the swing. It was hard to look at him, this man she'd loved for so long, who'd changed her life. More than once.

"Yes, of course I did. Lolly means a lot to me, you know that."

"She's very frail these days, Edward, and I don't think she'll be up to a visit, but I will tell her you came."

He nodded and turned to look down at the harbor. "I'm thinking about marrying Carolyn. I want you to know that—that it really wasn't just some sordid affair."

"Is that supposed to—" Oh, what did it matter anymore? There was nothing to argue about here. They were as through as through could be.

"I also want you to know that I can understand how it must seem—that I fell in love with a woman who has a child. My therapist told me it must feel like a double betrayal to you. But it's not like I planned to be involved in her daughter's life—that was separate. Or supposed to be."

Isabel mentally shook her head, resisting the I-knew-it-made-no-sense smile. "Ah, so Carolyn realized that you had no intention of playing stepdaddy and she ended things. Said she was a package deal." *And good for her.* "Is that right?" No wonder he was suddenly in the mood for a six-hour drive; his life was falling apart.

He nodded and stared down at the floor.

"Well, Edward, I guess this is how you'll really know, then. If you really do love her. Because if you do, you won't walk away."

Like you did to me.

The unsaid words hung in the air between them for a moment; she'd known this man long enough to tell that he'd heard her say them in her head.

"I also wanted you to know I'm sorry for everything, Iz.

You were my best friend for a very long time, and it's been . . . hard adjusting to life without you, even if I'm with someone else. That probably sounds ridiculous."

"I know what you mean. It was very hard for me, at first, being separated from you, being separate. But I've learned some important things about myself. Very good things. I like the life I have up here now. Very much so."

"I'm glad, then. That— Well, you know what I mean. I'm just glad that you're happy."

I am happy, she realized. A beautiful breeze ruffled through her hair, and for a second she lifted her chin into it.

He sat down next to her, his hands on his thighs. His hands were as bare as hers, wedding-ring-free. "I know you signed the divorce papers that my lawyer sent. So in a couple of months, that'll be it." He glanced over at her. "Fifteen years. With the divorce settlement, you'll be able to finally build that screened-in back porch Lolly always used to talk about. And then some."

"If I had a glass, I would toast you to the future, Edward." Huh. Back in August she would have smashed it over his head.

He glanced at her. "Being up here has really agreed with you, Iz. Zen Isabel was not exactly what I was expecting."

She wanted to tell him what he could do with his approval. But she just politely smiled.

He stood up and walked over to the railing, looking out at the harbor again. "I miss this view. I forgot how much it does for the soul." He turned around, his hands in his pockets. "I'll put the house on the market. You can have what you want."

"I'll drive down with June on her day off next week. There are some pieces I'd love for the inn. You can set up an estate sale for what you don't want."

He nodded. "I always liked this place. Even though you

hated it for a while there." He started down the porch steps. At his car, he turned toward her, then looked up at the inn, at the pretty second-floor deck and the sign proclaiming it THE THREE CAPTAINS' INN with the etching of the three seafarers. "I'm glad you're back here."

I am too. "I wish you well, Edward." She meant it.

He slid his sunglasses on and got behind the wheel of the black Mercedes. As he drove away, she realized she never did find out who had sent the anonymous note.

A friend she hadn't known she had.

Two days after her past came and left in the form of her soon-to-be-ex-husband, Isabel found herself in the inn's kitchen with Alexa Dean, teaching the girl how to make crepes. Alexa had gotten into a fight with another girl in her Family and Consumer Science cooking elective at her high school. Apparently, the classmate had told Alexa that Alexa's French toast looked as "gross as you are," resulting in Alexa's throwing a handful of sugar at the girl. More wet and dry ingredients had been thrown, and both girls had been suspended for a day and had to make up the lesson by making French toast, pancakes, or crepes for the entire class and serving them. Alexa was also sentenced to six thirty-minute sessions after school with the guidance counselor on how to make better choices and deal with anger. Since Alexa's French toast had been "totally gross" (per Alexa), she'd asked Isabel to teach her how to make those amazing crepes she'd had when the Deans had stayed at the Three Captains'.

Kat had taught Isabel well; both sets of guests that morning had requested seconds of Isabel's crepes—one with whipped cream and strawberry sauce; the other chocolate-filled—if it was no trouble. It had been no trouble at all. Isabel loved making fancy and down-home breakfasts to order and preparing pots of tea and coffee. Isabel a doter. Who'd have thought?

"So guess what I did today," Alexa said, mixing the flour, eggs, and milk in a silver bowl. They stood at the table in the center of the kitchen, Norah Jones on the radio, Happy chasing after sticks that Charlie was throwing in the backyard. Isabel loved the sight of Alexa in her kitchen, the teen in jeans and three layered long-sleeved T-shirts, a tangle of long necklaces, her burnished brown hair, almost the same color as her father's, falling down her back.

"Aced a test?" Isabel said.

"Well, I did get a B-plus on my essay on *A Tree Grows in Brooklyn.*" Alexa pointed in the bowl. "Is this mixed enough?"

Isabel glanced into the bowl. "Perfect. And that's great about your essay." They followed the steps for the remaining ingredients, then got the pan ready. "I loved that book."

Alexa poured some batter into the butter-coated pan. "Remember how I told you I joined the School Cares committee? It's this group of students that gets assigned to help other kids with stuff. There's this girl, Micheline—isn't that the coolest name?—and her parents just told her, like yesterday, that they're splitting up and separating for a while. So after my 'mad-management' session, the guidance counselor asked if I'd be Micheline's mentor. Isn't that cool? We met during lunch today and got to sit outside on a private bench. We talked for almost an hour. I think I made her feel better."

Isabel explained how to flip the crepe so it wouldn't burn, then pulled Alexa into a quick hug. "That is fantastic of you. I'll bet you made a real difference in that girl's day—in her *life.*"

Alexa beamed. In a few minutes, they had a dozen crepes ready for drizzling and filling. Alexa pointed at Isabel's apron. "I just got half my mess on you. You even have batter on the ends of your hair now."

"That's how cooking should be. Messy."

Alexa smiled, a beautiful sight. It might take a while, but Isabel thought the girl would be just fine. "You were right about it feeling good to help people who are going through something you went through, something you're still going through. And besides it actually feeling good, I liked being the smart one. Do you know what I mean?"

"I know exactly what you mean."

Despite what had happened to her and Edward, he'd helped her when she desperately needed help, at a time that she'd turned away, not toward, her family. For that, she'd always be grateful to him. She was glad she'd always have those memories to counter the bad when she thought of him.

For the next hour, Isabel and Alexa talked about everything from *A Tree Grows in Brooklyn* to why boys pulled bra straps and laughed. They ate their crepes—strawberry, chocolate, and apricot—and drank iced tea, and Isabel could have spent another hour with Alexa when she heard Kat saying, "Right through there," and a woman came through the swinging doors into the kitchen.

"Hi, Mom," Alexa said. "I'm gonna go say bye to Happy. Back in a sec."

As Alexa went out the back door and ran over to Happy, Charlie gave her his stick to throw. She and Alexa's mother watched Happy go racing after the stick, Alexa's laughter coming through the windows on the sweet breeze.

"It's so nice to finally meet you," Isabel said. She introduced herself and shook hands with Alexa's mother, an attractive brunette named Valerie.

Griffin's ex-wife.

"I owe you a big thank-you," Valerie said. "Alexa's told me a lot about you, the things you talk about. You've really helped get through to her."

Isabel smiled. "I was a lot like her. She's going to be fine."

"Well, thank you. Very much."

Alexa came back in and scooped up the box of extra crepes she'd made. They said their good-byes, Isabel's heart as full as her stomach.

On Wednesday night, Isabel and Griffin had his house to themselves. She loved his house, a one-story stone cottage with nooks and crannies and a plaque declaring it built in the 1830s. She loved the sturdy square rooms with built-in bookcases and the stone fireplace in the living room that took up an entire wall. She loved Emmy's tidy room, her collection of ZhuZhu pets and a WordGirl coloring book and a box of Crayolas on the pink-and-purple, round, braided rug by her bed. She even loved Alexa's messy room, the tangle of sweaters on her bed. A jumble of cosmetics on her pretty, white iron dressing table, a photograph of Griffin, Alexa, and Emmy tucked inside the edging of the big round mirror.

Isabel loved being there, in this house, with this man. Just months ago, she'd felt as if she belonged nowhere. Now she had the Three Captains', which was home. She had her family, who felt like home. And something magical was happening between her and Griffin.

They made dinner together, pasta with peas and pancetta in pink cream sauce, and Griffin had bought a loaf of incredible bread from the Italian Bakery. There was wine. And talking. Lots of talking.

But there was mostly romance.

After dinner, they sat outside on the stone steps of his house and looked at the bay. From this side of the harbor she could almost see the Three Captains' Inn up on its hill.

"Sometimes I'd sit out here and look for the weather vane," Griffin said, his thigh against hers. "It made me feel connected to you to see it."

She was too happy to speak, so she smiled at him and took his hand and held it on her thigh.

He kissed her then, a kiss that was as sweet as it was hot, and she wrapped her arms around him and kissed him back with everything inside her. He took her hand and led her through the living room and down the hall.

His bedroom. She could remember cleaning his room at the inn, taking off his sheets, smelling his pillowcase, and wondering what it would feel like to be under him. On top of him.

Within minutes, she knew. And it was everything she'd fantasized.

The next day, as Isabel sat at a child's table in the game room of the children's wing of Coastal General Hospital, playing Chutes and Ladders with a four-year-old patient, her weary mother having gone to the cafeteria to get some coffee, all Isabel could think about was that someday she would have her own child. Whether a biological child or an adopted child or a stepchild. She would have her own child to love, to mother.

And she'd be a good mother. She had no doubt about that. And not because her supervising nurse had said so not once but twice over the past couple weeks. Or because Griffin had said so when they'd finally taken that walk—a few walks now—the night after she'd broken through with Alexa.

She knew it because she *loved*. Because she'd held a bedside vigil in her aunt's hospital room the night Lolly had been admitted with the life-threatening infection coursing through her weakened body. Because she'd held Kat, who'd been scared out of her mind, Isabel's heart breaking for her dear, sweet cousin. Because she'd comforted her sister. Kept her arm around Pearl. She loved these people. She *loved*.

That was what you needed to do to be a mother, above all else, Isabel knew. You needed to love. Everything else came from that.

On her way out after her shift, Isabel stopped in front of the nursery window to marvel at the tiny faces peeking out from under their white caps and striped blankets. Just two months ago, she'd stood here in tears, unsure of who she was.

She smiled at Baby Girl Putter. *You decide who you are,* she said to her sweet face as the infant slept. *Never let anyone tell you who you are.*

That night, Isabel peeked in on Lolly, who lay fast asleep in bed even though it was barely seven thirty. Between the infection and the second round of chemo, which she'd finally been cleared for, Lolly was so tired that it was getting more and more difficult for her to get around. She had a walker and enjoyed sitting at the picture window of her bedroom, which faced the backyard. She loved watching Charlie and Happy play fetch. Once, she'd burst into laughter when the stick had landed on the leaves that Kat had raked up and they'd gone flying up in a beautiful swirl of reds and yellows and oranges, Happy barking and Charlie twirling around with his hands up, the leaves raining down on him.

Kat lay on the chaise they'd brought in a few weeks ago, once they'd decided on round-the-clock care for Lolly. The day nurse and then either Isabel, Kat, or June at night. Kat lay propped up with her sketchpad and pencils. She was drawing a wedding cake. Her own? Kat wasn't talking much these days about Oliver or Matteo; all questions were met with "Do you want a cinnamon-chip scone?" So Isabel and June let Kat have her privacy. Whatever Kat chose to do, Isabel knew she'd make the decision for the right reason. And that was what mattered most.

Pearl popped her head in and said she was here to sit with Lolly for an hour, so Isabel and Kat gave her hugs and then headed into the parlor, where June was down on her knees, picking up crumbs and cheese from a guest's tumbled-over cheese-and-crackers plate. Isabel and Kat helped clean up, then sat in their favorite Movie Night spots, though they hadn't watched a movie in the parlor in weeks.

Isabel looked at the library of DVDs, the well-loved, often-used Meryl Streep collection taking up an entire shelf. "Lolly said this morning that she wants to watch *Out of Africa* this Friday." She got up and set it aside, then sat back down on the love seat.

Kat started to cry. "She's dying, I know it. That's her favorite Meryl Streep movie. It's sacred like *Sophie's Choice* to her. She only saw *Out of Africa* once and said it meant so much to her that she could never watch it again. So if she asked to see it, it means she knows . . ."

Isabel and June both got up and sat on the floor next to Kat's beanbag. "She's just going through a rough patch. You know Suzanne, two houses down? Her mother has breast cancer and also had the same infection as Lolly and came through. She went through three more rounds of chemo."

"But my mom is going to die," Kat whispered. "Maybe not next week or next month, even, but her doctors say I need to accept a three-month range."

Isabel closed her eyes. "God, how does anyone accept that?"

"We have to," June said, her eyes tearing up.

Isabel squeezed her sister's hand. "I can't even begin to imagine waking up here every morning without seeing Lolly walking through the halls, in the kitchen, out on the porch. She *is* this place."

Kat looked at Isabel. "*Will* you be waking up here every morning?"

"Yes. If you'll have me. There's nothing I want more than to live at the Three Captains' and run the inn. I love it. Everything about it. Isn't that amazing? The place I couldn't wait to get away from when I was eighteen, the place I came to twice a year on holidays, kicking and screaming, is now my sanctuary. I love dealing with the guests, making breakfasts, working with the inn associations. I even like cleaning."

"That means a lot," Kat said. "It means everything, actually. It means I can leave the Three Captains' without worrying or having to hire a manager. I don't think Lolly would like that—a stranger running the place. And no way would we ever sell the inn, right?"

"Well, that would be your decision," June said. "But I'd never want you to sell. I know I'm not much help around here, but I love the place too and will help out whenever I'm not at the bookstore."

"It would be *our* decision," Kat said. "Even if Lolly left the inn to only me, which I doubt she'd do, I wouldn't do anything without agreement from both of you. This place is ours."

Ours. Isabel liked the sound of that.

CHAPTER 20

June

"My great-aunt might be going to heaven soon," Charlie said to Eleanor and Steven Smith as he showed them Happy's doghouse on Monday afternoon. "So that's why Happy is allowed to sleep in the inn. Sometimes he likes to sleep with me, but sometimes I find him laying next to Lolly. And she doesn't even feed him treats."

"He must really like your great-aunt Lolly, then," Eleanor said, her green eyes full of compassion.

"Want to see Happy do tricks?" Charlie asked. "My aunt Isabel's friend is an animal doctor and taught him tons of stuff. Happy, give me your paw."

Happy did as commanded and received claps from Charlie's grandparents. After a few more tricks, they all headed inside to the parlor for refreshments, coffee and lemonade and the cakes Kat had baked for the occasion. The Smiths had stayed as complimentary guests in the Bluebird Room and had gotten the royal treatment. Isabel's Irish breakfast, which they were thrilled to see on the menu. Kat's scones. Charlie's happy chatter and affection. Maine guidebooks from Books Brothers from June. And a lovely welcome from Lolly, whom Kat had briefly wheeled into the yard. June, Charlie, and the Smiths had spent the day sightseeing around town, taking a lunch cruise around the bay, and walking around the beautiful Botanical Gardens. By seven, dusk had fallen, and after coffee, hugs, and a plan to visit again in a couple of weeks, they said good-bye to the Smiths.

With Isabel and Charlie playing Connect Four in the parlor, June went down the hall to Lolly's room, tapped on the door, and poked her head in. Lolly was in bed, looking at a photo album open on her lap, Happy at the end of the bed, a paw up on Lolly's leg. Pearl sat beside her in the upholstered chair, knitting. Every time June saw Lolly in the hospital bed, all June could think about was how small her aunt looked; she'd lost at least thirty pounds since the diagnosis. Lolly had also lost a lot of hair and had started tying pretty scarfs bandana-style around her head. June's heart pinged at the effort it took Lolly to shift a bit in bed. Her aunt had such little energy these days that they'd put off Movie Night last Friday. Maybe this Friday. June wanted Movie Night to go on forever, the four of them—five counting Pearl—sitting around the television, watching Meryl Streep transport them to another place, making them laugh, making them cry, making them think. And talk. June wanted to talk to her family forever.

She smoothed the quilt, pale yellow and dotted with faded-orange sea stars, which used to belong to her mother. "I just wanted to thank you for everything today, Aunt Lolly. You were wonderful to the Smiths."

"I can tell they're good people," Lolly said.

Pearl nodded. "Just lovely."

"You did good, June," Lolly said. "Finding them for Charlie. It wasn't only brave, but it was the right thing to do. Sometimes one thing is taken away but you get something else, something really wonderful."

"Like when I lost Mom and Dad and got you," June whispered. Lolly's eyes filled with tears, and June rested her head against her shoulder. "I love you, Lolly."

"I love you too," Lolly whispered, her eyes beginning to close.

June kissed her aunt on the cheek and blew one to Pearl. The moment she closed the door behind her, she burst into tears and quickly tried to collect herself.

Her aunt was dying.

She could hear Charlie's excited voice in the parlor. June dabbed under her eyes and took a deep breath, then headed in.

"You won again!" Isabel said as Charlie pointed out his four red game pieces in a row. "I can't beat you."

"You can try again tomorrow night," he said, beaming.

"Ready for bed, kiddo?" June asked.

After Charlie's "Aww, can't I stay up for at least thirty more minutes?" he hugged Isabel and then found Kat, who was sitting in the kitchen with Oliver and having some kind of serious conversation, for her good-night hug. Next was Lolly, who got a kiss on the cheek, and Pearl, who got a hug. Finally, a hug for Happy, who nuzzled Charlie's face.

"I really, really, really like my new grandparents," Charlie said to June as they headed up to his room. It was almost seven thirty. Time for a quick story and then lights-out on a wonderful and busy day for a little boy.

Charlie changed into his pajamas and brushed his teeth, then scooted under the covers. June sat beside him, reaching for *Charlotte's Web*, which she'd been reading to him the last few nights. Last night, the Smiths had read to him, each grandparent reading one chapter each. June had been so overcome at one point, at the sight of them sitting in chairs beside his bed, their expressions so full of joy, as though they'd been given the gift of their lives, that she'd had to step outside for a moment.

"Mommy, can you tell me a story instead? I want to hear the story about how you and Daddy met and why you liked each other."

"That's one of my favorites," she said, leaning down to kiss his head, soft with silky dark hair.

Sometimes one thing is taken away but you get something else, something really wonderful.

As June tiptoed out of Charlie's room and shut the door gently behind her, Lolly's words kept coming back to her.

She'd gotten many wonderful something-elses. She'd lost her parents and had gotten Lolly. She'd lost her great love and had gotten Charlie. She'd lost her job and home and had gotten the inn—and her family back. She'd lost her dream and gotten Charlie's grandparents.

She'd lost the fantasy she'd had for seven years and gotten the reality of Henry Books's love.

It was time to tell him how she felt. All she knew for sure was that, heart, mind, and soul, she was free. She had no words now, but when she saw him, she'd *know.*

June knew from running into Bean, the Books Brothers salesclerk, the other day that Henry had taken over June's job and kept the shop open until eight every night of the week. So she figured she'd find him either in the store or close by on his boat, where Bean could call him in if she needed him. Business always picked up with the after-dinner crowd, even now that the harbor crowd had thinned considerably since Labor Day weekend had come and gone weeks ago.

As she neared Books Brothers, she realized how much she'd missed the shop. It had always been the place that had given her security, safety. Now, as she pulled open the door with the little canoe-like handle, it was just pure comfort and joy that she felt.

The bell jangled over her head. The store was about to close, but still pretty busy.

Bean smiled at June and pointed toward the back. "You're just in time for the celebration."

"What are we celebrating?" she asked, but a woman came up to the checkout counter and took Bean's attention.

Henry wasn't in his office. She could feel the anticipation building inside her at just the thought of seeing him, of walking right up to him and kissing him. If he was celebrating a great day's sales, all the better. She went through the back door and the door to the pier, and there Henry was, but he wasn't alone.

He was embracing Vanessa. Her arms were wrapped around him, a diamond ring glinting on her finger.

June froze. No. No. No. She was too late and now he was back with Vanessa for good.

Her stomach dropped and her legs felt like rubber. She started backing away, but Vanessa, in a slinky black dress and shiny green Doc Martens, came walking toward her.

"He's all yours," Vanessa said with a cold smile as she pushed past June with a hard bump to her shoulder.

What?

June looked at Henry, standing there watching her. She stood still, frozen to the spot, and he came toward her. "So you and Vanessa aren't engaged?"

He half laughed. "No. But she's engaged to her mechanic. 'When you know, you know,' she said."

Relief flooded through June. Henry hadn't proposed to Vanessa Gull. June wasn't too late. "I agree with that."

He was staring at her. "Are you okay, June?"

She stepped closer and put her arms around his neck to see what he'd do. He wrapped his arms around her neck. "I'm more than okay. And I'm ready to come back, if you'll have me."

"Oh, I'll have you," he said, his smile, his expression, so full of emotion that June just pressed her head against his shoulder.

I'm in bed with Henry Books. In the middle of the afternoon, June thought, unable to hold in her huge smile.

"What are you all smiles about?" he asked, leaning over her and trailing kisses along her collarbone.

She took in his tanned, broad shoulders and chest, the slightly long hair, the Clint Eastwood crinkles around his intense brown eyes. He was so beautiful, so sexy, so everything she'd ever dared fantasize about. And here he was, real as real could be. "I just still can't believe I'm here. That *we're* here. How can something so incredibly right and perfect and comfortable feel so . . . magical?"

"I know just what you mean."

Last night, they'd gone from standing on the pier to kissing like crazy in his living room, then he led her by the hand into his bedroom, where they showed each other exactly how they felt, with years of pent-up passion behind it. He'd walked her home in the wee hours so she could be at the inn before Charlie woke up, and she'd loved the way Isabel and Kat had rushed her with happy questions the moment she'd tiptoed into the bedroom at five in the morning. Yes, being with Henry *was* everything she'd ever imagined. And more.

She'd gone to work that morning, floating around the shop to the point that Bean had said, "You sure are happy about something," and June had laughed. She sure was. Her relationship with Henry felt both sparkling new, full of the shy, tentative beginning sweetness, and old and comfortable, as if she'd been lying naked beside him for years. As she'd spent the morning making her Must Reads display, creating an *If you liked this, you'll love this* shelf, and jotting down plans for a children's book club at the store, she couldn't get him, their evening, out of her mind. She wanted to run down the pier to him. But she'd wait. They had plans that afternoon that would hopefully end with their being back in his bed on the boat, the stars watching over them.

Those plans started at four o'clock, when she and Henry left for the Boothbay Regional alumni association annual all-year get-together, which June had never before gone to. Both Isabel and Kat (who always went with Oliver) were attending, and so were Marley and Kip, so June figured she'd go, after all, and take a hot date. Not only couldn't she give a flying fig what her classmates thought of her anymore, she'd walk into that reunion with her head held high. She was proud of her life since graduation from high school.

Of course, the first group of people June saw when she walked in, her arm wrapped around handsome Henry, was Pauline Altman and her gang of worshippers.

"Look, it's Juney Nash," Pauline called out. "The girl who very narrowly beat me for valedictorian is *finally* showing her face at a reunion."

Had she been bothered by this twit all these years? June rolled her eyes at Pauline, gave Marley and Kip, dancing cheek to cheek on the dance floor, a smile and a wave, and joined her sister and cousin by the bar. Isabel looked gorgeous in a pale yellow jersey wrap dress that June was pretty sure had come out of Kat's closet. Kat was twirling the little umbrella in her drink, staring into space. Or thinking deeply. It was hard to tell. June could see Oliver with a group of guys.

As Henry went to order drinks, Isabel whispered, "I *love* seeing you two together."

Kat twirled her umbrella. "Talk about a reunion, huh? The three of us. You and Henry Books. Everything is as it was meant to be. Well, except for my mother's health." *And me and Oliver,* June could hear Kat thinking as Kat's gaze drifted over toward Oliver. Her cousin's expression wasn't full of love or excitement or joy as she watched her fiancé, who was laughing hard at something someone had just said.

Oh, Kat, June thought. *You'll figure it out and you'll do what's right for you. I know it.*

As Henry brought over their drinks, June took her glass and clinked her sister's and cousin's. "To family," she said, and Isabel and Kat clinked back.

"And to love," June said to Henry, clinking his glass.

The next afternoon, Charlie and Happy held races in the backyard as June, Lolly, Isabel, and Kat had a late lunch, compliments of Isabel, who'd checked in two sets of guests and whipped up her now famous potato and cheese blintzes for the family. Charlie ate his usual four bites and ran off to feed Happy, then lay down on a blanket with his big pad of construction paper and box of crayons and markers.

Lolly was in a wheelchair, her color good, her spirits high, as she ate two potato blintzes with sour cream and applesauce—a good sign. She had an appetite. June ate way too many blintzes, but they were so good. Charlie came running over holding a big piece of yellow paper. "Look," he said, holding up the paper for everyone to see. "I needed a bigger piece of paper to make some more changes to the family tree."

In addition to his father's name, his grandparents' and uncle's names, Charlie had added *Grifen, the dog dokter* (adorably misspelled all around) next to Isabel's name, and *Henry Books* next to June's name.

"I have an awesome family," Charlie said, beaming.

"Yeah, you sure do," June said, and everyone around the table agreed.

CHAPTER 21

Kat

"**Kat! He e-mailed!**" Isabel shrieked.

Isabel never shrieked.

Kat peeled open an eye in her dark bedroom and glanced at the clock on her bedside table. Just before five thirty in the morning. The sun wasn't even up yet. She pulled her pillow over her head.

Isabel flung it off. "He e-mailed!"

"Huh? Who?"

Isabel was beaming. "I just sat down at your desk to check the high temp for today and saw your e-mail box—message in bold from one Harrison Ferry!"

Kat threw the quilt off and rushed over to her desk. She didn't even bother sitting down. She and Isabel hunched over and read.

Dear Kat,

I'm terribly sorry that it's taken me so long to write back. I'm on leave this semester, doing research for a book, and though I've been checking my Bowdoin email, your email seems to have gone to the spam folder. Anyway, I'm so sorry to hear about your mother's health. Not a day has gone by in all these years that I haven't thought of Lolly. I'd like to come soon as you say it's all right. I live in Brunswick, so can come at a moment's notice.

I'm very glad you got in touch.

Yours, Harrison Ferry

Kat grabbed Isabel into a hug, then they glanced at each other and hugged again. " 'Not a day has gone by in all these years that I haven't thought of Lolly,' " Kat repeated. She felt like jumping up and down.

"He sounds very kind," Isabel said. "What a relief."

Kat sat down and wrote back. That he should come whenever was good for him, today, tomorrow?

He wrote back within twenty minutes. He was coming this evening.

Kat brought a breakfast tray into her mother's room, scrambled eggs and sourdough toast, which Lolly loved, a dish of berries and a cup of chamomile tea. June had been on night duty and was awake and reading a thick novel on the chaise when Kat had poked her head in an hour ago. Lolly was too tired to get into her wheelchair and join in the happy chatter in the kitchen, so Isabel had prepared a plate.

"Mmm, smells so good, I'm gonna go have some," June said, kissing Lolly's cheek before heading toward the door. "I hope there's bacon."

"If Charlie didn't eat it all," Lolly said with a laugh. "Better run."

As June came around the bed, Kat whispered, "Isabel has something big to tell you," and June zipped out.

Kat placed the tray over Lolly's slight figure and sat down on the edge of the bed. *Just tell her. No song and dance,* as her mother always said. *Just say it.*

"Does smell delicious," Lolly said, taking a bite of sourdough toast.

"Mom, you're going to have a special visitor tonight," Kat blurted out, her eyes closed. She opened them to find Lolly choosing between a strawberry and a blueberry.

"Who?"

"Harrison Ferry."

Her mother put down the strawberry. "What?"

"I e-mailed him and he's coming."

"You e-mailed him and he's coming?" Lolly repeated. "Harrison is coming here?"

Kat nodded and braced herself.

"He knows about the cancer?"

"He knows, Mom."

"Harrison is coming?" Lolly's blue eyes filled with tears. Her hand went to her mouth and she turned her head away, facing the windows. June had opened the curtains before she'd left on the gray, drizzly day.

Kat held her breath, unsure if her mother would rail at her for contacting him behind her back, nosing into Lolly's business, and how she wished she'd never told Kat.

"Will you help me look nice?"

Kat let out one hell of a breath. "You always look nice, Mom. But I'll help you look dazzling."

Lolly's smile seemed to come from somewhere deep inside her, and Kat knew she'd done the right thing.

Harrison Ferry reminded Kat of what an older, professorial brother of Pierce Brosnan might look like. In his late fifties, he was quite handsome, tall and lanky, with dark hair almost shot through completely with gray. He was both distinguished and sea-captain-like at the same time. He came bearing a beautiful bouquet of purple irises. Kat didn't spend too much time thinking about her mother and this man in love fifteen years ago, trysting away while Kat's father had taken her to state fairs, the way Meryl Streep's husband had with his children in *The Bridges of Madison County*. Her mother had loved this man and that was what mattered.

Lolly had told Kat to bring him into her room when he arrived so that they'd have some privacy. For the past few hours, Isabel, June, and Kat had fluttered about Lolly, holding up different head scarves for her approval, lightly applying makeup, a hint of powder and sunny bronzer to her cheeks, a bit of brown mascara, special eyebrow powder to feather in her sparse brows, the gentlest spritz of her favorite perfume, Chanel No. 19. They hadn't had to do much to doll up Lolly's bedroom; they'd done just that for the past few weeks, making sure there were always fresh flowers, the prettiest bedding evoking Lolly's beloved Atlantic Ocean, and cheery art on the walls, including some framed originals by Charlie Nash, age seven.

Kat had left Harrison in the parlor with a glass of Pellegrino and dashed to Lolly's room and shut the door behind her. "He's here, Mom."

Lolly sucked in a breath. "I'm ready."

Kat nodded and went back into the parlor. "Lolly's in her bedroom," she told Harrison. "It's difficult for her to get around these days." Bouquet in hand, he followed Kat down the hall. She left him to tap on the door, standing just around the bend, her heart in her throat.

She heard her mother's intake of breath, the whispered "Harrison," and then the gush of tears. She had no doubt that Harrison Ferry sat on her mother's bedside, taking her into his arms and holding her.

For the past two days, Harrison had come every evening, bringing Lolly books and flowers and chocolates and a special telescope she could use to see the constellations from her bed. He was planning on staying the weekend at the inn—with Lolly. Kat had been worried that Harrison would be married with children, not that she wished him the lack of a family, but it turned out that he was divorced; he'd gotten married a year after he and Lolly had broken up for good, but the marriage hadn't lasted. His presence clearly made her mother happy; Lolly often had the same goofy expression on her face as June and Isabel did.

Goofy happy was good.

Kat relieved the day nurse at twelve thirty to take her lunch hour and brought in a tray of French onion soup and grilled-cheese-and-tomato sandwiches for her and her mother.

Lolly reached into the drawer of her end table and pulled out an envelope. "Kat, I have something for you. A gift."

"Mom, you didn't have to get me anything. You've given me *everything*."

"Open it."

Inside was a one-way plane ticket to Paris. Open-ended. In Kat's name.

Kat stared at it. *One-way.*

"I've been watching you, Kat. And listening—closely. I know we haven't always been close, but I know you. I know you and I love you and all I want for you, all I really want for you, is to be happy."

Kat leaned down and gently hugged her mother, unable to stop the tears that were slipping down her cheeks. "Oh, Mom."

"I'm not telling you what to do either way, Kat. All I care about is that you're happy. If that means going to Paris alone for a year—maybe even forever—or if it means marrying Oliver or if it means getting to know that handsome Dr. Viola better . . . it's your choice. But *you* decide that on your time, on your terms. No one else's. Especially not mine."

Thank you, thank you, thank you. "I love you, Mom." Kat leaned down and hugged Lolly, her heart bursting.

"Just promise me one thing, Kat."

"Anything."

"Promise me no regrets. Regrets are the worst thing you can take with you in the end."

Kat was so overwhelmed by love for her mother that she couldn't speak. She just held on to Lolly's hand. "I promise, Mom," she finally said. "No regrets, no matter what." Because she'd make her choices and respect them.

"Your father would be so proud of you."

Kat lay down beside her mother and held her hand, a peace settling inside her for the first time in a long, long time.

Kat used to be a champion sleeper. She could sleep through lawn-mower services that tended to come at the crack of dawn. She slept through early-bird guests in the backyard, sipping their tea and chattering excitedly about their plans for the day. She slept through crickets and showers running, through Isabel's snoring, through June's clicks of her computer mouse as she'd searched for Charlie's father.

But lately, she'd wake up in the middle of the night, not in a cold sweat or anything, but unsure what had woken her. And then she'd think about Oliver, hearing his *Well, do you want to marry me?* over and over in her head. Then she'd see Matteo's sexy face, hear his invitation to move to New York and see what was between them.

It was just after 1:00 a.m., and sick of tossing and turning, Kat quietly got out of bed so as not to wake her cousins and padded downstairs to the parlor. She took a novel from the shelves, and a *Real Simple* magazine, but ended up sitting on the beanbag, flipping channels on TV. Nothing caught her attention. She rooted in Lolly's DVD collection and came across *Julie & Julia* misfiled in the Susan Sarandon section.

Julie & Julia. Kat flipped over the case and read the description on the back. How had she missed seeing this when it first came out a few years ago? Meryl Streep as a young Julia Child in Paris, learning to cook at Le Cordon Bleu. Julie Powell, young, married, and emotionally lost in New York City, looking for *something*. And deciding to cook every one of Julia Child's five-hundred-plus recipes in *Mastering the Art of French Cooking.* A movie based on two true stories. Kat's heart leapt. The perfect movie for tonight. She went into the kitchen to make a pot of tea and took one of her lemon cupcakes from the EAT ME container on the counter, then settled back in the parlor on her beanbag.

Suddenly she was in Paris in the late forties and fifties with Julia Child, who had enrolled in the famed cooking school with no training, and soon mastered the art of French cooking with her "opening of the soul and spirit." Once again, Meryl Streep brought a character, Julia Child, alive in such a way that Kat forgot she was watching Meryl Streep, forgot she was watching a movie. She was right there with Julia in Paris, City of Lights, city of dreams. Where Kat wanted to be more than she wanted anything else.

Such as getting married. Such as settling down in Boothbay Harbor—for the forseeable future, anyway. She did believe in her heart of hearts that her mother would be as happy to see Kat go off and live her dream as she would to see Kat marry the boy who'd been by her side since age five. Her mother truly did want her to choose her future for the right reasons only. Kat knew that now with certainty.

She got goose bumps when Julie Powell's husband reassured her that she *could* take on this big project, that she *could* make every single recipe in Julia's masterpiece of a French cookbook, all 524 in a year, because she, like everyone else, had to start *somewhere,* because "Julia Child wasn't always Julia Child." It was something Oliver would say.

So did that mean Oliver would wish her bon voyage? Or that she should ask him to come with her?

What she did know was that the best line of the movie belonged to Meryl Streep, as Julia Child told her husband early on in her training that he should have seen the way the men in her class were looking at her as she made mistake after mistake—because they didn't yet know she was fearless.

Fearless. That was what Kat wanted to be. She liked the piece of her that hadn't dwelled on her mother's confession about the night Kat's father died. The piece that had e-mailed Harrison Ferry without a clue who he was or what her e-mail would lead to. It was a start in the right direction, following her heart instead of fear.

At two forty-five, Kat went back upstairs and slipped into bed, drifting off to thoughts of flipping crepes in a famed French pastry school.

October began brilliantly, with bright sunshine and sixty-six perfect degrees. The day was so postcard-perfect that even stepping inside the hospital for Lolly's tests couldn't bring Kat down. It had been two days since her mother had given her the one-way, open-ended ticket to Paris, and though Kat hadn't made any decisions, she wasn't anxiety ridden. She'd even slept until seven the past two days. One reason was that her mother was in good spirits because her heart, mind, and soul were at peace, and Kat, with her secret one-way ticket hidden under her mattress, felt carefree for the first time in a long, long time.

As the nurse took her mother's vitals, Kat excused herself to get them both a cup of hot tea from the snack bar. Matteo and a group of doctors had come out of a room down the hall, and when he saw her, he smiled and waved. The sight of him made her stomach do its usual flip-flop.

"I'm on my way to get tea for me and Lolly," she said. "Have a minute to join me?"

She hadn't seen him in a while. He called often, and they'd had a quick lunch last week at the hospital when she'd explained she'd have to postpone his father's muffin lessons until her mother was a bit stronger, but otherwise Kat had kept away from both Matteo and Oliver. Oliver couldn't understand it and left short, angry texts like *Don't get u lately at all,* and Matteo left voice mails talking about white blood cells that had gotten more technical, less personal. Maybe he was pulling away too.

Turns out she was wrong. "I've been thinking a lot about you lately, Kat," he said as she held the spigot of hot water over the Earl Grey tea bag in a large cup. "I've been trying to keep my distance because I know you have a decision to make about— Getting married," he finally said. "But I think there's something very real between us."

There wasn't, she realized now. There was something inside her, something that he'd stirred, something that made it crystal clear that she shouldn't be marrying anyone or running off to New York with anyone. Matteo, with the call of Europe in his voice, had awakened her deepest desires—to do what she'd always been afraid to do. Leave Boothbay Harbor. Taste her way through Paris and Rome and Barcelona, take a class with a master baker. Decide for herself who she was. Whom she would love.

As she watched Matteo's mouth move as he talked, the mouth she'd watched so often, unable to take her eyes off it, longing to kiss those lips, she realized he was like Clint Eastwood in *The Bridges of Madison County,* asking her to leave with no real understanding of—or concern for—what she'd be leaving. She didn't have a husband and children, of course, and she knew her mother didn't have much time left on this earth. But another man wasn't the answer either.

She needed to stretch those wings of hers, fly away, and maybe then she'd be ready to come back and marry Oliver—if he'd even have her. Or maybe she would find herself in New York, ready to kiss those Italian lips of Matteo's.

But for now, she was her own girl.

Kat sat on Oliver's couch and opened her mouth to tell him that she just wasn't ready to marry him, to marry anyone, but nothing came out. It was one thing to mess around with herself, be a confused, ambivalent idiot; it was another to hurt Oliver, who'd been her best friend for as long as she could remember.

"I have something for you," he said, getting up and going over to the desk under the window. He handed her a piece of paper.

"What is it?"

"Read it."

She scanned the sheet and gasped; it was an online receipt for a six-week patisserie course at a famed culinary school in Paris. Start date: January 4.

"There's a reason people throw around that old cliché about if it's meant to be, blah, blah, blah," he said. "Maybe we'll end up together, maybe we won't. Maybe you'll never come back from Paris, or you'll come back with some beret-wearing French husband. Or maybe you'll come back, ready to settle down, and I'll be here, or maybe I'll have met some-one else. I don't know, Kat. I just know that you're supposed to go to Paris and apprentice in some fancy bakery. I know you're not ready to get married. And I know that I love you and need to let you go."

He was wishing her bon voyage. Just as she thought he

would. "God, Oliver, you're as true-blue as my father said you were when I was ten."

He took her hands and held them. "Because I'm your best friend, Kat. Maybe that's all I've ever been and I pressed the issue of an us when you've really only ever loved me as a friend. I proposed at your weakest moment; I know that."

"Oliver, I—"

He shook his head. "Go to Paris. No matter what happens, Kat, I'll always love you in here," he said, hand over his heart. "Always have, always will."

"Me too," she whispered, and hugged him fiercely.

On Friday night, the full moon so low in the sky that Kat could see it glowing through the kitchen window, she added the initials along the edges of the chocolate layer cake—*L* for Lolly, *I* for Isabel, *J* for June, *C* for Charlie, *K* for Kat, and *P* for Pearl. Kat brought the cake into Lolly's room, where everyone was gathered for Movie Night.

"Is that *P* for me?" Pearl asked from her chair on the far side of Lolly's bed.

"Sure is," Kat said, slicing Pearl's piece with its white *P* and handing her a plate. "You're part of this family, aren't you?"

Pearl beamed.

"Is your beau joining us, Aunt Lolly?" Isabel asked, settling her *I* slice on her lap.

Lolly blushed. "No. He's planning on arriving afterward, around ten. I'm so excited to see him! My God, how happy I am to have him back in my life."

Kat glanced at her cousins and they shared a happy smile.

Lolly pointed the remote control at the television and hit PLAY. "And I'm excited to see *Out of Africa* again. This is my favorite movie of all time. So many lines undid me the first time around that I didn't think I could ever see it again. But I'm ready now."

"I love it too," Pearl said. "And I don't think there's ever been a more handsome man than Robert Redford in *Out of Africa*. He's breathtaking."

As Meryl Streep's reverent narration began, *I had a farm in Africa*, everyone was quiet and riveted to the screen. Meryl played the real-life Karen Blixen, a wealthy woman whose titled husband used her money to buy a coffee plantation in Africa, only to betray her. Meryl ended up loving the farm, putting so much of herself into it, and falling in love with a man more independent than even she was. But she asked more of Robert Redford than he was willing to give of himself, and to be true to herself, she had to give him up. In the end she lost almost everything: Her farm. Her great love. But never, ever her self-worth.

Lolly hit PAUSE three-quarters of the way through the film. She dabbed at tears under her eyes. "That was the line I've always thought about over the years. When, after all she's endured, all she's lost, Meryl says that just when she thinks she can't endure another moment of pain, she remembers how good things once were, and when she's sure she can't handle another second, she goes another second more and knows she can endure anything." Lolly's smile seemed so far away. "It's true." She hit PLAY again.

"I'm sitting here crying," June said, dabbing under her eyes with a tissue.

Isabel laughed. "Me too." She took a tissue from the box June handed her.

Kat held her mother's hand. She noticed she wasn't the only one sitting stock-still, not eating popcorn, barely breathing, as Meryl Streep, breaking her own heart, told Robert Redford—as beautiful as Pearl had said he was—that what he was offering wasn't enough for her.

"Oh, God, hit PAUSE." Isabel sat up straight. " 'I've learned there are some things worth having, but they come at a price, and I want to be one of them,'" she said, repeating Meryl Streep's words. "I'm going to write that down and carry it with me in my wallet."

Kat knew in that moment that what she'd been so ambivalent about all along wasn't getting married or staying in Boothbay Harbor. She'd been ambivalent about herself, who she was, deep down, what she thought she was worth.

She had her plane ticket. She had her pastry-course enrollment receipt. She had her family. And she had a person to become: herself.

Three days later, Lolly died in her sleep. Kat had woken up at 4:00 a.m. on the chaise, the cool air blowing the gauzy curtains horizontally. She'd gotten up to close the window, then checked on her mother, and she wasn't sure how she knew that Lolly was gone, that she wasn't just sleeping, but she knew. There was a stillness, an utter stillness.

She knelt at Lolly's bedside and said a prayer, then sobbed up the stairs to the attic bedroom and woke her cousins.

At the funeral, Pearl gave a beautiful eulogy and then, in her sweet, slow soprano, sang ABBA's "S.O.S.," which Meryl Streep had sung in the movie *Mamma Mia!* It was so touching that Kat found herself singing along in a whisper. June and Isabel, sitting on either side of her, held her hands and whispered the song with her.

Much later, when mostly everyone had gone home, Kat, Isabel, and June gathered in the parlor to light a candle for Lolly. *The Hours, Evening, Julia,* and *The Iron Lady* were set aside on top of the television as possibilities for that night's Movie Night, though none of them were sure they could watch a Meryl Streep movie without Lolly there. Not yet, anyway.

On the wall, to the right of the television, Kat had hung the gift she and her cousins had presented Lolly with two days before she'd died, a painting they'd commissioned from a photograph Lolly had taken of Isabel, June, and Kat in September, on the front steps of the inn. The three new captains, home together.

ACKNOWLEDGMENTS

Alexis Hurley, literary agent extraordinaire at InkWell Management, fierce advocate with a brilliant editorial eye, believed in this novel from the beginning. There isn't enough good chocolate in the world to say thanks for everything—and there's a lot of everything.

Because the universe works in wonderful ways, Karen Kosztolnyik, executive editor at Simon & Schuster/Gallery, is my editor and helped me shape and strengthen this novel with such care and affection for the characters. To many more books!

To Louise Burke and Jen Bergstrom at Gallery for believing in me and this book. Thank you, thank you, thank you.

A special thank-you to Kara Cesare, fairy godeditor.

To my friends and family, particularly my beloved son, who inspires me every minute of every day with his questions and smile and kid-energy. A movie lover as I am, he thinks Meryl Streep is cool because she was the voice of Mrs. Fox in *Fantastic Mr. Fox*.

A long time ago, I caught Meryl Streep on Inside the Actors Studio. When James Lipton got to his last question—"If heaven exists, what would you want to hear God say to you when you reach the Pearly Gates?"—Meryl, with a big sweep of her arms, answered, "Everybody in!" This sums up why I love her. I've been a fan of the beautiful and breathtakingly talented actress for as long as I can remember, and I thank Meryl Streep for her fifty-plus roles, for making me laugh and cry and think and believe. My novel is my tribute.

The Meryl Streep Movie Club

Reading Group Guide

INTRODUCTION

Three estranged women—two sisters and the cousin they grew up with after a haunting tragedy—find unexpected happiness in the most unexpected way: by watching Meryl Streep movies together. It is only when the three are summoned to their family matriarch's inn on the coast of Maine for an important announcement that they are able to reconnect through surprising and heartfelt discussions of movies such as *Out of Africa* and *Mamma Mia!* and discover who they really are and what they truly want.

With warmth, depth, and candor, Mia March skillfully opens the lives of these three very different women, each coping with their own challenges and secrets.

TOPICS & QUESTIONS FOR DISCUSSION

1. Consider the novel's epigraph, which is one of Meryl Streep's lines from the film *Out of Africa*: "Perhaps he knew, as I did not, that the Earth was made round so that we would not see too far down the road." What does this quote mean to you? How does it relate to the novel?

2. *The Meryl Streep Movie Club* brings together a collection of unique characters. Was there one character with whom you most identified? Discuss your favorite characters and why you felt drawn to each.

3. Isabel wants to use a "magic" ravioli recipe to help reignite a spark between herself and her husband, Edward. Do you have a special dish, place, song, or something that you think of as "magic" for you and someone you love?

4. In the prologue, readers indirectly learn that something devastating happened to Lolly's husband and Isabel

and June's parents on New Year's Eve. However, the specifics are not directly revealed until later in the novel. How did this intensify the revelation of what happened that New Year's Eve? Did you find this technique effective? Why or why not?

5. At the beginning of the novel, June, Isabel, Kat, and Lolly are all leading separate lives. What ultimately must happen for them to unite? What do they each have to let go of in order to reconnect with each other?

6. "And then one day, Edward said, you realize right in the middle of whatever you're doing that you're not thinking about it, and it gets better from there, becoming a piece of you instead of everything you are" (p. 11). Do you agree with this description of grief? Discuss the ways in which recovery from loss connects various characters in the novel.

7. "All that was left of John Smith was a face she'd never forget, a face she saw in Charlie's every day" (p. 29). Do you think it is possible to fall in love at first sight? Why or why not? Discuss June's character. How does her encounter with Charlie's father both haunt and enhance her life?

8. Isabel, June, Kat, Lolly, and even many of the minor characters hold heartache at the center of their lives— death, affairs, divorce, guilt, dropping out of college, being afraid to love. Do these difficulties make you care about or relate to the characters in a deep way? How do you think the context of the story determines your expectations and opinions of the characters?

9. "The feel of flour sifting through her fingers, of dough, warm and pliant and sweet-smelling in her hands, of chocolate chips and fruit, always lifted her heart in

the way movies did for her aunt. The way playing with Happy did for Isabel. And the way June looked when her son sat on her lap at meals, unable to get close enough to her" (p. 139). Do you have a hobby or favorite activity? Is there something that brings you as much peace as baking does for Kat? What do you think each characters' favorite activity says about them?

10. June's son, Charlie, does not know his father. He becomes more aware of not having a father, grand-parents, or family on his father's side when he is given a school assignment to complete his family tree and much of it is left empty. Did you agree with June's decision to seek out the man she only knew for two days and never saw again? Discuss why you think this may have been a good or bad decision.

11. Isabel and June's stories open the novel, and readers don't hear Kat's story until chapter three. Why do you think the author chose to introduce the sisters first? Would you have felt differently about them if we'd been invited to the inn first, to get to know Kat and Lolly before the sisters? Discuss your thoughts.

12. Lolly makes her big announcement on page 50 and shocks her daughter and two nieces. Did her news come as a surprise to you? What did the author do to set up this announcement and make it so dramatic?

13. How does the movie *The Bridges of Madison County* mirror the lives of the characters in the novel? Can watching a fictional account of something familiar be helpful? Can it be harmful? Compare and contrast the movie's themes, events, and characters with those of *The Meryl Streep Movie Club*.

14. Which do you think was more difficult and shocking to Isabel: Edward's betrayal or Lolly's news that she is dying of cancer? Which do you think would be more difficult to deal with?

15. Lolly and the girls find deep meaning even in comedies and musicals, such as when Lolly points out that she and Kat were in the same situation as the mother and daughter in *Mamma Mia!*—only their roles were switched. Identify and talk about other examples from the book in which a comedy or lighter film leads to a discussion of a serious topic.

16. Which Meryl Streep film described in the novel do you most identify with? Why? Are there any other Meryl Streep movies not included in the narrative that you think Lolly and the rest of the "club" would have enjoyed?

17. How did reading her mother's letters impact Isabel?

18. There is a moment toward the end of the book when Edward visits the inn and lets Isabel know that he still loves her, even though he wants to marry someone else. What does Isabel realize about her feelings toward Edward in this scene? What does she realize about herself? How might the scene have played out differently?

19. Lolly, Isabel, June, Kat, Pearl, and other guests meet regularly to watch their favorite Meryl Streep films and then discuss them. How is their club similar to your own book club experience? How does it differ?

20. Kat has always lived at the inn and fears being trapped there. Isabel, in contrast, always wanted to get away from the inn as a child and now wants nothing more than to stay. Are there any examples in your own life

where you wanted to get away from a place, person, or situation only to discover later that you wanted it back? Which of the new "three captains" do you envision remaining at the inn and following in Lolly's footsteps?

ENHANCE YOUR BOOK CLUB

1. At the beginning of *The Meryl Streep Movie Club*, there is a list of ten Meryl Streep movies, all of which are viewed by the characters in the novel. Select one to watch with your book club members. Do you find you can relate to some of the movie scenes and characters the way the women in the book did? Discuss the movie you watched with the group. Did watching the movies help to deepen the discussion of the book?

2. The author writes, "A Meryl Streep movie was as good as chicken soup, a best friend, a therapist, and a stiff drink" (p. 56). Do you have a favorite comfort—be it a movie, actor, book, writer, album, song, television show, or artist? Share your response with the group.

3. Isabel and June's mother kept copies of letters she sent to her daughters. Fifteen years after her death, they have the chance to read those letters. As adults, they revisit what their mother thought through her words—not just what they thought she thought. If you don't do so already, try keeping a journal. Start off with recording your thoughts and activities for a week and see if a habit forms! You may decide to continue writing in it regularly.

4. The Three Captains' Inn is a safe haven for the characters of the book. It is also a place where they reconnect in deeper and more meaningful ways than before.

Consider getting away to an inn, bed and breakfast, or another retreat with your discussion group, friends, or loved ones with whom you'd like to reconnect.

A CONVERSATION WITH MIA MARCH

1. **Why Meryl Streep? Was she an obvious choice from the start, or did you have a list of possible contenders? Could there have been an Audrey Hepburn or Elizabeth Taylor Movie Club?**

Meryl Streep was always the only choice. The novel was actually inspired by the very beautiful and incredibly talented actress, who has been a favorite of mine since I was a teenager. When I was around thirty, a family holiday visit was going the way holidays with family can sometimes go . . . . happy to be together, but some arguing over everything under the sun— from whether to put garlic in the mashed potatoes to something that was said twenty years before. You know those holidays, right? After dinner, my mother, grandmother, and I settled down with popcorn to watch *The Bridges of Madison County*—and whoa. The discussion afterward changed everything. We opened up to one another that night, understood things about one another we hadn't before. All because of the issues and emotions raised by the film—and by the acting talent of Meryl Streep. I never forgot that night. And some years later, while watching another Meryl Streep movie (*Heartburn*, one of my favorites of all time), I realized I had a story to tell. About how movies—and watching movies with others—can change your life in unexpected ways. That I could do that, and pay tribute to one of my idols, Meryl Streep, was a true labor of love.

2. **It seems that oftentimes people decide not to bring kids into the "cruel world" due to the difficulties, pain, and problems in the world. But Edward and Isabel make a pact as teenagers for a more specific reason—because they want to avoid turning their kids into "grieving orphans" like themselves. Did you find their reason more compelling?**

I'm so interested in exploring the complicated shades of gray in people. Edward and Isabel's pact was so sad to me (I cried as I wrote that scene, where as sixteen-year-olds they lay under that oak tree, hand in hand, staring up at the stars and making a decision from a place of terrible grief, a decision they carry into adulthood). As a teenager, I myself made decisions about the world based on my emotions and experiences—some that held me back from things I didn't even know I wanted until I was much older. That's what I wanted to examine in fiction: how you can sometimes get yourself stuck, but with change and growth you can pull yourself right out. Sometimes you can do it yourself, and sometimes you need help. And sometimes who helps is the one you least expect.

3. **You do a great job of writing intense moments, and then moving on—like in the prologue and Isabel's discovery at the end of chapter one. How do you decide, as a storyteller, where to break scenes and chapters? How do you know when to transition from one character to another?**

Thank you! Interestingly, I didn't write the prologue until after I finished writing the entire novel. The book opened with Isabel, and every time I started to read page one, I couldn't put my finger on what was poking me. Finally I realized I wanted to open with

Lolly, wanted to frame the novel with Lolly's voice and the night that changed everyone's lives. The prologue made me suck in my breath because of what happens, and within a few pages we're in Isabel's point of view, where she's so hopeful, so determined to save her marriage with memories of who she and Edward once were—and then it's all shot to pieces. As a writer, I'm drawn to looking at what happens when you're trying, trying, trying (even as Lolly was in the prologue), and then in a moment, everything changes, whether subtly or with a terrible clang. I think a writer just naturally *feels* when to move on, to a different character or to a different scene/setting. It's not conscious for me. That's one of things I love most about writing fiction: how mysterious it is.

4. **You work with multiple points of view. How do you decide which characters to channel for different scenes?**

Structurally, since I had three main characters and about three hundred manuscript pages, I envisioned they would watch nine Meryl Streep movies together—three movies for each character's point of view. And I *thought* I knew which movies would be viewed through which character's eyes—until I started writing. Another wonderful mystery of writing fiction! *The Bridges of Madison County* and *Heartburn* were both naturals for Isabel, as they deal with affairs, but when I started to write the *Mamma Mia!* scene, which I envisioned for June's point of view, I realized how deeply affected Kat would be for different reasons, and I rewrote that scene, then ended up changing it back. I always try to go with my first instinct, but there was lots of rearranging and sticky notes posted on the manuscript during my revision phase! The opening scene of chapter four, which is Isabel's second point-of-view chapter, was originally the end of chapter three and in Kat's point of view. But when I re-read it in manuscript form, I felt in my bones that as a *reader*, I wanted to be back in Isabel's head; I wanted to know what happened after she ran out of her husband's affair's home. And I thought it would be interesting to have Lolly's announcement occur in Isabel's point of view because Isabel was the most distant from Lolly. So much for first instincts!

5. **Your characters all seem like well-adjusted people, but they have a lot of pain in their lives. They have lost close loved ones at early ages, suffered affairs and betrayals, lost jobs and homes, dropped out of college and let go of dreams. Do you find that difficult situations make for more compelling writing? Or do you generally let events unfold on their own?**

Okay, I'll be really honest here. The thing I love most of all about writing fiction, why I write, is because I can work out issues, emotions, and experiences vicariously through my characters. None of the characters is based directly on me or anything that has happened in my life, but I've experienced loss and betrayal and change and all sorts of life occurrences, big and small, good and bad, and some things I wanted to explore through fiction. What would this character do with this pain? How do I wish something painful had unfolded in my own life? I can give anything to a character, make anything happen, within reason, of course, if it fits that character. Sometimes, though, something I *want* to happen doesn't ring true for the characters or story. When I set out to write the book, Kat *was* going to marry Oliver at the end. But when I got three-quarters of the way through, I knew she couldn't. And shouldn't. Not yet, anyway. I do think she'll come back from Paris and marry him. I want her to.

6. **In the prologue, you reference the film *When Harry Met Sally*. In chapter three, you introduce Kat, who is afraid to admit she's in love with her best friend. Was this a deliberate connection to the ongoing argument in the film regarding whether a man can be "just friends" with an attractive woman? What's your opinion on the subject and how did it influence your telling of these women's stories?**

When I was in my late twenties, one of my best friends was a wonderful guy named David. We met through a friend on a sort-of blind date, very quickly realized we had zero chemistry, and became great friends instead. One day, while bemoaning a relationship that didn't work out, he threw his hands up and said, "Why can't I just fall in love with *you*? That would be perfect." We both laughed over that. If only we could, life would be so easy. So yeah, I absolutely think men and women can be friends. BUT. But, but, but, when one of the friends gets a significant other, that S.O. might not be too comfortable about it. David soon fell madly in love with someone who was very unhappy about our friendship. Yadda, yadda, yadda, the friendship drifted away. I don't think I consciously brought up *When Harry Met Sally* (except that it's one of my favorite movies), but the notion of male/female friendship—with Oliver and Kat; with Matteo and Kat at first, with Henry and June—was certainly an undercurrent. Again the unconscious working in interesting ways!

7. **Do you have a place like the "alone closet" that you escape to? Or when you need to work out something in your story?**

My "alone closet" is the shower. There you are, absolutely naked, with hot water, soap and delicious-smelling shampoo. The shower is the best place to cry and think and dream.

8. **You've created characters with separate lives, but weave those lives together so they fit perfectly at the inn. Do you have a favorite character in this book?**

I love all the characters, was so emotionally invested in everyone, including Happy, the sweet stray dog, but I have a very special fondness for Henry Books. He's a bit in the background, but such a strong-and-silent-while-saying-so-much type with crinkly Clint Eastwood eyes.

9. **What made you decide to match Isabel with a reflection of herself in Griffin? Was it important for him to have experienced infidelity for him to really understand what she was going through? And for his daughter to be, in many ways, a reflection of who Isabel had once been?**

I knew I wanted Isabel to fall in love with a single father with his own complicated history, someone who'd "been there, done that," especially because the betrayal was so fresh for her, and to let her see for herself that Edward was wrong about her and her maternal instincts. At first I thought Griffin would have only a young child. But then fourteen-year-old Alexa, with her scowl and iPod and sad anger, came barreling through the doors of the Three Captains' Inn before I even made the connection between her and Isabel. As I was writing, especially the scene with Alexa sobbing in the Alone Closet, I realized that Alexa would represent a reinforcement for Isabel that she needed to forgive herself for the teenager she'd been, in all ways.

10. What came first: the characters, the plot, or the idea to frame a book around a Meryl Streep Movie Club? How did the elements all come together?

The idea of a fractured family of women watching movies together—particularly Meryl Streep movies—and how the ensuing discussions bring them back to one another (inspired by my own experience of watching *The Bridges of Madison County* with my mother and grandmother) came first. But then the main characters—Isabel and June and Kat, and Aunt Lolly, all came in a rush. I knew their names and their stories and the smallest details—like the stray dog that adopts Isabel just when she needs that unconditional love. The characters' stories came first before the movie selections, though. Given Isabel's and June's and Kat's individual stories, I looked at Meryl Streep movies that reflected what they were going through, what they had to deal with. The incredible collection of Meryl Streep films runs the gamut of emotions. I'd already seen all the films I reference in the book and then watched each at least twice again. There were a few movies I thought I'd have the characters watch, but then ended up not using, like the amazing *One True Thing*. (*Sophie's Choice* is sacred to me, as it is to Lolly.) Once I wrote the first movie scene, with the women watching *Bridges,* the discussion came so naturally because the characters' different reactions helped create and cement who they were, what they thought and believed, how they felt. The farther I got into writing, the more I understood each character through those discussions, and the easier the revision process became. That's the magic of movies.

11. Finally, the obvious question: what is your favorite Meryl Streep movie? Why?

My favorite is *Out of Africa*. Stunning and beautiful and heartbreaking and powerful and life affirming. Honestly, I can hear Meryl Streep's voice as Karen Blixen in my head: "I had a farm in Africa," and I can suddenly be transported to that coffee farm on the foot of the Ngong Hills. Knowing that the movie is based on a memoir, that it's an amazing woman's true life story, makes it all the more powerful. But Meryl Streep, the breathtakingly talented actress, brought that fiercely independent, brave, gifted, compassionate woman to life and had me on the edge of my seat, emotionally and otherwise for over two hours. And good Lord, is Robert Redford a thing to behold in this film.